What t

છ

Five Stars "Dying For Siena is a captivating tale of burgeoning love and self-belief as Faith discerns her inner beauty and aptitude for genius. Elizabeth Jennings suavely weaves the mysterious death of Kane into a revealing saga of self discovery and new beginnings. I joyously tag along with Faith and Nick and was sad to say good-bye. I hope Elizabeth Jennings continues to write about Siena and the Rossi Family." ~ *Dena, Fallen Angel Reviews*

"DYING FOR SIENA is a non-stop mystery that will keep you guessing until the very end. Elizabeth Jennings does an amazing job describing the sights, sounds, and excitement of Siena. You can practically envision it!" ~ *Chrissy Dionne, Romance Junkies*

"I cannot say enough about the way Ms. Jennings described the countryside of Siena interspersed seamlessly are scenes of the wonderful locale she chose for the backdrop of this engrossing who done it. This, along with the cast of characters from the other professors, to the cook staff at the monastery, are vividly brought to life on the pages. A slow, simmering romance develops between the two lead characters. Leaving the reader eager to find out both who did it and will they have their happily ever after?" ~ *Jenn, Reviewer for Coffee Time Romance*

"DYING FOR SIENA takes place during the Palio season in Siena, a popular bi-annual horse race where lots are drawn for the horses, and the town is filled with excitement. The thousand-year-old races pit different neighborhoods against each other, with the participants taking the race very seriously and resorting to almost anything to win. Readers can almost imagine themselves in beautiful Tuscany with its old buildings, blue sky, and friendly people. DYING FOR SIENA is an entertaining book that romantic suspense readers are sure to enjoy." ~ *Marilyn Heyman, Romance Reviews Today*

"Reading **Dying for Siena** was like going on a virtual vacation to Italy. Elizabeth Jennings' jaunty storytelling and enthusiasm were infectious, and I willingly followed her when she guided me through her Siena and showed me an Italian microcosm she obviously knows well and adores. I found Faith, Dante, and Nick to be likable and refreshingly normal characters." ~ *Ha, All About Romance*

Elizabeth Jennings
DYING FOR SIENA

Cerridwen Press

A Cerridwen Press Publication

www.cerridwenpress.com

Dying For Siena

ISBN #1419954598
ALL RIGHTS RESERVED.
Dying For Siena Copyright© 2005 Elizabeth Jennings
Edited by Kelli Kwiatkowski
Cover art by Syneca

Electronic book Publication July 2005
Trade Paperback Publication January 2006

Cerridwen Press is an imprint of Ellora's Cave Publishing, Inc.®

DYING FOR SIENA

ঙ

"Everything that can go wrong, will go wrong."
Murphy's Law

ဆ

"In the worst possible way."
Faith Murphy

Prologue

Never sleep with anyone crazier than yourself.

∞

The telephone rang.

Nick Rossi wanted to groan and roll over in bed but something told him to keep quiet and not make a move. The noise of the bell had almost been enough to take the top of his head off.

Through the greasily nauseous roiling going on inside, he tried to take stock, but it wasn't pretty.

His hair hurt. His eyelashes hurt. His toenails hurt. And everything else in between hurt.

The telephone rang again and hammered sharply pointed spikes into his skull. He tried to bring a hand up to his head, but there was something on his arm. Nick moved his hand — even that small movement caused pain — and touched a soft, springy mass. Hair. Human hair.

He hoped.

The way he was feeling, maybe he had spent the night with a very furry gremlin.

He opened one eye. Cautiously.

Nope. No gremlin. A girl.

She was sleeping with her back to him and all he could see was a finely drawn pale profile surrounded by a cloud of brandy-colored hair. He knew her. He knew he knew her. If only his brain could shoot him messages through the thick fog that fouled his head. As it was, merely trying to conjure up the memory of the face — and of last night — taxed his pain threshold.

The phone rang again, the bell echoing shrilly in his head for long seconds. Each second seemed like a lifetime. Everything was happening in an unsteady, sickening slow motion, as if he were on a boat. The girl turned over in bed, the rustling noise of the sheets sounding like thunder. She looked at him, wide-eyed, all fresh and innocent and not at all as if she should be in the bed of a hundred-year-old man, which is what he felt like.

He took in her features one by one, his brain too befuddled to be able to put the parts together. She had pale skin, with a spattering of freckles across her nose over high cheekbones. He knew — without knowing how he knew — that she blushed easily.

Her eyes were large, the same brandy color as her hair and the whites were milky-white, like a child's. Small straight nose, arching sandy eyebrows, lips which he knew were full, but were now compressed in a thin line.

It was an unusual face, not conventionally pretty but...arresting. He knew her, knew her well even, and her name was going to break through the cobwebs...any second now...

A loud noise made him start in pain. It was his answering machine kicking in. His recorded voice sounded preternaturally loud in the room. "Hi, this is Nick Rossi. Sorry I can't come to the phone, but if you leave a message and a phone number, I'll get back to you as soon as I can."

There was a hum, then a high, breathy, impossibly sexy female voice came on. "Nick, love, sorry I couldn't make our hot weekend, but I was held up. I hope you didn't go looking somewhere else for fun and excitement because, believe me, I'm going to make it up to you next weekend and I want you fresh." A loud phone kiss ended the message and Nick winced.

The girl bolted up in bed like a startled fawn and Nick tried to think of something to say. Hell, he just tried to think. Period. But nothing was happening up there.

"Y-You—" she stammered softly. "You…and I…last night…and all the time—you were supposed to be *with someone else*?"

"Er," he replied, trying to gain time while trying to jump-start his head. He couldn't think and his memory was shot, but his body was frantically sending him messages. About last night. Fragments of memory jockeyed tantalizingly for attention. The memories were entirely tactile and unbearably sweet. Soft limbs, sweet caresses, gentle words.

Who is she? It was on the tip of his furred tongue. He would remember in just a minute…

But he wasn't going to have that minute. She was hurriedly dressing, her movements jerky and awkward, as if she weren't used to dressing in front of someone. And he should be saying something, but what? He sat up in bed, regretting the movement instantly. By the time the room stopped spinning, she was fully dressed and halfway to the door.

He didn't know why he wanted to stop her, he only knew that he did. "No, wait, ah—" And then his mind pulled a blank. Utterly empty, like a desert plain.

She turned and her eyes widened even more. "Oh—my—*God*." She brought her small fist to her mouth. "You don't even remember my *name*."

"Don't be silly. Of course I do, ahm…" But it was too late. She had gone and the sound of the door slamming behind her was so painful he couldn't even breathe for a full minute.

By the time he could think again, he could hear the elevator slowly taking her down to the ground floor. Then, suddenly, his treacherous memory kicked in. Images from the previous night blossomed in his mind. It had been wonderful, extraordinary…and he had the horrible feeling that he had just cut himself off from the sweetest thing in his life.

"Faith," he groaned as he fell back onto the mattress. "Faith Murphy."

Chapter One

Smile, tomorrow will be worse.

&

Thirty hours later, Certosa di Ponteremoli near Siena, Italy.

Faith Murphy was expecting Professor Roland Kane to be cold and unresponsive to her request.

She wasn't expecting him to be dead.

At first, it wasn't entirely clear he was dead. The door to Professor Kane's cell had swung open unexpectedly at her tentative knock. Unsure what to do next, Faith peeked into the room where generations of monks had lived out lives of prayer and meditation.

The cell was familiar—an exact replica of the one she was inhabiting during the yearly Quantitative Methods Seminar at the *Certosa di Ponteremoli*. The cell was simple and spare as befitted the monastic life. One small metal cot, one laminated desk and wardrobe combination, one wicker-seat chair.

One full Professor of Applied Mathematics, stretched out on his back on the floor, eyes closed. At least he was fully dressed. Faith could remember once entering the office of Professor Harlan White, another mathematical genius, and finding him in the lotus position.

Naked.

It was like the old joke—why do universities have math departments? Because it's cheaper than institutionalizing them all.

To prove the point, Professor White's nakedness had been immediately forgotten once he had started talking about a new demographic model for social security.

So, for all she knew, Professor Kane was working out a new quantitative theory, stretched out on the terra-cotta tiles with the buttery Italian sunshine streaming in through the open window.

Indeed, what better place to meditate on the infinite than in this former Franciscan monastery perched picturesquely atop a Tuscan hill, with Siena a russet-turreted vision on the horizon and the very air stirring with the echoes of centuries of chants?

Of course, Professor Roland Kane, for all his genius, was anything but a monk. Though in mathematical terms he was a genius, in human terms he was a pig. A monstrously intelligent pig. A drunkard and a lecher and a despot and an opportunist.

And a pig.

And a genius.

Which was why Faith was here. Only Roland Kane had enough clout to get her a few minutes of Cray time, which she desperately needed for her paper. She had been shoehorned into the conference at the very last minute as a replacement for Tim Gresham, who had come down with the flu.

Some of her calculations were still incomplete. Otherwise, there was nothing on this earth that would have her knocking on Roland Kane's door at eight o'clock on a sunny Italian morning.

Faith stood in the doorway and made polite humming sounds. Then she coughed. Professor Kane didn't show a flicker of response. "I, ah—" Faith coughed again, louder. "Professor Kane?"

Faith took two steps into the room and wrinkled her nose. The smell of alcohol was heavy in the air. An unstoppered bottle of Glenfiddich, three-quarters empty, stood on the laminated plastic next to another full bottle, unopened.

Faith remembered the incredible fuss Roland Kane had made at Rome airport when the customs officer had halted him to check the clinking sounds in a carryon bag and discovered four bottles of Glenfiddich.

Four bottles for a three-day seminar. God forbid he should run out.

Bottle number one was almost finished by day one. Faith wondered whether they sold Glenfiddich in Italy. She also wondered what Professor Kane's liver looked like.

Faith stood in the doorway a moment longer, then stepped cautiously into the room. Professor Kane didn't seem to be paying her any attention, so she edged over to the left, rising a little on tiptoe, eager to get a look at the view through his window.

The St. Vincent's contingent had arrived late the previous night and, so far, all Faith had seen of Italy was Rome Fiumicino Airport, the Florence airport, and some of the Tuscan countryside from Florence to Siena from the minivan that had picked them up.

But it had been growing dark, and all she'd seen of fabled Tuscany was the rather dingy outskirts of Florence and a few hilltop towns on the darkening horizon. They had arrived at the *Certosa di Ponteremoli* well after dark, and their Italian hosts had been so anxious to feed them that they hadn't seen anything at all but the refectory room and the cell each mathematician had been assigned.

Her cell was on the other side of the large quadrangle where the monks had lived and prayed. It had a view over a small, charming cloister garden with an ivy-bedecked stone well. She was looking forward to sitting down with a book in the cloister after lunch, but now, right now, she wanted to see something of Tuscany in the daylight.

She shot another glance at Professor Kane. He still showed no flicker of response. *Probably out cold,* she thought disgustedly.

How could so much intellectual power be packed into such a miserable human being? Still, he was her boss, so she couldn't give in to her urge to haul back and kick him, as he so richly deserved. She stood on tiptoe and craned her neck to see out his window, barely suppressing an exclamation of awe. The view was like an impossibly beautiful painting by a Renaissance artist.

Beautiful trees marched up and down the gentle hills. They were tall, dark green, as slender and as elegant as church spires. *Cypresses,* she thought. In the distance topping the highest hill was Siena, golden-red and magical.

Faith stood for a long moment, transfixed by the scene. The intense colors, the landscape which looked as if an impossibly gifted gardener had planned it down to the finest, most meticulous detail, the bright, cloudless cobalt blue sky—everything called out to her and touched a chord deep in her heart she hadn't known existed. *There isn't a human being alive,* she thought, *whose very soul wouldn't thrill to that view.*

Well, maybe not the pig at her feet. Professor Kane's soul, she was certain, was completely impervious to beauty. As it was to kindness and responsibility. Faith flicked a glance down at him. He looked exactly like what he was—a self-centered monster.

His lean face was heavily crisscrossed with lines of cruelty and ill temper. *No soul at all there—merely a brain.* A brain that, for all its brilliance, was unable to appreciate the beauty beckoning from his window. *Otherwise, he wouldn't be passed out at my feet,* she thought in disgust.

At least he wasn't snoring. Faith frowned as she realized that. *Why wasn't he snoring? Wouldn't a drunk snore?* Her father certainly did, though admittedly Nick hadn't... She stopped herself. *Don't go there.* She didn't want to *think* of that. It had been humiliating enough living it.

She drew in a deep breath and tried to concentrate on Professor Kane. Horrible as the man was, it was certainly better to think of him than of Nick.

The thought was distasteful, but she had to wake him up. Last night Griffin Ball had said if it turned out that she needed Cray time, Kane would have to authorize the call to the computer center at St. Vincent's.

She'd been up all night, frantically trying to ready her paper, but a few vital calculations were missing and her laptop wasn't powerful enough.

She needed the Cray and this was a perfect time. It was 2:00 a.m. back in Deerfield and the Cray would, in all probability, be free. If she waited until Professor Kane sobered up, she'd likely find the Cray in use. So—though what she would really have liked to do was tiptoe back out of the room—she braced herself.

"Professor Kane?" That was no good. He hadn't even stirred. Faith cursed the fact she had a soft voice that didn't carry. Even though her classes were in a small classroom, she needed amplification for the lessons.

Faith cleared her throat and pitched her voice louder. "Professor Kane? Professor Kane, I'm sorry to bother you—"

Faith broke off and frowned. Her distaste for the man had kept her from looking too closely, but now that she focused on him, she could tell that there was something wrong. Very wrong.

His normally sallow complexion was ash-gray, the eyes deeply sunken into the bruised-looking flesh around them. His features were like wax, utterly still and immobile.

Faith wondered whether he had had a heart attack. No, that wasn't possible. Professor Kane didn't have a heart.

Maybe a stroke. That was more like it. He certainly had a brain.

Faith had read somewhere that you weren't supposed to practice first aid on stroke victims. She certainly hoped it was a stroke, and not a heart attack. The idea of giving Professor Kane mouth-to-mouth resuscitation made her skin crawl.

She looked at his chest, hoping to tell by sight alone whether he was breathing, and trying not to think about the fact she should be trying to get a pulse. She didn't want to touch him.

His chest didn't appear to be moving. For the first time, Faith noticed that Professor Kane's left hand was lying under him in what must have been a viciously uncomfortable position, and his right fist was clenched on his chest. The upper-left quadrant. So it might be a heart attack, after all.

With a sigh, Faith dropped to her knees beside him. She was going to have to touch him. It was her duty to help a fellow human being and Roland Kane *was* a human being, after all. In a manner of speaking.

She tried to lift his hand away from his chest to feel for his pulse, and found to her surprise that it wouldn't budge. His fist was clenched *around* something. It hadn't been immediately apparent because everything on his chest was gray — his shirt, his hand, what his hand was holding…

Then, suddenly, Faith's normally sharp mind finally snapped to attention. Her thought processes had been slowed and were fuzzy and vague from sleep deprivation. Well, after all, she'd been up most of the night on her computer, frantically trying to ready a half-finished paper after having flown across the Atlantic. And then, of course, she'd been up the night before *that* with Nick...

Stop that, she told her mind sternly. *Concentrate.* She studied Professor Kane's chest then reached out to the clenched hand. She couldn't pry it open. With great difficulty, she pulled his hand up and away from his chest, then stared.

The gray thing he was holding wasn't a pen or a laser pointer, as she'd thought. It was a knife. A stiletto, to be exact. A long, very sharp one. And it must have been plunged straight into Professor Kane's heart, for blood stained the shaft.

Well what do you know? Faith thought. *He had a heart, after all.*

Without really thinking, she tugged and the slim haft slid through Professor Kane's claw-like hand into hers.

Shock and horror coursed through her system as she slowly rose to her feet. Unsteadily, Faith stood and turned and reached for the door. She stopped on the threshold, stymied for a moment. The Quantitative Methods Week organized by the University of Siena and St. Vincent's was a yearly affair. She knew that Professor Kane, Griffin Ball, Madeleine Kobbel and Tim Gresham had been attending for years.

But it was her first time and she didn't know anyone. She didn't speak Italian. She didn't even know where the rest of the contingent had been lodged. She only knew where Professor Kane was because she'd checked last night.

The only thing she could think to do was report it to the authorities. But this was a foreign country and who knew what passed for authority here?

She'd seen the reception area last night—a small cubicle just inside the vast iron-studded wooden door to the monastery. Last night, there'd been a guard posted in the cubicle. Maybe that was authority enough.

Faith hurried down the stairs and along the portico rimming the quadrangle. A slight mist rose from the grassy center as the sun's rays started heating up the cool ground. It was going to be a hot day.

There was no one about and before she could wonder about that, she heard laughter and the clinking of silverware coming from one of the big, wrought iron-barred windows across the way. Where they'd had dinner last night, she remembered.

There's no one about because everyone's having breakfast, she thought, as she walked up the steep cobble-stoned incline to the guardhouse and the entrance to the monastery.

Just where she'd rather be this morning—having a real Italian espresso instead of scurrying off to report a murder. On that grim thought, Faith walked into the guardhouse.

"Excuse me."

A handsome, middle-aged man looked up from his newspaper with a smile. When he saw a pretty young woman, his smile became flirtatious. "*Si, signorina?*"

"I'd like to—" Faith coughed to loosen her tight throat. "I'd like to report a—a murder?"

The man's smile broadened, showing acres of strong, blindingly white teeth. "*Si, si.*"

He raised his hand and pointed to a wooden door across the way. Faith was halfway across the room when she saw what he was pointing at. She turned back with a sigh.

"No, no." Faith shook her head. "I don't need a bathroom. I have one of my own, thank you. No, I need to report a *murder.*" The guard looked at her blankly. Faith pantomimed a knife going into her chest. "A *murder.*" She knocked on her chest with the edge of her fist and the guard's eyes followed her hand with interest. "You know. Murder?"

"Muh-duh," the guard said amiably and shrugged his shoulders. He lifted his eyes reluctantly from her breasts and raised an eyebrow. Out of politeness, he beat his chest, too. Probably thinking this was some strange American gesture of goodwill.

"No, no." She knew it was ridiculous, but she raised her voice, as if that would make him understand. "Murder! Murder! A — man — has — been — murdered."

Exasperated, Faith put her hands around her neck and shook it. She jerked her head at an angle, rolled her eyes up and allowed her tongue to loll slightly out.

The guard's smile slipped and he eyed the door. "*Prego, signorina?*"

"*Mortus.*" Remnants of high school Latin swam up. She must be more tired than she'd realized not to have thought of it sooner. "*Homo mortus.*" She couldn't remember her numbers in Latin, though, so she reached behind the guard. He jerked back, wary now of the crazed foreigner.

"It's okay. You're not the dead man," Faith said reassuringly. There were forty small cubicles with hooks for the keys to the cells. Most of them were empty. She tapped number seventeen, Professor Kane's room.

"He's the one who's dead. Seventeen. Professor Roland Kane. *Mortus.*" Faith met the guard's eyes. Comprehension was dawning. She nodded and tapped seventeen again. "*Mortus.*"

The guard picked up the phone, never taking his eyes off her, punched out a three-digit number hastily and spoke in quick liquid tones into the receiver. Faith could catch only one word that sounded familiar. *Morto.* Dead.

Shaken, Faith sank down on a cane-bottomed chair. She tried to make it look natural, but her knees were weak. The reality of what she'd seen was starting to sink in.

Professor Kane was dead. Murdered. Faith wasn't surprised he'd died by someone's hand — she'd contemplated offing him herself any number of times, as had just about everyone on the faculty of St. Vincent's.

But there was an abyss between fantasizing about killing a nasty, overbearing man and actually doing it. Actually taking a knife and plunging it into a human heart. Perhaps holding it in place, watching the light in the eyes fade, watching the life drain away...

Faith shivered. She was alone in the cubicle now. The guard was outside the entrance pacing the wide, graveled driveway, all Latin insouciance gone.

She lifted her eyes and was startled to see a face staring back at her. The face was dead white, with pale freckles scattered over the nose and cheeks, and wide, light-brown eyes. Pale face, pale eyes. A ghost.

She knew she was seeing what Nick had seen the morning after the night before.

No wonder he hadn't remembered her name. Who could? She looked insubstantial — pale and lifeless. Plain and utterly forgettable. Faith looked away from the mirror, unable to bear the sight.

How could Nick remember her name? He was brimming with life. It flowed from his fingertips. He seemed to carry a force field around his large, strong frame. Even his coloring was vivid. Blue-black hair, bright blue eyes, olive skin with ruddy undertones.

Faith could see him now, his face alive with joy and excitement. Just being around him was like being at the circus. When she'd tagged along with Nick and Lou and all the assorted Rossis, she'd had to work to keep her eyes off him. Even now, if she closed her eyes, she could see his laughing, handsome face...

"*Signorina.*"

Faith's eyes flew open. She hadn't heard anyone come in. Shaken from finding Professor Kane, shaken from her thoughts of Nick, she just stared at the newcomer.

"Nick?" she breathed. "What on earth are you doing in—" she began, then bit her tongue.

The man standing in front of her was tall and well-built, with olive skin and bright blue eyes and as handsome as sin, just like Nick. But instead of blue-black hair, his hair was dark brown and he wasn't smiling. Nick always smiled.

"Not Nick," he said soberly in perfect English. "Dante. *Commissario* Dante Rossi. Of the Siena Police Department."

Chapter Two

Left to themselves, things tend to go from bad to worse.

ॐ

Deerfield, Massachusetts

Nick let the phone ring fifteen times. The shrill sound of the rings hurt his ears. For that matter, breathing still hurt.

His instinct was to lie down for a few days, maybe a few weeks, until he felt better, but he couldn't until he'd talked to Faith. Which, it appeared, wasn't going to be any time soon. He finally hung up, still hung over.

He'd been calling since the day before yesterday morning.

He'd sent flowers, but the florist had called to say there was nobody home to accept delivery.

He'd driven by, shielding his eyes against the nauseatingly bright sunshine, driving slowly because he was sure he still had an illegal amount of alcohol in his system even after two days.

He could just see the headlines if he'd been arrested while still steeped in alcohol. *Former Hunter Star Arrested For Drunk Driving*. And it would all be out.

The concussion, the letter from the doctor, the letter from the team manager. The sympathy, the calls from friends who would soon be former friends, bandwagon fans, newshounds hot after the scent of blood...

It was going to come out soon anyway. Nick Rossi's forced retirement from hockey was going to be big news and the calls were going to come sooner or later.

Later, as far as Nick was concerned. The later, the better.

It was why he wasn't answering the phone and why he had put his answering service in the spare room.

One of the spare rooms.

Ever since his sister Lou had had him buy into this luxury condo as an investment, he had more room — *rooms* — than he knew what to do with. He'd put the answering service in the room Lou called "The Botanical Gulag" because it was where he put all his plants after they'd died on him.

He didn't want to talk to anyone right now. His parents were at a conference in Miami, Lou was on an out-of-town business trip and the only other person he wanted to talk to would probably cut off her own finger before dialing his number.

Faith thought he hadn't remembered her name after an entire night spent making love. What Faith hadn't realized was that he couldn't remember his *own* name at the time.

After the team neurologist had told him, gently but firmly, that Nick would never play professional hockey again and that, if he were smart, a bracing game of tiddlywinks would be the extent of his competitive playing, he had gone out on a booze cruise and had basically emptied Deerfield of alcohol.

And Faith had ended up as road kill.

He picked up the phone and started punching out the numbers. Again. Faith had to come back to her apartment some time, didn't she?

Siena, Italy

Commissario Dante Rossi kept his voice low. "Miss Murphy?"

The young woman didn't answer for a moment. She was utterly white-faced and he supposed she might be in shock.

Finding a dead body would do that to a person. He was about ready to repeat the question when she answered in a steady voice.

"Yes, I'm Faith Murphy." She peered at him closely. "Rossi. *Commissario* Rossi. Are you Lou's cousin?"

He inclined his head. He leaned forward and took her hand gently in his. "The same. I was going to call the *Certosa* today. Lou called me to look out after you. A murder wasn't quite what she had in mind."

"No." Faith Murphy's smile was shaky. "No. It, ah, came as a shock to me, too."

"I imagine it did." Dante looked around the small reception area. The *Certosa* had changed since he and Nick had run wild as teenagers through the ruins of the old monastery. Now it was restored and elegant, even stately. He turned to the night porter and asked in Italian, "Where can I speak with the American lady in private?"

"More or less every room in the main cloisters is set up for the conference and the University of Siena people are everywhere. You'll have to go into the next courtyard. Go down the ramp and turn left, then right, then left again. Through the archway, fourth door on the right. There's a meeting room called the San Francesco room. That will give you some privacy, *Commissario*."

Dante narrowed his eyes. "Do I know you?"

The man grinned. "Egidio Pecci. You went to school with my boy Carlo."

"Ah, Carlo Pecci. From the Caterpillar." Now Dante remembered the laughing, black-haired boy he'd gotten into endless scrapes with. He resembled his father.

The family was from the Caterpillar *contrada,* one of the seventeen districts in Siena, seventeen little mini-states with their own flags, colors, symbols, mottos and songs, and all locked in an endless thousand-year-old battle to win a silken banner, the *Palio*, twice a year, in a horse race. Being from the Caterpillar was all right.

The Rossis were from the Snail *contrada*, which had been allies of the Caterpillars for going on seven hundred years. "What's Carlo doing now?"

The man's grin disappeared and he lifted his hands heavenward. "Gone," he said mournfully. "Carlo works for the *Monte dei Paschi* and they sent him to Milan."

In Siena, working for the *Monte dei Paschi*, the oldest bank in the world, was the equivalent of working for God. You followed His inscrutable ways, even when they meant exile. The way Egidio had said "Milan", Dante knew he might just as well have said his son had been posted to Devil's Island.

Dante understood. He, too, had been posted for three tedious, interminable years to the *Questura*, the police headquarters, of Bolzano, the northernmost city in Italy, practically in Austria's lap, where the food had been bad and the women Teutonic and boring. The four years in Naples with good, spicy food and bad, spicy women had been better. But it hadn't been Siena. He knew what exile from Siena was like.

"Too bad," he said sincerely, placing a hand on Egidio's shoulder.

"Particularly *this* year, when the Caterpillar is bound to win the *Palio*," Egidio said with a sly look at Dante.

"In your dreams, Caterpillar," Dante said cheerfully. "In your dreams."

He turned to the woman, sobering up immediately. She had been watching them carefully, big light-brown eyes moving from him to Egidio and back. Dante nodded to the door. "We can talk more easily in another room, *Signorina* Murphy. Over in the other cloister. Down the ramp, through the archway, fourth door to the right. It says *Sala San Francesco* on the door. I'll be right there."

After she had left, Dante leaned close to Egidio. "There used to be only this one entrance to the *Certosa*." Except for the west wall, which fifteen years ago presented few obstacles to agile teenagers. "Is that still the case?"

"Yes." Egidio turned and picked up a huge cast iron key, suitable for the lock of a medieval castle. He hefted it in his hand. "And I have the only key."

"Okay. I want you to make sure that no one from the *Certosa* leaves the premises until I say they can. Where's the body?"

"Room seventeen, the lady said," Egidio answered promptly. "That's on the first floor."

"In about fifteen minutes, my men from *La Scientifica* will be arriving. Tell them I'll be up straight away."

Egidio's mouth formed an O at the mention of the *Scientifica*, the Crime Scene Squad. He swallowed and nodded.

Dante knew that a thousand TV scenes of polished pros poring over a dead body were flashing before Egidio's eyes. Little did Egidio know that the Siena Crime Scene Squad saw murdered bodies about as often as the Snail *contrada* won the *Palio*. Which was never.

With a sigh, Dante made his way down the ramp, wishing the American had waited until after the *Palio* to get killed.

It was the heart of *Palio* season, the period the entire city waited for, dreamed of, schemed for all year round.

Today was the feast day of the patron saints of his *contrada*, Saints Peter and Paul. All of the Snails would be out in the streets celebrating, from the youngest to the oldest. It was the day in which kids, and the odd infatuated foreigner, would be baptized into the *contrada* at the little fountain that spouted wine whenever the Snail won.

Alas, wine hadn't flowed from the fountain in far too many years.

This morning would be the drawing of lots to assign the horses to each district, after the horses had a trial run around the unusual race track, the fan-shaped central square which turned into a golden track of magic twice a year.

It was a tradition stretching back a thousand years, one that would doubtless continue for another thousand. So whether Dante was there or not would make no difference whatsoever to the outcome. But he wanted to be there. He didn't want to be embroiled in the investigation of the death of a foreigner.

He wanted to watch the horses race, wanted to stand there listening to the old timers judging legs and breadth of chest and stoutness of heart. Word had it that the best horse of all was Lina, a bay. Who knew if fate would assign Lina to the Snail *contrada*?

Only ten *contradas* out of the seventeen raced at every *Palio*. There were two *Palios* a year, one in July and one in August. This year, the Snail was running in both. All Sienese took life one *Palio* at a time.

There was a chance in ten that fate would allow his Snail *contrada* to draw Lina. They already had the nastiest, craftiest jockey in Italy, Massimo Ceccherini, known to all as Nerbo, after the whip made of calves' phalluses the jockeys used in the race. Considering Nerbo's reputation as a skirt chaser— and catcher—the nickname was an apt one.

Maybe the goddess Fortuna, notorious bitch that she was, would smile on them this year.

God knew the Snail needed all the help fate could give it. The Snail was the *nonna*, the grandmother, of all the *contradas*, the *contrada* that had gone the longest without a victory.

Seventeen long years in the desert...seventeen long years with the grandmother's bonnet that was a mark of shame. Surely this year...

Murder is so...so un-Sienese, he thought, as he walked along the cloister skirting the central courtyard of the *Certosa.* Why risk spending your life in prison where the food was bad and the company worse just to kill someone?

Particularly since God or biology — depending upon your faith — would eventually take care of that problem in time. You just had to wait, that was all.

With a sigh, Dante walked toward Miss Murphy and his duty.

* * * * *

Fleeing four thousand miles from one Rossi only to find another Rossi and a dead man is perfect Murphy luck, Faith thought as she walked on the herringbone brick walkway.

The cloister was spectacular, as if the careless gods who botched looking after the Murphys were trying to make up for years and years of things gone wrong. A large grassy swath with an enormous oak so old the first branch was a hundred feet from the earth, a wishing well with an ornate wrought iron cupola, broad topiary evergreens, all ringed by the graceful arches of the arcade. And roses. Everywhere. In full, spectacular bloom.

The intense smell of roses, ancient tightly furled roses with bees hovering over them just waiting for the day to heat up enough to entice them to open, tickled her nose.

Trust Kane to get whacked in a gorgeous place.

Faith was sure her own fate was to end up a week-old dead body in some musty motel in Bumfuck, Nowhere, with the wind whistling down from the North Pole. She'd be dead for days and days, and they'd find her body by the smell.

Down the ramp. Through the archway, fourth door to the right. She entered the smaller courtyard — the one she'd seen from her window this morning, delicate and welcoming — and counted four doors. *Sala San Francesco,* a terra-cotta tablet informed her.

Faith knocked briefly, then walked in. It was high-ceilinged with cream-colored stucco walls and the vestiges of a fresco on one wall. Some anorexic saint willing improbable miracles.

There were chairs arranged in rows in front of a steel desk. Clearly, the room was used for lectures on some thorny topic, because the chairs looked lethally uncomfortable, with tiny hard seats and spindly legs. She thought of some of her obese students back home. They'd never get an education over here.

Behind her, she heard the door open then close.

The *Commissario,* whatever that was. Of the Siena police, he'd said. She didn't know what rank *Commissario* was, but it sounded pretty high.

Commissars in Soviet Russia had held the power of life and death over people, she remembered.

She hadn't even had time to contemplate the insane coincidence of having a Rossi show up to investigate Kane's murder. The same Rossi cousin Lou had urged her to call when she'd told Lou she was, improbably, going to Siena, Italy. At the very last minute yesterday, Kane had called to say Tim Gresham was sick and she was taking his place at the Quantitative Methods Seminar in Siena.

She had had two hours to pack and had met Lou as she was rushing out of the building they shared.

Sort of shared.

Faith low-rented a damp bedsit in the basement and Lou owned the spacious penthouse, but it was the same building so that counted. Lou's father taught at St. Vincent's and she'd met Lou at a university fundraiser. They'd discovered they lived in the same building and she and Lou had become friends.

Lou had introduced her to her brother Nick, who in turn had introduced her to sex — good sex, at any rate — which had led her to Siena and murder and another Rossi.

Nothing like circularity.

Just before leaving, Lou had pressed a piece of paper in her hand. "Here's my cousin's number. His name is Dante, and he's cute and fun and he's not married and I want you to call him, now." Lou's eyes had narrowed. "Wait. Knowing you, you won't, so *I'll* call him and have him call you. You'll like him."

Well, Faith hadn't had to call him after all. He'd come all on his own.

Ain't life grand?

Faith sat down in one of the spindly chairs and expected *Commissario* Rossi to take a seat behind the desk and play power politics, but he surprised her by grabbing one of the uncomfortable chairs and sitting next to her. He took out a notepad and pen.

"So, Miss Murphy," he began, "I understand you found a body this morning."

"A dead one." Faith nodded. "And you can call me Faith, if you want. I know your cousin Lou very well."

"Lucrezia." He smiled faintly.

Dear God, he looked so much like Nick it was scary.

"And you must call me Dante."

He was tall and well-built without giving the impression of being a mountain, like Nick did, but he had the same bright blue eyes, dark hair — chestnut instead of blue-black like Nick—and the same olive skin and strong features. No wonder she'd mistaken him for Nick.

"Lucrezia called me yesterday to say you were coming and to look you up. I was going to call today. I didn't imagine I'd be meeting you this way."

"No." Faith smiled faintly. "Not even Lou could think up this much excitement."

"I see you *do* know her well." He even had the Rossi charm. His English was excellent, with only a faint hint of an accent. He leaned forward. "So, Faith, what happened?"

It was smooth and friendly, but Faith was under no illusions that this was anything but a police interrogation.

"Nothing actually happened, in the sense of action. The man was dead after all." She spoke slowly. Dear God, she was so tired. "I knocked on Professor Kane's door at eight o'clock this morning."

Reflexively, Faith looked down at her wristwatch. Only an hour and a half ago. It felt like a century. "I needed to ask for some information. His door was ajar so, when I didn't get an answer, I pushed it open slightly. Then I saw him stretched out on the floor." Her lips tightened. "I thought he was drunk."

"Hmm." He looked down at his notepad. "You must have known him well to make such an assumption."

"Well, I've worked under Professor Kane for a year now, so I was aware of...of his habits."

Dante Rossi wrote quickly in his notepad, bold, certain strokes, unlike Nick who wrote painstakingly slowly, a letter at a time.

A bird chirruped loudly outside, interrupting the silence. Faith swayed in her chair with exhaustion. Part of it was hunger—she hadn't eaten much last night and hadn't had breakfast yet—part of it was sleep deprivation, but a goodly portion of it was emotional burnout.

Too many things happening all at once, none of them good.

The luck of the Murphys, holding true.

Dante looked up, pen hovering.

Faith took a deep breath and let it out slowly. Pinwheels danced across her eyes and she shut them for a moment. Which wasn't good, because she saw Roland Kane's ill-tempered features in vivid color. Her eyes snapped open. Seeing Dante Rossi instead of Kane was a distinct improvement.

"And?" he prodded.

"So, I walked in and, um, coughed."

"To get his attention?"

Faith looked at him, startled. "That's right."

He smiled. "You look surprised that I understand. I see you're used to Nick. He's a little slow."

That was Faith's cue to defend Nick. He was often the butt of family jokes and she'd heard them all—that he played hockey with a warped stick, that his think tank leaked, that he'd played too often without a helmet.

Nick wasn't dumb, just a little clueless at times.

Faith opened her mouth then closed it. Let Nick defend himself, the rat.

"And you didn't get his attention, right?"

Faith blinked. "Nick's?"

He sighed. "No. Professor Kane's."

"No." Faith frowned. Maybe Nick wasn't the only clueless one. "He was dead."

"Yes, of course he was. But you couldn't have known that at the time now, could you?"

His blue, blue eyes were laser-sharp. No, the man wasn't clueless and Faith decided she had better wake up and get her act together before she found herself in handcuffs.

"No," she admitted. "I couldn't. So what I did was cough and make little humming sounds."

"Did you shuffle your feet? That always works with the *Vice Questore*, my boss, when he's trying to ignore me." He smiled that charming Rossi smile.

"Yes, I shuffled. I was getting annoyed. Today's a big day and there's a lot of work to be done to prepare for the conference. Then I noticed he looked a little...odd."

"Odd?"

"Well, he *was* dead, after all. Anyway, as I looked at him, he seemed grayer than usual. And then I noticed he wasn't breathing."

Dante nodded. "That's a pretty good indication of death right there."

"Exactly. So I thought maybe he'd had a heart attack because his fist was clenched over his chest."

"Which fist?"

"The right. He was holding it clenched over his heart, which is why I thought he had had a heart attack. So I tried to pull his hand away and it came away with difficulty, which must mean —" She looked at him closely. "Rigor?"

"Maybe," he said calmly. "The coroner will tell us. So, Faith, we have you in a cell with a dead man and you pull his hand away from his chest. Yes?"

"Yes."

"And it came away with difficulty?"

"It came away with a knife. Not a knife so much as a...a stiletto. Very long and sharp."

"Did you touch the knife?"

Those blue eyes were watching her so carefully.

"I'm afraid I did," Faith said, and he sighed and made an annotation.

"Pity."

"Yes. I suppose that makes me suspect number one."

"No." His dark head was bent as he wrote.

He needed a haircut.

"Finding the body makes you suspect number one. Now."

She tried not to squirm as he lifted his head and skewered her with his sharp gaze.

"Let me get this straight. You knock on the victim's door at eight o'clock this morning, the door is open, you walk in and observe the victim. It takes you a few moments to realize he is deceased."

He was making her sound like an idiot. "I was very tired," she said in her defense. "I'd just made an intercontinental trip and I haven't been sleeping well lately." *Not to mention sleeping with your cousin*, she thought, and turned bright red.

He observed her carefully. "Okay," he said finally. "You're tired and it takes you a while to get your bearings, but then you do finally see that something is wrong and you...what? Kneel?"

"I—I guess so." Faith closed her eyes for a moment so she could relive the scene. Closing her eyes felt so good she allowed her mind's eye to roam right out of the room and into the sky...

"Faith?"

Her eyes popped open. She straightened. "Sorry." Falling asleep while describing a murder to a police officer was not smart. "I hunkered down, but my knees didn't touch the floor." *Did knees leave knee prints?* she wondered. "Do knees leave knee prints?"

"No. Did you touch anything besides the knife?"

Had she touched anything else? "No. The door, the doorknob, Professor Kane's hand and the stiletto. That's about it."

"What did you do after you picked up the knife?"

"Dropped it. I wasn't expecting it. I thought he was clutching a pen or something. So when I saw what it was, and that there was blood on it…"

"Recent blood?"

"I beg your pardon?"

"Was the blood still dripping, or was it coagulated?"

"Oh, I see." Personally, Faith thought that, like a vampire's, Kane's blood couldn't coagulate. "Well, it didn't drip blood, if that's what you mean. So I dropped the knife and went down to tell someone that Professor Kane was dead."

"Murdered, you mean." His gaze was level, as was his voice.

"Yes. Murdered." Faith spread her hands. "You know the rest. I waited in the reception room while he called the police. You."

"Me." He rose and her eyes followed him up. He was very tall, almost as tall as Nick. "I'm going to have to ask you to be available for further questioning. We'll be wanting to talk to you again. And we'll be wanting to talk to your colleagues, as well. Please ask them to be available and not to leave the *Certosa* until I say so."

Faith rose, too. "Certainly."

He smiled faintly. "I'm sorry you've had such a...violent introduction to Italy. Lou will be on my case about this."

She was startled. "It's not your fault, *Commissario*."

"I told you. Please call me Dante." He sighed and tucked his notepad in his shirt pocket. "And of course she'll blame me. Lou could make rain seem my fault. And Nick's."

It was true. It was one of the things Faith most admired in Lou.

Dante held the door open for her and followed her out. He murmured a goodbye, and Faith went to break the news to her colleagues about the murder and to look for a cup of coffee.

Coffee first.

Chapter Three

After things have gone from bad to worse, the cycle will repeat itself.

❧

Commissario Dante Rossi really hated murder.

He had become a police officer because he loved upholding the peace. He hated it when the peace was broken.

A wayward husband or two, kids who got overly rowdy, some property damage, *Palio* fans from rival *contradas* getting into fist fights...those were perfectly normal events which could be easily put right.

But murder—well, nothing would put a death to rights. Not even the God he didn't believe in could bring someone back to life.

Dante heaved a huge sigh and turned his mind to the business at hand. Second stairs to the right, Egidio had said. His crime scene people would be arriving soon. He wanted to get there beforehand and gather first impressions, take the lay of the land, as it were.

He ran nimbly up the stairs and turned right, his boot heels echoing along the empty corridor as he counted off the cell numbers.

The door to cell seventeen was open so he looked in, pulling out surgical gloves from his pocket as he did so.

He couldn't remember the last time he had been required to wear latex gloves.

From outside in, from left to right, from ceiling to floor. He remembered that from his course on Crime Scene Techniques in Rome taught by Claudio Simoni, a man so old he had seemed mummified except for his sharp black eyes. "Observe, observe, observe," Simoni had repeated endlessly.

Well, there was nothing to observe from the doorway. This door had nothing whatsoever to distinguish it from any of the others in the long, empty corridor except for the small brass seventeen, a number that brought bad luck in Italy.

It had certainly brought bad luck to Roland Kane.

Dante nudged the door open slightly with his foot and it swung silently to the left. *Divide the room into four quadrants.* He could almost hear *Professore* Simoni's voice with its tobacco rasp. *Anterior, posterior, left, right. Where is the body?*

Neatly laid out on the median line, he mentally answered *Professore* Simoni. *Feet north, head south.*

The room reeked of alcohol. There was an open bottle of Glenfiddich whiskey on the laminated desk, half full, and a full bottle next to it. Dante sighed because he knew that the opened bottle—and the unopened bottle as well, just to be thorough—would have to go to the toxicology lab in Florence and it was likely they'd sit on it for days.

Dante leaned over and sniffed the air. There was a definite smell of alcohol—of whiskey—coming from the body as well, and he knew that the deceased's blood would have to go to Florence, too, since Siena didn't have a forensic toxicology lab. The blood was pure alcohol, judging from the smell.

He hunkered down and surveyed the body somberly. The dead man was about a meter seventy-five. He was stretched out on his back, dressed in a cheap, ill-cut suit with more polyester than cotton that no Italian male above the poverty line would be caught...well, dead in.

He wondered if the man would be buried in a similar suit. He wondered if the dead professor had anyone at home who even cared what he would be buried in.

Dante remembered when his Uncle Francesco had died seven years ago. Aunt Sara had insisted her husband be buried in a new suit and new shoes.

He had accompanied his cousins Laura and Andrea to buy the suit and they had picked it with exactly the same kind of care and disregard for expense that would have gone into buying a suit for a wedding. They had chosen pure cotton underwear and shoes that wouldn't pinch.

Professor Kane was lying supine with his right hand over his stomach. There was a long, sharp stiletto knife about a meter away. Dante examined it without touching it. *Schauble* was finely engraved on the haft.

It was a good German brand that produced excellent cutlery and knives. Sold both in Europe and in America. Only lab analysis would yield any information on the blood, and Forti, his lab tech, would be lifting any latents, though he knew Faith Murphy's fingerprints were already on it.

A dumb move for what looked like a smart woman. Unless she'd killed him.

If she had, touching the stiletto had been a very smart move. She'd instantly had a perfectly reasonable motive for her fingerprints being on the knife that had killed a man.

Dante had seen lots of dead bodies in his twelve years as a police officer, especially when he'd been stationed in Naples. The dead bodies he'd seen in Siena had been traffic accidents mostly. Overturned tractors. Once, horribly, a child drowned in a well fifteen days before. A few fires.

As a policeman, Dante had seen most of what life did to humans and his soul had hardened some.

But murder still gave him a primeval sense of dread — man usurping the natural order.

He wasn't a religious man — no Rossi was. From the patriarch, Senio, who still had his lithograph of Lenin — not in its heavy walnut frame on the living room wall anymore, since times had changed and not even the Communists were Communists now—on down. The lithograph was tucked away in Senio's sock drawer, though Dante suspected he took it out now and again to look at it.

Senio still drank to the Revolution on November 7th. From Senio to Michelangelo's youngest, unbaptized son, the Rossis were *mangiapreti*—priest-eaters, fiercely anticlerical. So, too, was Dante. He didn't believe in an afterlife. There was only *this* life—with all its sweetness and bitterness, to be drunk down to the dregs. There wasn't anything after this. There were no second chances. This was it.

This was certainly it for the man lying on his back in the sunlight-filled room. Outside the window of cell seventeen could be seen Siena, the graceful tower whose bell tolled constantly on the mornings of the *Palio*, the copper cupola of the cathedral gleaming in the distance, the brick walls shining red-gold in the sun.

The man had had one of the best views in the world, but he would never see it again.

He would never feel the summer sun's rays on his face again. He would never go strolling in the countryside again. He would never make love to a woman—or to a man if his tastes ran that way—again. He would never sip coffee in an outdoor square with friends again. Life had flown from his body.

The dead man didn't have a face that looked as if he had enjoyed many cups of coffee with friends.

How a murdered man had lived his life was the greatest clue to his death. Dante would be hearing a lot about Professor Roland Kane in the next few hours and days.

He would interview Professor Kane's colleagues. He would find out whether Kane's colleagues loved him, hated him or merely tolerated him. Uncle Lorenzo would be emailing him the professor's history, as would his close friend Sam Murray of the Deerfield PD. Sometimes the bare bones of a life were enough to know whether that life had been lived well—in peace with loved ones—or badly in constant strife.

Judging by the harsh lines crisscrossing Professor Kane's face, frown lines more than laugh lines, Dante was sure there couldn't have been too much love in the professor's life.

Hatred, then. Envy and jealousy and hostility. And once he had learned all there was to know about the dead man, as day follows night, Dante would know who had killed him.

There was a clatter in the hallway.

Shaking his head at the waste, Dante rose to let his men in.

He really, really hated murder.

Faith followed her nose back to the refectory, but Murphy luck was holding true. The waiters had cleared away the breakfast things and were already setting the tables for lunch.

A girl finds a dead body and she can't even get a cup of coffee, she thought in disgust. Maybe if she begged.

There were interesting plate-rattling sounds coming from the kitchen. She stuck her head into the spotless room where a chef was stirring something wonderfully savory in a pot and a waiter was chopping salad. They looked up.

"Coffee?" she asked. "*Caffè*? Please?"

Both men were extremely good-looking. The chef smiled and said, "*Sì, signorina.*" He immediately put a moka maker on the gas stove.

"*Grazie.*" She was getting the hang of Italian. Having so many attractive males around was certainly an incentive.

Any more thousand-watt smiles from dark, gorgeous faces and she'd be babbling.

A few minutes later, the waiter walked out with a little tray and an espresso cup. Faith's stomach growled in appreciation.

A whiff of cologne she didn't recognize but which probably cost more than she spent on underwear in a year, a flutter of an incredibly fine linen shirt, and Griffin Ball was sitting beside her, graciously accepting *her* coffee with a flirtatious smile at the handsome waiter.

With a movement of his elegant hand he pointed at the cup. "*Un altro caffè, per favore.*"

Trust him to speak Italian.

He opened the small packet of sugar on the saucer and carefully poured about a third of it into his cup and stirred. Slim and elegant, he made sure he stayed that way. He leaned his perfectly coiffed head forward. "Is it true, Faith? The staff here is talking but it seems so — so *unreal.* Kane dead sounds..."

"Too good to be true?"

Grif hid his smile behind a genteel cough. He was from the south and had impeccable manners. He also had a wicked sense of humor he emphasized by making his witty comments in a deep, southern drawl. He was sharp, elegant and urbane. He was the ideal of a mathematician, except he had no talent. All of that had gone to Kane, who was — had been — an animal.

"So." He leaned forward. "Is it true, what they're saying? Is he dead?"

"Well," she said, considering. "The last time I saw him, he had rigor mortis, a knife in his heart and he wasn't breathing. Looked pretty dead to me."

Besides Tim Gresham, Grif was her only friend in the math department. Moreover, he understood her perfectly, always. Their eyes met and they looked away, both a second from grinning.

In Faith's case, it would have been a nervous tic of a grin, born of stress and fatigue.

In Grif's case, it would probably have been a grin of vindication. Kane had made Grif's life miserable, too, though Grif wasn't as powerless as she had been. He came from a rich, well-connected southern family, and his partner, Carl, came from a rich, well-connected northern family.

Carl's father had donated enough to St. Vincent's to ensure Carl's suggestion that Griffin Ball, of the South Carolina Balls, be hired for a vacancy in the math faculty be taken seriously.

Grif had little math talent, but was a superb administrator and personnel manager, human skills Roland Kane was abysmal at. Kane had made Grif's life miserable because that was his nature. But deep in the convoluted recesses of Kane's mind, there must have been some recognition of how much he relied on Grif's people skills because Grif's job was always somehow secure, his second-rate skills as a mathematician notwithstanding.

Actually, Faith thought in surprise, Grif is at the moment de facto department head, something he had always wanted to be. The administration had made no bones about the fact that it preferred dealing with him rather than Kane. Admin would undoubtedly confirm the posting as soon as they got home.

Unless, of course, it was Grif who'd offed Kane in the first place.

Could be.

She watched him sipping his coffee—*her* coffee. He looked the way he always looked—cool and elegant and together. From the top of his well-cut hair to the tips of his expensive loafers, he looked like a successful academic, a man at the peak of his powers. But was that...glee she could see in his eyes?

Kane's death solved all of his problems. There was no doubt the academic council would appoint him next head of department, and Grif's life would be the smooth progression he had been born to. *He'd be a good department head, too,* Faith thought. *Fair and just.*

Had he murdered Kane to become department head?

"What are you thinking, Faith?" he asked, putting his cup down on the saucer without a whisper of sound. You had to be born rich to know how to do that. "Your thought processes scare me sometimes."

Me, too, she thought. "I was thinking about Kane."

"Listen, you don't suppose...he'll come back, do you?" Grif gave a little half laugh.

Faith pursed her lips. "From the dead?" If anyone could do it, Roland Kane could. He'd make a great Undead. "I don't think so, Griffin. He looked like he was in a pretty permanent state of death."

Grif smiled. "Well...good."

Faith's snicker was lost in a clatter of dishes from the kitchen and the sound of the door to the hallway opening and then slamming shut.

Quick, tense footsteps and Madeleine Kobbel was frowning down at her. She was breathless, as if she'd been running. "Faith, I heard Roland is dead. Is that true? What's going on?"

Her voice was tense. Her stance was tense. Everything about Madeleine Kobbel was tense. She even managed to have tense clothes—a stiff, unattractive dress in an unflattering deep blood red. Madeleine took a seat near Faith just as the waiter started to put another cup of coffee down. She took it from the waiter's hand and looked up with a tense smile. "*Mille grazie*," she said, and blew on the creamy surface and then gulped it down.

"Actually," Faith began, "that was my—"

"I needed that," Madeleine said.

Not this morning, you don't, Faith thought.

Madeleine was usually silent and retiring, but this morning she looked over-caffeinated and...wild.

Her long, gray hair seemed to lift in electrostatic waves around her face instead of hanging down in lank clumps as it usually did. An undertone of ruddiness underlay her usually sallow complexion. Madeleine had always given Faith the creeps. She wasn't surprised that death seemed to be Madeleine's G-spot.

"Someone said that you found him, Faith." Madeleine fairly vibrated in her chair. "Is that true? Is he really dead?"

Everyone seemed to be worried Kane would come back from the dead, which Faith understood completely. "Yes, Madeleine. I found him and yes, he's really dead. He won't be coming back any time soon."

She primmed her lips. "I didn't mean it *that* way. I meant—I meant *how*. He was perfectly all right yesterday. We all traveled together. How did he die?"

"Oddly enough, not by alcohol poisoning." A miracle, considering the amount of alcohol Kane had soaked up crossing the Atlantic. "He died by a sharp object through the heart."

Madeleine was looking at her strangely, her long, narrow, gray head cocked as if Faith had been speaking some arcane language. *Sharp? Object? Heart?*

"Someone stabbed him," Faith said, just to make it clear.

Madeleine's gasp sounded loud in the room. "He was — he was *murdered?*"

"That's right." Why Madeleine should sound so shocked was beyond Faith. If there was ever a man who asked for a knife through the heart every day of his life, it was Roland Kane. "He was murdered and the police want to talk to you."

"Who?" Grif straightened suddenly.

"Me?" Madeleine said at the same time. "Whatever for?"

Faith looked at both of them. She'd worked with them for a year, but she suddenly felt as if she'd never seen them before.

"The police want to talk to both of you. And as to why, well, I imagine if Kane was murdered, it follows that someone did it. *Q.E.D.* And — I'm just guessing here, I might be wrong — but they might actually want to know who did it."

"There's no call to be sarcastic, Faith." Madeleine's blade-like features took on a disapproving cast. "It's just that — it's just that there's a lot to do still, and the participants are slated to start arriving soon and —"

"And this will interfere with the organization. I understand. God forbid that murder interfere with our seminar." Faith ignored the narrow-eyed glare Madeleine threw her way and perked up at the sound of the waiter coming back in. "Still, I'm afraid the policeman insisted. His name is Dante Rossi and he's —" She stopped to think. "I guess he must be Lorenzo Rossi's nephew."

"Lorenzo Rossi from the economics department?" Grif asked.

"Yes. Dante Rossi. He's the police officer in charge and he speaks perfect English. And he's waiting for you. So go."

They wavered.

The waiter placed another cup on the table and Faith pulled the saucer toward her and placed a protective arm around it. She looked up. "You might not want to make him wait too long. I don't know if they have extradition laws in this country."

Dante Rossi yearned.

It was past noon and the drawing that would assign horses to the *contradas* for the *Palio* was about to begin.

Most of Siena was now in the central square, the *Piazza del Campo*, watching the horses race around the track ten at a time in a trial heat. The Snail's jockey, Nerbo, would be watching the legs of the horses for form and the eyes of the other jockeys for bribe potential.

The trial runs would be just about over and everyone in the *piazza* would have an idea about the best horse and the toughest jockey, and would be arguing at top volume with anyone within earshot.

Dante wanted to be there with every fiber of his being. Instead, he was watching his Crime Scene Unit troop in. Corrado was already blocking off the door with the red-and-white crime scene tape Dante secretly thought was so much more elegant than the American yellow-and-black.

Noon now. Six o'clock Eastern time in the States. He pulled out his cell phone and punched out Lou's number. She'd skin him alive if he didn't let her know that her friend Faith had gotten herself mixed up in a murder.

He let the phone ring for two minutes, but she wasn't home. She was probably away on a business trip. Oddly, Lou's answering service wasn't on. He hesitated for a moment before calling Nick. It was 6:00 a.m. after all, and knowing Nick, he'd had a hard night. Either playing on the ice or playing in bed.

To hell with it. He dialed Nick's number and got the answering service on the third ring.

"Nick, tell Lou I have some good news and some bad news. The good news is her friend Faith is, indeed, very cute. The bad news is that she's got herself mixed up in a murder."

He left a long message explaining everything, then snapped his cell phone closed just as a loud voice boomed, "*Commissario*, permission to enter the room, sir!"

Dante rolled his eyes then turned around. "Permission granted, Loiacono." His latest recruit, Inspector Carmine Loiacono, stiffened, snapping off a sharp salute, and Dante suppressed a sigh.

Carmine Loiacono had been shipped here by disgruntled city officials from Catania, Sicily, where he'd been a little too zealous in uncovering corruption in the local health district. The man was painfully eager to prove his mettle and to show that, notwithstanding local prejudices, southerners knew how to work.

Loiacono was a thorn in Dante's side because he was humorless and because he mangled the beautiful language of Tuscany. On the other hand, he did the work of four men.

"Let's start working the scene, Loiacono," Dante said and waited patiently for the bellowed *Sir!*

"*Sir!*" Loiacono shouted and Dante managed not to wince. Loiacono straightened to his one meter sixty-five-and-a-half centimeters—he had insisted the half centimeter be included in his file—and saluted.

"Okay, let's—" Dante's cell phone rang. He looked at the number on the display. It was Mike. The results of the *tratta* were starting to come in and his heart beat a little faster.

Loiacono, however, would never understand this. He had no conception of what Siena was about and would consider it dereliction of duty to worry about the *Palio* when there was a murder—*a murder!*—to investigate. He was already marching up and down the room, cheeks ruddy with excitement, tossing instructions as Carducci and Falugi trooped in.

"Inspector." Dante beckoned Loiacono over.

"*Sir!*"

Dante put a finger to his lips and Loiacono moved his head closer and whispered, "Sir."

Dante laid a heavy hand on his shoulder. Southerners were used to the heavy hand of authority, it was in their DNA. "I have to move into the corridor for a moment for an important phone call, Inspector." Dante pointed his thumb heavenward toward the Center of All Things for a bureaucrat. "Rome," he whispered. "The Ministry."

Loiacono stood to attention so stiffly, he quivered.

"Can you cover for me on such an important case, Inspector? Can I count on you?"

The cords in Loiacono's neck stood out. "Absolutely, *Commissario*. We'll work the scene. Dr. Guzzanti should be here soon, too. Have no fear, *Commissario*, everything will be done according to protocol!"

Dante had no doubt.

"Very good, Inspector," he said, making his voice deep. He turned and marched out of the room in almost military cadence in case Loiacono was watching and allowed himself to slump against the wall only when he'd turned the corner.

He had the number of Mike's cell phone on speed dial.

"*Pronto.*"

Dante could hardly hear his brother against the backdrop of thousands of people shouting.

He closed his eyes briefly and imagined it—the *campo* filled to the brim with excited Sienese who had just watched thirty or forty of the finest horses on the face of the earth race in packs of ten.

The extraction was a solemn ceremony, a blindfolded young boy in medieval dress extracting the names of the *contradas* one by one, each *contrada* assigned a horse.

As each horse was assigned, the inhabitants of that *contrada* would surround it and lead it off to the special stables that had been prepared.

There would be cries of exultation from the *contrada* assigned a brilliant horse, moans and even tears from the *contrada* that had drawn a *brenna,* a relatively poor horse. The *contrada's* rivals would then yell out baa-ing sounds to show the *contrada* had drawn a sheep instead of a horse.

It was pure chance, fate at its most ineluctable, which is why it was so important to even up what the fates doled out by putting together the craftiest arrangement of bribes and alliances possible.

A microcosm of Italian life.

Dante heard a garbled noise. "What?" He curved in toward the wall. Mike was trying to shout above the noise of the crowd. Dante pressed the phone closer to his ear. The roar of the crowd was like the ocean in a tempest.

"I said we drew Lina. Lina! Do you hear me?" Mike's voice was exultant, and Dante wanted to shout with joy.

"Lina!" His voice carried loudly in the empty corridor, echoing faintly, and he dropped his voice to a whisper. "Lina! That's great! My God, Mike, we're going to do it this year."

"Bet your ass, brother! Bet your ass!" Dante's normally staid, correct-to-a-fault brother became a wild man during the days of the *Palio.* Another wave of sound crashed over the phone. "I've got to go now. We're taking Lina back to the stables."

"Keep a close eye on her."

"You'd better believe it." The horse was being escorted by wildly exulting Snails to the special stables in the *contrada*. From now until the moment of the race itself, Lina would be anxiously watched day and night. Rivals had been known to slip laxatives in the feed of horses that weren't well watched.

"Who'd the Turtles draw?"

"Big bay named Cioccolato."

"He any good?"

"Yeah. Fast," Mike said, and Dante could hear the anxiety in his voice.

The only thing worse than not winning the *Palio* was watching your mortal enemy win it. The Snails and the Turtles had been enemies forever. But the Turtles weren't going to win this year.

Eat your hearts out, Turtles, Dante thought. *The* Palio *will be ours.*

"Keep an eye on Nerbo, too," Dante admonished. With a strong horse like Lina, the chances of the Snail winning the *Palio* had just increased dramatically. Nerbo would be inundated with offers of bribes and he was an avaricious son of a bitch. Hell of a rider, but he didn't have an honest bone in his body.

"Don't worry. We won't let anything slip past us." Another wave of sound. "Listen, Dante, I have to go." Mike rang off.

Dante closed his cell phone slowly. It was going to happen this year. He could feel it in his bones. This year, his *contrada* would take the *Palio*, a silken banner, home to the little *contrada* museum where it would be kept with the other *Palio* banners for a thousand years, and admired by generations of school kids. He couldn't wait to get back down into town. He wanted to see Lina for himself, in the little stables where she'd be pampered until…

"There you are, Dante!" a voice boomed. "I think you should be there when I examine the body. What are you doing hiding out here?"

"Speaking with Rome," Dante explained coolly as he turned around.

The medical examiner, Dr. Aldo Guzzanti, was watching him steadily, white bushy eyebrows drawn together. He was a tall, lanky man, with a deeply ironic view of life, and Dante liked him eleven months of the year. He knew Aldo Guzzanti very well. Not just in his official capacity as coroner, but in his official capacity as Enemy. Dr. Guzzanti was a Turtle.

"What does Rome have to do with this?" Alas, Guzzanti was not only an enemy but also highly intelligent.

"Ahm…" Dante thought quickly. "The dead man is an American. I had to talk to the embassy in Rome. Protocol, you know."

Guzzanti looked at him for a long moment. "Okay," he said finally. "Let's get going. Your inspector is practically panting with excitement. I've had to keep him from trying to pick latents up from the ceiling."

That sounded just like Loiacono.

"*Commissario*, sir! *Dottore!*" Loiacono bellowed as Dante and Guzzanti entered. "Photographer Pecci—" the lanky youth kneeling next to the body threw him a sardonic look and Dante raised his hand to shield his eyes against the bright flash of a bulb, "—has almost completed his photographic survey. Sir. He has taken photographs of the complete perimeter of the body and lambent photographs of the murder area."

"Last one," the photographer said, flashing the bright light and unfolding his length as he rose. He nodded to Dante. "The roll will be ready in an hour, *Commissario*."

"All right, Carlo," Dante said.

Carlo moonlighted as a photographer for weddings and christenings. The last time he'd been called in to photograph the scene of a crime had been eight months ago, at the site of a vandalized discotheque.

Dante looked around at the gray dust. He turned to Loiacono. "How about the prints? They finished?"

"Sir! Yes! Specialist Carducci and Specialist Falugi have dusted this room and the door. They've gone downstairs to fingerprint the suspects. There was a half-empty bottle of whiskey and they've taken it to the toxicology laboratory, where Toxicologist Simoni will analyze it." Like all southerners, Loiacono loved titles. Whatever a person's job, Loiacono managed to upgrade it to a title. Gas Station Attendant Manzini. Garage Mechanic Trotti. Dante fully expected him one day to refer to Wife Anna.

"There was an unopened bottle of whiskey as well, Inspector Loiacono," Dante said. "I want you to take that bottle and the half-empty bottle and any other bottles you might find and send them to Florence for analysis."

Loiacono's face fell. The person Loiacono so grandly called Toxicologist Simoni was actually a police cadet who had been sporadically studying for a degree in chemistry these past eight years.

Loiacono was always crushed when it was borne in on him that the Siena Police Department wasn't the American FBI. There *was* no toxicology lab, unless you counted the Bunsen burner used to brew coffee when the espresso maker broke down, and a perfectly useless microscope with scratched lenses pressed into service as a paperweight.

Everything went to Florence for analysis. *Where,* Dante thought irritably, *they took their own sweet time about responding.*

Guzzanti was kneeling by the body and had opened his black medical bag.

Dante hated everything pertaining to doctors and illness and had to school himself not to look away from the array of hideous instruments Guzzanti was placing on the floor.

Guzzanti snapped on latex gloves and examined the body carefully, head to toe.

"What do you think, Guzzanti?"

Guzzanti looked up. "Dead, Dante. He's definitely dead."

Guzzanti had always been ornery. Dante was suddenly very glad that he hadn't married Simona Guzzanti, good in bed as she had been. Having Guzzanti and his sharp tongue as a father-in-law would have been hell. "I mean, when did he die? Can you tell?"

Guzzanti touched the body for the first time, picking up the right hand and holding it, turning the body slightly. He unbuttoned the first button of the shirt to loosen it and lifted the body slightly to check the dead man's back.

"Okay, here's what I can tell upon visual examination. The body's cold, so algor mortis has already set in. But that happens immediately. Rigor has begun. Most likely he's been dead for at least eight hours, possibly more.

"The skin of his face, neck and hands is ashen, so blood has started to drain from the topmost part of the body. He has lividity on his back. He has a normal expression and there is no sign of a struggle. He may have been taken by surprise. The stiletto must've been slipped right between the fourth and fifth rib for an instant death. Not an easy thing to do."

Dante deeply, deeply wanted to get out of the room. "So…time of death?"

Guzzanti sighed. "I'll need to do a test for that." He reached into his bag and pulled out a thermometer. He looked up at Dante. "New method from the Americans, bless them. They don't know how to cook and can't manage to make a decent wine, but boy do they know their dead bodies. I'm going to measure the temperature of the body's liver."

"Liver!" Dante gaped. "But—but the liver is *inside* the body."

"Good going, Sherlock. Indeed it is. And that is why, *Commissario* Rossi," Guzzanti looked over his half-moon glasses as he stressed Dante's title, "I'm going to need your permission to remove the dead man's jacket and shirt, punch a hole in his side and measure the temperature of his liver."

Dante didn't know about the temperature of Roland Kane's liver, but he did know that the temperature of the room had suddenly shot up ten degrees. He tried desperately to think of some reason why Guzzanti couldn't do this, but it was hard to think with his stomach sliding greasily up his throat.

He deepened his voice. "I'm not certain I can give you permission at this time, Guzzanti, because it might violate the integrity of the crime scene, you understand, and—"

"Shut up, Dante," Guzzanti said, scrutinizing the bottom of his bag. "I'm going to need an extra pair of hands here."

Dante looked down at his own hands and put them behind his back. *No way.*

"Me, Doctor." Loiacono trembled with eagerness. "May I be allowed to assist you?"

"You may, Inspector. Put these on." Guzzanti held out a pair of latex gloves and Loiacono donned them.

"Okay." Guzzanti looked up. "This is what's going to happen. I am going to open up the man's jacket, pull up his shirt and undershirt, if he has one, and expose the lower right quadrant of his torso, find myself a nice intercostal space, take out a punching awl and punch a hole through the skin with enough force to reach the center of the right lobe of the liver. After which I will insert a thermometer into the hole and thence down to the liver. Any questions?"

"No, *sir!*" Loiacono shouted and dropped to his knees.

For one crazy moment, Dante thought Loiacono had had a religious epiphany, but he was only getting close to Guzzanti. Who was going to punch a hole in a man's liver. Right now. This minute. A trickle of sweat tickled its way down Dante's back.

"Remove the man's clothes, Inspector," Guzzanti ordered as he pulled out a long, thin instrument. "I need access to the liver. Very good," he said as Loiacono bared the right side of the man's abdomen.

Dante wanted desperately to look away, but he couldn't. He willed his cell phone to ring. Any interruption would do. An earthquake. Fire. Anything.

Guzzanti put a notepad and pen in Loiacono's hands. "Okay now, Inspector, please take notes." Guzzanti read off the thermometer. "Ambient temperature twenty-eight degrees, time thirteen hundred hours." He drew a line in the air from the body's nipple down to the edge of the rib cage. He pressed hard against the rib cage with his left hand, while lifting the awl in his right.

"This is the theory, Dante." He looked up and squinted. "Are you okay?"

"Fine," Dante assured him, and swallowed. "Perfect."

"All right. Now, this is the point of the exercise. After death, the body cools at a constant rate of half a degree per hour for the first twelve hours postmortem." He pressed the tip of the awl against the point indicated by his left hand. He pushed hard then, gripping the awl with both hands. He leaned down heavily. "Damn chest wall. Ah!"

With a pop, he broke through the skin, pressing down until the awl had penetrated to the hilt. He probed delicately, frowning. "*Gesù*, the guy's liver is like butter."

Dante's stomach roiled as he remembered eating *fegato alla veneziana* the evening before. The delicate, Venetian liver-and-onion dish was one of his favorites.

Guzzanti pulled back. "Okay, now. Take this, Inspector."

The awl emerged with a slight, sickening pop and Guzzanti handed it to Loiacono. He picked up the thermometer and inserted it into the hole, holding it there for three minutes, which he timed by looking at his wristwatch.

"Right, Loiacono, please record. At thirteen-oh-four hours, ambient temperature twenty-eight degrees, corpse hepatic temperature thirty-point-one degrees, which would indicate...let me see...circa twelve hours from moment of death."

Loiacono wrote fervidly, while Guzzanti swabbed the wound he'd made. He took a felt-tip pen and circled the puncture hole and put his initials next to the circle. "That's so no one can accuse me of having delivered a killing blow to the liver. Heh-heh."

Dante smiled sickly.

Guzzanti stood and pulled off his gloves. "Well, that was fun. Trust the Americans to provide the best entertainment. Do you want me to do a vitreous humor test, Dante?"

Saliva was pooling in Dante's mouth. He had to swallow. "Vitreous... What's that?"

"I stick a needle in the guy's eye and syringe out the liquid. 'Course the eyeball collapses, then," Guzzanti said cheerfully. "Another American technique, bless their souls."

"No, that won't be necessary," Dante said. "Loiacono, see to the cleaning up here. Then go downstairs and advise the Americans I want to talk to them, and arrange for their transport down to headquarters. Ask the magistrate for the authority to sequester the foreigners' passports, then collect them.

"As soon as Carducci's film is printed, I want copies on my desk. The Americans are from Deerfield, Massachusetts. It so happens I know the chief of police there. His name is Sam Murray. I want you to email him at hq@dpd.org with the names of the foreigners and ask him to email me what they have in their files. Print out the answers and leave them on my desk."

"Sir!" Loiacono's dark eyes gleamed. He liked police work, but he loved computers with a passion verging on the aberrant. Dante was sure he'd just made Loiacono's day.

Dante turned on his heel with dignity and walked carefully down to the communal bathrooms, where he relieved his stomach of last night's liver.

Chapter Four

Don't be misled by facts.

ஐ

Deerfield, Massachusetts

The good news was that the doorbell ringing didn't hurt anymore. The bad news was that it was his sister, Lou, at the door.

Nick stared at Lou for a moment, hating her because she looked so good. She was dressed in one of her usual designer outfits in some bright jewel color and not a hair on her dark head was out of place.

"I used to think of you as my big, handsome brute of a brother," she said idly from the doorframe. Her big dark blue eyes, so remarkably like his own, looked him up and down, taking in his unshaven chin, tousled hair and bare chest. "But I guess brute just about covers it now. Do your eyes hurt?"

"Everything hurts," Nick answered shortly. "Why?"

"I don't think I've ever seen quite that shade of red outside a fashion magazine before. How come you haven't called? I was worried."

Nick leaned against the doorjamb negligently, as if he were relaxed and had nothing else to do and not as if he'd fall down otherwise. "Had an out-of-town exhibition game."

"Well, that's no excuse for disappearing. Can I come in?"

"Can I stop you?" Nick countered, and turned away.

Lou sucked in a breath and Nick winced, knowing what she was seeing on his bare back. The pain of the bruises had lessened, but even he had whistled when he'd seen the vision of blues and greens, slowly turning yellow at the edges, in the mirror. There was even a little black here and there.

Lou had seen him in this shape before, but Nick knew she never got used to the sight.

"Christ," Lou muttered behind him, and Nick hobbled more quickly into the living room. The lecture was coming. Any minute now.

He only wished he could fortify his system with alcohol beforehand, but he'd probably exceeded his body's yearly quota.

"You can turn around, Nick," Lou said acidly. "You don't have to hide. I'm not going to say anything. If you want to beat yourself to a pulp, week after week, that's your business."

Nick slumped down into the sofa. Lou might hold off for a minute or two, but he wasn't counting on it. She hated hockey, and said so...often. To hear her tell it, it was basically pro wrestling with a stick.

"Well." Lou sat down next to him, frowned and lifted her hip. She reached under herself and pulled out a none-too-clean T-shirt. "Christ, you're an animal."

Nick rolled his eyes. "Sorry, Lou. It's the maid's year off."

She wrinkled her nose in disgust and tossed it over her shoulder. "Honestly, Nick. You're enough to give jocks a bad name. How can you live like this?" Lou's sharp eyes narrowed. "Listen, I swore to myself I wasn't going to ask, but...how *are* you?"

"You were right the first time. Don't ask." Nick felt weary and depressed.

"Too late." Lou was trying to keep her voice light. "I already did."

"I'm fine." Nick pursed his lips and studied his knees. "Just fine." He looked up to see if Lou was buying it. Unfortunately, her mind was even sharper than her eyes.

"Uh-huh," she said dryly. "And I've got a genuine Armani you can have for fifty bucks. Spill it."

He didn't have any choice. Lou was as tenacious as a bloodhound when she wanted something. He heaved a sigh. "I... It's like this." Nick started to tell her everything—the concussion, the medical tests, the doctors, the enforced retirement, Faith—but to his horror, his throat seized up. His tongue became a useless muscle in his mouth.

I can't play hockey. Ever again.

The words were there but they simply wouldn't come out. It was like looking at a train wreck. You saw the smoking ruins, could hear the cries of the wounded, but words simply couldn't describe it.

Lou was watching him with her I-love-you-but-you-exasperate-me look and she was probably about five seconds from torturing it out of him. Or tricking it out of him. Nick had never, ever been able to outthink his sister Lucrezia.

He struggled up from the couch and went to the bookcase, where he picked up a sheet of business-grade paper, folded three times to fit into an envelope. One lousy sheet of paper that had changed his life.

He sat back down, looking at the paper he held in his hands, wondering where to start.

There was silence for a long moment, then Lou said, gently, "What's wrong with your leg? You're limping."

Nick's throat eased. He could talk about that. "It's not my leg. It's the knee."

"The meniscus again?"

"Yeah."

"Christ, Nick, how many times have they operated on that knee?"

"Seven. The surgeon said next time I should just buy myself a new one."

"Maybe while you're at it, you should just buy yourself a new head," Lou said acidly. "What?" She'd seen him wince.

Here it comes, he thought. "Well, since we're on the subject…at the last game, I was backboarded and — "

"Wait, you were *what*?"

Nick smiled. Lou knew what he had in his bank account. She knew the name of every girlfriend he'd ever had. If she thought about it, she probably knew what color shorts he was wearing. And yet, though he'd been a professional hockey player for going on twelve years now, she'd systematically refused to learn even the basics of the game.

She'd once complained that there should be closed-captioning on TV for the hockey-impaired.

Here goes, he thought. "Someone drove me into the backboard…hard. It's an illegal move and the player got fined. But as I went under, I felt something crack in my knee. I went off to the bench for a minute and the coach pumped me full of painkillers and — ouch!"

Nick glared at Lou and rubbed his head where she'd whacked him with a rolled-up magazine. As if he wasn't banged up enough as it was. "What the hell was *that* for?"

"You felt something snap in your knee and you *went back into the game*?" Lou spoke through gritted teeth. "What on earth happened to you, Nick? You used to be such a smart little boy, before you grew up. Overgrew up. Then you turned into an idiot."

If she only knew how big a one, thought Nick. "Lou, you know what hockey's like. Unless a limb is actually hacked off, you play. But that's not the problem. The thing is, I also…uh…sort of…blacked out for a while. Probably not more than a second or two. But I forgot to tell the coach."

"Hold on." Lou's pretty face turned fierce. "You *blacked out*. And you," she thumped him over and over again with the magazine, "you forgot to tell the coach?"

Nick lifted his arms in defense. "Wait, it's not as crazy as it sounds. It was the middle of the game, and it was a close one, and I didn't realize until later that I'd actually lost consciousness for a while. It's a symptom of concussion, the doctor said. Not remembering."

Lou was sitting back on the couch, arms folded, eyes blue fire. "So when did you tell the coach, Einstein?"

Nick winced again. "Later. At the end of the game." He hung his head, then looked at her out of the corner of his eye. "We won the game. I scored the winning goal."

"With a concussion." Lou rolled her eyes.

Okay, so that wasn't the best tack to take with her.

Nick drew in a deep breath. His throat started tightening up again, the closer he got to the heart of the matter. "After the game, I told him about the blackout and coach ordered me into the hospital for a checkup. I was put through a variety of tests which were—not fun." Nick shivered at the memory of being enclosed in the MRI machine.

He was tough and he could take blood and broken bones with the best of them. But that silent, eerie machine like a coffin… It had been like being buried alive. "That was the day before yesterday." Nick studied his hands. Hands that would never hold a hockey stick again. At least not professionally.

"And?" Lou prodded. "What did the doctors say?"

This was it. Nick handed her the sheet of paper and sat back, closing his eyes.

Lou sucked in her breath as she read. Nick knew every word, from the heading—Clarence A. Sorenson, M.D., Specialist in Neurology—down to the last words. *We hereby advise that Nicholas Rossi be barred from competition athletics for the rest of his natural life.*

And in between were all the fun words describing possible consequences if he were allowed to continue playing—secondary concussion, cranial nerve damage, possible permanent neurological damage, possible cognitive deficits, biochemical changes at the cellular level.

And there it was. What Nick had tried to drink himself into a stupor to forget. Twelve years of his life down the drain because of an overenthusiastic adversary and a few moments of blackout.

"Oh, Nick," Lou breathed. She put her hand on her brother's bare shoulder. "Oh, Nick, I'm so sorry."

"Yeah, well…" Nick shrugged, trying not to think about the rest of his life. "Had to retire sometime." He tried on a smile. "Just didn't think it would be this soon."

Lou was looking at him and he knew she was reading every emotion he had. She'd always been able to do that. Just like their mother. "You know, Nick, maybe this accident is…is a blessing in disguise."

Nick blinked. "Say what?"

"Oh, Nick, just think of it. How long do you think you could have gone on? You're thirty-one years old. You could have played for what? Another seven, eight years? Ten, tops? And then what? You'd be forty and a has-been.

"A *rich* has-been," she added wryly. "But it would be too late to do much of anything else. You're young enough now to start putting that brain of yours to use." She knocked affectionately on his head. "I know you have one in there. It used to be a pretty serviceable one, too, before you started playing hockey."

"No jock jokes," Nick warned.

"No jock jokes." Lou smiled happily. "I'm going to go dump my collection into the garbage can. Now you can move on to the next thing."

Whatever that was.

"Life after hockey." Nick shook his head. He didn't want to admit it, but he felt better now that he'd told somebody. He even managed a smile. "Is there?"

"Oh, Nick." Lou scooted over and picked up his hand. He'd broken each and every finger. Some twice. He'd also broken his collarbone three times, his arm and his nose. That hadn't been such a bad thing—Lou said it saved him from pretty-boy looks. But everything else… "One of these days you were going to kill yourself. And for what? Wouldn't you like a real life? A real job? And a real woman, instead of those silicone bunnies with room-temperature I.Q.s you date?"

"Ouch." Nick slouched lower in the couch. "I haven't seen her in two months."

"Well, how about that Dee Dee? She's smart all right, but all she cares about is the fact that you're a famous athlete. And rich."

His love life was not something he wanted to get into right now. "Okay, okay—"

"What you really need is a smart, nice woman," Lou swept on relentlessly. "Someone who cares for you as a person, not someone who's blinded by your fame. Someone like—like Faith. She's smart and nice and funny and pretty in her own quiet way. And the way she looks at you—" If Lou hadn't been holding Nick's hand, she wouldn't have felt him jolt. "What?"

"Nothing." Nick withdrew his hand and rubbed it across the back of his neck. "Say," he said brightly. He stood up, staggering slightly and steadied himself with a hand on the back of the sofa. "You want something to drink? I don't think I have anything alcoholic left, not even shaving lotion, but there might be—"

Lou watched him carefully. "Nick? *Nick*?" She raised her voice as he hobbled as quickly as he could into the kitchen. She got up and followed him.

"Nick, did anything happen between you and Faith? Because she was acting funny yesterday when I mentioned your name... Nick, get your head out of that refrigerator!"

Nick straightened and gave a bright smile. "What was that? Here, I found a beer for you. It was under the lettuce."

Exasperated, Lou took the can of beer and set it on a counter with a bang. She crossed her arms and waited. When she started tapping her foot, Nick threw up his hands.

"Okay, okay. I blew it. Okay? Is that what you wanted to hear?"

"What I want to hear is what happened," Lou said grimly. "Now."

It wasn't easy, confessing to being a jerk. Especially to his sister. Nick knew it was going to hurt, so he hobbled back into the living room and sat down. Might as well be comfortable. He drew in a deep breath, then blew it out.

"Well, what happened was this. I was—I was blown away when the doctor said I'd never play again. I just couldn't get my mind 'round the thought. It was as if the bottom had dropped out of my life. So I decided to go out and get drunk. Stinking drunk. I got totally wasted."

Lou rolled her eyes. "Typical male reaction."

"Yeah, well, I'm still paying for it, so don't crow. Anyway, by the time I got done, I could barely walk. I stopped by your house for a little sympathy, but you weren't there." Nick tried to look accusingly at Lou. Maybe he could shift some of the blame around here.

Lou's gaze was level. "I've been busy. Some of us have serious jobs. Go on."

So that wasn't going to work. "Well, Faith walked into the building just then. I wanted company, so I asked her out for a drink and then—then things just went on from there."

"Things?"

"Yeah." Nick shifted uneasily. "You know. Things."

"You weren't..." Lou hesitated. "You weren't violent, were you?"

"Of course not," Nick snapped, annoyed. There were gaping holes in his memory, but what memories there were, were almost unbearably sweet—and unusually satisfying. Then his head shot up. "Why?"

"Well," Lou said, troubled, "I saw Faith yesterday, like I said. She was just coming into our building. I invited her up for a cup of coffee, and said I was going to stop by your house later and did she want to come along? She turned pale and got very upset. She said she couldn't tag along because she was leaving in a hurry. She was off to some conference, called in at the last minute. A mathematics conference in Italy. In Siena, of all places."

"Siena?" Nick's voice was sharp. "So that's why—" *That's why she wasn't answering.* He'd called a thousand times, had buzzed her doorbell until his own head had buzzed. "What's she doing in Siena?"

"A conference. I just told you that, Nick." Lou gave him a withering glare.

It's unfortunate, Nick thought, *that Lou's tongue is just as sharp as her eyes.*

"Start paying some attention here. This is your life."

"So..." Nick tried to keep his voice casual. "When is she coming back?" Maybe he could pick her up at the airport, pick up where they left off...

"Do you know," Lou frowned, "I didn't ask. I was too busy telling her how pretty Siena was and how much she was going to enjoy it. I told her all our Rossi cousins lived in Siena. I gave Dante a quick call and told him to look her up."

"Dante!" Nick half rose out of his chair, then put a hand to his head. He'd hurt himself with his own voice. "Why would you want to call *Dante*? Why not Mike?" Mike was on the other side of forty, overweight and happily married with two kids.

"Because." Lou glared at him. "Dante has more time to show her the sights. But you're evading, Nick. I want to know exactly what happened between you and Faith. And I especially want to know why Faith looked so unhappy when I mentioned your name."

But Nick wasn't listening. "If Dante puts the move on her, I swear I'll kill him." Nick's head swiveled at the sound of the phone and he groaned. "Get that, will you, Lou? I don't want to talk to anyone."

"Okay." Lou rose gracefully. "But don't think you're off the hook. Hello? Hello?" She hung up. "Wrong number. But come to think of it, I left you a message on your answering service. Have you been listening to your messages?"

"Ah…no."

"You shouldn't be let out loose." Lou looked around. "Where's the machine?"

"In the gulag. I didn't want to be disturbed."

Lou made an exasperated noise and disappeared. Nick was cautiously contemplating the idea of food for the first time in two days when Lou called out. "Nick, I think you'd better come here and listen to this."

"If it's Dee Dee, I don't want to know." Nick limped to the gulag. "She's annoying enough in person."

"No," Lou said slowly. "It wasn't Dee Dee. It was Dante." Her voice was odd.

"What?" he asked Lou. "What did he say? Is Faith all right? Has he been putting some moves on her?"

Instead of answering, Lou pressed the replay button and Dante's voice came on. "Nick, I have some good news and some bad news…"

"Ah, Faith Murphy. Just the person I was looking for," Leonardo Gori, the head of the Siena University Math Department, said.

Faith had just entered into the cloister after lunch. Lunch had been subdued, what with a murder and all. Luckily, it had been delicious, so nobody had been overly bothered by the lack of conversation.

She looked up at Professor Gori. She was in awe of him. He had a solid reputation as one of the most original thinkers in the field of econometrics. He was also the driving force behind the Siena Quantitative Methods Seminar, arguably one of the most important math seminars in the world. It also didn't hurt that he was incredibly good-looking, in a tweedy sort of way.

She was here as an interloper. What did he want with her?

Be cool, be suave, she told herself. "Ah—"

"Terrible business, this." He rocked back slightly on his chic loafers. "We're so sorry at the loss of Professor Kane."

"Ah—"

"Indeed," he said. "A great loss to mathematics. However, I'm afraid this will mean some reorganization of the conference as well. I was wondering whether I could have a word or two with you in private." Professor Gori smiled gently at her. "If you have the time, of course."

"Of course," Faith murmured. *Not have time for Leonardo Gori?* Unless, of course, he was going to tell her she wasn't welcome anymore, now she wasn't riding on Roland Kane's coattails.

He led them into a large room directly opposite the entrance. It was elaborately frescoed and was furnished with museum-quality antiques. Two very attractive secretaries were doing what looked like nothing at all. But they were doing it very elegantly.

Faith followed Professor Gori into an inner study, as heartbreakingly beautiful as the outer study, only less elaborate. A long antique refectory table, a throne-like straight-backed chair with iron studs bracketing the leather padding, another chair and a sideboard made up the decor.

"Please sit down," Professor Gori said, and Faith realized it was the second time he'd said it while she'd gone into a fugue over his furniture.

"Sorry," she murmured, sitting down gingerly on an antique chair that probably cost more than she would ever earn in her lifetime. It was sturdier than it looked, though, and she relaxed slightly.

He sat down behind another one of those amazing antique desks, where generations of monks had prayed or eaten or done whatever it was monks did.

"Well," he said, and stopped.

Faith tried to look serious and smart and relaxed, while bracing herself. Professor Gori was probably going to give her one of Roland Kane's patented stay-out-of-trouble-don't-bother-your-betters-stay-quiet-and-pretend-you're-not-there lectures.

"I'm delighted at this opportunity to talk to you, Doctor Murphy." He put his clasped hands on the table and smiled.

Faith started. Her doctorate was brand-new and she still wasn't used to the title. Not that anyone at Deerfield would call her doctor anyway. She just didn't look the part.

"Just Faith, please, professor," she said. Professor Gori was a big name internationally. The idea of him calling her doctor was ludicrous.

"Then you must call me Leonardo, Faith," he replied and smiled.

Faith blinked, completely floored. Calling Professor Gori "Leonardo" was like…was like calling the Pope "Benni". Not in this lifetime. "Oh, I couldn't—"

"Of course you must." He smiled again and Faith started paying attention.

He'd just been Professor Gori before. An important man in his field and head of one of the most prestigious university departments on earth. She had hardly considered him a human being—he was just another one of those remote and faceless male authority figures her life seemed to be so full of.

But now she looked more closely. Like everything else in this country, seemingly, he was good-looking. Not lavishly good-looking like the Rossis, true, but handsome in a rather austere manner.

Though the day was already heating up, he was in a tan polished cotton suit with a cream cotton shirt, and blue and yellow silk tie. He looked as if his sweat glands had been surgically removed.

But aside from his looks, there was a gentleness to his face, a kindness in his eyes, and she felt herself relaxing. Instinctively, she knew she didn't have to weigh every word and brace herself against nasty comments. He was as far from Roland Kane as was possible and still be of the same gender and species.

"I'm delighted you've finally decided to accept our invitation, Faith. We were very disappointed you couldn't come last year. I was very much looking forward to discussing the ideas on hysteresis you published in *Mathematica*. Your report on system dynamics is just fascinating. And I found your thesis on tipping behavior thoroughly compelling.

"As a matter of fact, that's what I wanted to discuss with you. Would you be willing to moderate our panel on tipping behavior? It's a topic of great interest nowadays and I feel you'd be best positioned to cover all angles. We'd want to cover economics and public health policy, and I know you've done some work on that."

He stopped and smiled at her, his head tilted inquisitively.

Faith blinked and barely stopped herself from looking around to see who he was addressing. Normally quick, it took her a moment to process what he'd said because it sounded so outlandish.

Would she be willing to moderate a panel of world-famous experts on one of the hottest topics around? Talk about cutting-edge research with some of the finest minds on earth?

Well...yes, as a matter of fact. She'd also be willing to accept a winning lottery ticket, marry Mel Gibson and accept the Nobel Peace Prize.

"Faith?" Professor Gori—Leonardo—was looking at her quizzically. "Would you have a problem with that? Because if you do, if you'd rather moderate another panel, pseudo-quantitation, say, that's fine, too. I just thought that maybe you'd—"

Faith was jolted out of her surprise-induced stupor. "No!" She lowered her voice. "Ah, no. No, that's not it at all.

I'd be…delighted to moderate the tipping panel. But…" She shook her head to see if she could loosen a few neurons.

She thought she'd heard him say…

"What was that about not accepting your invitation last year? I'm afraid I don't understand," she said.

This time last year she'd been finishing up her paper for *Mathematica*, working madly on her PhD, and doing the usual graduate student scut work—teaching no-brainer summer remedial classes for jocks—and getting ready to move to Deerfield.

Her contract had started on July first. She was absolutely positively certain that no invitation to Siena, Italy, had been forthcoming.

Leonardo frowned. "Well, as I said, we were really sorry you couldn't accept our invitation last year."

"Professor Gori…Leonardo. I didn't receive an invitation last year. Actually, I didn't receive an invitation this year either. I'm only here because Tim Gresham fell ill at the last minute. And Professor Kane made it quite clear he wasn't particularly happy I was along."

"I…see." He sat back and steepled his fingers, looking *très* European Intellectual. "Well, my dear, we most certainly did issue you an invitation to participate in the Quantitative Methods Seminar last year and this year. We sent the invitation care of Professor Kane, since we'd heard you would technically be under contract with St. Vincent's by the time the conference started.

"Professor Kane said that you were too busy with the move to Deerfield last year. And he said he couldn't spare you this year. We were very disappointed and made this known to Professor Kane. Forcefully. And I, personally, was delighted when I saw last night that you were able to come."

Faith was silent. She could feel her heart swell with resentment and anger that she hadn't been the one to slip a knife into Kane's black heart. Being invited to participate in the Quantitative Methods Seminar was considered a signal honor in her field. He knew that. Kane had kept her from it last year and had done his very best to make sure she couldn't come this year.

When she spoke, her voice was thick with repressed anger. "I was told about the trip here less than four hours before departure."

"I see," Leonardo said again. He gave a little sigh, an Italian masterpiece of subtle expressiveness. *Yes, Professor Kane was a shit*, that sigh said, *but he was also a colleague and important in our field and I can't come right out and say what I think of him.* "I'm afraid that Roland Kane, for all his brilliance as a mathematician, was a very difficult character."

"Yes," Faith said shortly, her jaw muscles bunching.

Another elegant, little sigh and a gentle straightening out of the razor-sharp crease of his trousers.

"Well," he said, looking down at his perfectly buffed and filed fingernails. "Sadly, Professor Kane's…temperament is no longer a problem. And I can assure you we are delighted to have you. Tell me, Faith," he leaned forward. "Did you read Dunhatton's paper on system dynamics?"

"Sure." Faith leaned forward, too. "I think it will have a number of interesting applications. For example, it would be fun to come up with a sort of management flight simulator — a little self-contained world, where we could use a company's input to define the parameters. The executive staff could try out decisions and see what the short-term and long-term fallout would be."

"Excellent." He beamed. "This year is going to be exceptionally interesting. We have Yamaki from Nogura and Jean-Pierre Daumier from The Pasteur Institute. You'll enjoy what he's done on the epidemiology of AIDS. It's going to be an interesting week." He picked up a dog-eared copy of the program. "Let's see, tomorrow we're going to have registration from eight to nine, though the desk will be open all morning. We'll have an early lunch here and then we're starting again at two.

"I'd like the work to be over by 5:00 because most of the participants will want to get down to Siena to see the trial heat of the *Palio*." He smiled at her blank look. "That's our local horse race. It's—" he pursed his lips, " —it's a deeply felt event in Siena. I'm sure you'll enjoy it.

"And coming back to our business, I suggest you co-chair Critical Points in Hysteresis with Murauer in room four, from 3:00 to 4:15, and moderate the Tipping Behavior Panel from 4:30 to 5:30. We'll see about the other days as we go along. Is that all right with you?"

Thoughts of Roland Kane's perfidy fled from her head and, for a second, Faith forgot how much she hated him.

It was happening. It was finally happening. Eighteen long, miserable years in Sophie and eight long, hard, empty years putting herself through school and graduate school, and then this last year at St. Vincent's under Kane, which had been unpleasant, to put it mildly.

Who the hell cared? It was over. She was in this gorgeous country on a beautiful summer day and this wonderful Italian man had just handed her the keys to the kingdom.

Is that all right with you? Leonardo's words echoed in her head.

She smiled and saw him blink. So, okay, maybe she didn't smile all that much. "That's just fine with me, Leonardo," she said softly. "Just fine."

"Well good." He reached across the desk and took her hand. "After work, we're organizing minibuses to take the participants down to Siena in the evenings to watch the trial races of the *Palio*, and I found seats for the participants for the big day itself." He beamed with pleasure.

Faith tried to think of something she cared less about than horse racing, but came up blank. Still, if Leonardo wanted her to watch a bunch of horses run around a track, fine. She'd have happily gone along if he wanted to show her the Cow Patty Museum. She'd even make ooh-ing sounds if he wanted.

"Well." He stood and Faith was so spaced out she sat for a moment, looking up at him, neck craned. Then she hastily scrambled to her feet.

"I think Paul Allen's just arrived. You might want to talk with him about coordination. We're very happy to have you with us, Faith."

He escorted her to the door and she walked out, dazed, into the dazzling sunshine. Into her newly dazzling life.

She'd need to read Dunhatton, Yamaki and Daumier off the net, and she'd need to put her notes on tipping behavior in order. She'd need to interface with the other members of the panel on hysteresis…

God, it was all so exciting.

This immense male cloud had been…lifted. She'd spent the first eighteen years of her life under a mean drunk — her father — and another long year under another mean drunk, Roland Kane. In between had been gray years of slog.

It was as if Kane's death had freed her to be herself, to be who she was meant to be.

The narrative of her life had just changed, and she had no idea what the story was going to be. Better than the last one, though, she knew.

Faith lifted her head and closed her eyes, delighted with the warm, fragrant sunshine, the gorgeous *Certosa*, the warm welcome she'd received. She drew in a deep breath and strode swiftly into her future, walking right into a man instead.

"Faith!"

"Tim!"

Her former lover held her by the arms, his face pale with shock. If her life was a book, Tim Gresham was the chapter on bad sex.

"What on earth are *you* doing here?" He sounded stunned.

She stepped back. "I could say the same thing." She peered at him closely. "Weren't you too sick to travel?"

He still looked sick. He was slightly gray and new lines crisscrossed his pale skin.

"Yeah, I had the flu. I *still* have the flu, for that matter. But the doctor said I could fly." He shook his head. "But—but I don't understand. What are you doing here?"

Faith was about ready to apologize for taking his place, but then she remembered that she wasn't taking his place. She was taking *her* place, a Faith-sized space all her own at the conference. Leonardo had said so.

"It's a long story, but basically, Kane told me to come. Here." She picked up his battered carryon. "Is this your luggage? I'll carry it up for you." He looked like he would have trouble carrying himself up the stairs. "The accommodations are one flight up—oh, of course, you've been here before. You'd know that." She sneaked another look at him. He looked really awful. "Maybe you might want to rest up for a while, Tim. Not much is happening today. Tim?"

He looked in deep shock. Jet lag took some people like that. Plus he had the flu. She took his arm gently. "Come on, let me just take you up—"

Tim shook his head. "Sorry. I'm just—it's just—" He blew out a long breath. "Listen, I think I should check in with Roland first, and then you're right. I think I'll go lie down for a while."

"Well, Tim, there might be a little problem with that." She steadied her grip on his arm. "Seeing as how Roland's dead."

She felt the jolt.

"Dead?" Tim breathed. His eyes rounded so much she could see the whites all around. "Of what? Heart attack?"

"Sort of." Was there a polite way to say it? "He was...killed. Someone knifed him. In the heart."

Tim's jaw snapped shut and he looked up into the sky as he processed the information. Tim had a good head on his shoulders. Not a good-*looking* head, but a good-thinking one. Faith could almost see his hard disk working.

"Jesus Christ!" he exclaimed in disgust. "Who the hell beat me to it?"

Chapter Five

Friends come and go but enemies accumulate.

※

Back in his office two hours later, Dante reflected again upon how much he really, really hated murder. It ate up time and resources as surely as it ate up the lives of its victims.

He looked down at the list on his desk of the people who had spent last night in the *Certosa di Ponteremoli*. The Americans—Faith Murphy, Griffin Ball and Madeleine Kobbel. The University of Siena staff, consisting of Egidio Pecci, the gardener—a none-too-bright geezer—and the sous-chef, who had spent the night to get a head start on breakfast.

Egidio had been asleep in his cot inside the small room just off the porter's lodge. He had no alibi and no one could vouch for him. On the other hand, why would he kill Roland Kane? Now, if Kane had belonged to the Giraffe *contrada*, the arch-rival of Egidio's Caterpillar contrada, Egidio might well have killed him. But a foreigner, an American, would have been right off Egidio's mental map.

The cook had left after preparing breakfast and had taken the day off. As soon as he could be found, he would be brought in for questioning, though Dante doubted he could shed any light on the matter. The cook worked for an independent catering company awarded the contract for the University of Siena in April. The entire catering staff was new to the *Certosa*.

It was possible—not probable, but possible—that a thief had scaled the walls and been caught in the act by Roland Kane and had killed him.

Dante had set Loiacono the task of taking imprints of all the shoe prints around the *Certosa* and matching them with the guests and the staff. Loiacono had approached the task with an unhealthy enthusiasm and Dante could be certain that he'd soon know everyone who had ever been near the *Certosa* in the past year.

It was a possibility it was a stranger, but Dante didn't believe it. In his experience, murder was an up close and personal crime, much more than robbery. No, he'd lay odds that someone Roland Kane knew, and knew well, had slipped a knife in his heart.

Which left Madeleine Kobbel, Griffin Ball and Faith Murphy, the woman who'd found the body. And who was also Nick and Lucrezia's friend. He'd already interviewed Faith Murphy, who'd proven herself to be intelligent and reasonable.

Protocol had it that she was still suspect number one, at least until he could interview the two other professors and, however far-fetched it might seem, the rest of the *Certosa* staff, but he was willing to bet anything—anything short of his *contrada's* victory, that is—that she was innocent.

He'd know more when Deerfield Police Department emailed him some information on the three.

But for now, he had to take everyone's statements.

"Cini!" he called.

Piero Cini stuck his dark head into Dante's office. He brushed at some crumbs on the short-sleeved shirt straining around his stomach. The pastries at Nannini's on the *Via di Sopra* were his downfall. "Yeah, boss?"

"Send in the woman professor." Dante checked the sheet again for the name. "Madeleine Kobbel."

"Right away, boss." Cini ambled away and Dante wondered with a sigh what this particular "right away" might mean. Cini had a very elastic sense of time. Nannini's was very, very close by, they made superb truffle-and-butter sandwiches, and it was nearing either late lunch or early afternoon snack time.

But he was wrong to be so cynical. Ten minutes after watching Cini's broad back retreat slowly down the stairs, Cini was back with a tall, middle-aged lady in tow.

Dante stood and walked around his desk. "Ah, Professor Kobbel," he said genially and shook her hand. "I'm *Commissario* Dante Rossi and I'm in charge of investigating the murder of your colleague, Professor Roland Kane." He put a gentle hand to her back and urged her forward. Not rushing her but not treating her like an invalid, either.

Dante was good with women. He liked women, all of them — grandmothers, little girls and everything in between. As a police officer, as a man, he always treated them, even the hard-bitten prostitutes pulled in on the occasional raid, as courteously as he could.

"Please be seated. This shouldn't take long. Here, take this chair." He settled her down in the high-backed Gothic revival chair he kept for just this purpose and sat down again behind his desk.

He saw her eyes drift up to the wall behind him, full of framed citations. It was extraordinarily impressive and he'd put them up for precisely that purpose.

The citations meant absolutely nothing. Some were for a job well done, but most were for existing. There were citations engraved in gold for taking a typing course, for a handwriting analysis course, for having been a judge at a firearms contest, for having participated in the police annual parade...you name it, though Dante had drawn the line at his dog's training course certificate.

The Italian state paid its minions a pitiful pittance and made up for it with fancy engraved citations and even fancier dress uniforms. Though the *carabinieri* had better uniforms than the police force. Designed by Armani, no less.

Dante observed Madeleine Kobbel in silence for a moment until her eyes came back to him.

"I realize this must be most painful to you, Professor Kobbel, to lose an esteemed colleague in such a violent fashion. I do apologize most sincerely, but you must understand that I must ask you some questions. It is my job."

Dante's English was excellent. The Rossi clan bounced back and forth across the Atlantic often. He'd spent most summers with Nick and Lucrezia, either here in Tuscany or in Massachusetts. He'd even spent his high school senior year abroad in Deerfield.

Colloquial English had helped his sex life no end. The world was full of pretty young Americans and English women, Australians and New Zealanders, and even the odd Canadian woman, who fell in love with Siena and couldn't believe their luck when they found a policeman knowledgeable about Siena's history who could explain things to them in their own language.

He got laid a lot thanks to English.

But now he kept his English slow and formal and stepped up the accent. It gave him time to think. If he wanted more information, he could pretend he hadn't understood and required further explanation.

The woman nodded her distinguished gray head. "I'll try to contain my grief, captain," she said dryly.

Dante searched her eyes and found no trace of grief, sadness or much of anything else. She met his gaze evenly and coolly.

As Faith Murphy had done.

Maybe mathematicians were like that. Maybe working with cold numbers all day turned them into cool numbers themselves.

Being so attuned to women, Dante felt he could read Madeleine Kobbel's history in her face.

She was decent-looking, with high cheekbones and unlined skin, but did absolutely nothing to enhance her looks. Her hair, which must have been dark brown once, had been allowed to go steel gray, which aged her. She had on no makeup. Her dress was dark red, long-sleeved and too warm for the day outside.

"So, Professor Kobbel…" He leaned back in his chair, relaxed, a man idly passing the time chatting with an intelligent woman. "How well did you know Professor Kane?"

"Well enough, captain," she replied evenly. "We were colleagues. The mathematics faculty at Deerfield is small. There are only seven of us, plus some teaching assistants like Faith. So we all know each other fairly well."

"How long have you worked in Deerfield, professor?"

"Five years in all. Four years on staff," she said. "I came in 2000 and I worked as Roland Kane's personal assistant for a year. He paid my salary out of his own pocket. That year he produced his *Theorems of Mathematics*, which has become a standard textbook. I liked Deerfield and I liked the environment at St. Vincent's. There was a job opening, I applied and I was accepted in 2001."

"So, the two of you wrote a book together?"

She was still a moment. "Only Roland's name appears on the book jacket," she said finally, her voice neutral.

"But would it be fair to say that you had… How shall I phrase it?" Dante pursed his lips. He thought about stroking his chin, but decided against it. Overkill. "That you had a—a certain…input into the book?"

"Oh, yes." Her voice was dry and she inclined her gray head. "It would be fair to say that."

Dante wondered whether stealing someone's academic work warranted murder.

He would have thought not, but years on the force had taught him otherwise. He'd once arrested a man in Naples who had burned down another man's house for winning at *briscola*, the local card game. Dante had learned long ago that the human heart was fathomless. And this was a female heart, the most enigmatic entity in nature.

Time to cut to the chase. "And what was Professor Kane like? Can you tell me something about the man? His character? His likes and dislikes?"

A faint smile creased her face. "As you will no doubt find out, Captain Rossi, if you haven't already, Professor Kane was a most unpleasant man. He liked power—both academic and personal—money and alcohol. He was more or less averse to everything else in life. He was intensely disliked by everyone who ever met him. He was an indifferent administrator, an uninspired teacher and a disloyal colleague."

Whoa, Dante thought. *Why don't you tell me what you really think?*

"He was also," Madeleine Kobbel added with a sigh, "a brilliant mathematician. He had, perhaps, too great a love for applied mathematics, for anything he hoped would earn him money or prestige or power, but nonetheless, he had an extraordinary intuitive grasp of problems. I wouldn't hesitate to define him as a genius."

So most likely it wasn't being a superior mathematician which had gotten Roland Kane killed. It was being an inferior human being.

"Did you, personally, dislike him?"

The corner of her mouth tilted upwards. "If you mean was he my favorite human being, then no. There was no way he could be, given the type of man he was. If the subtext to that question is 'did you kill him', then the answer is no once more."

"Hmm," Dante said neutrally. "Can you tell me about last night, Professor Kobbel? Who was there at the dinner table?"

"Well, except for the absence of Tim Gresham and the presence of Faith Murphy, the very same people we've been having dinner with on our first night in the *Certosa* for seven years. There was Roland, of course. And Griffin Ball, myself, Professor Gori—he's the head of the mathematics department at the University of Siena—"

Dante nodded noncommittally. He'd gone to school with Leonardo Gori's daughter, Raffaella. They had even had an unmemorable night of sex together years ago. The last time he'd seen her she'd gained thirty kilos and had three kids.

She'd looked happy, though. Dante shunted that thought aside the moment it popped into his head.

"Oh, and we usually have Richard Myers from the University of Middlesex in England, but he'd emailed to say he'd be arriving only on the day of the conference itself. Roland was particularly upset at that—Richard does a lot of the administrative work leading up to the conference and that meant Roland was going to actually have to do something himself."

"So, if I've got this straight, Professor Kobbel, at dinner last night at the *Certosa,* there was you, Professor Kane, Griffin Ball, Faith Murphy and Professor Gori."

Madeleine Kobbel nodded.

"And what was the atmosphere like at the dinner table?"

She frowned. "Atmosphere?"

"Yes. What did you talk about?"

"The upcoming conference mostly. Professor Gori asked about our flight and we also discussed what remained to be done before Friday's opening session. There is a great deal of hard work that goes into organizing a conference such as ours. And this year we have people coming from as far away as Japan. The Quantitative Methods Seminar is very well-known in our field."

"Were there any disagreements amongst the diners?"

"If you're intimating that one of us stood up, screamed 'I hate your guts!' at Roland and then left the table, only to slip a knife in his heart later, well…no, captain. There was nothing like that.

"Roland was his usual unpleasant self, but we're all used to that. And he'd had so much to drink on the flight over and during dinner that he wasn't too cogent anyway. I hardly noticed when he excused himself from the table and left."

"How soon after did you leave, Professor Kobbel?"

Hello. Unexpectedly, she blushed. It was fascinating to watch a young girl's blush steal over the features of a more-than-mature woman.

"I—ah, actually, now that I come to think about it, I must have left soon after him. It was after 10:00 p.m. and I'd had a hard day. I was jet-lagged and we'd already made plans with Professor Gori to meet the next day. So when Roland left, I thought that could be my cue to leave, too."

"You left soon after him—or with him, professor?"

"After. I could hear his footsteps ahead of me. Are you familiar with the layout of the *Certosa*, captain?"

Dante nodded his head. He'd once come very close to losing his virginity at the *Certosa* before it had been restored. He still had fond memories of the abbot's cell.

"Well, as you know, there's an arcade around the central courtyard. The rooms assigned to us are on the other side of the cloister from the refectory. I followed Roland around the cloister and up the stairs, but then our ways parted. My room was along the northern corridor and his was along the eastern side."

"So, the two of you didn't talk on your way up to the cells?"

"Why on earth should we? We'd spent almost twelve hours traveling together and we'd just had dinner together. And I repeat, he'd had so much to drink he wouldn't have made much sense anyway."

Dante watched her for a moment. She hadn't answered the question, but she didn't have that cagey look of a witness who'd lied and got away with it.

"So you retired…when, Professor Kobbel?"

She raised her eyes to the ceiling, reflecting. "Well, I guess it must have been about a quarter past ten. I was in bed by 10:40. I remember looking at my alarm clock before turning out the light."

"Did you happen to hear anything unusual during the night?"

"No, nothing. As I say, I was jet-lagged and I'd…ah…taken a melatonin pill to sleep better. I woke up around a quarter to eight and went downstairs for breakfast an hour later. It was around ten when I heard the news that…that something had happened to Roland."

A long, thin something. Plunged straight into Roland Kane's heart. Dante changed tack.

"So, I guess we can sum up by saying that you saw nothing, heard nothing and knew nothing. Am I correct?"

A corner of her mouth lifted. "Put that way, *Commissario*, I sound guilty as hell. But actually, that's the way it is. You'll find the same holds true for the others, as well. We were all tired from a long journey, we all had dinner together and we all went to sleep afterwards."

"Except one of you got up later and killed Professor Roland Kane."

Madeleine Kobbel started. "Well, ah—" she stammered. She shook her head sharply. "Surely it doesn't have to be one of *us* who—who killed Roland? Surely it could have been—I don't know...one of the staff perhaps? An outsider who sneaked in? Why one of us?"

He sighed. "Because, professor, ninety percent of homicides are committed by someone the victim knows. This year a new company won the contract to cater the conferences at the *Certosa*. The staff started in April and they had never met Professor Kane—or any of you for that matter—before.

"The *Certosa* was locked up last night. Of course, any building can be breached, but the walls are fifteen feet high and have glass embedded along the top. There are flower beds all around the perimeter of the walls and so far there are no signs of a break-in." Dante looked at her, all affability gone, a cop. "We're checking."

"Well." Madeleine Kobbel blinked slowly once. Twice. She opened her mouth then closed it again. She didn't look like a woman who was often at a loss for words. "Well, I, ah—" She sighed. "Put that way—"

"Put that way, Professor Kobbel, the list of suspects narrows considerably."

"Put that way I guess it does," she agreed.

"But we don't necessarily suspect *you*, Professor Kobbel." Dante put on his most charming smile. "And forensics will be telling us a little bit more about the method of the murder which will undoubtedly bring us closer to who killed him. In the meantime, Professor Kobbel, I have asked the Public Prosecutor's Office for a warrant to sequester your passports."

This was true and technically Dante had the approval of Marcello Sestini, the public prosecutor. The only thing was Marcello's lazy secretary, Sonia, wasn't going to draw up the warrants until tomorrow, something Madeleine Kobbel didn't necessarily have to know.

"I'm afraid I'll have to keep your passport and the passports of Miss Murphy and Professor Ball for the duration of our inquiry. I would also ask you not to leave the confines of Siena for the next few days."

"I'm hardly likely to, Captain Rossi," she said. "We've got a conference to organize and during the conference itself, we rarely even leave the *Certosa*."

"The conference isn't going to be called off?" Dante asked, eyes slightly narrowed.

For the first time, a true expression crossed Madeleine Kobbel's face—surprise. "Of course not," she said blankly. "We've been working for a year for this. Something as—" She clamped her lips shut.

Dante could figure out the rest of the sentence himself. *Something as trivial as murder certainly isn't going to stop us.*

"Well, professor, I trust you will receive your passports back in a few days," he said smoothly, rising. He stretched out his hand. Hers was dry and bony. "Thank you for your cooperation, Professor Kobbel. I might want to question you further in the next few days."

"That's fine, captain." There was a minute relaxing of the lines around her eyes, but she kept her expression calm. "I understand you're just doing your job. Am I allowed to go now?"

"Most certainly, Professor Kobbel. And I'd be grateful if you would send in Professor Ball." Dante made to accompany her, but kept behind a few steps. When her hand was on the door handle, he said, casually, "By the way, how did you know Roland Kane's heart was punctured? We certainly didn't give out that information."

Her hand tightened on the handle, then she released it and turned around. "Faith Murphy told me." She gave a tight, thin smile. "Good-bye, Captain Rossi." She walked out.

Dante stared at the closed door for a moment, thinking. The phone rang and he picked it up before it could ring again. "Rossi," he said.

"Michele, the pharmacist, saw Nerbo buying a new, expensive sweater. Armani," his brother Mike said without preamble.

Dante shut the file and sat up straight, electrified. "Damn."

Nerbo had absolutely no virtues save the fact he was a magnificent horseman. He was quick to anger, had problems holding down jobs and was in trouble more often than not. He was also totally incapable of handling money. Any money that crossed his small, tough, leathery palm was usually illicitly obtained and was immediately blown. If Nerbo was buying Armani, someone had bought Nerbo.

"Fucking Turtles," Mike said grimly. "How much do you think they sprung to bribe him?"

"I'm not too sure it was the Turtles," Dante said thoughtfully. "It might have been the Tower. If Nerbo had been bought by the Turtles now that we have Lina, he'd be pricing a Mercedes." The Turtles would pay any sum to keep the Snails from winning.

Dante took a perverse pleasure in knowing that the Turtles and the Snails had been archenemies for almost as long as there had been a *Palio*. He had no doubt whatsoever that his great-great-grandfather had complained regularly to his brother about those treacherous Turtles. It gave him a warm, solid feeling in the pit of his liver.

"Have someone keep an eye on Nerbo," he told his brother.

"Already did," Mike answered. "Michele's second son, Giancarlo. He failed two classes this year in high school and he's in the doghouse. Michele promised him that he'd forgive him and let him go to the beach after the *Palio* if he keeps tabs on Nerbo. Nerbo won't be able to take a shit without Giancarlo knowing about it."

Dante grunted. Michele didn't necessarily need to sic his son on Nerbo. The whole Snail *contrada* would be watching the jockey's every move.

As soon as all the details of a *Palio* had been decided upon by the drawing of the lottery, the *partiti* began—that ever more slippery series of formal and informal deals with the enemy of one's enemy *contrada*, forming temporary coalitions with other *contradas* to ensure that one's enemy not win, approaching a rival *contrada's* jockey...

There was a discreet knock on his door.

"Stay on top of the situation," he said to his brother and hung up.

"*Avanti*," he called out.

The door opened and an elegant man slipped in, closing the door quietly behind him.

Dante rose, all affability. "Professor Ball?"

"Griffin Ball," the man confirmed with a nod. "I understand you're *Commissario* Dante Rossi. I also understand you're Lorenzo Rossi's nephew. Your uncle is a very dear friend of mine. He's a wonderful man."

"That he is," Dante said as he indicated the chair for Ball to sit in, and sat down himself. "If you know Uncle Lorenzo, I imagine you also know my cousins, Niccolò and Lucrezia."

Ball frowned a moment, then smiled. "Nick and Lou. Sure. They're great. My partner, Carl, and I had them over for dinner recently. We had to be really inventive with the menu because Nick had just broken a finger."

"Niccolò has always just broken a bone," Dante replied. "I'm surprised he can stand upright."

While they were having their little chitchat, Dante studied the man carefully. He'd seen the man's passport. If he hadn't read the birth date, he wouldn't have put the man's age at much more than forty, but he was approaching sixty.

Ball was immaculately dressed in light tan chinos and a cream-colored, short-sleeved linen shirt. Despite the heat and the fact it was afternoon, his clothes were crisp and spotless. Ball straightened his trousers carefully so they wouldn't crease and Dante noticed the skin on his hands was smooth and unspotted.

Clearly, the man had made a pact with the devil. Or with an extremely clever plastic surgeon and very talented hairdresser. His dark brown hair was well-cut and showed no signs of white hairs. His skin was clear with only a few smile lines around his eyes.

Actually, Dante thought uneasily as he caught a glimpse of his reflection in the window, *Griffin Ball looks younger than I do.*

Dante had been meaning to make it to the barber for weeks now and his hair touched the back of his collar. It wasn't fashionably long, just slovenly long.

It was against the natural order of things for an American to be more elegant than an Italian. Unthinkable.

Dante brought his mind back to the business at hand. "So, Professor Ball, I wonder if you could go over the last twenty-four hours with me."

Ball folded his hands calmly. "Certainly, *Commissario*."

Griffin Ball's recollections of the trip and the dinner dovetailed with Madeleine Kobbel's. And he, too, had heard nothing, seen nothing and knew nothing.

Ball wound down and Dante sat back in his chair, carefully aligning his pen with the side of the notepad.

The two men looked at each other. Griffin Ball, like Faith Murphy and Madeleine Kobbel, was cool and apparently unflappable. Dante decided to see if he could conjure up a response.

"What was your relationship with the dead man, Professor Ball?"

"I beg your pardon?"

It wasn't a difficult question. "I said, what was your relationship with Roland Kane like? You worked together in the same department for…" Dante made a show of looking at the sheet of paper in front of him, though he knew the answer, "for eight years. That's long enough to get to know someone very well. Were the two of you friends?"

Ball smiled. "Clearly, you never met Roland Kane, Captain Rossi. I doubt whether Roland Kane ever had a friend. I doubt he even fully realized what friendship was. The man was so emotionally stunted I wouldn't hesitate to define him a sociopath."

"Harsh words, professor," Dante said mildly.

"And one never speaks ill of the dead, right? Well, in Roland Kane's case, it would be very hard to speak well of him. I'll spare you having to go check back with the authorities in Deerfield, *Commissario*, and tell you straightaway that I had good reason to hate Kane. Probably to kill him, too, if I were a violent man." He shifted elegantly in his chair. "Which I'm not."

Dante had always envied gays their style, as if they were all—every single one—Italian. Being an Italian heterosexual took a lot of work to keep up the image, and Dante wasn't always up to it. But any gay, from more or less any part of the world, managed to look more elegant than he did without breaking a sweat.

"I've had problems with Roland Kane since my arrival at St. Vincent's," Ball began. "And I bitterly regret the day I left Virginia."

Dante didn't have to check his notes. Griffin Ball had resigned his post as assistant professor at Virginia Tech and had been hired on the tenure track at St. Vincent's in September, 1996.

"I guess the weather in Virginia was better."

"Everything in Virginia was better," Ball answered sourly. "And to think, at the time I thought I was taking a step up. St. Vincent's has a world-class reputation in mathematics. Roland Kane wasn't present during the interview process. He never participates—sorry, he never *participated*—in any of the administrative tasks of the faculty. If he'd been there when I interviewed, you can be sure I'd never have accepted the job."

"You had...problems with Professor Kane," Dante said carefully.

"You could say that." Ball's mouth tightened. "I have two lawsuits against Kane pending—one for harassment and the other for assault. Roland Kane was undoubtedly the nastiest human being I've ever met, and I've met my share. Besides being a misogynist and an alcoholic, he was also a rabid homophobe. He made my life a living hell. I reported him several times to the dean and to the trustees of the university but to no avail.

"His harassment eventually became so serious I had to report him to the police. That was how I met your uncle, Lorenzo Rossi. He's the president of the staff committee and he was as disgusted as I was, bless his soul. He went to have a talk with Kane. I don't know what was said, but the worst of the harassment stopped."

"And yet you worked together," Dante said neutrally. "Every day. That must have been a strain."

"Well, to tell the truth I didn't see too much of Kane during the working day. He didn't actually teach many classes. And lately I think his drinking was getting out of control. He was skipping more classes than he taught.

"Mainly I saw him at faculty meetings, but he had to restrain himself with other people around. Mostly, he would try to corner me in the restrooms. He'd leave lurid notes for me, that kind of thing. Luckily, the worst of it stopped once Lorenzo had his talk."

"Yet you took it to court."

Ball straightened. "Damned right I did. Kane's behavior was inexcusable. I called for his resignation time and again, but whenever his situation got serious, he'd pull a rabbit out of a hat. He donated the copyright to a weather prediction software program to the university that earned St. Vincent's a lot of money.

"And the quantitative methods series of conferences gave the college a lot of luster. He had a genius for pushing a situation right up to the edge and then pulling back at the last possible second."

Ball's voice was even and his hands stayed calmly composed on his lap, but Dante could see a vein throbbing in his temple and his breathing had speeded up.

"Someone had to stand up to Kane, and that someone had to be me. I have tenure. I have a generous trust fund from my grandmother, and my partner is a very successful stockbroker. There wasn't anything Kane could really do to me. Unlike Faith."

Dante raised his eyebrows. "Murphy?"

"Yes, Faith Murphy. She's a lovely girl, and a very gifted mathematician, very gifted. Kane made her life miserable from day one. Faith comes from a very poor family and is on contract. Her entire existence is tenuous and Kane preyed on that. And there was a girl—" Ball stared into space. "Coral..." He snapped his fingers. "No, Candace. Candace Simmons. A student. She accused Kane of rape, but before the case could come to trial, she was institutionalized and the charges were dropped. Basically Kane got away with rape. Believe me, *Commissario* Rossi, whoever killed Roland Kane did humanity an immense service."

Ball was slightly flushed, his jaw tensed. Suddenly he smiled. "But it wasn't me."

"That, professor, remains to be seen," Dante replied.

Ball inclined his head. "Of course."

Dante drew in a deep breath. "We will keep your passport for the time being. You will get it back in a few days. I must ask you not to leave Siena until our investigation is complete."

Like Madeleine Kobbel, Ball looked startled at the idea. "Of course I won't leave Siena, captain. I'm here for the conference. It lasts until the second, by which time I'm sure you'll have made headway in your investigation."

By which time, Dante thought, *the Snail will have won.* "I'm sure we will have. I think that's about it for now. You might be called in for further questioning, but, in the meantime, you are free to go."

Ball nodded and rose gracefully, his pants falling softly, perfectly over his suede loafers.

How did the man do it?

The heat of the day had gathered in Dante's office, bearing down oppressively. Dante was sweating and his clothes stuck wherever his body touched the chair.

Every year the town council swore it would put air conditioning in the *Questura,* and every year the town council fell before it could approve the supplementary budget.

In the summer, Dante's office was like a furnace. Yet Griffin Ball looked cool and unruffled. *How did the man do it?* Dante wondered.

Ball walked quietly to the door and stopped. After a moment, he turned around. Dante lifted his head. "Was there something else, professor?"

Ball hesitated. "I know I shouldn't say this, *Commissario.* But...don't look too hard for Kane's murderer. Whoever did it should have a monument erected in his honor."

Chapter Six

Smile ... tomorrow will be worse.

&

The next morning, Faith slid into her seat and smiled at the black-coated waiter pouring more of the delicious coffee so strong it should be classified as a nutraceutical.

Even breakfast, normally a humdrum affair in her life consisting of lukewarm instant coffee and a supermarket donut, was delicious here.

There were croissants, called *cornetti*, still warm from the oven, star-shaped cookies with plum marmalade in the middle, sugary donuts the waiters called *bomboloni* and — on the other side of the diet pyramid — slices of thick, salty country ham and round, sweet melon balls.

Everyone looked up as if surprised to see her. They were frozen in a little breakfast tableau — Tim with bread crumbs from the saltless Tuscan bread spilling down his shirt, Grif, elegant as always with a little round pastry held up between thumb and forefinger, and Madeleine hunched over her plate, long grey hair swinging forward to hide her face.

"Faith." Grif, always the gentleman, stood while Faith took her seat.

For the thousandth time, Faith wished Grif were straight and that she had had a brief, passionate affair with him, rather than the short, bloodless affair she'd had with Tim.

Grif would have taken her out to some elegant restaurants, and he would have made her laugh and sigh while seducing her. She and Tim had shared a stringy takeout pizza in her apartment followed by very bad sex.

She and Nick had had very good sex, though, of course, her experience was limited, so maybe it hadn't been as spectacular as her memory insisted. Still, right up until the moment it had been made clear she was one of a faceless series, it had felt pretty special. More fool her. She didn't seem to have much luck with straight men.

"Sit down, Grif." Faith smiled. She picked up her cup, drained it and looked around. Before she could signal a waiter, a freshly brewed cup was slipped in front of her. "Can't fault the service here." She caught Grif's eye. "Beats the cafeteria back home, eh?"

"By a mile." Grif delicately patted his lips dry. "What did Leonardo want with you yesterday, Faith? Is something wrong?"

Much as Grif liked her, he had somehow picked up on the general aura Kane had created for her—that she was an accident just waiting to happen.

With real pleasure, Faith reached out for a *cornetto* and said, "Not at all. As a matter of fact, he asked me to chair the Tipping Behavior Panel." She felt slightly defiant as she looked up. Grif was looking thoughtful, and Tim seemed slightly shocked.

Madeleine put her cup down sharply in its saucer, two red spots on her sallow cheeks. "There must be some mistake," she said, frowning. "I was supposed to head that panel."

Faith tensed. "I'm afraid he didn't say anything about that at all, Madeleine. Are you sure? Professor Gori—Leonardo—doesn't seem to be the kind of man who would make mistakes like that."

Madeleine's lips tightened at Faith's use of Gori's first name. "Last year, I chaired the workshop on viral quantitation. So this year, of course I assumed I'd be chairing the panel on tipping behavior.

"This isn't fair, Faith. I'm afraid you'll have to go back to Professor Gori and say you weren't aware of the situation and that you can't chair the panel. I came prepared for this."

Say no? Over her dead body. Faith drew in an outraged breath, but Grif raised his hand before she could speak.

"Madeleine, the decision is not ours to make. Traditionally, Leonardo draws up the speakers' list and the workshop panels, and unless something is very wrong, we go along with it."

"Well, there's something wrong here." Madeleine's flat chest rose and fell quickly. "Having chaired last year's meeting, I just naturally assumed—"

"You *co*-chaired a panel on a different, though related, subject. That's not the same thing at all. And Faith is the only one here to have written a paper on tipping behavior. And a very good one, too." He nodded to Faith and she felt her outrage muscles—the ones running from her nape along her shoulders that had been getting such good exercise while working under Kane—relax slightly.

She had never been close to Madeleine, but by the same token, Madeleine had never gone out of her way to be nasty to her either. By St. Vincent's Math Department standards, that was practically a torrid love affair. Why was Madeleine being so difficult now?

Madeleine was already co-chairing another panel on pseudo-quantitation and, over the course of the past few years, had chaired and moderated her share of workshops and seminars.

It wasn't even as if she were an expert on tipping. Faith was.

Faith had been surprised Leonardo had taken the trouble to read her paper, but she was proud of it. Maybe she was lacking in just about everything a normal human being and a normal woman should have but, by God, she was a fine mathematician and had written a fine paper.

At some level, she'd been aware of the fact that part of Kane's hostility had stemmed from jealousy. Tim, Grif and Madeleine—they were all competent enough. Tim was a decent theoretician and Grif was an excellent teacher.

Madeleine—no one really understood what Madeleine was doing in the department, but Kane wanted her there and so she'd been there.

But none of them were as good as Kane had been. And none were as good as she was.

Faith looked around. A sunlit room in Tuscany, in a restored monastery, in the room where monks used to pray was as good a place as any for an epiphany. Something deep within her shifted, something old and rotten like a piece of ancient furniture moving away to make room for something new.

All her life she'd been put down. By her parents, for being alive. For having that chance at a happy life that had so spectacularly eluded them. At college, for being poor and gangly and overly bright. By Roland Kane, for being almost as good a mathematician as he was.

Even Nick, without meaning to, had dealt her a huge blow. He couldn't even remember her name after a night of lovemaking.

But, for the first time in her life, she had a glimpse of a life that was more than merely grimly hanging on by her fingertips. She might not be good at much, but she realized she was a talented mathematician.

And another talented mathematician, Leonardo Gori, had recognized it. If he had read her paper and been impressed, then maybe others had as well.

"*Ancora caffè?*"

Faith was jerked out of her thoughts by a handsome waiter hovering over her with a steaming silver coffeepot.

"*Si, grazie.*"

He bent over to pour, then stood and winked. "*Brava.*"

Faith winked back and was rewarded with a brilliant smile, a thousand watts of teeth.

"…not fair," a voice was whining.

With a sigh, Faith turned from the pleasant, mild flirtation to gaze at Madeleine across the table, still complaining to Grif. Madeleine shook her head, the long, gray strands around her ears making her look like a greyhound. "I'm going to speak to Leonardo about this."

"I wouldn't if I were you." Grif's voice was sharp, eyes sharper. "Kane's dead, and until the administration appoints his successor, I am *pro tem* department head and I absolutely forbid you to make a fuss about this, Madeleine."

Madeleine blinked. Grif rarely raised his voice and was rarely anything but lazily courteous. But now, Faith could almost see the glint of steel beneath his indolent southern charm.

"Well." Madeleine stood up abruptly, jarring the table, and Faith steadied her cup before it could slosh over. "That was clear. And it's also very clear whose side you're on." Shooting a look at Faith that was surprising in its venom, she turned and left.

"Wow." Tim's eyes blinked behind his thick glasses. Tim rarely noticed anything going on around him, but Madeleine's temper tantrum had broken through his usual distraction. He turned to Grif. "What was that all about?"

Grif sighed. "Jealousy."

"Of *Faith?*"

Faith could have slapped Tim for the tone of utter disbelief.

104

"Yes. Of Faith." Composed, Grif patted his lips with the snowy, blanket-sized napkin and smiled warmly at her. Eerily, his words echoed her thoughts. "Looks like this is *your* time now, Faith, my dear. I'm happy for you."

Tim's head swiveled. Grif. Faith. Then Grif again. His brow furrowed. "Huh?"

A tall, good-looking man in a uniform materialized beside her, accompanied by Leonardo Gori.

The man mouthed wonderful sounds in liquid tones at her. She frowned at Leonardo. It seemed so unfair to have a handsome man asking something—and she didn't know what.

Leonardo bent forward. "I'm sorry, Faith," he said unhappily. "But the *commissario* wants to talk to you again. He's willing to wait until the day's work is over. *Agente* Nicoletti here will wait for you and then accompany you downtown to the *Questura*."

The good news was she had a handsome young man waiting for her.

The bad news was maybe he wanted to arrest her.

* * * * *

Faith was waiting in a room with an incredible view at police headquarters, with a handsome, young, English-speaking agent taking down her vital statistics, when a dirty and crazed-looking Nick walked in. It was Faith's worst nightmare—Nick, seeing her in a vulnerable position. Standing in a foreign station house waiting to be questioned about a murder was about as vulnerable as you could get.

Dante strolled in. "Nick." He looked taken aback. "What are you doing here? You usually come to the August *Palio*. You're a month early."

Nick's jaw muscles bunched. He had a big jaw and it was like watching cats fight under a blanket. "All I wanted to do was see if Faith was all right." Nick pushed both hands through his disheveled hair. "I got your message and flew straight over." He looked over at Faith. "I came to rescue you, honey. Stop glaring at me."

Faith folded her arms under her breasts and looked out the window. "Go away, Nick. Nobody asked you to be here."

"No, nobody asked me to be here." Very gently, Nick put his hand on her arm and she jerked. "I wanted to be here because you were in trouble. I want to help you. Let me help you."

"I don't need any help, thank you very much." Faith's lips tightened as she pulled away. "I can get myself arrested for murder all on my own, without any help from anyone." Her eyes lifted to Dante. "Isn't that right, Dante?"

"Damn it, Faith." Nick rammed his hands through his hair. "Stop that. Being arrested for murder is no joke, and—"

"Ah, excuse me," Dante murmured, clearing his throat.

Nick rounded on his cousin. "What?"

"What?" Faith asked in alarm.

"Hey, easy." Dante held up his hands. "All I want to say is that one thing should be made clear here. Faith is not under arrest or even a major suspect. She's just in for questioning, since she found the body." Dante's voice was even as he looked back and forth between Faith Murphy and Nick. "I, ah, knew you were a friend of Lou's, Faith. I didn't realize you're a...friend of Nick's, too."

Faith looked out the window, arms still crossed over her chest. "I'm not," she said, just as Nick said, "Of course she is."

"Listen you—" she said, just as he said, "Don't be stupid—"

"Children, children." Dante held up his hands as two pairs of eyes, one dark blue, one golden brown, flashed daggers at him. "Behave yourselves."

Faith opened her mouth again to put Dante straight, but he waved at a chair. "Please, sit down, Faith. I'm afraid we're going to have to go over the terrain once again. I realize how annoying this must be for you, but it's a pure formality."

Nick took her elbow and Faith shot him a venomous glance. She looked down pointedly at his hand on her arm, as he tried to steer her chivalrously to the chair.

Ha! Faith thought. *Chivalry. The rat doesn't have a chivalrous bone in his body.*

Then she looked again at his hand — large, long-fingered, elegantly masculine. She had a sudden vision of his strong, deeply-tanned hands moving over her pale skin, touching her breasts, breaching her body, and she went hot then cold at the memory.

She looked up and saw Nick was thinking the same thing. His deep blue eyes were focused intensely on her and she could feel a blush rising.

Hard on the heels of that was the memory of her humiliation.

She had practically thrown herself at him, when he'd been so drunk a female *goat* would have done.

Nick hadn't even been aware he had been making love to *her*, Faith Murphy, as opposed to any other female fan. He had them falling into his bed in droves and the fact she'd been just as easy as any of the other over-endowed bimbettes who followed the Hunters players around burned her pride.

She pulled away again from Nick's hand with a hiss and sat down, turning her head away from him. She folded her hands in her lap and tried to compose herself. She drew a deep breath. "I'm ready when you are, Dante."

"Yes." Dante was trying not to smile as she glared at him.

Nick pulled up a chair next to her and she picked up her own chair and turned it so her back was to Nick.

"As I was saying, I realize this is ground we've already covered—"

"That's okay." Faith tried very hard not to think of Nick sitting next to her. Not to notice that he seemed to take up an inordinate amount of space in the interrogation room and that she could feel his body heat against her back. "I read murder mysteries. You're going to interrogate us all, over and over again, until you catch one of us up in a lie and that person confesses and you've solved your case. Fire away."

"Don't I wish it were always that easy," Dante murmured. "So—let's run through this once more. You arrived at the *Certosa* around 9:00 p.m. last night? With your group?" Dante frowned down at the notes he had on the table in front of him as if he could barely decipher the rudimentary markings in Assyrian. "Would you like to go over that with me again?"

Neatly done, Faith thought. She had no doubt whatsoever that *Commissario* Dante Rossi knew all about her, and the rest of the St. Vincent's group, and knew all about their movements.

"All right," she said on a sigh, rubbing her neck. It had been a long day. Very satisfying—until now—but long. She'd slept some last night, but she'd spent two sleepless nights before. On top of another sleepless night in bed with... Faith didn't look behind her. She could feel Nick's presence without having to see him.

All in all, it was no wonder she was stressed out. "Okay." She looked down in her lap and watched her fingers intertwine then separate as she gathered her thoughts.

Dante nodded and picked up a printed program. "All right. Here it says that the conference, the Seventh International Quantitative Methods Seminar," he read slowly from the program, "wasn't scheduled to start until today. So why did your group come early?"

"Because, traditionally, the University of Siena and St. Vincent's College run the seminar. It takes a lot of planning. The University of Siena takes care of most of the physical details like hospitality and catering, and both the universities are responsible for the running of the program. That's why we come over a day early. Or so I was told."

"Mmm-hm." Dante pursed his lips as he looked at the program as if he'd just noticed something. He frowned as he flipped through his notes. "I don't see your name on the program, Faith. And your name wasn't on the list of guests up at the *Certosa*."

Faith's heart started to pound. She could almost feel Nick's intense gaze behind her. She cleared her throat. "That's true. Ordinarily, I'm not part of the QM seminar." *Though I should've been*, she thought resentfully. The thought still rankled.

"The seminar has been run for seven years now by Professor Kane with the help of Madeleine Kobbel, Griffin Ball and Tim Gresham. But Tim Gresham came down with a bad case of flu and I—" Faith shrugged casually, "I was at loose ends. So they asked me if I could come to replace Tim. And I said sure."

"They?" Dante frowned.

"He." Faith sighed. "Professor Kane. And he wasn't gracious about it either. He let me know in no uncertain terms that I was a peon, not fit to tie the shoelaces of the Mensans."

"Mensans?"

"Members of Mensa. It's an organization that requires a genius IQ to join. Which I don't have. All I am is smart."

"I see." Dante pursed his lips. "So — you were allowed to tag along."

"That's about the size of it." Faith grimaced. "Professor Kane made that clear. Basically, he said I would be making coffee and running the photocopy machine. And if I was very, very lucky, a paper of mine could be added as a footnote to the proceedings." She shrugged. "But in academia, you grab your chances where you find them."

"Indeed. So, the four of you — Professor Kane, Madeleine Kobbel, Griffin Ball and yourself — leave for Siena via — " He looked up.

"Boston, Rome, Florence."

"Boston, Rome, Florence. From Logan Airport. All right. Did anything unusual happen on the flight?"

"Well…" Faith frowned. "Unusual. It depends on what you mean by unusual. Professor Kane got drunk and made a heavy pass at a pretty flight attendant. That's fairly unusual by my book, but apparently not for him. Madeleine — Professor Kobbel — said that he often made scenes like that."

Dante was writing in his notebook. "So he insulted a flight attendant. Did you happen to get her name?"

"Yes. I talked to her later. I thought I would calm her down. But she was calm enough. She said there was one every flight."

"One what?"

"Bastard. Her name was Karen Lewis and she couldn't have killed Professor Kane. She said she was due to fly back out of Rome two hours after we landed. You might want to check that."

"I might." Dante's mouth lifted in a half smile and he made a brief notation. "Did anything else happen on the flight?"

"No, that was about it on the flight itself, except that Professor Kane drank six of those small bottles of wine and ten-mini bottles of brandy. He had some trouble with customs at Fiumicino Airport. He'd brought four bottles of whiskey, and apparently that was over the allowance.

"Professor Kane threw a real fuss about paying extra duty. Showed his letter of invitation from the University of Siena. Told the customs official he knew the President of the Italian Republic. Told him he was a close friend of George Bush.

"He really pulled out all the stops." Faith winced. "He could be heard from the baggage claim area. And all for a savings of a grand total of twenty-seven dollars and fifty cents in excise tax."

"Hmm. Roland Kane seems to have had a knack for making enemies," Dante said. "Any other problems en route?"

"No. Alcohol and jet lag seemed to catch up with Professor Kane after that. He slept on the flight to Florence and dozed in the minivan. It was almost dark when we reached the *Certosa*. We were all assigned cells and we were given fifteen minutes to unpack because supper was being served in the refectory.

"All the meals at the *Certosa* are delicious. As was the snack I was served here today. Thank you, by the way." Faith shook her head in amazement. "If monks and prisoners eat like that, I hardly dare think what ordinary civilians get to eat."

"Doubtless you'll find out soon enough." Dante looked behind her. "When Faith has finished here, you might want to take her to Tullio's for a bite," he said to Nick. "She's had a hard day."

"Right."

Faith whirled around at the sound of Nick's deep voice and Nick raised his hands in self-defense at the heat he saw in her eyes.

Faith turned back, gripping the arms of her hardback chair. "I'm quite capable of feeding myself, Dante. There's no need whatsoever —"

"Nonsense." Without raising his voice, Dante managed to stop her, mid-tirade. "I'm taking off my policeman's hat here for just a moment. You're a friend of my cousin, Lou, and I see you're a friend of Nick's as well." He politely ignored Faith's unladylike snort. "You're a foreigner in my country and you've been subjected to the utmost stress. It would be unthinkable of me to allow you to be left to your own devices."

He smiled suddenly and Faith was bowled over by the charm of that smile. It disappeared as quickly as it had come. "Now," he said, his voice all business again, "let's go back to the night before last. You had dinner at the *Certosa*. Who was there?"

"Let's see." Faith tried to concentrate. It was all beginning to catch up with her — the lack of sleep, the shock of finding a dead man, the excitement of chairing a meeting of some of the greatest mathematical minds on the planet.

Faith hesitated for a moment, as if gathering her thoughts, but the truth was her thoughts were harder and harder to gather, like fireflies in summer. She felt numb and empty and a little sad.

She shook her head and tried to focus on what Dante had asked. "Besides Professor Kane, there was the head of the Siena University Math Department, Professor Gori. Leonardo. Nice man. He speaks excellent English. Then

Madeleine and Griffin and myself. And the waiters, of course.

"We ate a pasta dish and then veal cutlets and a salad. Then this really incredible ice cream. Professor Kane excused himself after the second course and, a few minutes later, so did Madeleine.

"Well, Kane didn't exactly excuse himself. He simply stood up abruptly and walked—or rather staggered—away. He'd drunk a whole bottle of Chianti himself. Quite frankly, I'm surprised he could stand."

"So Professor Kane left early, followed immediately by Professor Kobbel?"

"Yes."

"Is there anything…personal between Professor Kobbel and Professor Kane?"

"Personal? You mean like…sex?" Faith wrinkled her nose. The idea of anyone having sex with Roland Kane was repugnant in the extreme. "No, there was nothing personal between them. Not that I know of, anyway. Professor Kane wasn't fit for human intercourse. Of any kind.

"And believe me, I should think sex was the last thing on his mind. Particularly since, for some reason, he'd ordered himself another bottle of whiskey. As if four weren't going to be enough."

"He had? How do you know that?"

"I got a little lost after dinner trying to find my way back to my room. The corridors all look alike, and they aren't very well lit. Then I saw a maid walking down one of the corridors and I called out to her, but she didn't turn around, so I followed her 'round a corner. She stopped at Professor Kane's door and knocked. She was holding a tray with a bottle of whiskey on it."

"Are you sure she stopped at Professor Kane's door?"

"Yes. Number seventeen. I'd asked beforehand what his room number was because I knew I might have to ask him a favor."

But Kane had been so drunk he would have been incapable of paying attention, so she'd put it off until morning. *What if I hadn't?* Faith thought suddenly. What if she'd decided to go to his cell that night instead of in the morning?

Would she have surprised someone kneeling over him, stiletto point poised over his heart? Faith shivered at the thought then jumped as she felt Nick's large, warm hand on her shoulder.

"Are you cold, Faith?" he asked softly. "I could get you a sweater."

"No." Faith struggled for calm. "Thank you." It was easy to stay angry at Nick when he was his usual cocky, ebullient self. But when he showed his sweet side... She concentrated on the cop Rossi and tried to ignore the jock Rossi.

"Did you see Professor Kane when he opened the door?" Dante asked.

"Sort of." Faith frowned, trying to remember. "I heard the maid knocking and the door opening, but I'd got my bearings by then, realized I was in the wrong corridor and walked back to the right one. But it must've been Professor Kane who answered. Who else could it have been?"

"Do you remember what she looked like?"

"The maid?" Faith thought, then shook her head. "Nope. Sorry."

Dante leaned forward. "Think, Faith. What was she wearing?"

Faith snorted.

"What?"

"Close your eyes," she said.

He didn't question her. He simply closed his eyes and waited.

Faith smiled. "Now, what are *you* wearing?"

He sighed. "A tan cotton shirt, dark brown cotton pants, brown socks and loafers. The shirt isn't ironed very well, my mom refuses to do my ironing and I'm no damned good at it." His eyes opened. "Did I pass the test?"

"Perfect," Faith said. "Now close your eyes again. What is Nick wearing?"

Dante smiled, eyes closed. "Probably the first thing he found in his closet. A very rumpled T-shirt, faded jeans with a rip in the knee and sneakers. No socks. Nick, if Lou saw you like this, she'd have your hide."

"Well, if I'd known I was going to be attending a fashion parade—" Nick began heatedly.

Faith held her hand up. "That's enough, I've made my point. You can open your eyes, Dante. I want you to know I could never, ever do that. Unless I have a reason to focus on it, I don't remember what people look like, or what they're wearing or what they do."

She didn't mention that most times, unless it was about math, she didn't remember what people said, either. She gave a short laugh. "I rarely remember what *I'm* wearing on any given day."

"Okay, cops are trained to be observant," Dante said. "But surely you remember something about her. How tall was she?"

Faith shrugged.

"The windows of the corridors are about a meter and a half off the floor and are about two meters tall. How tall was she in comparison to the windows? Did her shoulders reach the bottom sill?"

Faith was amazed at a cop's thought processes. She would never have thought of that.

"Think back to that moment," Dante urged. "What were you thinking? Do you remember?"

Of Nick. She'd been thinking of Nick. Of how angry she was at him, of how exciting it had been to make love with him, of how much she missed him. She'd barely noticed the maid.

"Come on, Faith," Dante said softly. "Cast your mind back. You were tired, you'd just arrived in Italy, you'd had dinner, you were walking along, you see a woman and she's carrying a tray. What was on your mind?"

"Ah, I wasn't thinking of much. I was tired and jet-lagged. Oh, I do remember thinking that—" She stopped suddenly.

"You remember thinking?"

"Well…I remember thinking she wouldn't have to worry about Professor Kane harassing her. He'd have been too drunk to make a pass."

"Did most women around Professor Kane have those kinds of problems?"

"Anyone young and attractive," Faith said. "Pretty much. Two sexual harassment suits have been hushed up. There was talk of another young woman…Candace Simmons, I think her name was." Faith frowned as she tried to recall the gossip that had swirled around the school last fall. "But I think the charges were dropped. She's apparently in psychiatric care. A lot of women had problems with him."

"Did you?" Dante asked, his eyes sharp.

"He harassed me." Faith swallowed heavily. "But not sexually. He always said I was too plain to make love to. He didn't employ the term 'make love to' either."

"Why did he harass you?"

"I wasn't his first choice as assistant lecturer. His first choice was Loren Ing at Arizona State, who was working on meteorological models. Professor Kane thought he could sell Ing's package to commodities investors. But Dr. Ing accepted another position at the last minute. They didn't have any other candidates.

"Professor Kane was—" Faith tried to keep an even voice as she remembered the first horrible months at St. Vincent's, "—difficult. He made it known he didn't want me. That he thought I was an inferior mathematician from a fourth-rate school. That I wasn't fit to wash the floors at St. Vincent's.

"He wrote letters to the administration complaining about my teaching abilities. It was..." She swallowed and shrugged. "Hard. Then, after a while, I guess he lost interest. And I learned to stay out of his way."

"So what you're saying is that you would've had a motive for murdering him."

"Hey, wait a minute!" Nick said heatedly. "How can you—"

"Stop it, Nick," Faith said wearily, without turning around. "Your cousin is just doing his job." She met Dante's eyes. "I would say, Dante," she said clearly, "that just about anyone who has ever met Professor Roland Kane would have had a reason to kill him."

"I see." And he looked as if he did. "All right then, let's get back to the maid. You didn't see her face, and you didn't see Professor Kane open the door."

"No."

"All you saw was the back of a woman carrying a bottle of whiskey and stopping at Professor Kane's door."

"That's right." Faith clenched her hands on the chair arms and straightened. The temptation to slump was great, but she couldn't give into it, no matter how tired she was.

"What time did you go to Professor Kane's cell the next morning?" Dante asked, his voice casual.

"Early. I was up all night, working on my paper. It was only going to be a footnote. But I wanted it to be a *good* footnote."

"All night?" Dante was writing constantly now. He didn't look up. "Could you clarify that, please? You didn't go to bed at all?"

"I guess I started working on my paper around eleven. I was really tired. I thought I would just go over it quickly, but there were a number of problems and I got sucked in. By the time I realized that I wasn't going to get anywhere without a Cray to crunch my numbers, it was a quarter to six and it was already light. I set my alarm for 7:30 and just fell into bed."

"This...Cray." Dante looked up from his notes. "He's a colleague of yours?"

"Don't I wish." Faith smiled at the thought. "A Cray is a supercomputer. Nowadays, you can have serial computers working a problem and it's cheaper, but time-wise, a Cray is the best bet. It's very powerful and time on it is very expensive. We have one back at St. Vincent's, but only department heads can authorize its use. That would be Professor Kane."

"I see. So you decided to knock on his door at eight o'clock in the morning."

"8:05," Faith said. "I checked my watch. Uh, Dante?"

"Yes?"

"My laptop has a built-in clock in the hard disk. I mean all laptops do, of course, not just mine. I didn't mean to say that I have a special—" She was babbling. Fatigue and stress. She drew in a deep breath and tried to ignore the dizziness she felt.

"What I meant to say is that the time I was working—it's all recorded on the hard disk of my laptop. If you take the hard disk out and have it analyzed, you'll see that I was constantly at the keyboard until a quarter to six in the morning."

"Mm. How did you get into Professor Kane's cell, Faith?"

"Well, I knocked, of course, but the door was unlocked and off the latch. It swung open and I could see Professor Kane on the floor."

"And what did you think when you saw Professor Kane lying on the floor?"

"That he was dead drunk." Faith's lips tightened. "I told you that before."

"Yes, you did." He flipped back through his notes. "You considered that a reasonable assumption."

"Considering what I saw him drink over the course of the previous day, it was. I knew he was a heavy drinker, but I didn't realize he was that bad. Maybe he was worried. They say—"

"They say what, Faith?"

Faith sighed. Looked like she was the designated gossip-repeater. "They say Professor Kane lost a lot of money on a model he designed with a colleague to predict consumer trends. It was a flawed model and he sank a little of his money and a lot of other people's money into it. There was sort of a stink and then it blew over."

"I see." Dante looked up from his notes. "Where do you suppose I could find a list of investors?"

Faith shook her head wearily. There had been rumors someone in the English department had lost all his savings in the scheme and had blown his brains out. Roland Kane had left such a blighted legacy of suffering and unhappiness behind him. Who cared who killed him?

Then, unbidden, the image of his dead body swam before her eyes. Someone — probably someone she knew, and knew well — had stood close to him, slipped a stiletto into his heart and watched as the light in his eyes had died. *What kind of person could do that? Even to a man like Kane?*

"Faith?"

She started. "I'm sorry," she murmured wanly. "I missed your question. I guess I'm…a little tired."

"I can see that," Dante said kindly. He put down his pad and stood up. "I'll tell you what. Why don't you get a good night's sleep tonight and we can go over the last few points tomorrow. They're just details anyway." He straightened and lost his smile. "However, I am obliged to remind you that you may not leave the confines of the city of Siena and we will continue to hold your passport until further notice."

"Sure."

"Your purse and personal belongings are downstairs, in room Ten C. Why don't you go down and sign for them? I'll send Nick on down to you in a moment."

Faith shot to her feet and squared her shoulders. She looked him straight in the eye. "You needn't bother. I don't need or want Nick around me."

"Faith…" Nick growled from behind her, putting a hand on her shoulder. "You're dead on your feet. I'm not about to—"

"Take your hand off me, Nick," Faith said icily without turning around. "Dante, tell Nick to take his hand off me."

Amusement lit Dante's dark blue eyes. "Nick," he began, "take your hand off—"

Nick pulled his hand away as if she had become red-hot.

"All right!" he said, lifting his hands. "All right." He drew in a deep breath and blew it out again, struggling for patience. "Look, Faith, all I want to do is to help—"

But he was talking to thin air. Faith had left the room, closing the door quietly behind her.

Dante looked at Nick for a long moment, deciding that it was Rossi pumping time. He picked up the phone and punched an extension. "Keep Miss Murphy busy with formalities in Ten C for a quarter of an hour."

"Thanks, Dante." Nick rubbed a big hand over the back of his neck. "I owe you."

"Yes, you do. I let Miss Murphy go. Technically, I could've kept her in jail for thirty-six hours." Dante sat back in his chair and eyed his cousin.

"She didn't do it," Nick growled, his muscles tensing.

"I'm sure she didn't," Dante said agreeably, and Nick relaxed. "I'm just telling you what I have the power to do. But I'll have to question her again, and I'll have to keep her passport. Lucrezia didn't tell me you'd be coming. She said Miss Murphy was a friend of the family, but I didn't realize…"

"She's not your style, Nick. She seems like the kind of woman who can be hurt."

"I have no intention of hurting Faith," Nick said heatedly. "And you're making me out to be some no-brainer Romeo."

Dante raised his eyebrows and said nothing.

"I'm *not*," Nick said truculently, as if Dante had said something. "And anyway, I've…matured."

"It must've been a recent development. In the last week, say. Lou had me in stitches about your latest, Dee Dee. And the one before that…" Dante held up a hand to ward off Nick's sputtering protest. "Never mind. Here." He dug into his pocket and pulled out a set of keys and tossed them. Nick caught the set one-handed. "Use my car while you're here. I'll use Mike's old Fiat. Do you need anything else?"

"Clothes. I only have what's on my back."

"Grandma will insist you stay with her. You'll find some old clothes of mine there. Feel free to use whatever you want."

"Thanks. How's Gramps doing?"

Dante sighed. "Some days he's better than others. Mostly he sits in the sunshine and dozes. You'll see for yourself." He stood. "I like your Faith."

"Hands off, Dante," Nick bristled. "I'm looking after her now."

"She seems to be very resistant to the idea of being looked after by you." Dante's lips lifted in a half smile as he watched his cousin limp around the room. "I think she might be needing someone else to look after her. Though, come to think of it—" he scratched his chin, "—she seemed pretty good at taking care of herself."

"Well, if she's that good at taking care of herself, what's she doing all tangled up with a murder? All of this wouldn't have happened if she hadn't left my b—" Nick suddenly clammed up, pressing his lips tightly together.

They both contemplated the ceiling for a moment.

Dante laughed and stood up. "Go on down and get her and feed her. She looks like a strong wind would blow her over. I'll talk to her when she's rested."

"Right." Nick hobbled to the door and opened it.

"Oh, and Nick."

Nick turned and met Dante's sober gaze.

"Make sure she sleeps somewhere safe tonight. There's a murderer on the loose."

Chapter Seven

Mother Nature is a bitch.

∞

"Faith."

"Go away Nick," she said stonily as they both stepped outside the *Questura*.

"Goddammit!"

Faith looked up in surprise as Nick raked a big, scarred hand through his blue-black hair. She'd never heard him curse before, not even mildly.

He looked angry, which surprised her even more. She had supposed he usually worked out his aggressions on the ice because he always seemed so even-tempered.

Not now. Now he looked tired and exasperated, regretting his precipitous rush over the ocean. He looked like he'd rather be anywhere but here. With her. Her spine stiffened. "I told you before, Nick, go away. It was absolutely crazy of you to fly across the Atlantic for me. All that money wasted and you're probably in the middle of training or something—"

"We train in the fall," Nick interrupted.

"Whatever." A limp loop of hair fell over Faith's eye and she shoved it out of her face. She felt limp all over. "It was ridiculous to come out here just because—"

"I often come over at the end of June, beginning of July. Or else halfway through August. The race is run twice in the summer."

"Race? What race?"

Nick stuck his hands in his jeans pockets. "The *Palio*." At her blank look, he added, "It's a horse race, but it's more than a horse race...it's a way of life. A way of belonging to the city."

Faith couldn't imagine what he was talking about, then remembered Leonardo talking about some horse race.

"A family tradition," he ended lamely. "We all come over, sometimes in July, usually in August. Lou will be over in August and my parents will be, too."

Nick was interested in horses? Lou was interested in horses? As far as Faith knew, Lou was interested in money and clothes, and bullying Nick, their father and any man within a ten mile radius into doing what she wanted. "I...see."

"I just came over a day or two earlier than I would have anyway."

Great, Faith thought as the humiliation washed over her in waves. Nick had slept with her because he'd been drunk and thought she was someone else, and she'd made this big deal out of it. He'd come over to Siena because he came over every year around this time anyway, and she'd made a big deal out of that, too. She was suddenly reminded all over again why she loved math so much.

Numbers weren't people.

"Listen, Faith—" Nick began, two red spots of color on his high cheekbones.

"No, you listen to me." Faith had never wanted anything in her life as badly as she wanted to get away from Nick.

Not even getting out of Sophie and then getting her PhD had evoked the same yearning in her.

She'd longed for Nick for almost a year, knowing she could never have him. In comparison, getting out of Sophie and getting her PhD had been a piece of cake.

And then she'd landed Nick, briefly and humiliatingly, and all she could think of was how much she longed to toss him back.

She backed away. "Look, I'm tired and stressed, and hungry and thirsty and dirty. I need to get back to—" She broke off as Nick took her arm. "You're hurting me," she said icily.

"I'm not hurting you," he snapped. "Believe me, if I wanted to hurt you, by God you'd know it."

Faith rolled her eyes. "If I'm going to be kidnapped, can I at least know where you're taking me?"

"To eat." She could actually hear Nick's teeth grinding. "Not that you deserve being taken care of, or having someone worry about you. God forbid someone care that you look like you're about ready to faint." His features were hard, tense.

He was angry. *Fine,* Faith thought, as she stared blindly at the gorgeous shop windows. *Fine. Let him be angry.* She was angry, too.

Nick dug his fingers into her elbow and started walking. She had no choice. Thoughts and stomach churning, Faith walked with him. Faith didn't want to look at him, so she looked around and tried to resist her heart melting as she finally *saw* what she'd been looking at.

The afternoon had been spent inside the grimy, stuffy waiting room of the police station. It had smelled of sweat, dust and—oddly—lasagne, probably courtesy of a nearby restaurant. The afternoon had passed slowly in a stupor of tiredness and heat, and by the end of it, she had been too numb to think.

But she wasn't too numb to see.

The world had turned red-gold while she'd been in the room with closed shutters. The light was so intense she had to squint her eyes against the crimson sun shedding its dying rays over…perfection.

There was no other word for it. Deep red brick buildings, which were probably golden at high noon, rose straight and high from the cobblestone street. She could hardly take all the gorgeousness in all at once. Marble and stucco casements, wrought iron balconies, friendly green shutters. Swallows wheeled and cried overhead in the dying light.

Well, of course, why not? What she was seeing was as beautiful and as unreal as a film set. The set needed a soundtrack, and the birds and their raucous cries were providing just that.

Music, she thought. *We need some music…* And sure enough, the sounds of someone practicing a piano concerto drifted down from an open window.

Faith stood, taking it in, too overwhelmed to think beyond the moment, too tired to move in any direction. Too tired to react when Nick took her arm again.

She just stood there, soaking up the glow, Nick's tall, broad figure as much a part of the scenery as the earth-colored buildings, the oleander bushes in big terra-cotta pots with molded angels on the side, the pewter-colored cobblestones and the shafts of bronze sunlight with gilded dust motes dancing in the air.

Faith closed her eyes and savored the gentle evening breeze. Even her eyelids turned golden on the inside. For a moment, she felt an elemental connection with everything—the hand-made cobbles, the warm wind on her cheeks, the glow of the sun so strong it almost had weight. The hard, warm hand at her elbow.

For an instant, she imagined herself one of the swallows wheeling overhead. Imagined the freedom, whirling and banking over this lovely city…

"Come on," Nick said. "Let's go."

And just like that, she snapped back to reality. Back to a foreign country, back to the thought of a dead man killed by someone she knew, back to her deepest humiliation.

Nick had come for her because he felt guilty.

Sweet Nick.

He was incredibly tough on the ice, slashing and hacking his way through his opponents at thirty-five miles an hour, slicing over the ice like a fury. A ruthless and canny adversary, he had what the sports reporters called, simply, "the edge". That extra something that men who went into war and survived had.

Off the ice, he was a perfectly normal man, if you didn't count the fact that the many years spent playing hockey to the exclusion of much of anything else besides chasing skirts had left him a little…uninformed.

He was larger and stronger and tougher than most men, but he was a real softie when it came to his family. Lou and his mother rode roughshod over him. Even his father could get him to do anything.

And somehow she'd fallen into the category of family for him. All those evenings out with Lou and Nick and Rossi friends, tagging along in the background, watching Nick with the hockey groupie *du jour*, had turned her into wallpaper.

Rossi wallpaper.

So much in the background that, for Nick, she'd somehow become a female family member who needed looking after.

Nick was loyal to his family. Of course he'd be appalled at what he'd done. Which was only fair, since Faith was appalled at what *she'd* done.

Not that she hadn't enjoyed it.

She pulled away and started walking. She didn't even know in which direction she was supposed to go, but anywhere away from Nick sounded good.

He hobbled along beside her and she stepped up the pace.

Nick grabbed her elbow again in an unshakable grip. "Hold on. I can't keep up," he gritted, and Faith felt guilty.

She also felt angry and sad and lost, but right now guilty prevailed. With a huge sigh, she slowed her pace and he dropped his hand.

"I didn't know where I was going anyway," she confessed.

"Doesn't make any difference. You just follow the road. All the streets lead to where we're going."

Faith blinked, momentarily diverted from her misery. *All the streets lead to where we're going.* It was an interesting topological concept. Were they on a Möbius strip?

Faith matched her pace to Nick's as they turned left into a busier street. Nick was slow, too slow. He'd always had some injury or another in the year she'd known him. He'd shown up splinted, bandaged or strapped up so often she'd lost count.

But he was also a fast healer and, once the cast or the bandage came off, he was as good as new. If he was still limping, maybe something was seriously wrong.

She stopped herself from fretting. She didn't want to wonder and she didn't want to worry about him. *To hell with him.* She moved off.

"Hold it." Nick pulled her to a stop and Faith glanced at him in surprise.

They were on what seemed to pass for a main street in Siena, though there weren't any cars.

There had been no cars at all, she realized. They'd meandered down a narrow, cobble-stoned street filled with people and plants, the loudest sound that of kids playing street ball, then had turned left onto this broader street with gorgeous shops, cool and secret courtyards, mysterious ten-foot high wooden doors like the entrances to heaven.

Nick had stopped her at the corner of what looked like a dark alley angling off down to the right.

"Close your eyes," he ordered, and Faith stepped back.

"Nick," she murmured warily.

But Nick looked perfectly normal, not crazed with lust, and certainly not drunk.

"Close them. It's a surprise."

In spite of all that had happened, somewhere deep inside, she trusted him. She closed her eyes and felt Nick's warm, large hand clasp hers. He tugged and she stiffened.

"Come on," he said coaxingly. "I'm not going to let anything happen to you."

You already did, Faith thought, and stepped haltingly forward.

He turned them right, into the dark alleyway. The golden light seeping through her eyelids vanished and the air was noticeably cooler. Unexpectedly, the cobblestones beneath her feet slanted and she lost her footing for a moment.

"Steady there," Nick said and put an arm around her for a moment. She hated the unstoppable thrill that shot through her heart at his touch, and straightened away from him.

The road angled downward in broad shallow steps and they walked in silence. After a minute or two, she obeyed Nick's tug on her waist and stopped.

"Okay now," he said, his voice serious. His hand dropped away. "You can look. And be prepared."

Prepared for what? Puzzled, Faith opened her eyes and stared. And stared.

The alleyway was steep and narrow and dark, with high walls rising on either side, and at the end of the alleyway…

Like a painting, she thought, dazzled. Framed by the walls of the alleyway, the cobblestones and the cobalt blue sky overhead.

She moved slowly forward and the vista opened up more magically with each step. The square was bathed in intense light, the contrast with the dark alleyway making the colors even more vivid.

The square was shell-shaped, the exact shape it would have if God were to hold it in his cupped hands. It was made of rose-red brick, as were the buildings ringing it.

Circling the *piazza* was a ring of tawny earth, like a ring of gold. People were walking along it. Every once in a while, someone would stoop and gather a handful, as of gold dust.

It seemed impossible that such a large space could be so seamlessly beautiful, that there could be a place in the world where nothing was ugly or unsightly.

After a moment or two, Faith realized she'd stopped breathing. She sucked in warm, golden air and let it slowly out. Her breath hitched.

"Yeah."

Faith turned. Impossibly, she'd even forgotten Nick's presence beside her. "It's, it's…" She shook her head sharply, as if to loosen words up, but none came.

"Yeah." The corner of Nick's mouth went up in a half smile. His eyes lifted over her head to the square beyond. "I've seen it every year of my life and it still makes an impact. It's in every Sienese's blood. It's the center of the city and the center of their lives. Come on in."

She didn't need his hand at her back to move forward. The square beckoned like Oz.

Nick would have smiled at Faith's amazement if he hadn't felt so bad.

He'd been showing the *Piazza del Campo* off all his life and it always gave him a lift, particularly the view from the alleyway they were on, the *Chiasso del Bargello*. The view of the *piazza* had to be seen to be believed. For most Americans, it was right off the radar.

He was grateful Faith's astonishment had made her forget she was mad at him. He hated seeing that get-out-of-my-sight expression on her face. It was only now that things had changed that he realized how much he craved her looking at him with her usual...what? *Approval? Admiration? Something else?* he wondered uneasily.

Not that he wanted her in love with him, of course. She was just one of the guys...Lou's friend. But she was funny, smart and easy to be with. They joked a lot and she was great company. He wanted things back the way they were. Damn it, he wanted *her* back the way she was.

Well, he was the one who had made this mess, so he was the one who was going to have to clean it up. Starting now.

The cobblestones were a little uneven and Faith wasn't able to watch her feet because what she was seeing was so fascinating. She kept swiveling her head around on that long, slim neck of hers and stumbling over her own feet.

Nick gently took her upper arm and steered her down into the square and onto the *terra*, the tufa dirt that comprised the track for the *Palio*. When the horses weren't running trial heats, the track was filled with people and tables and chairs from the bars and restaurants ringing the *piazza.*

Her mouth was open and her eyes were slightly glazed and she didn't even notice he was holding on to her.

"This is neutral territory," he said, and she shifted those large brandy-colored eyes to look at him. "This square belongs to all of Siena, but the rest..." He grinned. "The rest of Siena belongs to its *contradas*."

Faith frowned. "*Contradas*?"

"Yup. Neighborhoods, though there's nothing neighborly about the way they feel about each other. Seventeen of them and each one is as individual as a fingerprint. Ornery, too. You see those flags waving from the flag-holders?"

She nodded.

"Each *contrada* has its own symbol. A couple of hundred years back, they'd have killed for those symbols. And they'll still shed blood over them come *Palio* time. The *contradas* include the She-Wolf, the Giraffe, the Owl, the Dragon. The Rossis belong to the Snail."

Faith thought of the Rossis, sleek, sinuous and gorgeous. "Should've been the Panthers," she murmured.

"God forbid," Nick shuddered. "They're north of us. And we hate them, of course, and they hate us. But we particularly hate the Turtles. We'd rather lose the race than see the Turtles win. We've been rivals for seven hundred years."

Her face shut down, smooth as a doll's. "My parents are from Belfast. We took a visit back to the old country when I was fifteen." She shrugged tensely. "They have hatreds that last for hundreds of years, too."

"Naw, it's not like that here. Sure, the rivalry gets a little...heated at times—" *And the blood could flow,* Nick thought with an inward smile, and often did. But it usually got mopped up quickly and forgiven over a glass of wine.

"Once the *Palio's* over, there's this huge victory dinner in the streets of the winning *contrada* and life goes right back to normal. Speaking of dinner, here we are."

They'd circled the square and plunged into another narrow street that angled upwards this time.

Ten yards up the steep incline, a large, gray, stone archway set into the wall led into a square courtyard with geraniums banked in terra-cotta pots around the perimeter. Tables were set out in the courtyard. It was early for the Sienese and nearly all the tables were still free. In an hour's time, the place would be jumping.

"Niccolò! *Mascalzone!*" a burly man shouted and rushed toward them. He pounded Nick on the back. "Good to see you, you rascal, you! Still killing them on the ice?"

"Tullio." Some of the pleasure Nick felt at seeing his old friend faded. He pounded back, because it was expected, and tried not to think about never being on the ice again.

"You're here a few days early. You going to help your cousins Michelangelo and Dante whip Turtle butt?" Tullio leaned close and Nick got a tantalizing whiff of garlic, truffles and Brunello. "We're going to show those fucking Turtles what's what, aren't we?"

Technically, Tullio was a Dragon and a potential rival, but the Dragons were the sworn enemies of the Turtles, too, and on the theory that your enemy's enemy was your friend, the Dragon and the Snail were allies. Sort of. This year.

"I don't think Michelangelo needs my help," Nick said. "And Dante's staying out of it, of course." Mike was the *capitano del popolo,* the leader, of the Snail *contrada*. For the purposes of the *Palio*, the *capitani del popolo* were the commanders in chief.

Tullio knew perfectly well that a police *commissario* shouldn't be involved in the mostly illegal wheeling and dealing that went into trying to secure a victory for your *contrada*.

Tullio also knew that Dante was happily involved up to his neck. Their eyes met and slid away in perfect understanding.

"And who is this lovely young lady?" Tullio boomed as he turned to Faith. "*Bella ragazza.* Much too good for you, Nick." Tullio frowned, taking in Faith's pallor and the bruised-looking skin under her eyes.

He stretched out a beefy arm to indicate the way and bustled behind them. He sat them, with enormous fuss and bother, in a small out-of-the-way table where they would still have privacy even when other diners started trooping in.

Then he and Nick started haggling over the meal, serious as judges.

It was only when Nick was assured that the *panzanella* was made with the freshest of spring onions, the crispiest of cucumbers, the greenest of tomatoes—*nostrane*, the lumpy but savory local variety—and the purest of virgin olive oil, made only from trees on the south side of Monte Cercina ("Every year, I set ten bottles of it aside for my grandmother," Tullio swore); that Faith's fish antipasto was made with seafood so fresh it was practically still swimming ("My brother-in-law drives to the Pisa fish market at four in the morning and brings them back alive."); that the *vitello tonnato* was made according to Artusi's nineteenth-century canon ("Baby veal boiled gently for hours until it melts in the mouth."); the mayonnaise made by hand by his sainted mother a quarter of an hour ago and the salad plucked from his own garden that very morning, did Nick sit back, satisfied.

"Now," Tullio said with a gleam in his eye. "The wine."

Nick and Tullio put their heads together again. In the end, Tullio disappeared and came back with a wisp of cobweb clinging to his cheek and a bottle of 1992 *Poggio Antico* white from his own special reserve. He poured a golden finger into the crystal glass and waited with a smug smile.

Nick sipped and closed his eyes as every cell in his battered body signaled acute pleasure. Tullio poured half a glass for Faith and she, too, closed her eyes in pleasure after the first sip.

A call came from inside the restaurant. "*Vengo!*" Tullio bellowed, and hurried off.

"Sorry to take the ordering out of your hands, Faith," Nick said as he topped their glasses. "But I thought it might be easier that way. Tullio takes pleasure in setting a fine table. I wouldn't cheat him out of fussing over the food. It's the way things are done here, and this way he got to describe every dish."

"In detail, it sounded like."

"The finest detail," Nick agreed. "Including where everything came from."

"Well, I certainly couldn't have done the ordering, not like that. Did you order fish for me?"

"That's right. You often order fish back home so I thought you might like it. Tullio makes a great seafood antipasto." Nick frowned. "How'd you know I ordered fish?"

"Well, I bought a little teach-yourself-Italian manual at the airport before leaving and studied it on the plane. And I did Latin in high school and I know French. *Poisson*, *pesce*. It's not that hard a leap. And Tullio's fish imitation was perfect, wriggling fins and all." She imitated Tullio's extravagant imitation of a fish.

"So putting all those things together, and with the body language..." She shrugged. "You'd have to be blind and deaf not to follow. Though I'm not too sure what Tullio was doing there toward the end."

"End?"

"When he made those noises and pawed the ground? Are we having steak?"

"Oh." Nick smiled. "The mozzarella for the *Caprese* salad. He wanted to assure me that the mozzarella was so fresh it practically mooed."

Faith laughed and Nick relaxed. It was good to see Faith laughing again. She had a skewed sense of humor that delighted him. Often, he found himself barking with laughter a minute or two after a murmured comment she made sank in. His dates usually laughed about five minutes after, when they got it, which wasn't often.

Tullio would take at least a quarter of an hour, twenty minutes to serve them. Faith was smiling. He'd never get a better shot at it.

He leaned forward and covered her hand with his, scowling when she slid it neatly back out from under his. "Listen, Faith, I think we need to talk about what happened. You know, the other night. I'm afraid I wasn't really —"

"Why are you limping?" she interrupted.

It took him a moment to change gears. "Limping?"

"Yeah. What gives?"

He didn't want to go there. Someday soon it would be public knowledge that he'd retired due to injuries, but not yet. It was childish, but somehow until it was official, it didn't have to be true. He shrugged. "Problem with the meniscus."

"Uh-uh." She narrowed her eyes. "You're hiding something, Nick. What is it?"

"I'm not hiding anything. I'm trying to apologize here, but I guess I'm not making much headway."

"Okay," she said crisply. "Apology accepted. Tell me what's wrong."

Horrifyingly, though she looked like the same sweet, gentle Faith as always, her voice had Lou-like overtones.

Before he could even think about it, his mouth opened. "The knee's nothing. It'll heal in a couple of weeks. It's my head that's the problem."

"Your head's always been the problem. What's so different about it now?"

He looked away. Diners were starting to trickle in. Darkness was fast approaching and Tullio came out to start lighting the candles on the table.

"Nick?"

He swallowed. "I, um, I..." The hot ball of grief tangled in his chest, stopping him from getting the words out. He pushed them out in a rush. "I had a concussion, a bad one. It's all right now, but I can't afford to ever have another one. I'd be running the risk of a coma or even death. The head doctor said I can't play hockey." His eyes lifted to hers. "Ever again."

Faith's mouth opened and her eyes rounded. "Oh, my God." She shook her head. "Oh, Nick, that must be terrible for—"

"I don't want your sympathy," Nick said fiercely, clamping down on his teeth so hard his jaw muscles worked.

She recoiled and her chin went up.

"Well, good, I'm glad, because you certainly don't have my sympathy," she snapped. "You've still got your health, you're incredibly good-looking, you have tons of money, and you have a wonderful family who loves you. I see no reason at all to feel sorry for you. I wouldn't dream of wasting my sympathy on you."

"Good, because I don't want it," he said heatedly.

"Good."

"Good."

Silence.

Nick looked up with a sly smile. "Incredibly good-looking, huh?"

"Shut up, Nick."

Except she wasn't looking at him, and was drawing wavy lines in the tablecloth with the tines of her fork.

"Look at me when you say that."

She took a deep breath and raised her eyes and said nothing.

"Ahhhh, Faith." Miserable, Nick pressed the heels of his hands to his eyes. "I want to go back. To the way it was…before."

"Nobody can go back, Nick. That's the nature of life. You can only go forward."

"Okay." He took his hands away. "Then let's go forward. I'm really, really sorry about what happened. The truth is, I was—"

"Drunk." Faith looked at him steadily. "As a skunk."

"Yeah. I guess you could tell."

"I had an inkling when you tried to pay for dinner with your Hunters security pass. You're such a celebrity, the manager was actually apologetic when he said, very seriously, that the restaurant couldn't accept security passes as a form of payment."

Nick didn't remember a thing about the dinner or even how they had wound up at his house. Though he did remember long, pale limbs and the feeling of bone-deep satisfaction.

"Don't look so sad, Nick. You were a very sweet drunk."

"You're smiling. I must've done something right."

Faith's light brown eyebrows drew together. "Is that what all this is about?" she asked icily. "You want to know what your performance was like? 'How'm I doing, coach?' Do you want me to tell you the earth moved? Do you want a score? Your rating on a scale of one to a hundred?"

Nick winced, wishing he didn't deserve that. "No, no. It's just—"

"Just what? You're making such a big deal out of this, Nick. We had sex. It was nice and now it's over. I don't know why we need to rehash it. And it's not as if it was your first time."

His cue. He leaned forward, looking her intently in the face. "Faith, listen to me." He looked away for a second, mouth tight, then brought his gaze back to her. "I really, really need to know this, so don't blow me off. Was it—was it *your* first time?"

Blood rushed to her face and she wanted to die, simply die, on the spot. Nick was so close to the truth it was humiliating. In all the ways that counted, Nick was the first.

She could hardly consider Tim Gresham's unsatisfactory and brief flailing around in her body as sex in any real sense of the term. More a roll in the spreadsheets than a roll in the hay. The heated discussion afterwards, about Truman's theories on factor analysis, had been infinitely more exciting than the sex.

"Of course not," she said haughtily, lifting her chin. "I've had—" she looked at him to see what he would buy, "— dozens of affairs. Dozens."

Nick's jaw muscles bunched.

She ticked off her fingers, as if silently totting all her lovers up, then opened her hands and shrugged her shoulders—sorry, too numerous to count. "Can't even remember their names."

"Look—" Nick bit off what he was going to say as Tullio himself smoothly slid two plates in front of them.

"*Buon appetito.*" He beamed at them, then rushed away.

Nick didn't even look at his plate. He shifted the plate away with a forefinger, planted his elbows on the table and leaned forward. "Okay. That's the way you want to play it, fine. But don't think that's the end—"

"Great stuff," Faith said around a forkful. "Wow. This is the first time I've ever had a cucumber with a specific taste as opposed to something cold and slimy. Can you get the recipe?"

She lifted her eyes to Nick, and he could read perfectly well that the subject was closed.

Okay, Nick thought. *That's it.* If that's the way she wanted it, fine. Fine. He shunted his guilty conscience aside. His women knew the score, he made sure of it. He didn't ordinarily have to beat himself up about having sex with a woman. Granted, he never chose anyone remotely like Faith and he knew why. She'd have been perfectly justified to beat his brains out, with what he'd done. Instead, she chose to pretend that nothing was wrong. But he knew—

Suddenly, with no warning, Nick was blasted away by sensory memories.

Long, silky limbs, milk-pale skin soft as a baby's cheek, wet and tight…

Christ! Nick shook his head, shaken at the intensity of the flashback. He was semi-aroused and disgusted at himself. *What had brought that on?* Maybe it was the concussion. That was the only explanation. This was Faith, good old Faith. Lou's friend. His friend, still. He hoped.

And because he wanted the friendship to continue, because he wanted her to know that he was her friend, too, he needed to ask the next question.

What she had told Dante about her first months on the job had shaken him. He'd had no idea…

All through last fall and last winter, while they'd seen each other a couple of times a week when his team wasn't on an away game, she hadn't let on. While he'd complained about his coach, and Lou had bitched endlessly about the guy two cubicles over in her office, Faith had listened to them in total sympathy, dispensing advice, and more often than not making them laugh with some ironic, totally dead-on comment about the coach's IQ and Lou's office-mate's creepiness. She hadn't let on by so much as a whisper that her boss was making her life a living hell.

"Why didn't you tell us you were being harassed?"

She looked up, surprised, the fork halfway to her mouth. She finished chewing and swallowed. "What?"

"By Kane. I heard what you told Dante. You should've told us you were going through a hard time. We had no idea."

Nick didn't know which was worse. The fact she hadn't told him and Lou about her troubles when they were all supposed to be friends, or the completely blank look on her face right now, as if sharing troubles was a completely unknown concept to her.

The idea made him angry. Damn it, everybody had to have someone to care when times were tough. Lou had threatened to remove Coach Benson's manhood with a dull spoon and the Rossi men had had a little talk with Lou's nemesis. Three tall, broad-shouldered men had instilled the fear of God — or better yet, the fear of Rossi revenge — into the creep. He'd behaved himself after that.

Who had gone to bat for Faith? He wanted to know, needed to know, someone had been on her side, since he hadn't.

"Did you at least tell your parents?"

And just like that, Faith shuttered down, tighter than a Batmobile, with eyes blank, mouth tight and skin gone even paler. Nick's balance slipped a little more. Good old Faith. Calm, rational, funny Faith had a whole side to her personality he had had no inkling of. *No family to back her up.* And her friends couldn't even tell when she was in trouble.

She was staring at him fiercely, like a wounded bird that didn't want to be touched, and a huge surge of emotion caught him square in the chest and he looked away so she wouldn't see it.

One thing he knew about Faith Murphy—she was astute. If she caught any whiff of the intense emotion he was feeling, she would mistake it for pity and clam up even more. It wasn't pity he was feeling, or at least not all he was feeling.

Valor. The Code of the Jock. When you fell down, you mopped up the blood and picked yourself right up again. And you never ever said that you hurt. It was what Faith had done. She had valor. The quiet, tough kind. She wasn't going to talk about it. Well, two could play at tough guy.

"So," he said genially, digging into the *vitello tonnato*. "Who do you think offed the prof?"

Faith blinked and he watched as every muscle relaxed. Clearly, murder was a much easier topic to deal with than sex or a harassing boss.

"I don't know," Faith said thoughtfully. "But whoever it was, he deserves a medal."

"Sounds like Kane would've had people lined up just waiting to do the job," Nick mused. "Knifing someone in the heart is just about as up close and personal as it gets." His eyes narrowed on her plate and he frowned. "What's the use of Tullio cooking up something really good for you if you're just going to stare at it?"

He watched pointedly until she put a forkful into her mouth. "That's it," he said with satisfaction.

"So...who's the guilty party? Unless..." He stopped and looked at her. "Unless you did it. Perfectly understandable if you had. I don't mind. Unless, of course, you develop a taste for it and come after *me* with a knife."

Faith gave a half laugh. "Truth is, I didn't do it, though I thought about it." She sighed. "A lot. Especially in the first few months. The man was insanely cruel. I imagine your cousin will order an autopsy. I'd like to know what Kane's brain is like—he's probably missing the hypothalamus."

"Is that where feelings are?"

"Why, yes." Faith blinked in surprise.

Nick finished off the last bite of his veal and pointed his fork at Faith. "There you go. You're as bad as Lou. She's always making cracks about dumb jocks. I'll have you know that even though I don't read that much, I did go to college—"

"Lou says you didn't go to college...that you went to sex camp," Faith said acidly, and Nick winced.

He held up his hands. "Okay, okay. Enough. So—who do you think did it?"

The humor died out of her eyes. "I don't know," she said, her voice dropping to a whisper. "I'm hoping it's an outsider, some tramp who got into the *Certosa*, but...bottom line, I don't know. It's much more likely it's one of us. Madeleine, Grif...I work with them every day. Professor Gori—he seems like such a nice, civilized man."

"Civilization's a thin shield," Nick said. "On the ice and off."

"Yes." She sighed. "I don't know, Nick. I just don't know. I could say to you that it's impossible the people I know could commit an act of violence, but then, I was the one who found the body and I saw it—the knife. The stiletto." She shivered. "Like a stake through the heart."

Nick covered her hand with his.

She let her hand rest under his for a moment, then shook it off. "Anyway, we've got your cousin on this guy's trail." She frowned. "Or the woman's trail."

"Dante." Nick finished off his wine and caught Tullio's eye. He mimed writing a check. "Dante's smart, but I don't think he's got too much experience with homicide."

"He's a cop. Of course he does."

"He's an Italian cop. More to the point—a Sienese cop. The Sienese have too pleasant a life to indulge in murder. I don't think there are any murders in Siena."

"What—people are better here?"

"Not better." Nick handed over a credit card. "Happier. More content. There's a difference." He signed, left a big tip and smiled at Tullio, exchanging a few words.

Faith glanced at her watch. "I need to be getting back to the *Certosa*. I think the door closes at ten."

"No, there'll be a police guard tonight. I asked. I'll get you to the *Certosa* and, if you can pack your bags quickly, you can be in bed by ten."

"Why should I pack and where will I be by ten?"

"Hmm?" Nick was walking along with a half-smile on his face. The *piazza* at night was like a fairytale land. A crescent moon was rising above the bell tower of city hall and two stars twinkled. One of them, doubtless Venus, was sending her wayward rays to mess with the minds of otherwise sane men and women.

There was a deep buzz, the conversation of hundreds of people, laughing and talking on a summer's night, accompanied by the percussion of hundreds of feet. The sound of it was almost a living thing.

"You'll be staying at my grandparents' place. They have a nice summer house in the country, not far from the *Certosa*.

Don't worry. I cleared it with Dante. And my grandparents are nice people, so you'll enjoy them."

"I have no doubt your grandparents are nice people. But I fail to understand why you think I'll be staying with them when I'm staying at the *Certosa*."

"Now, Faith," Nick said reasonably. "You don't think I'm going to let you stay in a building where there's a murderer on the loose, do you? Lou'd have my head."

"Well, since it's only there for decorative purposes, that's no great loss," Faith said between her teeth. "Listen, Nick, I can't imagine why you think you'd have a say over my sleeping arrangements. I am absolutely not staying with your grandparents. I am staying at the *Certosa*, where I'm in the middle of an important conference."

"Now, look—"

"No, you look." Faith wheeled and faced him. "Nick, get this through your head. You don't need to atone for anything. You don't need to hover over me or worry about me. And I certainly don't want you interfering with my job.

"This conference is my big chance to show what I can do. It's also a chance to network and get to know some of the people in my field without Professor Kane running interference. I want to—I *need* to—be on site as much as possible and not be ferried back and forth.

"This is my big chance and I won't have it ruined for me because you seem to harbor totally unjustified guilty feelings about a perfectly harmless roll in the hay. Have I made myself clear?"

"Totally," Nick said. "I'll see if they can let me sleep over at the *Certosa*."

Chapter Eight

If you're feeling good, you'll get over it.

ဆာ

All the warm, fuzzy feelings Faith had had for Nick had evaporated by the time they topped the last rise and the *Certosa* suddenly appeared — massive yet graceful, a powerful gem set off by the dark spears of cypress trees.

Neither spared the *Certosa* a glance.

They'd been arguing all the way and Faith was about ready to take a hockey stick to Nick's other leg. She'd pleaded and cajoled and threatened. When Nick said he would pretend to be a participant, she laughed. Nick's jaw had tightened, but he didn't give in.

"Look," she said finally, exasperated. "What am I going to do? I won't be able to deal with you. I'm going to be busy. I'm supposed to be helping with the organization. I've been given two meetings to co-chair, and I have to bone up on them and on the work of the other co-chairs. There's a lot of work involved and you'll just be in my way."

"I won't be in your way." Nick's jaw jutted. "I'll just sleep there and get out in the morning. I'm hooking up with Dante tomorrow morning anyway. You'll be okay in the daytime. Damn it, Faith, for someone who's so smart, you're being really dumb about this."

"Dumb? *Dumb*?" Faith's voice rose. "I'm being *dumb* because I don't want to trip over you during the most important days of my life? That's rich coming from *you*. The guy who took six years to get through high school."

"Five. Five years." Nick's overlarge jaw muscles bunched and he thumped the steering wheel.

She figured if he'd had more room, he probably would have used more body language. The car was too small for someone of Nick's size. When he'd squeezed into the driver's seat, he'd grunted and groped until he'd managed to find something under the seat that shot it back to its full extension. It was still a tight fit, but at least his knees didn't top the steering wheel.

He shifted a gear so hard it ratcheted. His entire profile was hard, tense.

He was angry. That was cool. Angry was cool. She was angry, too.

Thoughts and stomach churning, Faith stared blindly out the car window, seeing nothing, until Nick jerked the car to a stop, throwing her against the seat belt so hard it caught.

"Nice driving, ace."

Nick's jaw muscles bunched again and he threw her a sulphurous look. He unsnapped his seat belt and maneuvered his way out of the car. When Faith realized he was coming around the car to open her door, she shot out by herself and moved toward the entrance.

They were on the gravel driveway, and his shoes made a loud crunching sound as he followed her, his limp making the noise irregular. *Crunch*, crunch, *crunch*, crunch...

Faith had almost made it to the big wooden door when he growled and caught her arm. He turned her around and, when she opened her mouth to argue, he covered her mouth with his and her brain shorted.

Total static.

Plummeting from an IQ of one-forty-five to zero in point-three seconds.

She moved her mouth mindlessly under his, blasted by heat and lust. *Closer...*she needed him closer and she threw her arms around his thick, strong neck and tunneled her fingers in his hair.

Somewhere amidst the popping neurons, she knew that what they were doing would lead to mind-bending pleasure. She knew that for a fact.

Nick's big hand held her head for his kiss as he deepened it and she whimpered...

"Faith?"

She jolted and tried to pull away. Getting away from Nick's large hands was impossible.

"Faith?"

Oh God, Tim. With great reluctance, she pulled her lips away.

Nick bent again and she turned her head, wishing she didn't have to. But kissing Nick in front of Tim was too soap opera for her. Both men had been her lovers. Exactly once, but still...

Besides, she wasn't supposed to want to kiss Nick. She was supposed to be mad at him.

She pushed, hard, and Nick opened his hands.

Tim came forward, smoothing down his wispy hair that had escaped the small, thin ponytail at the nape of his neck. "Do you need help, Faith?"

If she did, Tim wasn't it. Looking at the two of them, she had a little moment of reality distortion. Tim — short and tubby and flabby. Nick — tall and strong and athletic. Did Tim actually think he could defend her against Nick?

"Okay." Nick shifted on his feet. "Who's this?"

"Uh, Nick Rossi, meet Tim Gresham. He's...uh, he's a colleague of mine. At the university."

Tim shot her a wounded gaze, as if she should have said — *this is Tim Gresham, with whom I have wild and crazy sex four times a day.*

"Tim, Nick plays — used to play — for the Hunters."

"A jock," Tim said, with exactly the same tone of voice with which he would have said "a leper".

"A nerd." Nick's voice was low and vicious. "Nice to meet you. Get lost."

Tim straightened and sucked in his little potbelly. Faith's mouth fell open. "Listen, Nick, you can't—"

"No, *you* listen," Nick said heatedly. "What the hell's the matter with you anyway? Do you realize that there's a murderer here? Someone killed your boss, have you forgotten that? So who's going to protect you — Mr. Geek here? For all you know, he's the one who offed your prof. Did you think of that?"

Tim's eyes went wide and he surged forward. "Why you overgrown—"

Faith shot out an arm to halt Tim. It wasn't hard.

"Actually, for your information, Tim was in the States and only just arrived, so he can't have killed anyone. Listen carefully, Nick. I am now going inside the *Certosa*, in Tim's company, where I will be perfectly safe."

"Over my dead body," Nick growled.

Tim puffed up. "That can be arranged, big guy."

Nick bristled. "Faith needs protection."

"I can do that."

"What the hell are you talking about? You look like you can't protect your hat in a wind."

"Oh yeah?" Tim stepped closer. "Just watch me."

Faith rolled her eyes. Tim came up to Nick's collarbone, and the most strenuous physical activity Faith had ever seen him engage in was peering at his computer screen.

Nick could punch out Tim's lights in a nanosecond, and watching Nick, muscles corded, neck tendons sticking out, he was a hair's breadth away from doing just that.

Something had to be done. She pressed her hand against Tim's chest. There was a second as she and Tim adjusted to the polite fiction that her hand was the only thing that stopped him from stepping forward and cleaning Nick's clock.

Tim was trembling under her hand.

Faith turned. "Listen, Nick. I'm going in now. I'm going to my room, where I will lock my door and no one will disturb me until tomorrow morning. Then I will go downstairs and have an excellent breakfast. Believe me, the only bad thing that can happen to me will be my laptop's batteries running out."

She turned on her heels and walked through the huge iron-hinged doors that only lacked a portcullis.

"You fucking weenie—"

"Listen, iceman, you can—"

Faith took one last look at them before rounding the corner—Nick huge and menacing, Tim, a rabid terrier, unwilling to let go. It was hard to think that she had had an affair with each of them.

She started climbing the stairs up to the second floor.

She definitely needed a Boyfriend Upgrade, Version 3.0.

Today is the first day of the rest of your life.

The next morning, after a sleepless night, Nick stared glumly at his red, jet-lagged eyes and un-chic, non-designer beard stubble in the bathroom mirror of his grandparents' country house and contemplated that greeting-card thought.

It didn't reassure him in the least. He couldn't even begin to think about the rest of his life and the changes that were coming.

He'd liked his life just fine the way it had been. On bright shiny rails, moving right into the future and he was the train just chugging along. Without hockey, he didn't have the faintest idea what to do with his day, his week, his year.

It had all been so neatly boxed up and tied with a ribbon for him.

Summers were for the yearly trip to Siena to see his cousins, scheme and yell for the Snails, and get drunk with an entire city district when they lost. Maybe beat up a few rowdy members of rival *contradas* in a friendly little tussle. The Snails had been losing since junior high.

But even losing the *Palio* was more fun than anything else except hockey. The *Palio* gave him exactly what he got on the ice — noise, crowds and excitement.

It was that feeling of going to war — without actually having to shoot at anyone or having anyone shoot at you.

The ends of summers were workouts at least four hours a day, keeping fit and having fun while staying out of trouble.

September was the exhibition season, training camp, more workouts. Keeping an eye on the youngsters coming up as they kept an eye on him, wanting his job, and him thinking, *Not yet, kids. Not yet.*

October to April...ah...The Season. Show time. With every nerve, every muscle in his body like an arrow aimed straight at winning. Which he did more times than not.

May and June were for playoffs until he left for Siena.

He'd been living this routine for twelve years now and was far from ready to let it go.

Nick picked up his grandfather's ancient razor and started hacking at the undergrowth on his face. He winced as it took some of his beard off by taking the skin underneath it as well.

He missed hockey and wanted it back. *What was there to look forward to now?* Not to mention the little fact that maybe he'd taken a blow too many to the head and he might end up like those punch-drunk boxers who had trouble enunciating and counting to ten without using their fingers.

He supposed he was better off than most men who had just lost their job. In fact, technically, he was rich, though he never thought of himself that way. His agent had been about to sign an eight million dollar season contract and though that had gone straight down the toilet, there'd been another one before it for five million dollars. He was worth zip now as an athlete, but he'd salted it away.

Or rather, Lou had.

He'd once confessed to Lou his horror at meeting up with Robert "Hulk" Gascoigne, who'd aced all his opponents on the ice while nailing everything in skirts within a thirty-mile radius all during the Nineties.

Hulk had buttonholed him after a practice session and Nick had had to peer hard to recognize the athlete in that three-hundred-and-fifty-pound body. Hulk had been dressed in a cheap suit that had the sick green sheen of an oil slick and had tried to sell him an insurance policy.

Horrified, wanting just to get away, Nick had bought the policy—he wasn't even sure if it was for fire or life or even his car—and had promptly lost his copy. Later in the locker room, his teammates had joked that he'd been "*blitzed by the Bulk*".

Lou had responded in typical Lou fashion, by taking his money right out of his hands and investing it all in what she called "pin-striped pork bellies", some newfangled type of commodities trading.

She took out a subscription to the *Wall Street Journal* in his name. The copies, gathering dust, were stacked in musty gray piles in his spare room.

She also gave him bewildering quarterly reports he couldn't pretend to follow. Lou blinded him with economics, but the bottom line was she knew what she was doing. Even he boggled at the figures given on the bottom of the quarterly and annual reports.

Of course, Lou being Lou, when she'd taken his money out of his hands, she had also been very miserly about what she let trickle back into them.

He was given an allowance. A very small allowance, which mysteriously became even smaller while he dated Dee Dee.

Nick was a seriously rich man. If he wanted to, he could probably spend the rest of his life without having to put in a single day's work.

It was a depressing thought.

Given his family, Nick wouldn't even be allowed to go to seed. Who on earth in his family would let him become a bum?

For a moment, he had a vision of himself in a dirty stained raincoat with a bottle of beer in a paper bag hanging out of a torn pocket, living in one of the two buildings that could technically be classified as slums in Deerfield.

The image didn't work. His family would never let it happen. Look what happened the one time he went on a bender — Lou had hounded him until he'd cleaned up.

So here he was — all riched up with nowhere to go.

Today is the first day of the rest of your life.

Yeah.

"So," Tim said over breakfast, "I guess Elvis has left the building." He sniggered over his *cornetto*. "Finally."

Paul Allen froze, his fork halfway to his mouth. Not much of his breakfast would have gone into his mouth, anyway, as most of it tended to end up in his beard. Immensely tall and gangly, he had a red beard down to the middle of his chest and it clearly had a positive charge for food.

He was a true eccentric, kind and brilliant. Faith had adored him on sight. He'd helped make the symposium she'd chaired yesterday afternoon a wild success and she would have lain down on train tracks for him.

She rolled her eyes. "Don't pay any attention to him, Paul. That was just a little math humor." She eyed Tim severely. "Very little math humor."

Paul shoveled more Tuscan ham and bread into his mouth and Faith's hands itched to wipe his mouth for him. "Odd chap, Kane, but there was no denying he was brilliant. I was quite taken with his model for traffic congestion. Very elegant, it was. I tried it on the traffic in Manchester, which is hideous, and it was like divination, only better."

Faith looked down at her plate, acid eating into her stomach.

"Actually," Grif patted his lips so elegantly with the paper napkin it could well have been the finest embroidered linen, "that wasn't Kane's model. That was Faith's."

Every head at the table swiveled toward her.

Faith felt the rush of blood to her head. She clutched the edge of the table. She'd worked for four months on the project only to have it whisked from under her nose by Kane and marketed to the City of Boston Traffic Administrator as his own.

She turned to Grif. "You knew?" she whispered.

"That Kane was using you? Using your work? Of course, my dear." Grif looked around the table—at Madeleine, who blushed and looked away, and at Tim, whose jaw muscles worked beneath his wispy beard. "Everyone knew. But no one had the courage to stand up to him, myself, alas, included. Such is the way of the world."

There was dead silence. Paul Allen drained his cappuccino in one gulp. He inclined his curiously elongated head to her. "Then, I guess we should be doubly congratulating Faith today. On the work that went into that marvelous time-traffic flow model and on her paper on tipping."

He raised an earthenware cup stained with oily fingerprints. "I say we drink a toast to Faith. Hear, hear!"

"To Faith! To Faith! *Salute*! *Santé*!" This last from Jean-Paul Daumier, a flirtatious Frenchman who'd brought some interesting epidemiological data from the Pasteur Institute.

Something soft and damp like a slug touched Faith's hand. Tim was holding her hand and looking at her out of adoring brown eyes. He leaned close and whispered, "Good for you, honey," and puckered his lips.

She turned her head fast, and the kiss meant for her mouth ended up on her ear.

If it was meant to signal that they were lovers, he was way off base. Firstly, because there wasn't one male around the table who could be made jealous, and secondly, because she had no intention of ever letting Tim in her bed again.

Once had been bad enough. It had been proof of the geek theorem that sex was merely a sublimation of the urge to do math.

Faith had always been quick to learn and she never made the same mistake twice. One pocket protector romance was enough.

She'd always been wary of men, but Tim had flown right under her radar. She hadn't seen the affair coming until it was right on top of her, so to speak.

Though Tim had been at St. Vincent's much longer than she had, he'd seemed as out of place as she was. They'd become friends, sharing jokes and whispered complaints about Kane.

They'd shared their unhappy childhoods. Faith, in Sophie, Indiana, with a drunken father and morosely depressed mother. Tim, all over the place, with a mother who practiced recreational marriage. His childhood had been so chaotic he'd had two last names and lived in four countries and ten cities before he'd turned eighteen.

There was nothing even remotely sexy about Tim with his wispy, blond hair pulled back in a dirty ponytail and "mouse potato" physique.

They had spent a lot of time together. One evening, they'd been sharing pizza and talking about coefficients for knowbots when all of a sudden, she'd found herself on her back and he'd been trying to stuff what felt like a marshmallow inside her.

It had been embarrassing, humiliating and—now that she'd experienced Nick—utterly futile.

She had a horrible feeling that nothing would ever compare to Nick. Maybe her peak sexual experience was already behind her.

Dante waited for Nick at the *Porta Camollia*, one of the gates to the city. He loved the ancient brick gate, fronted with a baroque frame of white marble. The gate sealed the city off from the hated Florentines.

Sienese hearts still burned with resentment at the loss of Siena's freedom to Florence six hundred years before. After the bitter defeat, the hated Florentines insisted on entering through the gate. When the Medicis entered Siena, the Sienese had been forced to add the huge inscription above the coat of arms of the Medici — "Siena Opens Its Great Heart to Visitors".

What a crock. The gate to the city had been opened under duress, at musket-point.

How many times Dante had seen tourists open their books, their faces softening as they read the translation of the Latin inscription, little realizing that the Sienese heart was anything but large, warm and welcoming. The Sienese heart was shriveled, cold and black. The inscription had been put up under threat of reprisal, and the Sienese still hated the Florentines for it six hundred years later.

Dante turned his back to the gate and slipped on his sunglasses, scanning the horizon.

It was, as it usually was at *Palio* time, a beautiful day. The morning sunshine glinted off the red-tiled roofs and made the brick buildings glow. Jasmine scented the air and he pulled in a deep, appreciative breath.

He leaned against the gate and made a mental bet with himself that Nick would come from *Via Piave*, the road that led to the *Certosa* and Faith. Dante was sure Nick would have made a long detour to see how she was doing this morning.

Sure enough, his Lancia hove into view, nipping smartly into an empty slot. Dante tried not to smile as Nick emerged with difficulty. His size and busted knee made the whole process laborious.

Nick waved and crossed the street, limping heavily.

He looked tired, Dante noted. Tired and defeated. He hated seeing Nick like that, but he understood completely.

Nick was a talented athlete who would never compete again. The whole family had ribbed him for his choice of career, but Dante had yelled himself hoarse many a time at a Hunters game, and his heart had swelled with pride and affection at Nick's powerful plays across the ice.

How would he feel if he couldn't be a policeman any more? Shuddering, he walked toward Nick. Didn't bear thinking about.

"Hey."

"Hey." Nick smiled wanly as Dante hugged him.

"Come on. The car's this way." Dante matched his stride to Nick's. "You can start becoming Sherlock Holmes right away."

Dante's theory was that Nick had to start right away finding something else to do. Why not tag along and see if he could be a cop?

"I won't be any good at it," Nick said glumly. "Hockey's the only thing I know how to do."

"You never know until you try," Dante said affably. "By the way, how's Faith holding up?"

Nick froze and shot him a narrow-eyed look. "You having me followed?"

"Nah." Dante laughed and tapped his head. He nudged Nick forward again. "Just old-fashioned deduction powers. It's why I'm super-cop and you're not."

Nick speeded up and Dante kept pace easily.

"So?" he repeated. "What's Faith doing?"

Nick gave up and drew in a deep breath. "Don't know. I stopped by this morning to check on her. She was rushing around with this sheaf of documents under her arm, babbling something about chairing a tipping panel."

"Tipping? You mean like a tip? For service?"

Nick shrugged. "Beats me. But whatever it is, it had her excited. She all but shooed me out of the *Certosa*. She said something about coming into town later this afternoon."

"That Rossi charm is slipping, cuz. You usually have them at your feet. She'll come around, though."

"Yeah? How do you figure that?"

Dante tapped his head as he got behind the wheel. "Superior deductive powers. Super-cop at work."

"Super-cop." Nick snorted and Dante was glad to see a faint smile. They'd always ribbed each other about their jobs. "In Siena. Big bad Siena. When was the last time you had a murder here? 1950?"

"Ah…" Dante headed out of town into the countryside toward *Le Scotte*, the hospital. "Don't remember."

"See?"

"Well, at the moment, we do have a murder to investigate. The intrepid Detective super-cop is now officially on his way to the county hospital to talk to the coroner, to dig up clues. God, that makes me sound like something out of Michael Connelly or Ed McBain."

Dante loved American noir mysteries. For a moment, he imagined himself in one of them—the Lone Knight cruising down dark mean streets, alienated and alone against the world…

Nah.

He was a highly integrated Sienese, member of a large and loving family, driving down a gorgeous country lane bordered by pencil-straight cypresses in the warm buttery sunlight, to investigate the first murder in Siena in…he couldn't remember how long. Certainly the last murder had been years before he'd come back from his stint in Naples.

"Hey, super-cop, why don't you stop for a moment?"

Dante shot a startled glance. "Where?"

They rounded a corner. "There." Nick pointed at a small brick building housing a coffee shop. "I haven't had breakfast yet and I remember they make good sandwiches."

Nick was hungry? Half an hour after leaving their grandmother's house? "*Nonna* actually let you out of the house without feeding you?"

Nick looked away guiltily. "Yeah, well, a third degree would've accompanied the food. And you know what she's like. The Gestapo were pikers in getting information next to her. Before I finished my coffee, she'd have grilled me about my injury, my love life and my plans. All of which suck."

Nick's right about Nonna, Dante thought. She was a gentle, loving woman, still beautiful at seventy, a fabulous cook with eyes that would drill like a laser right into your head when she wanted to find something out.

And she wasn't at all backward about giving advice. Nick was too shaky to deal with the smothering blanket of Rossi love right now. He needed some distance and space.

And a sandwich. Dante swerved to park in front of the little red brick building. He drummed his fingers on the steering wheel. "Make it snappy. Guzzanti's waiting for us."

Five minutes later, Nick was gingerly settling back in the passenger seat, a huge white bag in his hands. Knowing Nick, there were at least seven sandwiches in there. Nick extracted a sandwich of thick slices of country prosciutto, overly savory to offset the saltless bread.

By the time they pulled into the *Le Scotte* parking lot, Nick had polished one sandwich off and was rooting around for another.

Dante got out and stood for a moment in the balmy summer sun. The heat of the day had just started. It was a good heat, the kind that penetrated into the bones. He wanted to soak up that warmth before entering the dead zone of the hospital.

As hospitals went, it was pretty enough, he supposed. Brick and glass, not too big, not too tall, and built on an exquisite little hill with one of the best views of Siena.

Which didn't stop it from being a place of pain and misery. Blessedly, he'd only ever been in for the births of his nieces and nephews, and once when Michelangelo had broken his leg. Dante had the Tuscan's superstitious horror of sickness and death, and walked toward the side entrance with dread in his heart.

"Nice hospital," Nick said approvingly. "Good size. Can't be more than three hundred beds. Our hospital in Deerfield is ten stories tall and covers three acres. Like being in suburban hell."

"Since when do you know anything about medicine?" Dante asked. Like all the Rossis, Nick was as healthy as a horse.

"Get real." Nick rolled his eyes. "I'm a—" He stopped and swallowed. "I *was* a hockey player. We're in and out of hospitals the way you're in and out of restaurants. I've picked up a lot of medical knowledge over the years. Particularly anatomy. Hey," he mused, "Maybe I could become a doctor."

Dante's laugh came out harsher than he'd intended. Pushing through the big glass swing doors, he was assailed by the smell of alcohol and sickness. His skin prickled with dread and his stomach took a little warning leap. He needed something to take his mind off where he was.

"You? A doctor?" He laughed. "Yeah, right."

To Dante's chagrin, Nick didn't nudge him in the ribs and grin. Instead, Nick's mouth tightened, his shoulders hunched and Dante felt as if he'd kicked a puppy…a big one, a St. Bernard, but a puppy all the same.

Uneasy, Dante looked up at the big board showing which department was on what floor. He'd only been to see Guzzanti once before in his professional capacity, for the death of a child, which had turned out to be SIDS and not abuse.

Thank God he didn't have much call to visit the coroner.

"Third floor." Nick nudged his elbow. "You can walk it. I'll take the elevator."

Dante fervently believed in conservation of energy. His own. "I'll come with you."

Aldo Guzzanti's office was the third down on the right. Light from the floor-to-ceiling window at the end flooded the short corridor. Like every window in Siena, it framed a view worthy of a master painter. Gentle hills terraced with vines and olive trees, sun-baked red earth below, fiercely blue cloudless sky above. It was a beautiful day, much too gorgeous to be indoors…

With a sigh, Dante recognized his reluctance to talk with Guzzanti about dead bodies and reprimanded himself. He was here on business. He knocked and entered, knowing Guzzanti was expecting him.

"Dante." Aldo Guzzanti stood, stooping. Dante always avoided thinking how he had achieved his stoop—bending over *what*? They shook hands. He turned to Nick. "Inspector?"

"No." *Maybe. Someday,* Dante thought. "This is my cousin from America, Niccolò."

"Ah, yes. The hockey player. I seem to remember one summer," his eyes slid slyly to Dante, "the summer we won the *Palio.* 1992, it was. My daughter's last summer before university. And I seem to remember her talking—a lot—about Dante's American cousin. That would be you?"

Nick's cheekbones were flushed. "Yes, sir, that would be me. How is—" His eyes drifted up and to the left.

"Anna." Dealing with dead bodies had given Guzzanti a poker face. The amusement was all in his voice.

"Anna." Nick sighed in relief. "Yes, how is she?"

"Oh, fine, fine." Guzzanti smiled. "She's in Rome now, moving up through the ranks. She's a public prosecutor and her first big case will be next month. She's married to a doctor and they have two kids. Hellions, both of them, but we love them anyway."

"Well, give her my best."

Guzzanti's smile widened. "That I'll certainly do. So, Dante, we've got a dead body on our hands. A murdered dead body." He shook his head. "Haven't seen one of those in years."

"Foreigners." Dante shrugged. "What do you want?"

"Barbarians," Guzzanti agreed. He rubbed his hands together. "Well, I guess we can start," he said brightly. "Your cousin can come, too, if he wants." He turned and fixed Nick with a sharp gaze. "I must make a few things clear if you want to tag along, son. First of all—no fainting and no vomiting. If you feel woozy, you get out as quickly as you can."

"Sure," Nick said easily. "I've mopped up liters of blood, my own and teammates'. There's not much that turns my stomach, believe me."

Guzzanti nodded. "It's hard enough to clean up after the dead, and we don't like to worry about cleaning up after the living. So, now we can—"

"Just a minute." Dante tried to quell the panic he'd felt at Guzzanti's words. "I'm — we're here to pick up the results of the autopsy."

Guzzanti scratched his crown of gray hair. "Well," he drawled, "that would be kind of hard to do. Seeing as how the body hasn't been posted yet."

Dante frowned. "Not posted? Why not? What is this? The man should've been posted yesterday. Who knows what clues we're losing?"

Guzzanti sighed. "You're not losing anything. The American has been kept in the morgue under stable, ambient conditions. No deterioration has taken place. Trust me."

"Why wasn't the autopsy done before?" Dante could feel his heart racing and a cold sweat filming his torso. His family knew about his weak stomach and gave him some mild grief, but nobody really realized how weak it was. At the thought of witnessing an autopsy, his stomach seemed to float up his esophagus.

In all his years as a cop, he'd managed to adroitly avoid attending autopsies. Loiacono attended them religiously, but Dante couldn't figure out what a non-doctor could possibly get out of watching the process. He figured the doctor's report was more than good enough.

"The autopsy wasn't done before because we are understaffed and because we had not one but two cases of suspected Creutzfeld-Jacob disease."

Dante was horrified. "Mad cow disease?" he breathed. "Here? In Siena?" Just the other night he'd had a big, juicy, bootleg *bistecca fiorentina*. Maybe encephalopathy prions were even now settling in his brain, eating big holes.

"That's right." Guzzanti nodded grimly. "And I had the Local Health District Administrator, the head of this hospital, the heads of three trade unions, the head of the local farmers' cooperative, our senator and my wife breathing down my neck as we examined the brains centimeter by centimeter under a microscope. And I mean that literally."

Oh, God, Dante thought. "And?"

"Dementia praecox. Both of them."

"Whew." Dante didn't even want to *think* about an outbreak of mad cow disease.

"And that, gentlemen," Guzzanti declared, snapping his desk diary closed, "that is why we have one—" he glanced at the form he held in his hand, "—one American professor, presumably stabbed to death, though it is bad form to make pre-post guesses, who is still awaiting our scrutiny." He walked over to his office door and opened it. "If you'll come with me, we can start right away."

"Hey." Nick perked up. "We're going to watch an autopsy? Cool."

Not cool. Hot. Dante pulled at his shirt collar. "Wait a minute. Won't—won't our presence, um, compromise the body? Contaminate the evidence?"

"Dante." Nick shot him a look. "The guy's dead. And we're not going to spit or jerk off into his corpse—pardon me, Doctor—and leave foreign DNA. Our presence can't hurt anything." Nick stood, and Dante saw the first signs of interest that Nick had shown all morning. "Right, Doc?"

"Correct." Guzzanti stood impatiently in the doorway. "So gentlemen, if you'll follow me, we'll see to your murdered corpse." He opened his arms and ushered them out. "I'll tell you the truth. I'm looking forward to this. It's been much too long since I've actually had a case of murder to deal with. Very exciting."

Dante's guts did a slow roll.

Chapter Nine

Everything put together falls apart sooner or later.

જી

The pathology lab was underground.

Figured. Fitting for a hellish experience.

Dante's namesake had descended to hell, too, only with a different companion. Dante followed Guzzanti and an excited Nick with reluctance and rising gorge.

Guzzanti and Dante automatically adjusted their pace to Nick's limp. "So, Niccolò, what are you doing here with your cousin? It's Dante's job, but you don't necessarily have to be here. Watching an autopsy isn't exactly my idea of the perfect Sienese summer holiday. Particularly during *Palio* season when there's so much going on in town."

Amen, Dante thought. Nick was silent, so he answered. "Nick's...retired from ice hockey and trying to figure out what to do next. Since he's here, I thought I'd let him tag along. See if he'd like to become a cop."

"Retired, hmm?" Guzzanti cast shrewd eyes at Nick's limping leg with the brace. "Anterior cruciate? I thought the Americans were so good at sports medicine, athletes just bought themselves new knees."

"Not the knee," Nick said softly. "Secondary concussion."

Guzzanti's lips pursed and his eyes opened wide as he emitted a soundless whistle. "Bad news. Sorry."

Nick nodded stiffly and Dante's heart went out to him.

They passed the canteen where the hospital staff and the patients were going to have *pasta al pesto* for lunch, to judge by the smell.

The *obitorio*, the morgue, was right next door. They walked past a wall of steel lockers with pullout handles. Dante couldn't figure out what they were.

And then he could, and swallowed.

Through another door was a corridor, then a room with a big white sign above it. *Anatomia Patologica.*

Guzzanti held the door open for them, and Dante walked into a scene as hellacious as anything the other Dante had ever seen in his descent to the Inferno.

The autopsy room was large, with a heavy odor of dead meat and pesto overlaid by formalin and alcohol. Four large, rectangular stainless steel tables were in the four corners of the room. Three bodies in varying stages of butchery were lying on the slabs as gowned humans wearing face shields and wielding what looked like carpentry tools bent over them. It was impossible to detect the sex of anyone in the room, living or dead.

"Carlo!" Guzzanti called out. "What the hell is going on here?"

An amorphous body lifted its face shield. "A whole family found dead in San Rocco. Suspected asphyxiation." The shield banged back down again like a space warrior's.

"*Cristo.* The insurance company is going to be all over us," Guzzanti grumbled.

The door swung open again and two people in white lab coats walked in—a tiny woman with plain, sharp, serious features and huge Coke-bottle glasses dwarfing her face, and a large, broad-shouldered, thick-necked man almost as large as Nick.

"Right then," Guzzanti said briskly. "Let's get started. Sergio?"

A glum, middle-aged man detached himself from the shadows at the far end of the big room. He slouched, his hands deep in the pockets of his stained lab coat. Dante didn't even want to think about what had caused the stains.

"Yeah?" The man's voice was sullen, body language depressed.

"You can bring him in now, Sergio."

The man grunted and turned. Guzzanti smiled apologetically. "Our *diener*, Sergio."

"Your *diener* seems to have an attitude problem," Nick said, after the man had left the room.

Guzzanti sighed. "He's from the Wave."

"Ah," Nick and Dante said together. The Wave *contrada* wasn't running this year. Not running in the *Palio*, coupled with working with dead people for a living, would make anyone depressed.

Dante shuddered. He couldn't imagine a worse job, a worse life than dealing with dead people.

The door banged open, pulling Dante out of his thoughts. A stretcher with a dead body—presumably *his* dead victim, so he tried to straighten up and look interested instead of nauseated—rolled in, pushed by the *diener*, whose trip to the morgue had made him surlier than ever.

The back wheels caught in the jamb and Sergio rattled the stretcher angrily. One of the wheels had locked in a sideways position and he couldn't straighten it. The *diener* pushed and pulled, cursing a blue streak.

If Dante had been a religious man he would have made the sign of the cross at the imaginative sexual positions the *diener* had the Madonna assume. One particular curse involved a barrel of wine, and Dante looked up at the ceiling uneasily.

He didn't believe in God, but if there was one, He was as likely to make His presence felt now as at any other time.

Finally, with a rusty creak, the wheel turned around and the stretcher jumped into the room with a bang. The body shifted and the head hung limply over the edge. Impassively, Sergio reached out to deposit the head back on the stretcher with about as much emotion as a housewife putting a cantaloupe back on the greengrocer's shelf after having sniffed it.

"Ah, Sergio," Guzzanti said genially. "Over here, please."

The *diener* wheeled the stretcher sharply right. It turned with a creak, trundling along, pushed by Sergio's large, broad hands until he had it parked next to the steel table by the window.

He walked around the stretcher and the table, then reached across with his simian-long arms and tugged the body across. Two sharp yanks and the body had been pulled over to the steel table with as much emotion as a butcher shifting a side of beef.

Sergio efficiently stripped the body until it lay, naked and defenseless, on the metal slab, the puncture wound small but clearly visible.

Ashes to ashes, Dante thought with a shudder. Roland Kane might not have been much of a human being, but he'd still been human and, as such, deserving of pity for the state he was in now. Pity and horror vied in his chest.

"The block, Sergio," Guzzanti said.

The *diener* placed an arm under the body's neck and lifted. When the upper body was where sit-ups hurt, he slipped a block of plastic under the back and let the body fall back over the block.

Sergio looked over with a truculent scowl.

"That will be all, Sergio," Guzzanti said, and the *diener* gave a grunt and walked out. The door didn't slam behind him because it was pneumatically driven, but it wasn't for lack of trying.

"Not too merry a job," Dante observed.

"What, Sergio's?" Guzzanti asked. "It's not bad. He doesn't get any backtalk from his clients at least."

Guzzanti beckoned to the two young people. They arranged themselves solemnly at either side of the head of the body, hands clasped behind their backs, necks craned, waiting. They gave Dante the creeps, like vultures around a corpse.

"You don't mind if I allow these two students of mine to attend the autopsy, do you, Dante?" Guzzanti asked. "It's their first post, and a murder at that. Who knows when they'll get a chance to see another one? Of course," he frowned, looking at Nick, then Dante, "it's getting a little crowded around here, so maybe Nick could — "

"That's okay. I'll step back," Dante said swiftly. He moved back a step, then two. "Nick wants to see what being a cop is all about, after all. I'll yield my place to him."

Guzzanti looked at him curiously and shrugged. "As you please. You don't really need to watch because I'll be dictating my findings." He slipped his face shield on and fixed a little collar mike to the lapel of the lab coat. On a podium nearby was a file. He pressed a pedal with his foot and straightened.

"Okay, let's see what we have here. We have one — " he looked over to the file on the podium, " — one Roland Francis Kane, deceased. Sixty-two years old. One meter seventy-seven, seventy kilos. This is a man who kept his figure, even though the muscle tone looks poor.

"One puncture wound of a sharp instrument inserted antero-posteriorally. No noticeable distinguishing marks or abnormalities. Okay, lady and gentlemen, here we go." He picked up a scalpel and held it up to the light as if it were a jewel. The fluorescent light overhead reflected off the blue-gray surface.

Guzzanti turned to the two students, holding the scalpel as if it were a pencil. "Okay now, Ricci and Barzi. Pay attention because this will be on the exam." He waggled the hand holding the scalpel up and down, the maestro limbering up his baton hand. "You want to keep your wrist loose, so you can feel the feedback effect. You want to cut through the derma, down through the abdominal wall. We want to see what this man is made of, eh?"

Polite titters from the two students followed his little stab at amusing repartee. Dante thought they should just shut up, all of them, and get on with it.

"So," Guzzanti paused dramatically, scalpel high over Roland Kane's naked, ash-gray, sunken chest. He turned to the two students. "So you want to cut quickly and deep. Three strokes. From the sternum to the pubis, cutting around the navel."

Nick leaned forward with a frown. "Why?"

"Hmm?" Guzzanti's hand hovered over the chest, an artist wavering before making that first brush stroke which would turn the canvas from potentiality to art. "Why cut around the navel? Well, because the navel's tough to cut through. Grisly. Puts you off your slice, as it were."

Oh please, Dante thought.

Guzzanti swooped down with the scalpel, opening Kane up in three swift strokes, from left shoulder to breastbone, from right shoulder to breastbone, then from sternum to pubis, delicately cutting around the belly button, while Dante's stomach swooped up to his throat.

"Now this Y incision is an American cut," Guzzanti said chattily. "And ordinarily quite useless. It doesn't help us understand what the body's trying to tell us, and you have to swerve around the breasts in women. But in this case we've got a knife wound to explore and we don't want the incision interfering. That's right," he crooned as he sliced. "Nice and easy."

Dante couldn't watch the body, so he watched the faces. Guzzanti was rapt, the complete professional engrossed in a technical task. Nick looked fascinated as, gruesomely, he munched on the tomato and mozzarella sandwich he'd picked up.

Dante's peripheral vision told him that what was inside the body looked remarkably like the tomato and mozzarella… Hastily he looked at the two students.

The small woman was leaning forward eagerly, the overhead light glinting spookily off her unfashionable, oversized glasses.

The big man had broken out in a sweat, his skin hue remarkably like the institutional gray-green color on the walls above the white tiling. Dante felt a deep kinship with him.

Guzzanti took another, smaller scalpel in hand. He hooked his fingers under the skin at the sternum and pulled with his left, while skillfully flaying away the skin and underlying muscles with the scalpel.

"Test time," he said. "Anyone recognize this smell?"

The tiny woman lifted her face shield a moment and sniffed deeply, pursing her lips in concentration. "Somewhere between fish and beef." Her voice was as tiny as her body, high-pitched and breathless.

"The slightly fishy smell is the beginnings of decomposition." Guzzanti finished and pulled the flap he'd liberated up and over the body's head as Dante felt his stomach roil greasily. "Nick?"

Nick edged closer, holding his sandwich away from his body. His nostrils flared as he breathed deeply over the open body cavity. "Raw lamb," he said. "I really miss good lamb in the States. *Nonna* cooks it with a sprig of rosemary and garlic."

Dante's stomach lurched.

"Bingo," Guzzanti said. "Raw lamb."

The male medical student's eyes rolled to the back of his head and he toppled to the floor with a heavy thump.

"Sergio!" Guzzanti raised his voice and grunted in satisfaction as the *diener* walked in. Hands lifted, he pointed with his elbow to the floor. "Take him away. This guy's going to be something nice and safe like a dentist or a dermatologist when he grows up and graduates."

The *diener* bent, hooked his hands under the big man's armpits and heaved. Sergio couldn't have weighed more than seventy kilograms and the man must have been at least a hundred kilos. The *diener* managed to stagger to his feet and stand, but he was wobbling.

"I'll help you," Dante said. He positioned himself at the feet of the medical student. "On my three, lift. One, two, three!"

"Thanks," Sergio said grudgingly. He knew Dante was a Snail.

"Any time," Dante said, meaning every word. "Guzzanti, I'm going to see to this guy. If I'm not back soon, just carry on and we'll meet back in your office."

"Okay." Guzzanti looked up with a frown. "But you're going to miss the autopsy."

"Can't be helped." Dante allowed his voice to deepen. "Officers are sworn to avenge the dead, but above all to protect the living. Much as I'd like to stay, I can't. See you back in your office."

"In about an hour." Guzzanti had already lost interest in him, curved over the cadaver, hands in the open chest.

Dante had one last look, enough to give him nightmares for a week, and staggered out with the *diener*.

An hour and a half later, Nick and Guzzanti walked back into the pathologist's office, where Dante had surreptitiously skimmed the spines of the magazines and books lining Guzzanti's shelves. They were all in that unique place between horrifying and boring, causing Dante to marvel all over again at how the world was put together. Choosing to be a pathologist was as inexplicable to him as choosing not to live in Siena.

"That was really cool, Dante." Nick was looking more enthusiastic than he had all morning.

"Glad we could arrange a little entertainment for you, Nick."

"Your cousin seems to have acquired quite a little bit of anatomical knowledge, Dante." Guzzanti patted Nick on the back.

"That's probably because he's broken most of his bits of anatomy," Dante replied. Nick's injuries were family legend, though he always kept mum about them. Even this latest one—the career-ending one. Nick hadn't said more than two sentences about it.

Guzzanti hung up his white lab coat. "So how's Barzi?"

"Who?" Dante turned to him blankly.

"The med student," Guzzanti explained patiently. "The one who fainted."

"Oh, right. Well, if you're going to faint, I guess a hospital is a pretty good place to do it in. Last I saw him, he was being fawned over by two very pretty nurses."

"They take his blood pressure at least?"

"Among other things." Dante smiled.

One of the nurses had made a date with the student for a pizza at her house on Saturday night after he had spun a woeful tale of too many late nights up studying, with no one to cook for him.

No one to cook for you was the Italian male equivalent of homelessness.

Dante leaned forward. "So, what do you have for me, Guzzanti?"

"You want the long version or the short one?"

Dante looked at his watch. His brother would be at the San Marco right about now, drawing up strategies before the morning trial heat. A lot would depend on the events of the next few hours and he was stuck here in a hospital. "Short."

"All right. Well, it was an interesting autopsy, to say the least." Guzzanti opened a notebook. "First of all, I'm surprised he wasn't dead before the knife was actually slipped into his heart, right where it would do the most harm—"

"Between the fourth and fifth rib," Nick finished.

Guzzanti and Dante turned to him in surprise and Nick shrugged. "I broke the fourth and fifth ribs once and the doctor said I was really lucky a splinter didn't go into the heart. And I was paying attention during the autopsy."

Guzzanti smiled. "You're right there, Niccolò. It was between ribs four and five. But what was really interesting was the man's blood alcohol level. Three-hundred-and-fifty milligrams. Even without a knife between the ribs, Roland Kane should've been lying flat out on the floor. The man was comatose as the stiletto went in, so there was restricted bleeding in the pericardial sac."

Dante remembered that harsh, hard face. Kane would have been a mean drunk. "We have witnesses who say Kane had been drinking heavily over the past twelve hours."

"He was about as drunk as a man can get and still be alive," Guzzanti agreed. "Speaking of which, your murderer basically only hurried things along a little."

Dante frowned. "What do you mean?"

"I mean that his liver was cirrhotic and he had terminal-stage liver cancer. His liver weighed less than one-point-seven kilograms."

"Oh." Nick sat up. "So that's why the guy's liver was pale and rubbery. I was wondering. I mean I just assumed a human liver was like a cow's liver. Liver-colored, I mean. This guy's liver looked like a mass of pus."

Dante closed his eyes briefly. *Thank you, Nick.*

"Well, this guy's number was definitely up," Guzzanti said. "If the stiletto didn't get him, the alcohol would have. And if alcohol didn't get him, liver cancer would have. Take your pick. It was just a question of time. Someone must've hated him very much."

Dante shrugged. "That's usually the case with murder."

Guzzanti smiled. "Well, it's a good thing we restrict our hatreds to the *Palio*, isn't it? It uses up all the bad feelings and spares us all the murders."

It was something Dante believed with all his heart. His pencil hovered over his notepad. "So, we have…?"

"Proximate cause of death, puncture wound to pericardial sac and heart, immediate cause of death, loss of blood, and mechanism of death, shock." Guzzanti dictated and Dante wrote every word down.

"Okay." Dante snapped his notebook closed and, signaling to Nick, rose. "Thanks."

"Don't mention it." Guzzanti rose, too, and there was a subtle change in the air of the room.

Dante felt it, he knew Guzzanti felt it and just maybe Nick felt it, too, if he could feel anything through his fog of misery.

During the business of the crime scene and autopsy, they had cooperated as two professionals working for the Italian state were supposed to.

Now their business was over and they reverted back to their raw — their true — states. As rivals...no, more than rivals, as *enemies.* Snails had been hating Turtles for six centuries, the enmity reaching fever pitch during the *Palio* period, and it was now embedded in their DNA.

"Thanks again," Dante said. "I'll be seeing you around."

"No problem." Guzzanti's eyes gleamed wickedly behind his lenses. "And, of course, your horse will be seeing my horse. The back of him."

Nick got into the car awkwardly and waited until Dante had turned the key in the ignition. He braced his hand on the seat and turned to his cousin. "Funny, I've known you all my life and I didn't realize you had such a weak stomach. Ain't life strange? Who would've thought? And you a big, bad cop and all."

Dante's hands tightened on the steering wheel until his knuckles whitened. "I don't have a weak stomach."

"Could've fooled me." Nick's stomach was pure iron and he could afford to sound smug. He'd been engrossed in what Guzzanti was doing and had been surprised to look up into Dante's green, sweaty face.

Dante swerved out of the hospital parking lot. "I had to see to that guy who fainted."

"Uh-huh."

The car leaped forward onto the narrow country road that would take them back to Siena. "We're supposed to help citizens in distress. We took an oath."

"Right." Nick kept his voice bland. "Absolutely. But you missed some really good bits. Like when Guzzanti was handling the liver and it was so rotten it fell apart in his hands."

The car swerved, narrowly missing an oncoming Brava.

"Keep it up, Nick," Dante said grimly, "and I'm telling *Nonna* who broke that crystal vase she and *Nonno* bought on their honeymoon."

Nick shut up. Dante didn't scare him, but Nonna sure did.

"God, I wish I'd been the one to whack old Rolando," Tim said glumly.

Faith shot him a sympathetic look.

"Yeah, me too," she sighed. "But I had more reason to kill him than you did. For two years, he tried to keep me away from this—" Faith waved her hand, encompassing the flagstone arcaded terrace looking out over the formal gardens below them.

Nearby, tables had been set up for a late lunch, the smell of which had been tantalizing them for the past half hour. Coy cherubs stared down in perfect understanding of human temptation from the frescoed vaulted ceiling.

Since the hand she waved was also holding a glass of excellent chilled white wine, she supposed that was included, too.

Though Tim had officially been taken off the program, he'd nonetheless made himself incredibly useful, throwing himself into organizational details by Faith's side. She had almost forgiven him for being such a jerk last night, something both of them had studiously ignored all morning.

For some reason, Leonardo had seemed willing to let her deal with many of the arrangements of the conference. He had seemed distracted and absent-minded and spent most of his time on his cell phone. From the odd snatches of conversation, he seemed to be caught up in the frenzy of the local horse race, the *Palio*. It seemed an odd hobby, like collecting bottle caps or telephone cards, but she'd long ago learned never to question a mathematician's obsessions.

Time and again she'd found herself having to make important decisions. Leonardo had simply agreed with what she'd done, Grif had smiled and winked, and Madeleine had glowered.

Leonardo had arranged for a light luncheon to be served on the broad balcony at the back of the main building. Though the day had heated up, the vaulted arcades managed to trap just enough cool air for it to be pleasant.

Lunch would be served soon, and in the meantime, a trestle table covered with a blindingly white linen tablecloth held chilled white wine in coolers, tiny balls of mozzarella and thin slices of a spicy salami.

It was so delicious sitting in the shade on this hot day. Rambler roses climbed trellises halfway up the wall and the hot smell of roses filled her nostrils. Honeybees ambling lazily from blossom to blossom gave off a comforting buzz, contrasting nicely with the little buzz the wine was giving her.

Life was very, very good.

Faith gazed out over the garden. She'd never seen a formal landscaped garden before. In Sophie, any plants out in an open space in vases that weren't padlocked would have been boosted right away.

Below them were two ornamental ponds. Rimming them were huge terra-cotta vases with intricately chased reliefs around the rim. They were filled with some brightly flowered shrub she couldn't begin to name.

White gravel paths wound lazily around low hedges surrounding old roses in full blossom. It looked more like a work of art than of nature. It was like some superb movie director's idea of life, as opposed to the gritty indie director's version that her life had been up until now.

She could have been here last year, too, sipping white wine in paradise if it hadn't been for a man who was now, thankfully, dead.

Tim took a sip of his wine and smacked his lips. "What do you mean?"

"Hmmm?" She turned to him. She'd almost forgotten his presence.

"What do you mean, Roland tried to keep you out of here?"

Faith shook off her sensuous daze and narrowed her eyes as she looked hard at Tim. *Was he faking it?* Grif and Madeleine had been aware of what Kane was doing. That knowledge still burned bright and hot in her breast—that people she'd considered friends could betray her like that.

Had Tim betrayed her, too?

She gazed into her glass and swirled the wine around gently. It flowed back down in golden rivulets. "Legs" she remembered reading that this was called. A sign of a very good wine.

"Leonardo told me that I'd been invited to Siena last year and had been invited this year, too. Professor Gori—I mean, Leo—Leonardo…"

Tim raised an eyebrow as she stumbled over the name.

"Leonardo. That's what he asked me to call him. Anyway, Leonardo said he'd read my article on tipping behavior in *Mathematica*. You remember it, don't you, Tim?"

"Yes, sure I do," he said softly and looked her full in the eyes. It might be a trick of the soft early afternoon light, but his gaze seemed warmer than usual. "That was a really great article, Faith. I think you opened a big avenue of research there. Everyone's been very impressed by it."

Yeah. Right. Could've fooled me, Faith thought cynically. "Somehow Kane contained his enthusiasm. Anyway, on the basis of that article, Leonardo wanted me over here last year. But Kane said I was too busy with the move to St. Vincent's.

"And this year I was invited again, and he declined for me again. Only you got sick and he needed someone to do his scut work for him and he decided I could tag along. So I guess I have to thank you for that."

"For being sick as a dog?" Tim grimaced. "Happy to oblige. Any time."

"This could've been my second year here, Tim. Everybody knows how important the Quantitative Methods Seminar is. That son of a—" She looked away.

"I can't believe Kane could do something that underhanded." Tim stopped for a moment. "What am I saying? Of course he'd be capable of doing it. But why? His position is—was—safe enough. You certainly weren't any threat to him. That was a gratuitous piece of nastiness. Over the top, even for him."

"Did you know? Did you know he turned the invitation down for me?" The words were blurted out. Faith tried to keep the bitterness out of her voice. She shouldn't be putting him on the spot, but she had to. She had a right to know. And after all, they'd been lovers. Sort of. "Because Madeleine and

Grif did. And they never let on. Not a word. Not a whisper. I had no idea."

Tim touched her hand briefly. "I didn't know, Faith. Honest. But I can't say that if I had known you'd been invited, I could've changed Roland's mind or done something about it. You know what he's like. What he was like." He closed his eyes. "God, it feels good to talk about him in the past tense."

"Doesn't it?"

Tim shifted uneasily. "You know, old Kane really had it in for you, Faith. I could never understand why."

Slumped in the cane-backed chair, Tim stared down thoughtfully at his wine, twirling the stem of the glass slowly between his palms. A sudden, light breeze from the garden lifted a wispy lock of dirty-blond hair in a rose-scented gust.

He looked back up at her, his expression troubled. "He made your life hell from the moment you arrived. I guess everyone knew what was going on—me included—but there wasn't much anyone could do about it."

Faith sighed. "I know. And the police know about it, too. I suppose it's one of the reasons I'm suspect number one."

"What?" Tim straightened, galvanized. "What on earth do you mean, you're suspect number one? Are the police here insane? One look at you and it's clear you couldn't have murdered anyone."

As opposed to thinking about it. Tim was so sweet. "Well, you have to look at it from their point of view. I had a motive. We all had a motive, it's true, but I had a biggie. I was the one who found the body and my fingerprints are all over the knife. What else can they think?"

"That's the craziest thing I ever heard. Why would you—" He stopped suddenly.

Faith smiled. "Their point precisely. I had good reason to. On the other hand, they're beginning to realize that just about anyone who crossed Kane's path had reason to kill him. Still, what they have isn't enough to arrest me, let alone indict me, so I guess they're just sitting back for a minute and seeing if maybe my guilty conscience will drive me crazy like Lady Macbeth."

"I haven't seen you compulsively scrubbing your hands lately. That's a good sign." Tim leaned forward. "So...what was it like?"

"What was what like?"

"Finding old Kane dead." He shivered. "I mean, not to carp at the generosity and humanitarianism of whoever did the deed but still...to find a dead body like that. What was it like? What did he look like? Was there a struggle?"

Kane's lifeless body flashed in front of her eyes. "No, I don't think so. He was just lying there on the floor, flat on his back. Actually, at first I didn't even realize he was dead. I thought he'd simply passed out on the floor the night before and hadn't woken up out of his stupor yet.

"He'd consumed an amazing amount of alcohol. He drank his way across the Atlantic, drank his way from Rome to Florence, drank his way from Florence to Siena and drank his way through dinner. Then he ordered another bottle of whiskey from his room before going to bed.

"Wait...that's funny." Faith frowned. "Come to think of it, why did he need another bottle of whiskey? He'd brought four into the country. Not even Kane could drink four bottles of whiskey in one day and live."

"Maybe it was a gift from the *Certosa*. Sort of like a welcome gift."

"Of whiskey? To an alcoholic?"

"Maybe Leonardo doesn't know he's an alcoholic."

"Maybe," Faith said. She doubted it, though. Leonardo struck her as a very savvy man. Still, if she hadn't realized the extent of Kane's problem, it was likely Leonardo hadn't either. The echo of a voice sounded in her head and she realized Tim had asked a question.

"What?"

"I said, what made you think he'd ordered the whiskey?"

"Oh. Well, the evening before, I saw a maid deliver a bottle of whiskey to Kane's room. If it was a gift from the *Certosa*, surely they would've put it in his room. So he must've ordered it. But that doesn't make much sense.

"He had a stock of whiskey bottles, so why—" Faith's voice trailed off as she thought it through. But no matter how many ways she turned it, it didn't make much sense. She was a trained mathematician and she hated it when things didn't compute.

The head waiter appeared and clapped his hands twice, sharply. "*A tavola!*" he called.

Faith and Tim both jumped.

Tim's head swiveled around. "Good. Lunch is ready," he said. "You're in for a real treat, Faith. The cook here is fantastic."

Faith smiled. Tim loved his food. If he had more money he'd have been a foodie. "I know. You forget, I've already had a couple of meals here." They walked over to the tables. Tim linked arms with her and she leaned companionably into him. Good old Tim. He was a lousy lover, but maybe not such a bad friend.

"You know, Faith," he said as the waiters pulled out their chairs for them, "the police haven't realized another motive of yours. Keeping you away from this food is reason enough to off anyone."

She laughed, suddenly glad she was alive and Kane was dead. "Just make sure you don't tell the *commissario* that."

Chapter Ten

If you're feeling good, don't worry — you'll get over it.

ॐ

Back in Siena, Dante mopped up the last of the wine sauce with a crust of bread. "Attilio should be beatified," he said as he put the bread in his mouth. His eyes closed reverently. Some things were almost too good to be of this earth.

Nick picked up another fried artichoke and popped it into his mouth. "Hmm. Almost makes you think there's something to religion."

"Well, let's not go overboard." Dante poured a generous dollop of *Brunello di Montalcino* into Nick's glass. It was the best wine in all the world and guaranteed to pull a dead man out of the doldrums. "Though I must say, if I *did* have to choose a religion, it would definitely have to be Catholicism...for aesthetic reasons. What other religion lets you celebrate with wine? Speaking of religion, did I ever tell you about the Buddhist colony here?"

"Nope." Nick settled back to listen. His expression was serious and Dante very much wanted to put a smile on his face.

"Well, there's this Buddhist colony near Bagnolo," Dante began. "It was founded about eight years ago. Probably about fifty people. They keep pretty much to themselves. Dress in saffron robes, are close to the land and lead very simple lives. The usual.

"Which would be very inspiring to all us materialistic clods, if the whole thing weren't paid for by the million euro trust fund of their founder, who also happens to be the Conte di Salvemini."

Nick raised his eyebrows. "Isn't that the guy whose mom ran away with the—"

"The same. Which probably explains the Buddhism. Anyway, we're called out to *La Rondinaia*, the family villa, because they've been having a few break-ins at night. So we go and check things out. Turns out it was a disgruntled member of the sect—some drab, pale, young man who wanted to take over and rule the other drab pale youngsters.

"But while we were checking things out, we learned a few things about how they live, including hygiene." Dante shuddered at the memory. "And—do you know that they *import* their food?"

Nick's eyes opened wide. "Whatever for?"

Dante shrugged. "The local produce isn't spiritual enough for them? I don't know."

"Well, that's crazy."

"You better believe it. Here they are, in the midst of the greatest bounty on earth and they import their lentils from Bombay. I ask you."

Nick shook his head, but Dante could tell he wasn't really listening. He was toying with his glass, lost in thought.

Dante looked away, allowing Nick a moment's privacy. He knew what Nick was thinking about.

He could read Nick easily. Though they had been separated by an ocean, in essence they'd grown up together. They'd spent all their summers together, either here in Siena or in Deerfield. Dante felt closer to Nick than he did to Mike, who was ten years older and had been married forever.

The Rossis had always given Nick a hard time about being a jock, but the truth was they were all proud of him. Nick was a natural-born athlete, had been all his life.

Watching him hobble around was like watching a cat with a broken leg. Heart-wrenching. Though it was the concussion that had done Nick in.

Yesterday, Dante had looked up secondary concussion in the *Merck Manual* in the *Questura's* reference library and had winced at reading about "near-complete damage to forebrain functions" and "chronic vegetative state".

Nick was never playing again. Dante would tie him to a post first.

Nick's athletic career was over and, in all the ways that counted to him, Nick had lost his life. Unusual for a Rossi, Nick had never been that good in school. He'd made it through college only because of Lou's coaching. And Nick had never shown even the remotest interest in anything other than hockey.

He was a young man. In spite of his injuries, he was as healthy as a horse. Like all the Rossis, he'd live forever.

But as what?

"Listen." Dante leaned forward, ready to give Nick the little Rossi pep talk, the one about how no matter what he was, what he did, no matter what was happening in his life, his family loved him—when his cell phone rang. *Damn!* Just as he was getting started.

He listened carefully, then said he'd be back to the office right away. Snapping the mouthpiece closed, Dante signaled Attilio for the bill, ready for a fight.

Attilio's son Cecco had gotten mixed up with a bad crowd the summer before last. He'd been doing soft drugs and was barreling straight toward the hard stuff—and hard time—when Dante straightened him out. Completely off the record.

Dante had come down hard on the boy, but now Cecco was studying economics at the university and helping his dad out in the restaurant in the evenings and weekends.

Attilio refused to accept payment for Dante's meals, which was annoying because the food was so good. Dante was forced to restrict himself to Attilio's fare once a month.

After he and Attilio had gone through their usual tussle, and Attilio had won, as usual, Dante hooked arms with Nick and they walked out into the *Via Fosso*. It was a ten-minute walk along the *Banchi di Sopra* to the *Questura*, but he veered left, taking the *Chiasso Largo* down to the *piazza*.

There was something there sure to lift Nick's spirits.

They walked under the cool dark archway and emerged into the blinding sunlight of the *Piazza del Campo*.

The *piazza* was dressed for the big event. As had happened literally a thousand times before, a tawny-colored ring of earth circled the square.

"*La terra in piazza,*" Nick murmured.

"Yeah," Dante answered. *The earth has gone down.* Overnight the square had turned from silver to gold. Nick had already seen it, but Dante was sure he hadn't seen it with his heart and mind.

They stood at the top of the *piazza*, above the *Fonte Gaia*. Half of Siena had come out, it seemed. It was the last day before the *Palio,* and excitement and anticipation pulsed in the golden air.

For a Sienese, the *Palio* lasted all year. Each *contrada* kept its members busy from one end of the year to the other. Meetings, the baptism in the *contrada* of the infants born that year, planning the menus for the dinners, the endless scheming against rival *contradas*...it lasted all year and no one was left out. No one left behind.

And now the preparations were reaching a fever pitch as the dirt had gone down and the square was turned into the world's oldest, trickiest racetrack. With the world's craftiest, most low-life jockeys wielding whips made of calf phalluses…what was not to love about it?

The *Palio* was steeped in tradition, every second of it. Even the dirt was traditional—carefully kept in the vaults of the *comune* and brought out twice a year, for the races.

The Sienese weren't a reverent people, but they reserved a special place in their hard, flinty hearts for the *terra in piazza*. It was finely ground *tufa* stone, the color of a lion's mane, dampened and then tamped down by thousands of feet. It was the solemn duty of every inhabitant of the city to come and *calpestare la terra*, to tread the earth until it became as smooth as silk and as hard as marble, hard enough for the horses to race on.

The earth had mystical, magic properties. In ancient times, any Sienese citizen sent into exile brought with him a small vial of *terra senese.*

Nick and Lou had been born in America, but by blood and by custom they were Sienese. Their mother had had a small bottle of Siena earth by her bedside in the hospital when they were born. And so they had been born in the *contrada* of the Snail. In Deerfield.

No true-blooded Sienese could see the track for the *Palio* set up and be indifferent. There was a saying for sufferers of depression around the end of June—don't worry, soon there will be *la terra in piazza.*

Sure enough, Nick was smiling.

Dante was supposed to go as quickly as possible to the *Questura*, but this was just as important.

He slowly walked Nick once around the piazza on the circular track, connecting Nick with five centuries of his family's and his city's history.

When they drew even with the *Chiasso del Bargello*, Dante stooped and gathered a pinch of the earth and gave it to Nick. Nick closed his fist around the tawny earth, hard. He stood with his head bowed, then looked up into Dante's eyes.

And right then, right there, Dante knew Nick would be all right. He was back.

"My men have tracked down the maid Faith saw the night Professor Kane was murdered. She might have some additional information for us. Let's get going," he said. "We've got a murder to investigate."

They walked companionably up the *Via di Città* and turned right into the *Via del Castoro*.

Coming up to the *Questura* from the *Via del Castoro* never failed to thrill Dante. Surely no other police station in the world could compare. Ahead, two medieval arches led the eye straight into the cathedral square. A narrow shimmering view of the terra-cotta tracings and bronze tiles of the cupola of the cathedral was visible between the high walls of the street.

The right side of the street was formed by the façade of the *Questura's* tall amber wall. Dante loved that it was such an integral part of the street, of the city, like a natural outcropping instead of a hated foreign body.

He'd seen a lot of police stations in Italy and America and they were usually apart from the city, architecturally and psychologically. Not his *Questura*. It was as much a part of the thousand-year-old scene as a branch was to a tree.

Dante remembered his four years at the Naples *Questura* fondly. The food and the women had been extraordinary. The *Questura* building in Naples was famous, a landmark of the city, set in the enormous *Piazza Matteotti*, not far from the Bay of Naples. It was a Fascist-era art deco relic faced in white marble and possessed of an eerie beauty that dissipated the closer you came and saw how shabby it was.

Nonetheless, the *Questura* building had been erected to inspire awe and fear, a stern reminder to the people that here are the police. Behave yourselves. Or else.

Of course, the Neapolitans never did, which constituted a goodly portion of their charm.

That wasn't the message the *Questura* here gave. Not in Siena. People entered and left the Siena *Questura* as casually as if it were the local butcher's shop or the hairdresser's, with no reverence and no fear.

It pleased Dante to the profoundest reaches of his soul that it was so.

Passing by the sentry who was busy arguing good-naturedly with one of the *ispettori*, Dante started up the stairs to the interrogation room. At the last minute, he remembered Nick's knee and took the stairs slowly, one at a time, instead of his usual three.

The interrogation room was on the third floor. Dante loved his Ed McBain and Michael Connelly novels. Steve Carella and Harry Bosch always managed to outmaneuver and outthink the bad guys in the interrogation room, mainly by keeping the bad guys uncomfortable.

American police procedural writers often took great delight in describing how interrogations were to be carried out in a state of near sensory deprivation, in shabby rooms smelling of smoke and sweat. The few stimuli were supposed to be bad. Bad coffee, bad lighting, grime. Windowless, airless, cheerless rooms.

Nothing could be further from the third floor room universally considered the interrogation room in Siena because it had a rather obvious two-way mirror.

Like all the rooms in the *Questura*, it was airy with a high ceiling and a glorious view. Not of the cathedral, which was the inspectors' privilege, but over the rooftops of the Eagle *contrada*.

Also, by unspoken agreement, it was where the stationhouse coffee machine was kept. A gleaming Alessi espresso maker kept stoked by twice-weekly offerings of freshly-ground Arabica from Ugo, the proprietor of the corner bar.

The coffee offered to potential criminals was some of the best in Italy.

The woman sitting on a chair and cheerfully chatting with *Ispettrice* Corsi didn't look like a criminal at all.

In fact, Dante noticed as he pulled back his shoulders and pulled in the annoying gut he was starting to develop and which he was going to start exercising away—any day now—she looked like a young Sophia Loren.

"*Commissario.*" Rita Corsi rose, smiling. The other woman rose, too. "Come meet my husband's second cousin, Sara Tommasi. Sara, this is *Commissario* Dante Rossi and—" She looked inquiringly at Nick.

"My cousin, Nick Rossi," Dante said brusquely. "He's...helping us in our inquiries. With the Americans, you know." He pursed his lips and looked wise, as if calling in outsiders to help with police inquiries was perfectly normal.

Rita nodded and Sara Tommasi smiled at both of them, noticeably more warmly at Nick, Dante was annoyed to see.

"Well..." Dante pointed to a chair for Nick and motioned for the beauteous *Signorina* Tommasi to take a seat. She did so in a way that took chair-sitting to new sensuous heights.

"Why don't we get started?" Dante circled the desk and sat behind it, signifying power and hierarchy—and because he had a much better view of *Signorina* Tommasi's décolletage from there.

He was a fervent believer in taking life's little pleasures where one could.

"*Signorina* Tommasi, we've had the devil's own time tracking you down. Were you unaware of the fact the police wished to speak with you? We contacted your employer, Stella Catering, and we left messages on your answering service at home.

"Your boss gave us your parents' number and no one answered there. It was only thanks to the good offices of *Ispettrice* Corsi here," Dante nodded at Rita, "that we were finally able to get in touch with you."

"I'm sorry, *Commissario* Rossi." Sara Tommasi's voice was low and pleasant. "I had no idea. I got word on the evening of the 28th that my grandmother was ill. She lives in San Casciano and they took her to the hospital in Florence, Careggi.

"My parents and I have been there ever since. I had some free days coming, so I just took them." She bit down on a luscious lower lip and her eyes took on a sheen. "*Nonna* is very ill. None of us have been thinking of anything but her."

"I...see." Dante tried to keep his voice brusque and businesslike, but it was hard. He had a *nonna*, and he loved her, too. "I hope she's doing better."

"She is," Sara replied. "She's a little better now, though she's not out of danger. So," she looked at Rita, Nick and then Dante, "I'd like to get back to her as soon as I can, please. Rita got in touch with me and I drove here immediately, but I'd like to go back this afternoon. What is all this about?"

"It's about late in the evening of the 28th, *Signorina* Tommasi," Dante replied evenly. He watched her carefully, her magnificent breasts for the moment forgotten. If Faith was telling the truth, Sara Tommasi was the last person to see Roland Kane alive and as such was a material witness. "You were on duty at the *Certosa* that evening, am I correct?"

She nodded, eyes wide.

"And after dinner, around 10:00 p.m., you delivered a bottle of whiskey to room seventeen, occupied by a certain Professor Roland Kane, one of the Americans—"

Dante stopped. Sara Tommasi was shaking her head. "What is it, *Signorina* Tommasi?"

"I got the call from my mother around 5:00 p.m., *Commissario*. My mother said *Nonna* had been taken to the hospital. I called Paolo, a colleague who works at Stella Catering, and asked him to cover for me. I set the tables, helped the cook out in the kitchen until Paolo arrived and then left.

"I don't know exactly what time I left but it can't have been much later than 5:30. By a quarter to seven I was in *Nonna's* room at the hospital. You can check with the hospital staff. You can check with my family. For that matter, you can check with Paolo, too."

Dante leaned forward. "*Signorina* Tommasi, please think carefully about what you're saying. I understand that with the shock about your grandmother's illness, things might seem a bit confused. Are you certain you left at 5:30? Because we have an eyewitness who says she saw you after ten o'clock on the second floor, where the guests sleep. Delivering a bottle of whiskey."

"Me?" The woman's eyes rounded. "You're wrong, *Commissario*. Even if I hadn't been called to Florence, we're usually done clearing away by ten, and anyway, it's not the *Certosa's* policy to offer room service. Any guests who have special requests are supposed to address the administration. I'm sorry. It certainly wasn't me delivering a bottle of—what was it?"

"Whiskey." Dante pinched the bridge of his nose. A wise man skirted obstacles. "*Signorina* Tommasi, were you the only woman on staff that evening?"

"Yes. Actually, there are only two women in our cooperative, Stella Catering. We just started up last year, and winning the bid for catering for conferences up at the *Certosa* was our first big—"

Dante stopped the history of Stella Catering in full stride. "So could it have been your female colleague who was seen at the *Certosa*? Maybe she replaced you instead of Paolo."

Sara smiled, the mysterious smile of *La Gioconda*, the Mona Lisa who'd been born not far from Siena. "Not likely, *Commissario*. Anna gave birth a week ago. To the most darling little boy. Why, he's already smiling, can you believe it? Strapping little boy, too. He weighed—"

Dante leaned forward. "Let me see if I can get this straight. We have an eyewitness who is willing to swear under oath that a female employee at the *Certosa*—" Dante pulled out his notebook and flipped a few pages, "—dressed in a black-and-white uniform and wearing white gloves—"

Sara Tommasi snorted, a most unladylike sound.

Dante looked up from his notes. "Yes?" he asked politely.

"The *Certosa* is nice, but it isn't the Excelsior Hotel. None of us wear uniforms unless it's an official dinner. And I certainly don't wear white gloves."

Dante looked up at the ceiling and then out the window. It was the hottest part of the afternoon, when even the pigeons took refuge in the shade under the eaves. The big windows were open, the rooftops gray-red in the hard afternoon sunlight. The view always helped him think. "If it wasn't you at the *Certosa*, *Signorina* Tommasi," he said, knowing what the answer would be, "then who was it?"

She shrugged, smooth shoulders rising and falling. "Who knows?"

Dante looked over at Nick, whose face was as grim as he knew his was. Someone was lying. Either Faith Murphy or Sara Tommasi. If Sara's relatives or this Paolo could vouch for her, then Faith Murphy had just moved up in the Murder Suspect Sweepstakes.

Dante took down the name of the waiter who had replaced her, the name of the two owners of Stella Catering and the number of Sara Tommasi's parents.

"*Commissario*?" Cini stood in the doorway, eyes widening as he saw Sara Tommasi. He stared, slightly slack-jawed.

"Over here, Cini," Dante said dryly.

Cini's head snapped around to him. "Eh? Oh! Yes, sir. You have a phone call in your office from Florence, sir." He stood to attention, but his eyes wandered Sara's way.

Dante pushed himself up from his desk, grabbing the numbers Sara Tommasi had given him.

Cini's eyes were riveted again on the young woman as if they were magnets and she was made of iron filings. Gorgeous, brunette iron filings.

"Cini, while I take the call, why don't you stay in here and…keep an eye on things?"

"Yes, *sir*!" Cini moved enthusiastically into the room.

Nick was watching the scene with a half-smile on his face.

Dante knew Cini needed a little boost to his love life. He hadn't dated since he'd been jilted a couple of months ago by the daughter of Dante's high school math teacher. Maybe he should clear the decks for Cini.

"Nick—why don't you wait for me downstairs at the corner bar? I won't be long."

"Absolutely." Nick got to his feet and hobbled to the door.

"See you in about ten minutes," Dante said, in the tiny little vestibule just off the landing.

Nick nodded, moved past the big locker where the officers kept their weapons and started down the ancient, uneven staircase.

Dante watched him for a second, then, hating himself for sounding like his mother, and Aunt Lidia, and Aunt Beatrice and *Nonna*, called out, "Be careful going down. The steps are steep."

Nick didn't turn around. He just lifted his hand to show he'd heard and continued his slow way down the stairs, one at a time.

Dante opened his office door and breathed in deeply. Someone had had the good sense to open his windows. He could smell what was going on in the neighborhood. Freshly ground coffee, suntan lotion, tomato sauce cooking, jasmine in full bloom, dust, heat...the heady smells of Siena in the summer.

A flash of yellow caught his eye. The Eagle banner, a two-headed eagle on a gold background, fluttered in the breeze.

The banners lined the *Via di Città* up to the "border" with the Forest *contrada*, crackling when the wind rose in the evenings and forming a gold corridor four meters up. Two blocks east, the corridor turned green and orange with the colors of the Forest, and two blocks west, the Panther's red and blue banners proclaimed the switch of an allegiance from one step to the next.

It reminded Dante of those houses in *Alto Adige* where the living room was in Italy and the bedroom was in Austria.

He heard the sound of a foot connecting solidly with a football and the cries of young boys going up in a cheer.

Another generation of kids was playing football the next block over in the *Quattro Canti*, the Four Corners. No doubt they were as delighted to play under the noses of the cops as he had been when he'd been a boy.

By the time the bored officer standing guard duty at the *Questura* had ambled his way down the *Via del Castoro* over to the Four Corners, the ball would have disappeared, as would most of the boys, into the labyrinth of streets around the cathedral.

It was a game that had been playing itself out for generations and would continue to do so as long as there were children, and cops, in Siena.

A violin sounded up, then a viola. *Palazzo Chigi* was only a few rooftops away. The Chigiana Music Festival was about to start and the musicians were practicing. Though he knew he had barbaric tastes in music, Dante had very, very fond memories of a certain Californian viola player.

He leaned out the window for a moment, wishing with all his heart that he were at the San Marco *Compagnia Militare*, the red-brick building that was the heart and soul of his *contrada*, with the photographs of his father, his grandfather and his great-grandfather up on the wall.

"Siena doesn't have crime," he remembered his boss saying to a visiting politician from Rome. "It has the *Palio* instead."

But, with a sigh, he realized that, notwithstanding his best efforts, a crime had been committed and he had to see to solving it.

He picked up the phone. "Oh, there you are *Commissario*," the operator said in relief. "Please hold, you have a call from the Florence *Questura*."

A moment later, a deep voice came on the line. "Dante, how are you, you son of a bitch? How are the ladies? You keeping them busy?"

Dante smiled. He always enjoyed the company of Marco Ricci. They'd trained together at the Academy in Rome and had done their best at night to lay all the pretty girls and drink all the white Castelli Romani wine in Rome.

"I do my best. But there are so many of them, Marco, and only one of me."

Marco's heartfelt sigh was only a little theatrical. "Lucky you. I remember…" His voice suddenly turned brisk. "Never mind, I'm married now. Listen, I called because I have the toxicology results of that bottle of whiskey you sent over for us to analyze, and there's a little surprise."

Dante sat down and picked up a pen. "This case has been nothing but surprises so far, but what can you expect when foreigners are involved."

"That's the truth. So listen, I'll fax you the results and send you the original by courier, but right now take note of the fact that the bottle of whiskey had enough gamma hydroxybutyrate to drop a horse."

Dante's pen hovered. "Uh, would you want to repeat that?"

"Gamma hydroxybutyrate. Otherwise known as Liquid E, Organic Quaalude and other cute street names. Sold as Temazipan and Rohypnol. It's not too common over here yet, thank God. "In America it's what's known as a—" Dante could hear him shuffling papers, "—a date rape drug." Marco's voice spoke the English words hesitantly, and he pronounced the words "date rape" as if they had four syllables. "That means—"

"I know what it means, Marco." Dante was trying to square a date rape drug with the distinctly unattractive man he'd seen stretched out on his cell floor.

"That's right, I forgot. You're practically an American."

"Yeah. So it's a date rape drug? How potent?"

Marco's voice turned grim. "As potent as they come. I checked it out. It's a hypnotic and an anesthetic. There have been a hundred-and-twenty deaths in America so far. Mostly young girls whose drinks had been spiked. I haven't heard of any middle-aged men. It's been a controlled substance since March, 2000.

"A few drops of gamma hydroxybutyrate added to a drink can make a young girl lose consciousness within a quarter of an hour. A dose of— how much did your guy weigh?"

"Seventy kilos."

Dante could hear scribbling. "A dose of four milligrams would induce respiratory distress, seizures, coma and possibly death. The bottle contained enough GHB to administer five milligrams per glass. Someone seriously disliked your victim."

"A knife in the heart is a pretty good sign of that, I think."

As he was talking, Dante was flipping through the documentation he'd built up during the investigation. The file was thick and dense, another reason why he hated murder.

He finally found the copy of the autopsy report, and he had to still his stomach as he remembered the autopsy. His finger ran down the blood tests.

"Listen, we've got a pretty good medical examiner at *Le Scotte*. And he didn't find anything in the blood but alcohol. Actually, more alcohol than blood. How's that?"

"Well, GHB is called a 'stealth drug'. Apparently it's very hard to detect. When was the autopsy performed?"

Dante did a quick calculation in his head. "About thirty-six hours postmortem."

"That's it then. It would have been metabolized if—"

"If?"

"Well, that's the weird thing, Dante. If he'd imbibed any GHB. Which I doubt he did. The bottle you sent us was full."

"Could the victim have drunk a little bit? Just enough to — you know, push him over?"

"Nope. The bottle was a seventy-centiliter bottle and there were seventy centiliters of liquid inside. Someone had eased up the excise tax tab, poured some of the whiskey out, topped it up with GHB, probably with a syringe, then stuck the tab back down."

"Did you —"

"Yes, we sent it to Rome."

They both knew the Rome state police laboratory was the only place in Italy that could carry out DNA testing. There had been talk of setting up another laboratory in Milan, but so far — like many things in Italy — it had remained just that — talk.

"But this is clearly a guy who reads his thrillers. There were no fingerprints on the bottle — none. Zip. So I think he might've had the smarts not to lick the tab. He probably used a wet sponge. At any rate, I know the head of the lab in Rome and he owes me a favor. He'll send me the results as soon as they come in. He won't sit on it like they usually do."

"This is strange," Dante said slowly.

"You better believe it. Someone goes to great lengths to poison a bottle and the victim doesn't even have the good taste to drink it."

"It would've been overkill. The guy had a three-hundred-and-fifty blood alcohol."

Dante could almost hear Marco wince. "Christ."

"Yeah."

"It's a weird case, isn't it?"

Dante sighed. "Yeah."

Murders weren't usually weird, not in Italy. They were pretty straightforward, or at least that had been his experience in the four years he'd spent at the Naples *Questura*. There had been a murder every three days there, on average, and none of them had been strange. Brutal maybe, but not strange. Most of them were mob killings, the who and the why and the how as clear as a bullet to the back of the neck, and the rest were passion killings. In that case, it was the murderer who usually called in the police, and they would arrive to find the distraught wife or appalled husband still holding the pistol, crying over the loss of the loved one.

As if the police were priests, the killer would start babbling a confession as soon as they walked in the door, looking hopefully at them as if they had the power of absolution.

This wasn't anything like that.

"Foreigners," he said again.

"Tell me about it. Last March we started getting hysterical phone calls from little old ladies living in *San Lorenzo*. You know—the marketplace?"

It was the central fruit and vegetable market in Florence and home to the elderly poor and recent immigrants. "Sure."

"Well, they were shouting about bloodbaths and screaming children, so we got over there real quick. You know what we saw?"

Bloodbaths. Dante's stomach gave a little warning twinge. "Do I want to hear this?"

"Come on, Dante. Turns out it was *Eid Al Adha*, this Muslim religious holiday which has to be celebrated by sacrificing goats. Abundantly. You haven't lived until you've seen a tiny sixth-floor apartment turned into a slaughterhouse. There was so much blood we had to wear rubber boots."

Dante's stomach slid greasily up his throat. He swallowed and it moved back down. Grudgingly. "That's really, ah, interesting, Marco, but I have to go now. Listen, get that DNA report to me as soon as you have it, okay ?"

"Absolutely. What horse did your *contrada* draw?" Marco had always loved the *Palio*.

"Lina."

"Good horse. And who's your jockey?"

"Nerbo."

"He's the best," Marco said approvingly. "Nasty, with a lot of dirty tricks up his sleeve. Well, this might be the Snail's year," Marco said genially.

Dante hung up on Marco's chuckle. He tapped his pen against the desktop once, then twice, sharply.

The bottle of whiskey Sara Tommasi swore she hadn't delivered to Roland Kane's door had been poisoned. But not drunk. He let the possibilities settle in his mind, then lifted the receiver of the phone and dialed the first number on the sheet of paper in front of him.

Fifteen minutes and three phone calls later, he put the phone back down. Paolo Tucci, the owners of Stella Catering and Sara Tommasi's parents all swore Sara had left the *Certosa* at 5:30 p.m. If it was a conspiracy, it was a seamless one.

When he stuck his head into the interrogation room, he saw Cini behind the young woman, his arms crossed over her waist. Dante narrowed his eyes. "Cini?"

Cini jumped and moved three meters away from Sara. He stood stiffly at attention.

"Sir. I was just...just showing Sara—*Signorina* Tommasi—how we in the police force...how we subdue criminals. Sir." He was beet red.

"Well, you might want to show *Signorina* Tommasi how we in the police force walk out the door." Dante wondered if the police force had a special hold for that. "Accompany her up to the *Certosa* and have her wait in the archive room. The receptionist will show you which room it is. Wait outside, and when we're finished, you can accompany *Signorina* Tommasi to Florence. To the—" He switched his gaze. "To the hospital?"

She nodded.

"To the hospital at Careggi. Is that clear, Cini? Cini? You might want to look at me when I'm giving you orders."

Cini's head swiveled and he turned an even deeper shade of red.

"Yes, sir," he mumbled. "Very clear."

Dante walked out to the little antechamber which held the gun lockers and entered his combination in the lock. He reached into the little tray and, for the first time in days, put on his shoulder holster. He hated the damn thing because it meant he had to wear a jacket in this heat.

Dante sprinted down the stairs. Nick was waiting for him at Ugo's corner bar.

Dante parted the long plastic strings that served as a transparent door in the summer and peeped in. Ugo was regaling Nick with a blow-by-blow account of the Eagle's victory three years ago. Dante had heard it at least three hundred times.

"Nick," he said, "let's go. Sorry, Ugo."

Ugo had his hand in the air, which meant that he was now imitating the jockey on the third lap of the track. In three years, the words and the gestures had remained unwavering, like a liturgy.

Nick dug into his pocket and paid for his cappuccino, then met Dante at the door. "So—what's up?"

Dante started up the *Via di Città*. "What's up is that the bottle of whiskey brought to the murdered man's cell by a maid only Faith Murphy saw was poisoned."

"Hey," Nick stopped in his tracks. "That doesn't mean Faith poisoned it."

Dante nudged him forward again, not an easy thing to do with someone of Nick's heft. "Maybe. Maybe not. To tell the truth, I don't see her doing that either. But there's something really screwed up here and I hate it when it's like that." He veered left into the *Via delle Terme*, going as quickly as Nick's knee would allow. Nick followed obediently.

"Where are we going?"

Dante hesitated, knowing Nick wasn't going to like what was coming.

"To where it began," he said. "To the *Certosa*."

The Certosa *has never looked lovelier,* Nick thought, as they pulled into the graveled driveway. It had only been turned into a conference center in the past ten years. He remembered as a kid spending his summers in Italy, coming to the ruins of the ancient monastery with his cousins. Mike knew the caretaker and, for a bottle or two of *Nonno's* excellent Gallo Nero, the caretaker would unlock the creaky gate and allow the kids in for an hour or two.

Dante had dated the chief restorer of the *Certosa* a few years ago, a pretty girl who had been much too sweet for Dante. Nick remembered her saying that the restoration team was proud nothing structural had been changed—not even the lock on the gate.

The restored *Certosa* was soberly elegant now, but it had had a wild and glorious ramshackle beauty all those summers ago. The cousins had run wild in the cloisters, avoiding the rats' nests and piles of bricks lain untouched since the Middle Ages.

Nick winced now at the thought of running his hands along powdery painted walls, enjoying the feeling of crumbling stucco. He realized now that he'd probably destroyed whole strips of priceless frescoes, just as they'd dumped the shards of what had been centuries-old terra-cotta vases in corners so they could play soccer undisturbed along the corridors.

It had been wild and wonderful then just as it was cool and beautiful now. All of Siena was dotted with warm and wonderful memories for him. He couldn't ever remember being unhappy here.

Is this where I belong? Nick wondered as he followed Dante's swift progress through the arcades of the main courtyard. Was his family's adventure in America about to run its course?

Nick's own father and mother were talking more and more about moving to Siena when his father retired next year. If they did, Lou would follow. Without making an issue of it, she would probably find a way to get a job in Siena or Florence for a year or two, which would stretch into forever. She was so good at her job they would fight over her services in the Gobi Desert. And Lou being Lou, she'd be knee-deep in suitors before the year was out.

Nick would be left alone over in Deerfield.

He had plenty of friends, but most of them were hockey players or sports writers or managers. He knew the score. Overnight, he had gone from being a big man in the game to being a has-been. Everyone would try hard to keep in touch, but the pull of the game would tug them away.

Nick shook his head. He hardly recognized his own brain. He never ever thought about the future until it was right on top of him.

He followed Dante through a narrow archway into a smaller cloister. A burst of laughter came from an open doorway in the eastern corner. They turned left.

It wasn't like him to have such somber thoughts. It was as if the Nick-shaped slot he'd inhabited all his life had suddenly disappeared.

He stopped in the doorway as another burst of laughter echoed in the hot, dusty air, and stared at the tableau.

It looked like Faith had found a little slot all her own.

She was surrounded by men, and damned if they didn't look a lot like admirers. He recognized Professor Gori—Dante had dated *his* daughter, too—and that slimy creep, Tim something. Her other colleague—what was his name? Something dumb like Griffen. There were two weedy-looking guys and a Japanese man, nodding and bowing and grinning.

Nerdy geeks, all of them, except for Gori and that Griffen guy. They looked like elegant geeks.

They were crowded around an overhead projector. Faith held a pen and was going down bullet points, the pen and her slender hand projected hugely overhead on the white screen.

"And here we have tipping," Faith said and, crazily, there was an audible murmur of approval. Like a flock of very odd birds, all the men bent their heads and tapped into their handheld computers.

Faith's big, light-brown eyes were alight with intelligence and humor, and Nick was suddenly floored with how wildly attractive she looked just then, hair a red-brown nimbus around her face, cheekbones and forehead slightly sunburned, wide mouth curved in a smile.

In the throes of lust when first dating Dee Dee, Nick had once commented on how gorgeous she was. Lou had shocked him by saying Faith was prettier. Nick had laughed at the time, but it was true, he had discovered.

He'd rarely seen Dee Dee without makeup, not even in bed. The few times he'd managed to catch a glimpse of her unadorned face, she seemed like a different person. Eyes small and too close together. And her nose—well, it was definitely a bit...piggish. Dee Dee made up for it with good makeup, tight clothes and pretty hair out of a bottle.

Dee Dee, in ten years' time, would be puffy and over the hill. Faith, he could clearly see, would probably look even better. She'd probably fill out some. Like *Nonna*, she had the kind of facial structure that aged well.

Right now, she was sexy and vibrantly alive as she held the undivided attention of all the men in the room, whose collective IQ was probably as high as the amount of money he had in the bank.

Faith made a comment, something crazy about... He leaned forward to hear better. Was she talking about *hysterias*? Whatever it was, was sparking another round of laughter. Nick shook his head. No wonder the geeks had stayed away from the jocks in college. They didn't even speak the same language.

A bell rang and Faith turned, murmuring something in that dry tone of hers. The room erupted into laughter again and Faith looked up. She froze when she saw Nick at the back of the room.

Her body language had been smooth, even elegant, but now her movements became jerky. Her mouth tightened and she declared the session adjourned.

Nick realized all over again how much he'd hurt her.

He waited patiently as ten or twelve of the geeks huddled around Faith like groupies around a rock star. He was surprised they didn't ask for autographs, though one of them *did* ask her to write something on the blackboard. She did, some impenetrable symbols, and the man nodded, humming a little.

Nick couldn't read anything of what she'd written — it was in math and God knew he had enough trouble with English.

He'd been slightly dyslexic as a child. Luckily, his parents were loving, attentive and smart. He got help early, but he distinctly remembered that feeling of helplessness in school — everyone understanding but him. Even now, when he got too tired or anxious, the words danced about on the page.

Faith certainly didn't have that problem.

Actually, Faith didn't have any problems at all that he could see. Kane's death had liberated her. She was going to be successful and she was on the verge of understanding what a desirable woman she was. Kane's death had done that. For a moment, Nick almost wished Faith really had offed him. It would have been poetic justice.

He hung back as Dante walked forward into the little flock of mathematicians.

"Faith," Dante said, his voice somber, "I need to talk to you again."

One of the geeks stepped forward, the one Nick particularly hated. The one who thought he had a claim on Faith. Tim — Tim Something. Tim Something glared at Dante. "What's this about?"

Dante barely glanced at him. "I need to talk to Miss Murphy," he repeated.

"Well, we're in the middle of work here and we need to talk to Faith, too."

"Yeah."

"Oui."

"Si."

"*Hai.*"

The men's voices formed a chorus.

"What is this, Dante?" Leonardo Gori asked with a frown. "We're busy here. Whatever it is, won't it keep?"

"It's a little matter of murder, Leonardo, and no, I'm sorry, but it won't keep." He beckoned with his hand. "Now, Faith, come with me, please."

Nick was used to seeing Dante as his cousin, his best friend, a guy he'd practically grown up with. Good-natured and kind beneath his casual exterior. But this was a new Dante — Dante the Cop.

Leonardo Gori shut up.

Without a word, Faith put down the pen and moved forward. She walked past him silently and followed Dante out of the room. If Nick had told her to follow *him*, she would have turned in the opposite direction.

If this was the effect you got, Nick thought, *then maybe I should become a cop.*

Chapter Eleven

Anything that begins well, ends badly.
Anything that begins badly, ends worse.

&

Faith watched the two Rossi cousins' broad backs as she followed them into the central cloister. She stifled a sigh. She'd been having such a good time with her colleagues, but Murphys didn't have good times for very long. It was some kind of law. Unwritten, but unyielding. She should have known that.

They passed through two big wooden doors, the cop Rossi shouldering them open, the jock waiting for her to pass then following hard at her heels, then another set of glass doors which opened onto a corridor. They must be somewhere near the kitchen because she could smell cooking.

Roast beef for dinner, she thought.

They went through the third and last door on the left. Coming in from the dim hallway, Faith had to shield her eyes.

They were in a corner room of the monastery and light flooded in through four large windows. Like the other rooms, it had high ceilings, but there the resemblance ended. It was sparsely furnished with cheap utilitarian furniture, and was a replica of the room Dante had first interrogated her in. Clearly, the *Certosa* kept a few rooms sparely decorated just to interrogate her in.

No pink putti on the ceiling. No antique furniture. Just a metal, Formica-topped table and six matching Formica chairs, pure vintage Seventies, and a gray-green metal bookcase holding document classifiers, each folder with the date written in pen on a label. The dates ran from 1973 through 1991 when, presumably, some form of computerization had taken place.

Perched on the edge of one of those lethally uncomfortable-looking chairs was an attractive, dark-haired woman.

Her glance moved briefly and without interest over Faith, then immediately to the two Rossi men. She beamed at both, and Faith bristled before she remembered that Nick wasn't hers. Had never been, never would be hers.

Faith stopped a few paces into the room and looked at Dante. This was his show.

"Please sit down, Faith." As he had the first time he'd questioned her, he didn't take a chair to sit behind the table, to show authority, but sat down in the nearest chair.

Nick leaned his shoulders against the wall, hands deep in the pockets of his loose tan cotton trousers.

Dante gestured to the woman. "This is Sara Tommasi, Faith. She's one of the waitstaff working at the *Certosa* while the conference is on."

Faith nodded to the woman and received a chilly smile in return.

"Now, I want you to tell us once again about the night you saw Miss Tommasi, the night Professor Kane was murdered. I want you to tell us every detail. Don't leave anything out."

Faith frowned. "I'm afraid I don't understand. When did I see Miss Tomas— What was the name again?"

"Tommasi. And we need to know—"

The woman broke out in angry and voluble Italian. It was quick and liquid. Faith recognized the words *mai*—"never"—and "whiskey". The *commissario* heard the woman out until she wound down, more out of a lack of breath than of things left unsaid. He nodded once, briskly, and turned back to Faith.

"Now, about the night Professor Kane was murdered. I trust you haven't forgotten it already."

Faith looked around. Her glance crossed Nick's who was watching her steadily. Her heart—treacherous organ—thumped hard and her gaze shot back to Dante.

"No." She shook her head. "I remember."

"Well, then, do you want to run through it for me again?"

"All right. We all ate together—"

"No, later," Dante interrupted her. "When you were going to bed. You saw a maid bring a bottle of whiskey to Professor Kane's room."

"That's right." Faith was mystified. This must have been the fifth time she'd told this story. It wasn't even a story, it was an incident. "I left soon after Professor Kane...retired." *Stumbled to his bed would be more like it.* "My bedroom is on the other side of the cloister, but I got lost and went down Professor Kane's corridor by mistake. The corridor was empty except for a maid carrying a bottle of whiskey on a tray."

"And how could you tell it was whiskey?"

As if Rory Murphy's daughter couldn't recognize a whiskey bottle at a hundred paces.

"She—the maid—she wasn't holding it right in front of her body. She was holding it a little off to the side." Awkwardly, Faith mimed holding a tray on the flat of her hand. "Whiskey bottles usually have distinctive shapes. And I recognized the label."

"Which was?"

"Glennfiddich. Everyone knew it was Professor Kane's favorite brand. He always kept a bottle of it in his office. It's got this huge red deer on the label. I've seen it a thousand times. Believe me, you couldn't mistake it for anything else. It wasn't a bottle of water or anything."

Dante leaned forward, watching her intently. "And did the maid notice you?"

Faith looked up at the ceiling, trying to remember all the details of that evening — the unexpected heat, the maid walking toward Roland Kane's room, the long walk back to her cell. What she mainly remembered was being tired.

She frowned. "I don't — I don't really think so. Well, no, now that I come to think of it. I had on sneakers still. You know — from the trip? So I don't think she did. Or at least, if she did notice someone else was in the corridor, she didn't turn around."

"So...I guess it would be your word against hers then. That she'd brought a bottle of whiskey to Professor Kane's room, as you suggested."

Faith felt rather than saw Nick stir. Dante shot him a steel-edged glance and he subsided back against the wall.

"Yes, I — I guess so," Faith said.

"Because — " Dante leaned forward, elbows on knees. He looked at her and at the sultry woman. "Because Miss Tommasi maintains she didn't deliver anything to Professor Kane's room that night."

"If she says she didn't, then I'm sure she didn't," Faith said evenly.

"And yet, you say you saw her delivering the bottle that evening. At around 10:00 p.m."

"I said I saw a maid delivering a bottle of whiskey. I have no idea if it was Miss Tommasi." Faith studied the other woman in the room. She was a beauty and Faith frowned.

A beauty. There was something about that…a beautiful woman. She closed her eyes, trying to remember — and suddenly, everything snapped into focus. She had a vivid vision of that night, the tiredness, the stillness of the *Certosa*, the silence. Not a creepy stillness and silence, but the silence of peace and serenity. Walking to her cell feeling happy to be in Italy, sad about Nick.

Seeing a lone woman walking down the corridor to Roland Kane's room. Thinking, *He won't be bothering her. Because —* "This isn't the woman I saw that night."

She heard Nick draw in a sharp breath. Dante's eyes narrowed. "What do you mean?"

"Exactly what I said. The woman I saw was short and…tubby."

"Tubby?" Dante repeated the word, as if uncertain of its meaning.

"Overweight. Her legs — She had big calves. They were short and bunched while she walked. And she had gray hair, gathered in a bun at the nape of her neck. She had a thick neck and no waistline. Believe me, Dante, when I say it wasn't this lady."

He sat back. "Well, it's beginning to look as if, indeed, it wasn't this lady." He rubbed his chin. "I'm sorry to say Miss Tommasi denies she brought a bottle of whiskey — or anything else for that matter — to Professor Kane's room.

"The problem is, there aren't any other women on the waitstaff. *Signorina* Tommasi is the only one. So, if you didn't see *Signorina* Tommasi bringing Professor Kane his bottle of whiskey, then who is it exactly you did see?"

Faith felt as if she were walking a tightrope. She'd been yanked back into Roland Kane's death and wanted desperately to move back on the other side of the divide. She drew in a long breath. Another. "I don't know, Dante," she said slowly. "I just don't know."

"Could it have been the other woman in your group, Madeleine Kobbel? After all, she knew the professor well."

Faith shook her head. "No. Professor Kobbel is tall and slender, and that woman was short and stout. They had entirely different physiques. I would certainly have recognized Madeleine from the back. But why is this so important? Does it really matter who took the bottle of whiskey to Professor Kane's room?"

"It matters when that bottle was full of a drug that would've killed a horse and certainly would've killed Professor Kane if he hadn't already been dead."

Dante dropped that little bomb into the room and complete silence descended. After a moment or two, Faith remembered to breathe. "Drug?"

"Drug." Dante nodded.

"In the—"

"Whiskey bottle. The same whiskey bottle which a mysterious woman only you seem to have witnessed brought to Professor Kane's door."

Uh-oh.

Beside her Nick lifted his shoulders from the wall. "Dante—"

"Shut up, Nick," Dante said pleasantly. "Now, Faith, I'll ask you once again. Who was the woman you observed bringing what turned out to be a poisoned whiskey bottle to room seventeen on the night of the 28th of June?"

"I don't know," Faith whispered. She spread her hands, then brought them together in her lap. They weren't trembling, but she was trembling, deep inside. "I really don't know. What drug was it?"

"Rohypnol. It's a—"

"Date rape drug. I know."

Dante's eyes narrowed. "And just how do you know that?"

"I tutor university students. There isn't anything about controlled substances we don't get to know about. Theoretically, of course. But still, we get the whole pharmacopoeia. And you're saying it wasn't the drug in the whiskey that killed him?"

"No," Dante said dryly. "It was the knife in his heart that killed him. Closely followed by an unholy amount of alcohol. If he'd actually drunk the laced whiskey, it would have been overkill. So to speak."

"Pity," Faith mused. "Death by Rohypnol would've been poetic justice. Since human justice didn't have time to run its course."

"I don't suppose you'd care to explain that?"

"Remember I said Professor Kane was charged with raping one of the freshman students? He laced her drink— *allegedly* laced her drink—with Rohypnol and raped her. Allegedly raped her. Charges were brought, but then dropped because the girl was hospitalized with a nervous breakdown and couldn't testify."

Dante closed his notebook. "So anyone wanting to exact revenge on that rape couldn't do better than to lace a bottle of his favorite brand of whiskey with this drug?"

"Yes. Though sticking a knife in his heart came a pretty close second," Faith said dryly.

Dante didn't answer, just sat looking at her for a long time. Faith tried not to fidget. She might be in trouble here. It occurred to her that the woman she'd seen carrying a bottle of poisoned whiskey might be the murderer. Murderess. It also occurred to her—and doubtless to Dante as well—that she was the only witness and that he had to take her at her word.

A deep-seated flush of resentment started to rise and she suppressed it ruthlessly.

The Quantitative Methods Seminar was her big chance. It had already changed her professional life, given her a showcase. Things were moving for her, very quickly.

Leonardo had already talked about letting her moderate the closing session tomorrow and had all but invited her to submit a chapter for an upcoming textbook on quantitative methods.

It would be hard to do all that sitting in jail.

She was well aware of the fact she had been given the opportunity of a lifetime. She was also well aware of the fact she was being given this opportunity precisely because Roland Kane was dead.

She'd had the motive, and if she'd wanted, the means. She was the only one who'd seen the outsider. They had to take her word for it—the word of a woman who had ample motive to kill.

Dante would be smart to take her in.

Faith sat quietly and watched him. He was looking at her just as intently, as if his eyes could walk around her head, seeing what was inside. She sincerely hoped he couldn't.

"Okay, Faith," he said on a sigh. "You're free to go now."

She hadn't been aware of holding her breath. She shot out of the chair and out the door.

"Faith, wait up!" Nick hobbled a little faster over the herringbone brick walkway, cursing. "Faith!"

He heard a faint sigh and she slowly turned around. She did it gracefully, her long skirt belling and her long hair curving out to fall in a wave on her shoulders.

Nick hated that expression on her face, like a porcelain doll's—eyes blank, mouth still. He was used to seeing her animated with all that ferocious intelligence brought to bear on the stupidities of the world. Looking at him with a smile on her face, making him laugh, too.

He kept his voice neutral. "Well, that was interesting, back there."

"Mm," Faith agreed. She started walking again, but at a pace he could keep up with. "Poisoned bottles. Mysterious women. I'm surprised your cousin let me go. I might be a dangerous criminal. I could be plotting my next murder right now." She looked up at him, tight-lipped and grim, and Nick had an uneasy feeling about who she'd off next...

"Faith, he's just doing his job."

She didn't say anything until they reached the corner. She sighed. "Yes, I know. I suppose I can't blame—"

"Faith!" A comic figure jumped out from one of the meeting rooms. He rushed to Faith and bent to take her hand. "Mahvelous talk you gave yesterday, my dear, simply *mahhvelous.*"

Who the hell spoke like that? Like some idiot in a bad film.

"We'll be discussing it for months back at Manchester. I loved the way you brought in nonlinear probability for S-shaped growth. And the implications you drew for hysteresis—magnificent!"

While he babbled, Nick studied him.

He was tall and gangly with shoulders no wider than his hips. Wispy red hair on top of a narrow face with pale, powdery skin. A sparse red beard grew down to the first purple button on his amazingly ugly print shirt.

There were bits of lunch in the beard. Nick could recognize pieces of what looked like fettuccine and almost an entire cherry tomato. Nick's eyes traveled down the unkempt body to the man's amazingly long feet in white socks and sandals.

It was illegal to dress like that in Italy. They threw you out of the country when you went around looking like that.

The guy was jabbering, again something about tipping — what *was* it with these people? — and still holding Faith's hand. Nick noticed Faith wasn't pulling her hand back either. No, she kept it engulfed in the guy's huge ham with the cracked fingernails and she was smiling at him.

Smiling! And talking. Math talk Nick couldn't follow.

And this creep wasn't letting go of her hand.

Nick had had enough.

He coughed and nudged Faith's elbow, hard enough to shake the nerd's grasp. The geek turned and stared at him, blinking. "I *say*."

"You say *what*?" Nick asked softly, moving right up into his face, almost stepping on the hole in the guy's sock.

The geek was a few inches taller, but Nick had at least seventy pounds of pure muscle on him. The man's sparse ginger eyebrows drew together. Puzzled, the geek turned to Faith. "Faith?"

Faith sighed. "It's okay, Paul. He's a — "

Nick moved even closer. "Friend. He's Faith's friend. *Close* friend, if you get my drift. You might want to remember that."

He heard Faith draw in an outraged breath. "Nick Rossi! You apologize right now!"

"Apologize?" Nick bared his teeth in a smile. "Sure," he said. "Why not? I'm sorry she's my friend because she's been giving me nothing but grief lately, but she is *my* friend and there you are." He grabbed Faith's hand and limped away as quickly as possible.

Faith tried to tug her hand away, but one thing Nick had going for him was strength. He might not have smarts, he might not have a sophisticated mind, he might not even have a job, but he had strength and, by God, she wasn't going to pull away from him. He made sure he wasn't hurting her, but he also made sure she couldn't pull away.

Grimly, he headed for the exit, limping up the ramp. He nodded his head at Egidio, the gatekeeper, who walked out from behind his desk to stand in the doorway, unabashedly watching the proceedings.

Luckily, Dante had insisted they take separate cars. They'd made quite a little procession going up the hill, first Dante in his fancy police *Stato Lancia*, then himself in *Nonno's* ancient Dedra.

Now he held Faith's hand tightly and practically dragged her to the Dedra.

Faith jerked her hand so hard he had to let go or she'd hurt herself. She leaned against the front fender.

Her chest wasn't as generous as that of Sara Tommasi's, but Nick remembered it very fondly. Her breasts had been small and round and milk-white. And had tasted like a small cone of vanilla ice cream. He closed his eyes, slightly dizzy.

It was either the secondary effects of the concussion or his memories of the night with Faith.

It didn't matter. Both were dangerous.

"Okay," Faith said to Nick, crossing her arms over her chest. They were just outside the *Certosa* gates, in the corner formed by the stucco façade and the fieldstone wall of the Romanesque chapel.

She was uncomfortable. The gravel of the walkway leading to the high arched brick entrance was hurting her feet. She lifted a hand to shade her eyes against the bright gold of the early afternoon sun. She'd left her sunglasses inside with her briefcase, and remembering that she'd been rudely pulled away from her briefcase — and her life — made her angry.

"Right now you're going to give me a very good reason why you just chased off the head of the math department of Manchester University, who happens to be a top man in our field and the editor of *Quantimath*. A leading publication, by the way, which now has an article of mine on system dynamics under consideration. My career is happening here, Nick. Right here. Right now. Just because you don't have one any more doesn't mean I don't get a shot at mine."

Faith saw Nick wince and regretted her crack about careers. For a second or two. But damn it, Nick had *had* his career. He'd already had his chance to show what he could do in his field — to shine. And he was probably a multimillionaire to boot. He'd done it while the time was right for him.

Mathematicians were like athletes, they did their best work young. This was her time. She'd done some very good work, but it had all somehow remained unnoticed.

She was just now beginning to suspect that the reason was Roland Kane.

But Roland Kane was dead. There was nothing to stop her now. Unless you counted a very angry and very large former hockey player.

A muscle was working angrily in Nick's jaw. It was extremely unfortunate it only added to Nick's attraction. There didn't seem to be very many things that detracted from it. Even drunk and bristly and clueless, he had been overwhelmingly sexy that last morning.

And even now, surly and sober and clean-shaven, she had to stop herself from swaying toward him.

"What was I doing?" he answered angrily. "What do you think I was doing? I see some wirehead with hygiene problems getting in your face and talking about becoming hysterical, what do you think I'm going to do? Wait until he goes postal?"

Faith was startled. Nick's thought processes were sometimes so hard to follow. Paul Allen hysterical was ridicu — Ahhh. Her brow smoothed out.

"Paul wasn't talking about being hysterical, Nick. He was talking about hysteresis. It's the history dependence of physical and virtual systems, and he's done some interesting work on the epsilon expansion — "

Nick's jaw muscles clenched tightly, like runners under the skin. "Never mind," she said with a smile.

"That's right, go ahead and make fun of me because I'm just a dumb jock," he said heatedly. "But I'm *not* dumb." His head stuck out aggressively, big chin tilted up. He looked like an attractive bulldog. "Just because I haven't heard of hysteric...hystero — "

"Hysteresis," Faith murmured.

"Whatever," he shot back. "Whoever heard of that anyway? It's a ridiculous word. Stupid word. I'm not dumb for not knowing what it is."

"No one called you stupid, Nick." It was true. She had never made the mistake of thinking him dumb, even in his stupidest jock mode. Nick's family made fun of him, but Nick was far from being stupid. It was, alas, another of his fatal charms — a completely non-theoretical, totally reality-based, street-wise intelligence.

"Listen up, Faith, because I'm going to say this once. They're running a trial heat of the *Palio* at six o'clock and you're coming with me. You're getting in my car and staying in the car with me.

"You're going to walk the streets of Siena with me until we get to *Piazza del Campo* and then you're going to stay there—*with me*—until the end of the horse race and then we're going to grab a bite to eat. Together. Then I will drive you back up to the *Certosa*."

He said all of that pugnaciously, shifting his considerable bulk from foot to foot in full rhino mode, with exactly the same expression as when he shot a puck past five adversaries on the ice straight into the net at thirty-five miles an hour.

He looked as if he were willing to carry her off if she said no.

Well, now, let's see. After the most satisfying day of her life, in the most beautiful place she'd ever been in, did she want to go down to the most gorgeous square on earth to watch a trial heat of the most famous horse race in the world with the most gorgeous man she'd ever seen?

Yes. "Okay," she said.

Nick was standing stiffly on the balls of his feet, fists bunched, a ferocious scowl on his face. "What?" His scowl deepened. "What did you say?"

"I said okay. You want to go down to the central square, that's fine. The rest of the conference team is going down anyway, so I can hook up with them later. All the afternoon meetings are over." She squinted up into Nick's frowning face, directly against the bright afternoon sunlight. The light hurt her eyes. "But first, I need to go pick up my sunglasses. I left them in my briefcase in the meeting room."

The scowl lightened. "Okay." The martial stance eased a little, and his weight rocked back on his heels. "Okay, let's go get your sunglasses."

"You can wait here—" Faith began, then took another look at his face. "Never mind. Come on. I need to gather my things anyway."

It was 4:30 p.m. and the conference was over for the day. There were a few participants Faith recognized lazing around in the shade of the portico, speaking quietly. Two men sitting on the low retaining wall saw her, smiled and got up. Faith felt Nick stiffen, the two looked at her, at him, then sat down again.

She sighed.

The *Sala Delle Volte* where she'd presided over the workshop was empty. Her footsteps echoed on the ancient terra-cotta tiles.

Faith drew in a deep breath as she walked down the aisle created between the rows of blue, upholstered chairs. Someone had forgotten to turn off the overhead projector and she could smell the faint smell of ozone that electrical appliances sometimes gave off. There was a faint and familiar tang of unwashed mathematician, with an overlay of Armani for Men. Doubtless Leonardo Gori. Or maybe the French guy.

At the far end was a fresco of The Last Supper, but instead of the usual lugubrious depiction, it looked like the painting of twelve men having a good time, eating and drinking. One of them looked a little pained, as if he had a touch of gas. He certainly didn't look guilt-ridden or tragic, definitely the happiest Judas she'd even seen. The long walls were covered in frescoes too, still-bright scenes of Adam and Eve in the Garden of Eden, frolicking in what looked suspiciously like the formal gardens of the *Certosa*.

She loved this room. This was the room in which her life turned around. Like many mathematicians, Faith harbored doubts about the reality — the corporeality — of the real world. The theory that there were a billion parallel worlds in which a billion parallel Faiths were having a billion different lives made a lot of sense to her.

Well, in this room, she had slipped into an alternate universe. A better one, one more suited to her talents, where she would be happier and more fulfilled.

Faith picked up her sunglasses and saw her briefcase sitting against the wall. She would just nip up to her room and leave it there. Maybe while she was up in her room, she would take the time to splash on some cologne, run a comb through her hair, change outfits…

It was going to be a fun evening. The first of many, many more to come, she was sure. Her real life was beginning. She was in the right universe.

She was smiling as she pulled her bulging briefcase up on the table that had served as a podium. She laid it flat, snapped open the locks and froze.

Nick had been looking around the room, puzzling over the frescoes, but he suddenly zeroed in on her face.

"Faith?" he said.

She tried to swallow, tried to get the words out.

"Hey." Nick walked to her. "You're white, honey. What happened? Is the heat—"

Then his eyes fell on her open briefcase and he swore, suddenly and viciously. He snatched the sheet of white A4 paper lying neatly on top of her documents, diskettes and books.

Don't touch it, Faith wanted to say, but nothing would come out of her mouth.

It was too late to worry about fingerprints, anyway, as Nick was poring over the words, reading them over and over again. He said something in Italian…probably a repeat of what he'd said in English. He cupped her elbow with one hand, and put the other hand, the one holding the sheet of paper, behind his back. Probably thinking to shield her from its contents.

But she knew. She had a good memory and there weren't many words, anyway. A simple message, laser printed in capital letters.

GET OUT OF HERE, FAITH. REMEMBER WHAT HAPPENED TO ROLAND.

Magnificent evening. The day before the *Palio* and Lina looked in great shape, darkly glossy, high-spirited and elegant, muscles quivering with anticipation. Nerbo, wearing the bright yellow and red silks of the Snails, was controlling her easily with his knees, careful of her delicate mouth.

Knees and hands were all the jockeys ever had as they rode bareback during the trial heats and the *Palio*. But hands and knees were all the *Palio* jockeys ever needed.

The other jockeys steered clear of Lina, and of Nerbo. High up on the mare's withers, he looked tough and mean and invincible.

Briciola, the Turtles' jockey, was visibly drunk, holding the reins stiffly, giving the horse mixed signals. The only thing better than winning was seeing the Turtles lose. Both things were going to happen this *Palio*. Dante could see it. All was right with the world.

It was going to happen. Dante could feel it in his bones. Seventeen long, long years in the wilderness of defeat, his beloved Snails plunged into darkness and mourning after each *Palio* loss. The sniggering comments, the mournful faces, all would be wiped out in the minute and a half it would take Lina and Nerbo to career around the *piazza* and take home the silk banner. Seventy-five seconds of glory.

He felt a sharp nudge and turned to see the weather-beaten face of Gigi Pucci, the oldest Snail butcher. Gigi had lost his wife last year. They had been childless, so he had made the Snail the beneficiary of his hundred thousand euro life insurance policy. "Looking good, eh, Dante?"

"Looking good." Dante smiled and slapped him on his burly shoulder. It was finally looking good. After all these years.

Dante closed his eyes, tuning out the late afternoon sun turning the wall of buildings that impossibly beautiful shade of gold that stunned foreigners and even — at times — touched the flinty Tuscan hearts of the Sienese. Tuning out the raucously blasphemous comments of the men around him and the high-pitched, excited comments of the women. Tuning out everything but what was in his heart.

Looking good.

After seventeen years of bad luck and bad horses and bad judgment, enduring countless sly comments from the other *contradaioli*, finally, finally the Snail was turning the corner.

Dante had been sixteen the last time the Snail had won the *Palio*. But he could remember every moment, every second.

The excellent start out of the ropes, the heartwrenching surge around the *piazza*, the celebratory firing of the gun signaling victory. The roar that had gone up from the Snail contingent, the silk banner of the *Palio* being handed down reverently into the hands of the *contradaioli*, the jockey heading for the celebratory *Te Deum* Mass at the cathedral on the strong shoulders of the youngsters of the *contrada*.

The rest of Siena with doused lights, drapes drawn, shutters closed. In mourning.

Every single Snail was drunk until dawn, most on the wine that flowed from the *contrada* fountain instead of water, only when the Snail won. The next morning a parade of hungover Snails leading the winning horse, with gilded hooves, and mane and tail braided, in a celebratory parade around the city, drums rolling, flags waving.

The September victory dinner. Five thousand people eating and laughing and drinking in the streets of the Snail, celebrating the *Palio*. Later, the victory dinner celebrating the pole of the *Palio* banner. Another victory dinner celebrating the cup of the pole of the *Palio*.

It had been much too long since the last victory.

The square was almost as crowded as the day of the race itself, excitement fairly vibrating in the air. With a roar from the crowd, the horses emerged from the *Palazzo Pubblico*, stepping lightly, almost mincing, jockeys easily riding bareback.

Prime horseflesh, delicate yet tough, responsive to the thousands of eyes, the almost palpable excitement of the crowd. One by one they emerged into the sunlight from the covered courtyard, in an order established eight hundred years before. When the Turtles' jockey moved into the sunlight, the crowd around Dante—Snails all—erupted in boos. Briciola's hard, bony face scowled and he slumped in the saddle.

The Tower, the Panther, and—

There they were! Nerbo and Lina. The cheers and whistles around Dante almost deafened him, though he himself was cheering and whistling harder than most.

Now the horses were lining up between the two ropes, the hardest part of the *Palio*. The horses, quivering, ears pricked, were as excited as the crowd.

Training the horses to line up calmly while remaining ready to take off at the drop of the rope was tantamount to keeping a candle lit while setting off a nuclear reactor.

It didn't matter who won the trial heat, but a good takeoff, a good run, rounding the dangerous curves safely were important—the eyes of the crowd would be on jockey and horse to see how they fared.

Finally, all nine horses were lined up, the tenth on the outer perimeter ten paces back, allowed to enter at a gallop.

The crowd fell silent as the horses pranced in place, the jockeys trying to keep them from touching the *canapo,* the rope. Expectation was ripe in the golden air. Dante could see the *mossiere,* the starter, move toward the medieval machine that would drop the ropes. The starter stretched out his hand and Dante could feel his nerves stretching, too.

In about a minute and a half, two tops, it would be over…

"Dante."

The deep voice behind him wrenched him out of his concentration. He swiveled with a frown. This was *not* the time…

It was Nick with a pale Faith beside him. "I really need to talk to you, Dante."

"Just a minute, Nick."

The horses knew the time was near. The jockeys had to work to keep them in line. Lina raised her head and whinnied. Dante could see the whites of her eyes.

"Now, Dante." Nick thrust a crumpled sheet of paper in his hand. "I need you to read this *now.*"

Seconds now… Dante's heart was thundering in time with the six or seven thousand other Snails in the square, eyes riveted on Lina, who was starting to shy backwards.

"Please, Dante." Nick pushed on the back of Dante's head. Hard. Angling it downwards.

"Hey," Dante said, angry, but the word was drowned out by the *mortaretto's* bang and the roar of the crowd. *They were off!*

Nick's mouth was close to his ear and somehow his voice carried over the delirium of the crowd. "Faith found that in her briefcase. Read it."

First lap, and Saturno, the Panthers' horse, was in the lead. But he was already flagging. Lina was third, and had taken the *San Martino* curve, possibly the most dangerous horse track curve in the world, with sublime elegance.

"Read!" Nick hissed, and jabbed Dante hard in the side with his elbow.

Second lap. Lina was slowly drawing even without breaking a sweat, Nerbo barely tapping her hindquarters with the whip. In following the horses around the racetrack, Dante's eyes fell on Nick's grim face.

There wasn't a man in the world he would look away from a trial heat of the *Palio* for, except Nick. Not even for Mike. With the crowd's wild cries in his ears, he straightened out the crumpled paper.

He read the message once, then twice as the heat finished, and the crowd erupted. Lina had won. The other Snails jumped up and down in delight as his heart sank. A grizzled geezer tried to give Dante a whiskery kiss, but he elbowed him aside.

He looked again at the message.

"Oh, shit," he said, but his voice was drowned out by the roar of the crowd.

Chapter Twelve

When things just can't get any worse, they will.

&

"So what can you tell me? Huh? Who the hell wrote that note? There's got to be a way to tell who the bastard is."

Nick hovered belligerently over Dante, who elbowed him away. "Back off, Niccolò."

"Okay." Nick stepped back half an inch, but craned his chin that same half-inch forward. "So? Who wrote it? Can you tell?"

Nick didn't care when Dante rolled his eyes and sighed heavily for the benefit of his fellow cops. He didn't care that they thought he was obsessed. He was. He knew he was.

They were on the third floor of the *Questura*, one floor above Dante's office. Any other time, he'd be looking around with interest. The place was crammed with odd-looking equipment and he imagined this was the heart of where Dante and his crew sleuthed.

But right now he was more interested in finding out who'd written a threatening note to Faith. Just the memory of those stark words on a white sheet of paper was enough to make him break out in a sweat.

He'd left Faith down on the ground floor, and he and Dante had given the two *ispettori* there strict instructions to keep her in their sight. Then he had doggedly followed Dante up the stairs, bad leg or not.

"Who wrote it?" he asked again.

The note in question was now a crumpled piece of paper covered in gray powder on a Formica-topped table.

Dante turned to the frowning young man who had placed it on the table in pincers. "Mario?"

The man shrugged. "Can't tell, boss. The paper has been handled so much we can't get a clear print. We'll send it to Florence. They have a better lab." He waited politely for Dante and the others to snort, since Siena didn't *have* a lab worthy of the name. "But if they can lift something useful from this, it will be a miracle." He looked at Nick. "Amateurs." His voice was thick with disgust.

"Hey!" Nick rose, upset. "What the—"

"Cut it out." Dante put his hand on Nick's shoulder and pressed. Hard. Nick sat down. "What could've been a very crucial piece of evidence has been crushed and smeared beyond any possible reading of it." He eyed Nick sternly.

"Crime scene evidence mustn't be tampered with. Even if we found a clear print of someone who isn't you and isn't Faith, and that's going to be a real long shot, we wouldn't be able to go to court with it." He snorted. "Nice going, Nick."

Nick was devastated. With a sick lurch in his stomach, he remembered crushing the paper in his hands in fury, then smoothing it out again later with the flat of his palms. He'd folded it up and put it in his pocket, then taken it out a couple of times, holding it flat so he could read the message and get enraged all over again. He remembered crushing the paper over and over again in his pocket as he searched desperately for Dante in the crowd.

Hell, and he'd watched the O.J. Simpson trial almost every day. Because of his stupidity, a murderer might get off scot-free. He hung his head.

Christ, he hadn't been thinking. The only thing on his mind had been to race down to Siena, plow his way through the excited crowds in the *piazza* to find Dante and be in on the arrest.

"Hey." Dante slapped the back of his chair and frowned. "Stop it. There's no fun in jumping on you and chewing you out if you're going to get all depressed and morose on me." He waited a beat. "Nick?"

Nick raised his head. "Sorry," he said between gritted teeth. "I am so sorry." His head whipped around as the tech picked up his hand.

"We need these for reference," the tech said, as he took the prints of each finger, first the left hand then the right, and placed the cardboard strips in a holder. "We need to be able to exclude you. We already have *Signorina* Murphy's prints on file."

"Sure," Nick said miserably.

He looked up as Dante squeezed his shoulder.

"Hey, for your information, people who write threatening notes almost never go through with it."

Almost never. Nick pinched his nose, then realized he was probably leaving ink blotches on his skin. "And that's supposed to make me feel better?"

"Yeah, that's supposed to make you feel better. Go on downstairs, pick up Faith and we'll meet at the *cenone* later tonight."

Nick perked up a little. Incredibly, he'd forgotten that the *cenone*, the good luck dinner held in the streets of all the *contradas* the day before the big race, was tonight. He'd rarely missed one, not even the year he'd busted up his shoulder and had had to travel in a body cast.

Good food, better wine, lots of flirting and shouting out insults to the rival *contradas*, kids sneaking sips of wine, geezers sneaking kisses. The best night of the year, except for the celebratory dinner—that the Snails hadn't celebrated in seventeen years.

"Well, that got you smiling. Come on, get out of here and let me finish up. We'll meet at the *Fonte Gaia* in about—" Dante checked his watch, "—in about two hours, okay? Faith will love it and afterwards you can drive her back to the *Certosa*."

"Before I go, tell me you can at least find out where the note originated. I read somewhere that you can figure out what machine typed a message, then find who used the typewriter."

Dante snorted. "The book where you read that must be a few decades old, when people still used typewriters, and anyway, that was only possible when the typewriter had a defect which matched the defect on the typed page. This note was laser printed, perfectly. Perfect fonts. Perfect toner. There is nothing to distinguish the type of print. There are ten thousand completely compatible printers within a radius of ten kilometers. The *Certosa* has eight printers—all laser. I checked just now."

"So we can't know where it was printed."

Dante sighed. "Nope. And the paper was standard A4, eighty gram weight. Two thousand reams of that paper are sold in Siena every day. And before you say anything, yes, I checked."

"So where do we go from here?"

"I don't know about you," Dante said, fingering his chin. "But I'm going home for a shower and a shave, then to the San Marco." Dante clasped his shoulder. "Come on, Nick, loosen up. Go down and get Faith, celebrate and then drive her back to the *Certosa*. Make sure she locks her—excuse me." The phone rang and Dante picked it up.

"Rossi here." He listened with a frown for a moment, then his face cleared and he nodded his head. "Okay. Right away." He put the phone down and turned to Nick with a grin.

"That was Giorgetti downstairs and he sounded desperate. He wants you to pick up Faith and get her out of here as quickly as possible because she's creaming him at chess and he's never going to live it down."

Faith's opponent was incredibly handsome, even when losing badly at chess. All the police officers in the central station were ridiculously good-looking, which she thought was a bit of a waste in a policeman. What do you need a cute cop for?

Actually, everyone she'd seen so far in this country was impossibly, outrageously, extravagantly good-looking. She'd once read a short story describing a dinner party so elegant everyone looked Italian. She'd never understood that line before.

I do now, she thought, as the young officer flashed a white, thousand-toothed smile. *A nervous smile,* she thought with satisfaction. *And well he should be nervous.*

"Check and mate." She sat back with a gratified sigh.

There was a whoop of derisive laughter from the other police officers milling around the small entrance with the glassed-in reception cage in the corner. The officer in the cage leaned out and shouted a question and received a laughing reply.

The body language of the responding officers could have been read by a Martian. The American lady had whupped Officer Giacometti's ass, and they were all delighted.

The whuppee grinned sheepishly and reached across the chessboard to shake her hand. His grip was firm and dry, and she had to remove her own hand since he was holding it a few seconds too long.

"That's enough, Kasparova," Dante said, and she looked up in surprise at the two Rossi cousins, one smiling and one scowling. "You've created quite enough havoc amongst my men for tonight. I want you and Nick out of here, right now."

The *Questura* was closed to the public after 7:30 p.m., so he unlocked the door himself and shooed them out.

Before Faith could blink, they were out in the fading light of another beautiful Sienese sunset.

She'd been to the *Questura* so often lately she knew the way home. Without question, she turned left and started walking down to the *Via di Città*.

Nick was limping more heavily than usual and, though she didn't want it to, her heart turned over in her chest. Watching a limping Nick was like seeing a wounded panther. He didn't deserve her sympathy, the rat, but he had it, nonetheless.

She took his arm casually and was distressed to note that Nick leaned heavily on her. Casually, as if she wanted to peruse the nonexistent shop windows in the short stretch of street, she slowed down to his speed.

"Did our eagle-eyed sleuths find anything out? Whose prints were on the paper?" She'd calmed down, having figured out who had probably written the note.

"Don't know," Nick answered sourly. "I smudged all the prints beyond recognition. I even crushed the paper then smoothed it out." He shook his head in disgust. "Basically, I destroyed any chance of finding out who printed it out and left it in your briefcase."

Faith looked at him sharply. He wasn't sleeping well and he wasn't shaving well either. That Dick Tracy lantern jaw was stippled with cuts and scrapes, the red scabs matching the red of his eyes. He looked tired and dispirited.

With a pang, Faith realized he blamed himself for the lack of fingerprints.

"Come on, Nick," she said softly.

Lou usually jolted Nick out of his rare down moods with sarcasm and an elbow to the ribs, but he was looking so...so un-Nick, a kinder approach might be better. "Anyone smart enough to print something out and put it in my briefcase unnoticed with an entire gaggle of scientists swirling around, is certainly going to have the smarts to use gloves. Probably those thin latex ones that aren't visible if you don't look too closely. I'm as sure as sure can be that the only prints on that piece of paper are ours."

"We could've nailed the guy. You've got a nutcase loose and he's probably dangerous."

"For writing a note? Oh, come on, Nick."

"For writing a note and murdering that professor of yours."

"He wasn't my professor and anyway, it's a long jump from printing out a note to sticking a knife in someone's heart. No, I don't think if we found the author of the note that we'd necessarily have the murderer. So stop worrying about it." She breathed in the sweet evening air and patted his arm. "Relax now, and enjoy the evening."

"I should've been more careful," he muttered.

Faith abandoned kindness and subtlety. They were pointless around Nick anyway. Once he got an idea into his head, it took a hammer to get it out. "Weren't you listening to what I said? Chances are there weren't any fingerprints to be found. Who is going to write a threatening note and leave fingerprints on it? That would be crazy."

Nick breathed out heavily. "You think so?"

She nodded. "And that's not all." Faith's lips tightened. "I think I know who wrote it."

"You do?" Nick stopped dead in the center of the narrow street. Two people bumped into him and broke out in

Italian vituperation. The volume was impressive. He didn't even budge. "Well, why the hell didn't you say so?"

He gestured with a large hand back up the street.

"Christ, Faith, I just spent an hour while Dante and his men went over that sheet with a fine-toothed comb. I can't begin to tell you how awful I felt when they said they couldn't lift prints.

"And it didn't make any goddamn difference because you knew who did it? What's the matter with you? Why the hell didn't you tell Dante?"

Faith's spine straightened. "Whoa. I didn't say I *knew* who did it. All I said was that I have my suspicions. And I'm certainly not going to talk to a police officer about a hunch."

Nick ran a hand through his dark hair, leaving it sticking out all over his head, making him seem even more like a madman. With his limp, his red eyes, bloody scabs on his large jaw and wild hair, he looked like something an Italian Vittorio Frankenstein might have put together—a wildly attractive monster.

"Well?" he demanded.

Faith tugged on his arm. He'd been standing stockstill in the middle of the busy pedestrian street so long people had started flowing around him as naturally as if he'd been a fountain or a bench. As immovable as a rock and twice as thick. Come on, Nick. Let's see if you can walk and talk at the same time."

She pulled at his arm again and he moved forward slowly, like an ocean liner being tugged out of port. "That's it. One step at a time, left, right, left… See, that's not so hard."

He shot her a fulminating look and she grinned as they moved slowly down the steepest part of the gradient, which would take them to the *Piazza del Campo*.

"You gonna tell me who?" he grumbled.

She sighed. "It's pure speculation, you understand, and I certainly won't repeat this in front of Dante, and don't you dare tell him, but...I think Madeleine left me that note."

"Madeleine...that lanky lady with the beaky nose and gray hair?"

Lanky lady with a beaky nose and gray hair was the best description of Madeleine she had ever heard. "That's the one, yeah. She's been acting very strangely these past few days. And she seems to be obsessed with the fact I—well, that things have been going well for me."

Going well was an understatement. Moderating two panels, being asked to submit another paper to *Quantimath,* Leonardo Gori singling her out for special treatment, her friendship with Paul Allen. She was on a roll.

"She's jealous?"

"Well," Faith grappled with the unfamiliar yet thrilling thought that someone might be jealous of *her.* "Um, I think so. She has more seniority than I do, she's on the staff committee and, for some reason, she was in Kane's good graces. But she isn't going anywhere with her career and she isn't—" Faith stopped. *She isn't as good as I am,* was what she was going to say. It sounded so unlike anything she'd ever say, how could she—

"She isn't as good as I am," a strange voice said, and she almost looked around to see who said that outrageously vain thing.

Nick stopped and nodded, as if she had stated something obvious. "So she sees someone she thought weak coming up from behind, fast, and sticks out the stick to trip them up. Oldest trick in the book."

Faith blinked. "Well, yes. In a manner of speaking." She tugged at his arm again. "Come on, Nick. We can't just stand in the middle of the street all afternoon while you ponder the politics of the math department of St. Vincent's."

"If it's old Beak Nose who wrote that note, I can live with it." Nick started lumbering forward. "She seems harmless enough. It's the thought of anyone else—"

"Oh, Faith! Do wait for us!" an English voice called out.

Faith turned and saw Paul and Tim scampering down the steepest part of the *Via di Città*.

What a pair, she thought, *and how utterly un-Italian they look.* One wildly tall and gangly with a red beard down to the middle of his chest, dressed in cheerfully absurd clothes, a brilliant clown. The other, short and flabby, in a beige shirt and beige shorts, wispy beige hair caught in a thin ponytail, thick beige legs pumping to keep up with Paul.

She couldn't help it. She glanced to her right at Nick, so tall and broad and perfectly formed. So outrageously handsome, looking so completely at home on an Italian street. Then she looked back at Tim.

Nick looked as perfect as the buildings surrounding them—an otherworldly, unattainable perfection.

Tim was beigely clumsy. Inept.

That both men had been her lovers struck her as absurd.

Tim had caught her gaze, moving from Nick's perfect form to himself, to his ugly, bowed legs and, as their eyes met, she saw a flash of hot anger in Tim's.

He had caught her comparing him to Nick and had seen that he'd come out wanting. A flash of a moment that changed everything.

How many times had she herself suffered that? Some man talking to her whose eye had been suddenly caught by a beautiful woman walking by and who then politely turned back to her, already bored? And she could clearly read in his eyes that she had been compared and found wanting. That he wanted to be anywhere but here. That he wanted her to disappear off the face of the earth.

It was the way of the world and it was cruel.

Tim had paled and stopped near a storefront. Paul leaned down and Tim craned his neck as he said something to him. Paul nodded his head once and, with one last look at her, Tim veered off into a side street.

I've hurt him, Faith thought sadly.

Paul waved at her and came striding down the street, his red hair damp and wild around his shoulders. "I'm so glad I caught up with you. Leonardo wanted to talk to you. I said I'd seen you and we went out to look for you, but you'd just...left."

He looked puzzled, as he often did, at the wayward behavior of humans. Faith had been there and then she hadn't and he couldn't seem to connect the two. Faith knew he had no sense whatsoever of time, and in his head, she had disappeared in an instant.

"But you're here now—" he beamed, "—so let's go. Leonardo's saving us a place in his *contrada*. The Eagle. Jolly good name, what?" He laughed, a loud bray. He smacked large, liver-colored lips. "Fabulous food. Leonardo took us to his *contrada* last year."

He frowned. "Or was it the year before last? Never mind. Anyway, he said to be sure to bring you with, if we saw you. So, off we go."

He had taken her gently by the arm, his huge hand curving easily around her biceps, and had started walking.

Leonardo wanted her at the dinner.

There was an etiquette to conferences.

During the conference itself, all participants were equal. But after the conference, only a select few were invited by the host, it being understood that was where contacts were established. Where careers were made.

And she was being asked to sit with The Chosen.

"What did you think of Kabusaki's paper? Interesting notion, what?" Paul pulled her forward and she followed, smiling.

"I think it smacked of some smart undergraduate's thinking," Faith said. "Kabusaki has never shown any signs of original thought before."

Paul threw back his head and brayed to the soft Sienese sky. "Too right, love. And I know who the undergraduate is and where he lives. Brilliant guy." He winked at her. "He'll be invited next year, too, just like you."

Too. Which meant…Paul Allen thinks I am brilliant.

Or did it? Maybe she was reading too much into what was essentially a casual comment. That was easy to do. Maybe he'd meant—

Faith realized they were walking around the curve of buildings that hid the *Piazza del Campo*, and that she'd left Nick behind. She stopped. Paul stopped, too, and looked back, then looked down at her.

"Do you want that chap to eat with us?" he asked doubtfully. He was speaking to her, but his braying voice carried.

Nick was standing behind them on the slope leading down.

"Nick?" Faith called out. "Do you want to come with us?"

She knew what the situation looked like. Two people politely asking a third—an intruder—to join them.

On the one hand, she'd like to eat with Nick. On the other, this was the last night of the conference and she wanted to network, and it would be hard with him distracting her.

Nick swallowed, his throat working up and down visible from a distance. "No," he called out. "Thanks anyway. Do you need a ride back—"

"Not to worry," Paul boomed. "There's a minibus going back up at midnight."

"Okay." Nick smiled weakly. "All right. See you tomorrow. Enjoy the evening."

"You, too," Faith called out. Paul took her arm again and moved her along. She had to scamper to keep up with his long legs.

"There's a thing Leonardo wants to talk to you about. I think you might find it interesting. We've been planning this for the past couple of years and now it's coming to fruition. I'll be interested to know what you think."

"Mm." Faith was barely listening. She craned her neck and saw Nick, still standing in the center of the road, watching them walk away.

He looked lost, and lonely.

"Chio-chio-chiocciola!"
"Chio-chio-chiocciola!"

"Where's Nick?" Mike leaned over to shout in his brother's ear over the noise of the Snails' happy cheers.

"Over there. Avoiding Serenella Gattini's breasts." Dante's fork, on which was speared a slice of boar sausage, pointed to the table set up on the far right of the street. "And brooding."

Serenella was the *contrada* vamp. She was doing her best to attract Nick's attention, all but thrusting her breasts in his face, but Nick wasn't having any. He was sitting and frowning down at the wine in his glass. Luckily, it was a very good one, a *Vernaccia di San Gimignano*, which, at any other time, would have kept him happy. Certainly capable of appreciating breasts.

Mike grinned. "Brooding? Over that girl Lou keeps calling about? Faith?"

"Yeah. She got a threatening letter this afternoon and it threw Nick for a loop."

Mike swung his head around. "A threatening letter?"

Briefly, Dante filled his brother in. Mike did his best to concentrate, but after a minute or two, he was listening with only half an ear, his eyes wandering over the happy crowd. Now was no time to worry about murder and threats.

Dante couldn't agree more. He leaned back in his chair at the podium and surveyed his kingdom. And a rich and satisfying one it was, too.

Trestle tables had been set up along the *Via San Marco* and the *Via della Diana*. There were between five and six hundred people sitting at the tables under the red-and-yellow banners of the Snail, the red-and-yellow bandanas of the Snail around their necks, yelling the Snail cheer.

"*Chio-chio-chiocciola!*"

"*Chio-chio-chiocciola!*"

Mike started singing with the crowd, wildly off-key. He was drinking and eating too much, but he could, since his wife, Loredana, wasn't around to breathe down his neck and recite his cholesterol count like a chant.

Loredana had been born in the Forest *contrada*. Though most of the year Dante thought she was a great sister-in-law, wife and mother, she morphed right into The Enemy come *Palio* time.

She always stayed at her parents' house with the daughter, Carlotta, during the last week before the *Palio* and on the big day itself. The son, Alessandro, stayed with Mike.

Contrada tensions ran too high during the *Palio* for two people of differing *contradas* to share a roof. Or a bed.

Which was fine. Loredana's father, Alberto Conti, was the *capitano* of the Forest *contrada* this year and would have had no compunctions about using his daughter for espionage.

Loredana would have reported right back to her father about whom Mike was seeing and how much was being offered for bribes to which *contradas'* jockeys.

The Forest and the Snail had never been mortal enemies—indeed they'd been tepid allies since 1790—but come *Palio* time, all bets were off.

Right now Loredana was sitting down in *Via Franciosa* wearing a bandana with the green-and-orange colors of the Forest, screaming her head off. *Se-Se-Selva!*

In the years of the Snails' drought, Loredana had come home five times after a Forest win, looking insufferably smug. That had to end.

Tomorrow.

"Chio-chio-chiocciola!"

"Chio-chio-chiocciola!"

The chant went up again from a long table full of teenaged girls. The boys of the *contrada*, pressed into waiter duty, hustled about filling glasses with Chianti and passing out slices of fried polenta from long, steel serving platters.

Dante picked up one of the slices, still hot from the pan, and slipped it into his mouth. It was oily and salty, and crunchy and delicious.

The Snail women had been arguing and planning the menu for seven months now. If the Fates continued to look kindly upon the Snail, the *contrada* would be celebrating tomorrow's victory for the better part of next year.

It would be expensive.

The *Palio* was probably the only horse race in the world where the victor pays. All the bribes offered were nominal — to be paid up only if the *contrada* won. The Snail had a huge war chest, built up over the past years of not winning.

Dante calculated that winning the race this year would cost a hell of a lot of money. Everyone knew the Snail wanted a win badly, and had the horse and the jockey to do it for her, and prices had inflated accordingly. It could cost upwards of a hundred thousand euros to bribe other jockeys and celebrate the win.

Worth every penny.

Celebrations would last all year. Come September would be the victory banquet, where the Snail would host over five thousand people. The guest of honor would be Lina, the winning horse, tethered to the podium of notables and fed a special meal of oats and sugar from the traditional pewter platter.

Through the long winter months, there would be more dinners, seminars on the exact details of the seventy-five second run, with a second-by-second recounting of the glorious event. The school kids of the *contrada* would paint endless posters, which would have pride of place along the San Marco Center's walls. Old men would reminisce, tears in their rheumy eyes, gnarled hands around a shot glass of *grappa*.

Snails would walk a little taller for a year. Snail women would become more beautiful, Snail men more dashing. The glorious win would be fodder for conversation a hundred — a thousand — years from now.

The square was alive with the raucous sounds of *contrada* chants, full-voiced boasts about tomorrow's certain win. Men and women flirted in the dying evening light. The banners overhead ruffled and snapped in the evening air. The breeze made the candles on the long tables flicker.

Except for the clothes, it was a scene that could have taken place five or fifty or five hundred years ago with the same faces, same chants, same behavior. For almost a thousand years, the people of Siena had been celebrating the days of the *Palio* exactly as they were now — by eating, drinking, arguing and laughing.

This time tomorrow night wine would flow from the *contrada* fountain instead of water.

Life didn't get any better than this. Dante put all thoughts of murder and Nick's love life out of his mind and raised his voice.

"*Chio-chio-chiocciola!*"
"*Chio-chio-chiocciola!*"

"*A-a-aquila!*"
"*A-a-aquila!*"

Four streets up, Faith sat at the long table in the cathedral square, smack in the middle of Leonardo Gori's *contrada*, the *Aquila*, the Eagle. She was cheering lustily along with everyone else at the street-length table, wedged tightly in between Leonardo's elegant frame and Paul Allen's gangly length.

Leonardo was looking considerably less polished and cool now, the sweat-stained yellow-and-black *contrada* bandana hanging limply from his neck, eyes wild with excitement.

"*A-a-aquila!*"

Faith chewed a local specialty — *finocchiona* — a light pink sausage made with fennel seed. After the first tentative bite, she'd loved it.

The cheer ended as the next course arrived, a platter of fried vegetables. Faith picked up a fried artichoke, light as air, put it in her mouth and nearly moaned.

Amazing.

The whole scene was amazing. It was the world's largest outdoor restaurant—a whole city neighborhood eating in the streets—hundreds of people wild with yellow-and-black fervor.

Everything and everyone vibrated with excitement, the yellow-and-black silk flags with double-headed eagles flapping overhead, the bright banners hanging from the window sills, the people with yellow-and-black bandanas around their necks almost too excited to sit in their seats and eat.

From further on down the street, a group would start up a song that would be picked up along the huge table's length. It was clearly a song about love, as the girls would sing a refrain and the boys would pick it up, throwing the words back in a slightly different version.

Anticipation and excitement were in the air, and happiness, too.

Faith savored the unusual feelings.

With the bandana around her neck, she had been unquestioningly accepted by the Eagles as one of their own. It didn't matter that she couldn't speak the language and had to answer fevered comments with a shrug and a smile.

The women simply smiled back at her and the men, from the codger across the table to the serving boy who couldn't have been more than fifteen, flirted outrageously, while making sure her plate was kept piled up with food and her glass full of a delicious country wine.

Faith found herself using the flirtation lobe of her brain, atrophied up until now. It was wonderful.

She loved the feeling of being in a group of people all rooting for the same thing. The biggest communal undertaking in Sophie was vandalizing telephone booths, with boosting hubcaps a close second.

But Sophie was then, and Siena was now.

She drew in a deep, happy breath.

The servers were moving down the tables, stepping around the children who ran between their legs. Everyone was a parent as skinned knees were tended to and rowdy fights were stopped by the nearest adult.

Something wildly aromatic was ladled into her dish. Rice, only not any kind of rice she'd ever eaten before.

Leonardo leaned over his plate and took a deep sniff of appreciation. "This is one of the traditional dishes of Siena. *Riso Fratacchione*. The rice of the monks. Monks were known for liking their food. The rice is cooked with the local sausage, *pecorino* cheese and chili peppers. An ancient recipe." He forked a bite into his mouth and closed his eyes. "*Dio mio,*" he murmured. "It's enough to make a non-believer take vows."

Faith smiled and chewed, then closed her eyes, too. Indeed it was.

Paul leaned forward, craning his long neck to talk to Leonardo. "I say, Leonardo, the conference went well this year, don't you think? I thought there were some interesting papers…particularly Faith's." He looked at her warmly. "Jolly good paper that was.

"I e-mailed it to Sanders Whitby and he'll be getting in touch with you about it. He might be asking you to do some follow-up research."

Half of Paul's *risotto* was in his beard, but Faith could forgive him that. She could forgive Paul anything, even his clothes. Sanders Whitby was one of the alpha geeks at that citadel of geekdom, MIT. Whitby was a mover and a shaker. That Paul had brought her paper to his attention was not only incredibly kind but also a major career boost. She felt a rush of gratitude.

"Thanks. Here." She reached for a straw-covered flask, one of many that dotted the tables. "Have some more wine."

"Absolutely." Paul wiped his mouth and beard, leaving only vestiges of the liver patè *crostini* and a few kernels of rice. He downed the glass in three long swallows.

"Marvelous," he sighed. "Even better than last year. Somehow everything here gets better every year." He winked at Faith. "You'll see."

A thrill rushed through her. Did this mean she would be asked back to the Quantitative Methods Seminar next year? It was almost too much to hope for. She knew she'd acquitted herself well, but there were plenty of bright mathematicians in the world. Having attended the Siena seminar even once was more than she'd ever expected.

Paul leaned forward again. "What do you think, Leonardo? Do you think we'll be seeing Faith again next year?"

"Oh, I don't know." Leonardo smiled secretively. "Depends."

On who else had published an interesting paper. On the cross-links Leonardo might have established with other universities in the meantime. On the moon and the tides, for all she knew. Faith understood completely and tried not to feel disappointed Leonardo hadn't immediately said that, of course, she would be here next year.

Leonardo forked in the last large bite of *risotto* and patted his lips elegantly with the paper napkin. He sat back with a pleased sigh and his cheeks blew out delicately in a suppressed belch.

"Have you heard of the *Monte dei Paschi*, Faith?"

Monte dei Paschi…Monte dei Paschi… She'd seen the sign everywhere around Siena.

"A…bank?" she asked.

"Not just *a* bank," Leonardo corrected. "*The* bank. Certainly around here. The oldest bank in the world. It was founded in 1470, and it's been successful ever since. How do you suppose they achieved that? Success for almost six hundred years?"

Faith opened her mouth and closed it.

Leonardo went on. "By staying ahead, my dear. By anticipating events. By riding the crest of the wave." He poured himself some more wine, sipping it appreciatively. "And what's the newest wave?" he went on. "The latest thing? What has to be understood if you want to survive economically in the twenty-first century?"

"The dotcom revolution. The new economy," Faith answered dutifully. "Even if it's tanked, it has to be understood." She shrugged. Any dummy knew that.

"*Esatto!*" Leonardo cried. "Very good, my dear." He patted her hand and leaned closer. "The *Monte dei Paschi*, which has a long and glorious tradition of knowing exactly when to strike and how, has decided that now is the right time to study the new economy. After the dotcom crash, before the next upswell that will muddy the waters again.

"So it is setting up a foundation called the New Economy Foundation, right here in Siena, to study the econometrics of the information revolution. The foundation will be very generously endowed. Very generously. We're calling in the top econometricians in the world. Wanasaki, Morgensen, Kublokov and many others. Plus guest speakers will be coming from the world of the new economy itself. Bill Gates has agreed to come. The head of the Foundation will be Renato Cozzu."

Faith's eyebrows rose. The Sardinian telecom wizard was legendary. He had parlayed a small computer dealership into one of the largest telecommunications industries in the world and had then sold it, when the lire still existed, for an amount of lire too big to fit onto a pocket calculator.

"The Foundation will be working closely with the University of Siena Math Department. I will be vice president of the Foundation."

"Sounds interesting." That was an understatement. It sounded like a groundbreaking event. What a privilege to be one of the first to hear of it.

"Yes, very." Leonardo poured her some more wine.

She sipped, getting a little buzz from the alcohol, a bigger buzz from the feeling on the inside of something new and big.

"We're calling in the best people we can find to carry out one-year study programs within the Foundation. And that's why, my dear Faith—" He filled her glass again.

How had her glass gotten empty so soon?

"That's why Renato and I thought we'd like to offer you a year's contract, starting now. He was quite taken with your paper."

"That's nice—" she started, then stopped. Everything stopped for an instant. Brain, heart, breath. Her eyes widened. "A year's— You want...*me?*"

"Now you mustn't worry about your job at St. Vincent's, my dear." Leonardo patted her hand. "I've already spoken with Griffin and he's willing to suspend your contract for a year, with a guaranteed job after the year is over. He said it was worth it to the department to have someone from St. Vincent's working on such an important project."

Faith's head swam. "Leonardo, I don't know what to say. I just—"

"Well, you say yes, of course." He frowned at her. "We do understand you'll have to give up your apartment, your job and your friends for a full year, but we can make it worth your while. We were thinking of a stipend of fifty thousand dollars for the year."

She choked. Her salary last year had been on the stingy side of twenty thousand dollars and it covered bread, but not butter, and certainly not jam. Fifty thousand dollars would mean walking in tall corn.

She would have to give up a one-room, basement apartment the landlord called a studio apartment but which had originally been the laundry room. It was damp and cold in the winter, and damp and hot in the summer. Her friends... The only real friends she had were Lou and Nick, and they came over here often anyway.

"We would pay for an apartment in the center of Siena and settling-in costs. Say...ten thousand? Tax-free, of course. Americans abroad don't pay taxes on the first seventy thousand dollars, so the money would be free and clear."

"This is so sudden." She shook her head, wondering if the alcohol had damaged her brain. "It's hard to—"

"We'll pay your trip back, so you can wrap things up in Deerfield. Business class, of course."

"Of course," she murmured. She'd never flown anything but cattle class.

A group of youngsters sitting at the next table over burst into song. The way she was feeling, it should have been the theme from *Rocky*, but a *contrada* song did just fine. Just fine.

"Ah, that's settled then." Leonardo sat back in his chair with a sigh and pulled a green bottle from a bucket of ice under his chair. "*Pinot Brut,*" he said reverently, and popped the cork. He gestured to one of the boys, who brought some champagne flutes on the run.

Paul had been talking to Jean-Pierre on his right, but turned his head at the pop. "So she accepted, eh? Jolly good. It's going to be an interesting mix of people at the Foundation. I guess we'll be seeing a lot of you, Faith. I'm going to be a Foundation consultant."

He held out his big hand and Leonardo put a flute in it. Paul downed it in one swallow. "Ah, fine stuff. I'm really looking forward to spending a lot of time here." He winked at Faith and held the glass out again.

"You knew?" she asked. "You knew Leonardo was going to ask me? Is that what you were talking about?"

"Sure," he said, sipping his second glass more slowly. "Leonardo asked me what I thought about the idea, and I said absolutely." He flicked food from his beard and his wild, intelligent eyes lit up. "I have a colleague at Cambridge who's working on nonlinear economic behavior. He'll be coming in for week-long seminars. You'll like him. He said he wanted to work on a project with you."

Leonardo poured some *spumante* for Jean-Pierre and slid it down the table. "*Félicitations, chérie,*" Jean-Pierre said, lifting his flute.

Up the hill, Grif saw the *spumante* and celebratory air and grinned. He clasped his hands and raised them over his shoulders like a prizefighter who'd won the championship. Grif turned to Madeleine sitting next to him and said something.

Madeleine straightened and shot Faith a vicious look, chilling her. Then Faith shrugged. The hostility was Madeleine's problem, not hers.

Leonardo nodded to Grif and shot his thumb in the air. He turned to Faith. "Griffin was certain you'd say yes, my dear. But I haven't actually heard *you* say it. So what's your answer? Will you accept a year's contract at the New Economy Foundation?"

A man's voice called something out and the table around her erupted in laughter and cheers, the noise echoing off the walls.

It was almost night. Only a faint glow remained in the sky. The street was lit by torches fixed into slots in the ground and candles on the tables. It would have been a romantic, dreamy scene except for the nervous energy erupting all around her. She'd never felt so alive in all her life.

"Yes," Faith said. "Oh, yes."

Chapter Thirteen

Don't lose heart... They might want to cut it out.

৪৩

The morning of the *Palio* found Dante at his desk at 7:00 a.m. without his cappuccino and *cornetto*. He'd had no choice but to come into the office in that sorry state at what, for him, was the crack of dawn.

Where on earth could he stop for breakfast?

There wasn't a bar in town where he wouldn't have been detained for at least an hour, chewing over probabilities and jockey peculiarities or—in his own *contrada*—exulting in the certain upcoming win. He didn't want to waste any time today. He wanted to be out and free by eleven to watch the last trial heat at 12:30 p.m.

Otherwise there was nothing in this world which would have him sitting at his desk at seven—on an empty stomach!—instead of lying in his bed, preferably with a partner. A pretty one.

He had walked into the *Questura* with the bravado of the utterly virtuous and had been disgruntled to see Loiacono already in the big, airy, communal office all the inspectors shared, hunched over some papers.

Dante stuck his head through the door. "*Ciao,* Loiacono."

The southerner looked up and blinked owlishly as if torn from his thoughts, and Dante could see that it took Loiacono a moment to register his presence. Then he shot to his feet before Dante could say, "Don't rise."

"I'll be in my office," Dante told him. *But not before making myself some coffee*, he thought, and headed for the interrogation room.

"*Commissario*, there's something I think you should read." Loiacono picked up the papers from his desk and swiveled like a robot to follow Dante's progress.

Probably the thousandth ministerial circular this year, Dante thought with a sigh. They seemed to have the power of Holy Writ for Loiacono.

"Uh-huh," he said without enthusiasm. "Just as soon as—"

"The Deerfield Police Department e-mailed some information on the Americans up at the *Certosa*," Loiacono interrupted. "Sir, I was just now looking through it."

Dante had been reaching up for the *Lavazza* coffee kept next to the 1998 edition of the *Civil Code* that no one ever read. "Deerfield?" He dropped back to his heels, the coffee forgotten. "I didn't know you could read English, Loiacono."

Loiacono stood stiffly. "Seven years at the Naples British Institute. Night classes, sir."

Even his voice sounded stiff. Dante squelched a sigh. Now he'd gone and ruffled those sensitive southern feathers and was going to have to repair the damage. On an empty stomach, to boot.

"Well, I must've missed that in your file, Loiacono. But be sure that I'll mention your superior knowledge of English in my report to the *Vice Questore*, and that it's been of invaluable service to the case. The *Vice Questore* will be delighted that we have, ah—" Was he laying it on too thick? "That we have such forward-looking officers in our service." Dante wound down.

Loiacono hadn't changed expression.

"So—what did Deerfield say? Anything interesting?"

"Very." Loiacono looked grim. He always looked grim, but there was a special quality to it this morning. "Very interesting. It looks like Madeleine Kobbel neglected to tell us she was married to Professor Roland Kane."

At the *Certosa*, Nick leaned against the wall, arms crossed, staring at Faith's closed and locked door, as he had been doing for the last two hours.

He'd watched the dawn from the big windows facing one of the smaller inner courtyards, as the sky turned from pale gray to robin's egg blue. It would be bright cobalt by the midday trial heat, and would be light blue tinged with red-gold by late afternoon.

Restless, he jingled the keys to his grandparents' house, the keys to his grandfather's Dedra and the heavy euro coins in his pocket. A door to one of the rooms facing the courtyard downstairs slammed shut and he could hear voices drifting up.

An old man in overalls shambled out with a hose and started watering the plants—roses and some other flowering bushes Nick couldn't even begin to identify. The sharp smells of heat and dirt and water drifted up—the smells of Italy in summer.

It was the day of the July *Palio*. He'd been in Siena on this day or the day of the August *Palio* at least twenty-five times in his life, and each and every time he'd been happy. Consumed with eagerness if the Snail was running, simply excited at the pageantry when it wasn't, but always, always happy. Not being happy was so foreign to him it was almost like being in another country.

It was humbling, right now, to realize how happy he'd been all his life, how blessed he'd been in his family and profession, how easy things had always been for him, what a smooth progression his life had been up until now.

Faith hadn't been so lucky and yet she'd faced her difficulties with a degree of courage and grit and humility that shamed him. He'd been off balance for days now, withdrawn and…sulking. That was the only word for it. The first real hardships of life and he'd stumbled, almost fallen, and had to be picked up by his family.

No more. He still had no idea what he was going to do with the rest of his life, and he might drift for a while, but no more sulking, no more feeling sorry for himself.

He would take it one day at a time, one task at a time. And task number one, right now, was seeing that Faith got back to the States safely.

Last night he had convinced Egidio Pecci, the porter, to let him have the empty room next to Faith's. He'd slept fitfully, one ear cocked for trouble next door, and had risen at dawn, restless, worried about Faith.

She was alive and unharmed, though. Of that he was sure.

Half an hour ago, he'd heard the window shutters opening, then the shower running. And, delightfully, he'd heard her voice raised in song, some pretty Irish ballad.

Her voice was soft and tentative but lovely, which didn't surprise him. He was beginning to realize she did a lot of things well. She might hide her light under a bushel, but it was a strong light. And a stupid bushel.

Quick approaching footsteps and then her door opened.

"Nick!" She stopped on the threshold, eyes wide. "What on earth are you doing here?"

"Making sure you're okay," he muttered as his muscles tensed. He was going to catch hell for this.

Her eyebrows drew together. "Have you been out here all night?"

It felt like it. "No. Egidio let me sleep in the room next door." He shifted his weight off his bad knee and stuck his jaw out. "The room next to yours was empty and I felt better sleeping there than at my grandparents'. I'm sorry if you think I'm interfering, but I just needed to know that you were safe."

He winced and braced himself for the coming tirade. All the usual stuff about how she didn't need him and she was fine and he was in her way and he should go. "I'll be going back to town soon, don't worry."

"Thanks, Nick." To his astonishment, her face softened. She bent to lock the door and turned back to him. There was a smile on her face, one of the very few directed at him he had seen lately. "As you can see, I'm alive."

She certainly was.

There was something different about her this morning. She was wearing a red sundress he'd never seen before and her hair was up, but that wasn't it. She had high color beyond the light tan the Sienese sun had given her and she vibrated with excitement, a spring ready to be sprung.

She walked over to him and, to his surprise, took his arm. "Come on. If you were my guard dog all last night, the least I can do is offer you a nice breakfast. And the *Certosa* breakfasts are about the best around."

Cautiously gauging her mood, Nick let himself smile down at her. "That's because you haven't had breakfast at *Nannini's* yet. I swear they make the best coffee and pastries in the world. Too bad you won't have a chance to try them out. You're leaving tomorrow morning, aren't you?"

Did she squeeze his arm? On the off chance that she had, he tucked her hand more closely into the crook of his elbow.

"Mm," she said ambiguously and started descending the stairs, slowly, so he could keep up.

She was still smiling. This must be some kind of record. He decided to push his luck a little. "You folks, ah, going to see the *Palio*? You can't miss it. It's quite a sight. It would be a shame to come all the way over here and leave without seeing it. Who knows when you'll come by this way again?"

Her smile deepened and she looked up at him. In the early morning light her light brown eyes looked tawny, like fine brandy, and just as intoxicating.

"You never know," she said as they reached the ground floor.

They crossed the flowering quadrangle and walked through the small archway leading to the main courtyard. They both stopped as if on cue to admire the scene — bright green grass, towering dark green and brown oak, brick walkway. The big ancient oak tree in the center was so huge its canopy covered the sky while they walked under it toward the refectory.

Even if he didn't know where the refectory was, he could have found it by smell and sound. The fragrance of freshly brewed espresso and warm *cornetti* was a counterpoint to the sounds of dishes clattering and male voices raised in laughter.

Faith raised her head to the sky and breathed in deeply. Her throat arched, soft and smooth, and his hand itched to touch it. Just once, just run his finger along its smooth, pale length to see if her skin was as soft as he remembered. He clenched his teeth and put his hand in his pocket.

Up ahead, heavy terra-cotta planters on the arched walkway a floor above spilled bright red flowers down several feet like a vibrant, colored curtain. The delicate, lacy blossoms swayed gently in the morning breeze. Nick slowed his pace to enjoy the contrast of the red flowers against the red highlights the bright, early morning sun picked out in Faith's hair.

Instead of entering the ground floor walkway through one of the four entrances cut into the low wall, Faith stopped and patted the broad gray stone surface of the wall. "Sit down. I have an idea. It's so beautiful outside, why don't we have our coffee here? I'll ask one of the waiters if they'd be willing to serve us out here on a tray. They might. They've all been so nice."

She smiled up at him, slim and vibrant in the morning light, and he thought the waiters would probably run into Siena to get her coffee, if she asked.

"Sounds great."

It did, too, because out here it might be easier to carve out a little private time with her without having to share her with the geeks still in the breakfast room, inhaling *cornetti* or whatever it was geeks ate.

Already in the courtyard there was probably enough brainpower to run a third world country. There were at least five geeks lounging in the cloisters, eyeing Faith, clearly hoping to catch a word with her. His glare kept them away.

There would probably be another thirty of them inside, and there'd be no hope of sitting at a table alone with Faith for more than a minute. Yeah, it was better to stay out here.

He brushed the gray slab of stone, which still retained the cool of the night, and sat down heavily. His knee really hurt.

Faith came out from the refectory empty-handed and he stood. Obviously, it wasn't going to be possible to have their coffee outside, so… He smiled appreciatively and shook his head in wonder.

Two waiters were following Faith, one carrying a little round table and the other carrying two cane-bottomed chairs. While one waiter set up the table on the grass, whisking a cotton tablecloth over it, the other disappeared for a moment, returning with a filled tray.

"*Ecco signorina,*" the first waiter said, with a broad sweep of his arm. He pulled back a chair and waited. Faith smiled as she sat and glanced up at him.

"*Grazie.* To both of you."

They bowed and went back inside.

"Don't just stand there, Nick," she said serenely as she poured two cups of coffee for them. There were four *cornetti,* slices of bread, pats of butter, a small jar of honey and a pot of steaming milk. "Come have breakfast."

The waiter had put the chairs facing each other, but he wanted to sit next to her. He pulled the chair over and sat down. "You put something in the water here? Either that or you've cast a spell on them. Tuscans aren't usually so obliging."

Faith laughed. "Maybe they're being so nice because they know that soon they'll see the back of us. The conference is over, except for a few ceremonial speeches. By eleven they'll be sweeping out the conference rooms. Then we're going down to see your precious *Palio*." She nudged a *cornetto* onto his plate. "From all the fuss, you'd think it was the second coming."

"Oh, better." Nick stuffed a big bite of pastry in his mouth and chewed happily. It wasn't *Nannini's*, but still worlds better than the rubbery donuts his corner coffee shop in Deerfield served up. "I don't imagine the second coming will be pretty to look at."

"Nope. I'm sure the *Palio* will be better." Faith sipped from her cup, closing her eyes and sighing.

Nick sidled closer with his chair. Now was the time to take a shot at it.

"Listen, Faith, I know you want to be with your geeks — sorry, your colleagues — but I'd love to have you watch the race with me. We have a cousin, actually not quite a cousin, his mother grew up with—" He waved his hand impatiently. "Never mind. Anyway, we always watch the *Palio* from his balcony, which gives right out onto the *piazza*."

He smiled tentatively. "Best seats in the house. And you can go to the bathroom, something you can't do out in the square."

Her eyes had slowly opened and she was listening with a faint smile on her face. "Well." She shook her head. "Bathroom rights sound like a deal-clincher." She pulled in a breath and let it out slowly.

"Tell you what, Nick, I'll talk to Leonardo about it. I think the business part of the conference is over. If he thinks it's okay for me to desert him this afternoon, I'd love to watch the *Palio* from your cousin's balcony. I think we're all going down this morning for the trial heat."

"The last one. It's called the *provaccia.*"

"Tell me about it. The—pro...what?"

Nick smiled. He was on familiar ground here. "*Provaccia.* It's the last trial heat before the race and less exciting than the other ones. Basically they just canter the horses around the square. The jockeys don't want to tire the horses out. It's the *Palio* that's the important thing."

"And the *Palio* itself is at what—6:00 p.m.?"

"6:30 p.m. The August one starts at 6:00 p.m. because the sun sets earlier."

She shook her head. "Two big horse races in the space of six weeks. Weird."

Across the way, Paul Allen, in red and orange shorts and not much else, was talking earnestly with a skinny Japanese man who came to his breastbone. Allen stooped to take off his enormous sandals, whacked them together, sole to sole, and threw his head back, braying with laughter.

Nick's eyes slid back to Faith. "You hang around with guys like that and you find two *Palios* weird?"

She poured more coffee into her cup, added sugar and stirred. She was playing it cool, but was having trouble suppressing a smile. "He's probably discussing amicable numbers. He's an expert."

Allen had slipped his sandals back on, on the wrong feet, and had opened his immensely long arms. He flapped them vigorously.

"Jesus." Nick shook his head. "What kind of numbers are those?"

Faith put her index fingers to her lips, considering. "Takanara's English is very sketchy. I think Paul's trying to tell Takanara that he's flying back home tomorrow. Paul—" She sighed. "Paul's neurons pop to a different drummer."

"Do they ever." Nick dismissed the crazy geek from his mind. He cut a *cornetto* in half. "Here, try this. It's great." He nudged the pastry against her lips. "Open up."

She obliged, and chewed and sighed. "Good," she murmured.

Nick watched her swallow and had to swallow himself. *Christ, she's lovely.* Why hadn't he ever noticed that last winter? He'd gone out with Lou and Faith at least a couple times a month all winter, and he'd never really looked at her.

She was driving him crazy. Like the roses in the growing heat of the day, she gave off an intoxicating smell of soap, shampoo and the warm skin of woman.

She raised her face, smiling into the morning's warmth. She was so pretty, long pale neck gleaming, smooth slender shoulders bare except for the skimpy straps of her sundress. The dress she was wearing was very revealing. For one thing, it revealed she wasn't wearing a bra.

The material was soft and clingy and he could see her small nipples pushing against the fabric and was blown away by sensory memories of taking those nipples into his mouth. His hand cupping that soft mound. Her hair fanned out over his pillow, her moans…

"Lean over." He barely recognized his voice. It sounded thick and distant.

She didn't jump or look quizzical. As if it were the most normal thing in the world for a man to be blasted by lust in her presence, she looked over and her mouth lifted in a half smile. "Nick," she murmured.

"Here." He was reduced to monosyllables. "Now." He hooked a finger into the bodice of that revealing dress and pulled. She didn't resist. She moved slowly but steadily toward him and he felt as if she were moving through water, it was that slow.

Finally, finally, there she was, her mouth against his, and he opened his mouth over hers. "Come closer," he whispered.

He put his hands on the metal armrests and pulled her and the chair toward him. The way he was feeling, he would have pulled the entire *Certosa* toward him if it meant getting closer to her.

Faith sighed and moved her tongue against his…

The loud crash drove them apart. Nick jumped to his feet and pulled Faith behind him. She peeped out from his side and they both stared at the heavy terra-cotta planter now in shards, the earth strewn around it in a star from the force of the impact. It had fallen exactly where Faith had been sitting five seconds before.

The sound of running footsteps sounded loud in the shocked silence.

"I saw it! Up there!" Paul Allen shouted, pointing up to the second floor where the planter had been, and took off with surprising speed for the corner stairs. He disappeared up them in an instant, the skinny Japanese hard at his heels.

Nick contemplated following him, but nerdy though he might be, Paul Allen didn't have a bum knee and could probably run faster than he could. Besides, he could feel Faith trembling behind him and he didn't want to leave her alone and scared.

He turned, blocking Faith's view, but she'd seen enough. So had he.

The vase and earth must have weighed a hundred pounds. Dropped from a height of twenty feet, it would have been enough to kill Faith if it had landed on her. If he hadn't been dying to kiss her, it would have fallen straight on her head and cracked her skull like an eggshell.

Nick turned and took her in his arms, and, with a whimper, she burrowed there. He put a hand to her head and dropped a kiss on her hair. She couldn't feel it, but that didn't matter. All that mattered was that she was alive. His arms tightened.

"I say!" Allen descended the stairs, his pale face blotched with red patches of emotion and anger. "Be still, you!"

He was holding a wriggling Madeleine Kobbel by a huge hand wrapped around her right biceps. He could have wrapped his hand twice around her arm.

The woman was jerking and pulling, but there must have been more muscle than Nick gave him credit for in those long skinny arms, because Allen didn't give an inch. He wrapped his other hand around her left arm and held her at arm's length.

"Let — me — *go!*" Kobbel jerked again and aimed a vicious kick at his prominent, white, hairless shinbone.

Allen's face was splotchier than before and he was breathing heavily.

"Easy there." His arms were so long she had no hope of reaching him. "Settle down now, Madeleine."

She was breathing heavily. "Let me go, you English bastard," she snarled, and tried to wrench herself away.

Allen blinked, surprised. "Actually, my dear," he said seriously, "my parents have been married since 1957, well before I was born."

She screamed in frustration and wrenched so hard he had to open his hands in order not to hurt her. She screeched and rushed forward, hands out in claws. She was almost at Allen's surprised eyes when Nick grabbed her by the waist from behind. She writhed in his grasp.

"Stop it," he said coldly.

Something about his voice and the strength of his hold must have penetrated her hysteria, because she subsided, sobbing and shaking. He looked down at the shattered vase.

She tried to aim a kick at him and he put a little muscle into his grasp. "Watch it, lady. You almost killed Faith, and I'm not feeling very charitable at the moment."

Kobbel straightened and wiped her face with shaking hands. "I—I don't know what you're talking about. I was walking along the corridor when this madman—" She glared at Allen. "When he grabbed me and pulled me downstairs."

Her head twisted as she looked at them—Paul Allen, the Japanese guy, Faith, and finally at Nick. Her mouth turned down. She shot a venomous look at Paul Allen. "I'm going to sue you for assault, and you—" She glared up at Nick.

She sounded vicious but sane, so he opened his hands and she stepped back.

"I can just see the headlines back home. *'Athlete Manhandles Woman'*. Your career will be over in an instant. I can guarantee that."

"Too late for that," Nick said. "And I wouldn't be so quick to lawyer up, lady. My cousin's a cop, and what do you want to bet that he'll find your fingerprints all over that vase."

They all looked solemnly down at the vase, smashed to smithereens. Nick doubted very much that any shards large enough to hold fingerprints were left, but he was a firm believer in the adage, when in doubt, lie.

He pulled out his cell phone and punched in Dante's number. "Dante? Yeah. You might want to come up to the *Certosa*. I think we've found your murderer."

Chapter Fourteen

If you think the problem is bad now, wait until it's solved.

&

In the excitement, the conference was *de facto* adjourned. In the breakfast room, a shocked Leonardo declared the closing session over before it began and announced that Faith Murphy would be drafting the final report, to be published in the proceedings.

Faith, taken totally unawares, had nodded sagaciously, then realized like a bludgeon upside the head that she'd just said okay to listening to sixty hours of taped discussions, transcribing the proceedings and drafting a twenty-page report.

No one was even listening to Leonardo make his announcements. Madeleine Kobbel, Roland Kane, possible motives for murder, where to have a good lunch in town and the upcoming *Palio*—these were the topics of conversation. The participants seemed to find it all "jolly entertaining", in Paul Allen's words.

In less time than Faith would have imagined possible, Dante and his minions had come up, carefully gathered the tangled mass of shards and dirt and mangled flowers—she could hardly look at the mess without shuddering—handcuffed Madeleine, who was now hysterically crying, and driven off with her, Nick, Paul Allen and Takanara.

She didn't mind Dante driving off with Madeleine, but unfortunately he insisted on driving off with Nick, too. Nick had been visibly reluctant to go, which warmed her heart. He'd left her his cell phone number and they'd made an appointment to meet at *Piazza del Campo ventiquattro*, twenty-four, at 4:00 p.m. to see the race.

The abandoned agenda didn't disturb anyone. The mathematicians found the attempted murder infinitely more interesting than the morning's scheduled program.

Particularly since the waiters had set up a little, impromptu banquet in the courtyard ferrying coffee and sandwiches for the police officers. The participants had ripped right in, too, and it had had the ghostly feel of a phantom coffee break at a nonexistent conference.

Faith's hand had been patted innumerable times and she'd been asked over and over again if she was all right. She clearly was, and the patting was getting annoying.

Particularly annoying was Tim, who must have asked her a thousand times if she was okay, and who insisted on having her tell him over and over again exactly what had happened.

Since Faith had had to give him a heavily edited version of the truth, it was getting tedious. Not to mention the fact she was anticipating more of the kisses she'd edited out of her story for Tim.

He stuck by her side like a leech. *Indeed,* she thought irritably, *he looks like a worm, with his beige hair and beige T-shirt and beige shorts and beige legs. Soft and somehow slimy.*

She knew she was being uncharitable, but she couldn't help it.

"I'm *fine*, Tim," she said sharply for the hundredth time.

They were being herded into four minivans by Leonardo, who had given up on even pretending that a little work could be done today and had arranged to ferry them all down to Siena.

"I was so scared for you," Tim said simply, and she shut up.

It wasn't his fault he wasn't Nick. Why was she so irritated with him?

She scooted over to the far side of the minivan and Tim climbed in after her.

Faith sighed. "Thanks, Tim. But in the end, no harm was done."

His jaw tightened. "Maybe. But that wasn't her intention."

No, Madeleine's intention had been to crack her skull. And she'd almost succeeded. Faith hadn't asked it yet, but now she had to. "Why me? What did I ever do to her? I thought we were friends?"

"Why you?" Tim turned in his seat to look her full in the face.

The van was dipping and rocking back on its suspension as the other conference participants climbed in. Finally the driver slid the van's door shut and started the engine.

"Jealousy. And Leonardo offering you the job at the New Economy Foundation just tipped her into insanity."

"Jesus." Faith stared at Tim. She hadn't seen Tim last night at the *cenone* and hadn't had a chance to talk to him this morning. "How did you know about that?"

He smiled. "Math jungle drums. Fastest communication vector known to man.. No, actually, Grif told me over breakfast. I think it's great, Faith. And you really deserve it."

While Faith heartened to Tim's unusual praise, he sneaked in a chance to lean over and peck her on the cheek, and took her hand.

He smiled, showing dull, gray teeth. "I love Siena," he said. "And if you're going to be spending a year here, that'll be my chance to come over more often."

Faith withdrew her hand and barely stopped herself from rolling her eyes. *Damn him!* Tim obviously wasn't reading her face language, her body language or her language language. She couldn't speak her thoughts out loud in a van full of colleagues, so she looked out the window instead.

It was the diplomatic choice, and had the added advantage that the countryside was much better looking than Tim Gresham.

"So, Professor Kobbel, you have a lot of explaining to do." Dante felt like a character in a Hercule Poirot story at the denouement of the novel.

They should have been in the darkened library of an English country manor, rain lashing the windows, his elbow propped on the mantelpiece. Instead, they were in his sunny office, window open to the view of rooftops stretching away toward *Via di Città*.

Kobbel had finally stopped weeping hysterically, for which he was profoundly grateful. Dante was well aware of the many weaknesses of his character. One of the greatest was he couldn't stand to see a woman crying. Even a lying, murdering woman's tears could unman him.

Dante had sat rigidly in his chair, jaws and hands clenched, while she'd wept tears of rage and frustration. Finally, finally, the storm passed and she sat quietly, head bowed, fingers picking at the stiff fabric of her skirt.

Now he could talk to her rationally. He leaned forward. He wanted to start slowly, work his way up to attempted murder and then the real thing. "Professor Kobbel, this morning Faith Murphy was almost killed by a terra-cotta vase dropped from a great height. She missed death by inches. That is attempted murder and it is a serious crime in this country. It carries a mandatory sentence of seven years in jail."

Her jaw worked upwards, giving her face a mulish cast. "Well, I'm sorry it happened, but it has nothing to do with me. I was upstairs in my room, minding my own business when all the commotion down in the courtyard attracted my attention—"

Dante sighed. "Before you go any further, professor, I think you should know that the vase broke in shards large enough to show fingerprints. And my fingerprint tech has found a match."

He was lying through his teeth. The vase had shattered into tiny pieces and dust. Even if the pieces had been larger, terra-cotta was much too porous a medium to take prints.

And anyway, his fingerprint tech, Lionello Pucci, who had taken a six-week course in Rome a few months ago and was still enthusiastically, though profitlessly, reviewing the course material, would never have been able to make a match. The pieces would have had to go to Florence, where it would have taken them days to give an answer.

Nonetheless, Madeleine Kobbel had paled on cue and he had his answer.

Any further comments would be superfluous. He put on his knowing, can't-get-anything-past-a-cop look and waited. And sure enough—

"It's not fair. She's only here in Siena on sufferance because Tim couldn't come. Roland wanted her to help with the organizing and administration. Faith's a nobody. A *nobody!*

"A TA, for Christ's sake, and not even a good one at that. She's boring in class and her students can barely hear her. She doesn't contribute anything to the running of the course. She never speaks up in admin meetings. People never even know she's there.

"Okay," she shrugged irritably, "so maybe she's written a few interesting papers, but so what? She's a nobody and all of a sudden she comes over here and she's a — she's a *star*. It's not fair."

And so you try to drop fifty kilos of vase and dirt and geraniums on her head, Dante thought. But that was only the *antipasto*. Time to move on to the main course.

He tapped a pen on his blotter. "It seems, Professor Kobbel, that you neglected to tell us something. Something very important."

She looked up, eyes red-rimmed, lids half-lowered. Heavy lines bracketed her mouth. She was looking singularly unattractive and Dante felt sorry for her. Being bony and plain was hard enough, without the prospect of spending at least twenty years for the attempted murder of Faith Murphy and the murder of Roland Kane in the *Volterra* prison, where she would come out bonier and plainer and sixty-seven years old.

"Why didn't you tell me you were married to Roland Kane?"

She looked utterly surprised, as if he'd suddenly started discussing soccer scores. Her brow creased. "What?"

Dante tapped the paper in front of him. "You were married to Roland Kane from 1985 to 1989. The two of you lived in San Francisco, where he was a Professor Emeritus at City College and you were a teaching assistant. I've been investigating Roland Kane's murder and have spoken to you on several occasions. Didn't you think your marriage to him was noteworthy? That you should've mentioned it?"

She shrugged and brushed long, gray bangs away from her brow. "It was a long time ago."

Dante's back teeth ground. "That might be, but it's still very pertinent. What happened?"

She looked startled again. "What do you mean?"

"The marriage ended. Why?"

"You've spoken with people...Roland's colleagues, *Commissario* Rossi. You must have a good idea why the marriage broke down. It was impossible being married to him. It only lasted as long as it did because of—" She stopped and bit her lip.

Dante didn't have to look down at the report on his desk. "Because of the child. A girl."

Her eyes lifted to his and he could see an ancient, wild grief there. It was such an intense, intimate look into her, into the very heart and soul of her that he wanted to avert his eyes. The part of his heart that could never be closed to a woman shifted and opened a little.

"Lauren," she whispered. She swallowed and Dante watched her thin throat contract. "Lauren was born with multiple birth defects. I had to quit working to take care of her. She needed a lot of medical attention and the hospital bills mounted up.

"Roland behaved very badly. He moved out of the house the day I came home from the hospital with Lauren. He couldn't stand to look at her. We stayed married because his job had medical benefits. He filed for divorce the day she died."

Dante knew the sick pity he felt didn't show on his face. He'd never even come close to marriage, had always been careful with protection, and was as sure as any man could be about that sort of thing that there were no kids of his running around. He also knew that the day he got married and had children...that was it—he'd be no more capable of deserting them than he could fly to the moon. No Rossi could.

"And yet you joined him in Massachusetts years later."

Madeleine Kobbel gave a short laugh. "I was going nowhere academically, and my three-year hiatus hadn't helped. When Roland called me out of the blue, I thought—"

Her hands twisted in her lap. "I thought he'd, I don't know...repented."

Her hands flew up like pale, bony birds. "I thought somehow he was sorry for the way he'd behaved. That's insane, of course," she added bitterly. "Roland doesn't— didn't—feel anything."

And as a direct consequence of that, he'd died, Dante thought.

"I was without a job," she continued. "So I was more than willing to come to Massachusetts. Only I didn't get a job in Deerfield either. Not right away anyway. Roland wanted me to do his scut work on his book for him. The typing, the editing, doing the minor calculations.

"I'd been out of the academic world for many years by that point. My career was over. So when he arranged a job on the staff at St. Vincent's, of course I said yes. It was perfect for him. I was utterly beholden to him and could be counted on to do what he wanted. He was a hateful man."

This last was said in a low, vicious whisper. Her jaw muscles bunched as she sat staring at her hands. Dante let the silence seep into the room. Outside his window, the streets were quiet, that peculiar quiet of the day of the *Palio*, when the whole city held its breath, waiting, waiting.

"So hateful you killed him."

"No." Her hair swung back and forth as she shook her head. "No, I hated him, but I was dependent on him. I'd be without a job if it weren't for him. And now that he's dead, I'll lose my job. God knows where I'll find another one. Certainly not in the academic world."

It was a good try. Dante recognized that. And maybe a line her defense lawyer would take. And no doubt she'd have all the time in the world to reflect on Roland Kane's sins as she stared out the windows of the prison at the moonscape around *Volterra*.

"Professor Kobbel," Dante said, rising.

Her eyes followed him up.

"I am going to read you your rights and call the American consulate in Florence to see that you get legal representation. An English-speaking counsel will be here in a few hours.

"In the meantime, I am calling the public prosecutor in to take your statement. You will, of course, be free to elect a legal counsel of your choice at a later stage when—"

"You really think I killed Roland, don't you?"

Dante didn't answer.

"If you think I did, you're barking up the wrong tree. And letting the real murderer get off. I didn't want to have to say this, *Commissario* Rossi, but I have a cast-iron alibi for the night Roland Kane was murdered." Pink tinged the sallow skin stretched tightly over her cheeks. "I was in bed with my lover of seven years, the porter up at the *Certosa*, Egidio Pecci. I was with him all night. He'd be willing to swear to that."

Dante sat back down again, abruptly.

Where is everyone? Faith thought. There was an expectant hush in the streets of Siena. She could hear footsteps a street away. It was high noon on a day that the city apparently waited for all year, and there wasn't a soul in sight. The sun beat down on the gray paving stones of the city streets as if it had a weight and heft all its own. Faith tried to keep in the shade, scurrying from shadow to shadow.

"What's going on?" she asked. "Where is everyone? The whole place is deserted, it's weird."

She and Tim had separated from the rest of their colleagues, or rather, Tim had herded her away. She still felt mildly guilty about her treatment of him and had allowed herself to be spirited away.

Tim was being charming company, morphing back into the old ironic Tim she'd known, not the sappy and clumsy suitor he'd been over the past few days, hovering at her side and throwing her longing glances.

And he was proving surprisingly knowledgeable about Siena and its history.

"Where is everyone? They're down in the *piazza* watching the last trial heat. Hey, careful. Watch your step." Tim smiled and took her elbow to steer her around a mound of horse droppings, then dropped her arm immediately, to her relief. "On the day of the *Palio*, horse poop brings good luck, but stepping in it is overkill. And I'm sure the good luck doesn't apply to foreigners. Nothing applies to foreigners in this city, it's all inward-looking." He stopped and fastidiously scraped off a bit of manure clinging to the edge of his right sandal. "Did you know that on the day of the race the horses are brought into the *contrada* church and blessed?"

Faith laughed. "You're joking."

"Nope. They're brought in by the jockeys. The horse is given some hay and munches it while the priest says some Catholic mumbo jumbo over it, then sprinkles it with holy water, kisses it on the nose and says, 'Go forth, little horse, and come back victorious.' Swear to God."

He grinned. "I've seen it three times in the *contrada* church of the Eagle, *San Giovanni Battista*. We're in the Eagle *contrada* right now. It's great watching the ceremony—the priest and the jockey standing around soberly in this elegant, little baroque church listening to Mass and this horse, munching on hay and farting."

A horse in church, being blessed by a priest. It sounded...fun. Worlds away from the Catholicism of Faith's parents, narrow-minded and mean.

"And the best bit is when the horse poops." Tim grinned. "Everyone goes 'Ahhhh'. Because it's a sign of good luck."

"Like pigeon droppings," Faith laughed.

"Yeah, only bigger and better. Hey! Look at that." They'd been meandering around the back streets, seeking shade, when suddenly the street opened up in front of them and the birthday cake façade of the cathedral rose tall and imposing, ornate and unreal.

Faith narrowed her eyes against the blinding glare, wishing she'd thought to bring along her sunglasses. She blinked sweat out of her eyes.

Fanciful spires topped the towers and fierce, white marble gargoyles stared down at them, disapproving of the passersby for eight hundred years. The bell tower to the right had narrow black and white stripes rising dizzily to the top. The stripes floated and vibrated like an optical illusion in the glare of the sun.

She had her bearings now. Across the immense square to the right, past a huge, mysterious arch, was the police station. And Nick.

Faith tried not to sigh. She needed to take her mind off Nick. Her emotions were still raw and unsure, flustered, rising suddenly at odd moments like the pigeons fluttering high up in the air at a stranger's footsteps, only to settle back down somewhere else.

Nick seemed to think something had been settled between them in her days here, but she had no idea what her feelings were, beyond an intense desire for him. But if there had been no future for them before, a year in Siena was a tombstone on any foolish hopes she might have harbored in the deepest reaches of her heart.

Sober thoughts for a glorious day. She had to shake the somber mood.

The door of the cathedral was open, bits of gold and marble glinting in the cool darkness within. It was enticingly mysterious.

She elbowed Tim. "Do you know I haven't been inside the cathedral yet? I can't believe it. That's usually the first place I go to in a city…not that I've traveled that much."

"Well, you've been busy."

Had she ever. A murder, a huge step up in her career, a fabulous job offer, new friends. "Yeah." She turned to him. "Come on, let's go look inside."

"Okay," Tim said agreeably. "No, wait. It's bound to be full of tourists and crazed members of the Eagle *contrada*, praying for victory, probably bargaining their grandmothers' souls for a win. I've got something better to show you." And he made off on a diagonal tangent across the huge square.

She really wanted to see the inside of the cathedral, but she thought, *What the hell.* It occurred to her with a burst of joy that she had a whole year in which to scrutinize every square inch of the cathedral, if she wanted. There was no rush. She followed Tim.

They scurried in a near crouch, the sun an almost living thing beating down on them. Faith gasped as they dove into the relative coolness of the tall, elegant wall separating the cathedral from the *Questura*.

"Wow." She caught her breath, almost hissing as it burned her lungs. Her bones were melting.

She wasn't built for this. She had northern Irish genes. Her people were a race known for being enemies of sunlight. It wasn't natural for someone with Belfast DNA to be out in the sun. To her certain knowledge, her parents had never ever had a tan.

"People are going to stand out in this sun all afternoon to watch a horse race?"

"Nuts," Tim agreed. "But still, it's worth it. The *Palio's* really glorious. Here we are."

Where? Faith frowned as she glanced up at the marble plaque. *Museo dell'Opera del Duomo.* Well, *duomo* meant cathedral, she was assuming opera didn't mean singing and *museo* was easy. Except closing herself up in a museum held no appeal. No appeal at all.

"This is where they keep the original artworks and statues from the façade and some artifacts from inside the cathedral. They're eight hundred years old and deteriorating, so they put them in a museum."

"A museum? Maybe some other time, Tim, but right now —"

"It's a great place, better than the inside of the cathedral. And the best thing is that it will be empty now. Everyone's going to start congregating in the cathedral square soon and we'll have the place to ourselves."

Tim plowed right over her. He grabbed her hand and plunged through the tall Gothic opening into the cool lobby within. He was digging in his pants for the ticket money before she could catch her breath.

"Come on." He grabbed her hand again and followed a bright red arrow up the stairs.

With a sigh, Faith followed. It was pleasantly cool inside and was indeed empty. They walked through room after room, their footsteps echoing on the flagstones. It was almost eerie, seeing the marble statues that had once adorned the façade of the cathedral, safe forever from the lashes of wind and rain, lined up against the walls as they walked through. A John the Baptist, a Mary Magdalene, Moses, even Plato. The necks of the statues were craned forward awkwardly.

"That's because the statues were placed in niches way up high," Tim answered her question. "So the sculptor had to make sure the face would be visible from down below. Hey, isn't she beautiful? That's a sibyl."

Indeed, the statue was beautiful, a serene marble woman with eyes fixed far in the distance.

Tim was rushing through the rooms, sprinting up the stairs to the floor above. Faith followed more slowly, watching Tim's short legs disappear around a bend and feeling vaguely uneasy. For the moment, she was completely alone. Even the guards seemed to have disappeared.

She had a sudden sense of remoteness, as if she were watching the scene from outside her body. Here's Faith Murphy, of Sophie, Indiana, climbing the exquisite stairs of an exquisite building in an exquisite city far, far away from home.

From what home once was. From what never was home, never would be home.

No wonder she was feeling a bit alienated. So much had happened in the past few days, so much had changed, that of course she felt changed with it. Going to bed with Nick, crossing the Atlantic, finding a dead body...

This floor was a series of large rooms with vaulted ceilings, arching into the distance. She could see Tim two rooms down.

As she followed him, she was suddenly overwhelmed with sensory memories of her first night in Italy—the bone tiredness, the heat, the disorientation of jet lag. She was walking down a corridor now as she had then, but what a difference. She felt like a different person and—she thought as she caught a glancing look at her reflection in the glass covering a medieval triptych—she *looked* like a different person.

Tim was in front of a huge wooden panel with a gilt background and a black-robed Madonna holding an amazingly adult-looking Christ child on her lap. The olive-skinned Madonna had her head bent to the side and her eyes fixed on a far-off horizon, an expression of inexpressible sorrow on her face, as if she knew what was going to happen to the sober-looking child she was holding.

She was surrounded by saints, to judge by the gold halos enclosing their heads like a muff, instead of a circlet overhead, as she was used to. The faces resembled the faces she'd been seeing in the streets of Siena. The painting was majestic, overwhelmingly beautiful and unbearably sad.

"This is the *Maestà*," Tim enthused. "One of the greatest paintings of its time. It's made with gold leaf and lapis lazuli dust and cost three thousand florins at the time. That would be almost a million dollars now. When it was finished, the entire city escorted it from the artist's studio to the cathedral, where it was kept up until recently."

Faith kept cutting between the amazing painting and amazing Tim. He was spouting art historical information as if there were a tape inside his pudgy chest. Whoever thought he was interested in art history? In the year she'd known him, he had only ever shown an interest in math, food and briefly — very briefly — her private parts.

The painting was gorgeous and what Tim was saying was interesting, but today wasn't a day to be stuck inside a museum sucking up historical information. It was delightful to know she could come back here any time she wanted during the course of the entire year.

In the meantime, she wanted to be back out in the dust and heat, watching the people, waiting for the *Palio*. Waiting to be with Nick.

"Listen, Tim," she said, "maybe we should go back out now. Didn't you say people were going to start gathering for the parade in historical costume? I'd like to see that and maybe grab a bite to eat."

She wasn't meeting Nick until 4:00 p.m. and she was suddenly ravenous. A little *trattoria* in a secluded square, eating *panzanella* in the shade...

"Okay, okay." He smiled, but she could see a nerve twitching in his cheek.

If she didn't know him better, she'd say he was high on something. He was certainly wired.

"Just one more thing to show you. You'll like it."

Faith had a sudden overwhelming desire to get out. The museum was dark, and she wanted the light. Empty, and she wanted people. "Another time, Tim. Come on, let's go now."

"Yeah, yeah." He wasn't listening. He grabbed her hand again and pulled her down another corridor.

Faith tried to drag her feet, but he was surprisingly strong. Also, he seemed to be obsessed with showing off his knowledge of Siena. Maybe out of jealousy of Nick. Shrugging, she gave up resistance and followed him.

Certainly, he had reason to be jealous of Nick. It was uncharitable of her to think it, but the two weren't even on the same planet in terms of attraction. And it wasn't just the physical attraction. Apart from being gorgeous, Nick had an ease with himself and others Tim couldn't even hope to match.

It was unfair and she knew it. Nature had favored Nick in every way there was. He was beautifully made and athletically gifted. He had a sunny personality. He had a wonderful family and they loved him. Nothing had ever gone wrong in his life.

All right, he had to stop playing hockey, but that would have happened sooner or later anyway. That it had happened now would allow him to do something else with his life, instead of happening ten years from now, when it might be too late.

Even in misfortune, Nick was fortunate.

A Murphy belonged on Tim's side of the tracks, not Nick's.

Tim had pulled her through a door, dropped her hand and forged ahead. With a sigh, she followed him.

Unexpectedly, the door led outside. Her eyes took a moment to adjust from the gloom of the museum to the glare of outdoors. As everything came into focus, she realized she was something like six stories up off the ground, on a narrow walkway, inside a great marble arch suspended in the bright blue sky.

Tim was in the middle of the tall, narrow arch, silhouetted against the brilliant, cloudless sky, elbows resting on the marble balustrade. He beckoned her over and she rested her elbow companionably next to his.

"Beautiful, huh?"

It was beautiful. Faith looked down at the people far below, tiny in comparison to the immense bulk of the cathedral filling the sky in front of them.

Tim looked sideways and upwards, his eye following the marble facing of the inside of the arch. "Actually we're in a window, believe it or not. This is the *facciatone*. The big façade. It was supposed to be the façade of the new cathedral, the largest in the world. Look." He pointed to the side of the cathedral across a vast space. "That was supposed to be the back of the cathedral and we're in the façade and all that space was going to be the central nave. You've got a great bird's-eye view from up here."

A throaty warble and whirring of wings and she was staring at a pigeon perched on one of a series of small stone tablets jutting out along the wall to the right and left of the arch. The pigeon stared at her unblinkingly, then took a delicate step to the right to come to rest on the next tablet.

"Pigeon's eye view is more like it." Faith turned her head to discover Tim had moved closer and was staring at her with the same unblinking intensity as the pigeon had done. Unobtrusively, with a smile on her face, Faith moved toward the arch's side.

What was she doing here with Tim when she wanted to be with Nick? Again, she felt that sense of unease, but more intense this time. Behind her was the *Questura*, where Nick was.

What's Nick doing? Is he helping Dante take Madeleine's confession?

Tim brushed her arm and she shifted. Tim moved again. Unease prickled in her veins.

Would Nick have finished? It was about one. Surely he was going to grab a bite to eat before meeting her at 4:00 p.m. in the *Piazza del Campo*. She had a violent wish to see him limping up the street, crossing Cathedral Square.

When would he be free? How long would it take them to take Madeleine's statement?

"About what?" Tim asked, and she realized she'd spoken the thought aloud.

Faith turned her head. "About the murder. I wonder how long it'll take her to confess to Roland's murder."

Tim's smile broadened and she recoiled from the expression in his muddy brown eyes. "Well, that's the thing, Faith," he said, leaning close. *Madeleine didn't kill Roland. I did.*

Chapter Fifteen

All great discoveries are made by mistake.

&

"What does 'date rape drug' mean?" Carmine Loiacono's strong Sicilian accent mangled the English words.

Nick leaned over his shoulder. While waiting for Dante to do his cop thing, he'd been roped in by Loiacono to translate the full text of the files sent by the Deerfield police department on Roland Kane, Griffin Ball, Faith Murphy, Madeleine Kobbel and Tim Gresham.

Loiacono's English was grammatically correct, but Sam Murray's version of English strained his vocabulary. Nick had eagerly accepted Loiacono's request for help to keep his mind off the woman in Dante's office.

He'd never hit a woman in his life, but he had been tempted. Had he been tempted.

Madeleine Kobbel had almost killed Faith. Nick didn't give a damn about the fact she'd probably killed the professor, too. The important thing was right now he could be arranging for Faith's body to be transported back to the States, and to the family who didn't love her. But he wasn't, thank God.

The files Deerfield PD had sent were interesting, with an official and unofficial version. There was dirt on everyone except, he was glad to see, Faith. Griffin Ball had once been arrested for lewd behavior while intoxicated on a gay beach in Florida. His family was rich and powerful and, in the end, the charges had been dropped. He had twice sued Roland Kane for harassment.

Madeleine Kobbel had been married to Roland Kane in the Eighties. There had been a child, a girl with multiple birth defects. Nick noted that Roland Kane had filed for divorce the day his daughter died. He shook his head. He never understood men who didn't stand by their families. He never would.

The mother of Tim Gresham, the man Nick loved to hate, had been married five times. Tim had been adopted once by an Englishman, John Dunham, and had lived a few years in England until his mother married again. They moved back to the States where his mother had married a Barry Simmons. At the age of eighteen, Tim had changed his name back to his biological father's, Gresham.

For an instant, Nick had a pang of sympathy for the creep. Having four stepfathers and two nationalities can't have been easy. Then he remembered Tim's proprietary attitude toward Faith and his sympathy evaporated.

"*Allora*?" Carmine Loiacono's sharply intelligent face was turned up to his.

Nick snapped out of his reverie. "Date rape drug? It's a drug put in the drink of an unsuspecting woman and it renders her either unconscious or incapable of resistance. They have no memory of what happened when they wake up." He'd heard the stories, of spiking a girl's drink and then using her when she was unconscious. The thought made him sick. "Why? Why are you asking?"

"That's why." Loiacono pointed to the printout in front of him. Roland Kane's file. Nick read slowly. Now here was an interesting set of data. Roland Kane had cut a wide swath in life, leaving behind burnt earth. Multiple law suits, charges of fraud, harassment...

Loiacono tapped the file impatiently. Nick was a slow reader, so he scrolled down, focusing on where Loiacono's finger was.

Nick read out loud slowly, sight translating for Loiacono.

"October 27, 2004. Roland Kane accused of raping Candace Simmons, a freshman student at St. Vincent's. Massive amounts of gamma hydroxybutyrate—" he stumbled over the word, "—were found in the bloodstream of the victim—"

"Wait!"

Nick looked up, frowning, at Loiacono's shout.

Contrary to American prejudice, southern Italians were anything but voluble, dramatic and over-emotional. Until recently, they had lived in a poor and dangerous world where one wrong word to the wrong person, an attitude of disrespect, could get you a bullet in the back from the local version of a sawed-off shotgun, the *lupara*. They kept their emotions reined in.

But now Loiacono, normally so stiff and formal, was shouting and waving his hands.

"Gamma hydroxybutyrate, GHB…" He was pawing wildly through a sheaf of documents. "*Ecco!*" He thrust a sheet into Nick's hands. "Look at that!"

"That" was a computer printout of some kind of medical analysis from the Florence toxicology lab in Careggi. Nick tried to run his eyes down the page quickly, but the words and numbers had no meaning and the dot matrix printer had been running out of ink. The faint words shimmered on the page.

"What?" Nick asked plaintively.

"There! There!" Loiacono jabbed at the paper so hard it tore. "See?"

Nick didn't. Then he did. Gamma hydroxybutyrate had been found in an unopened bottle of whiskey on Roland Kane's desk. He frowned and read further. No GHB found in

Roland Kane's blood. "Someone tried to poison him, but didn't?"

"Strange, no?" Loiacono was quivering like a bloodhound on the scent.

"It seems to me that someone wanted to poison the man with his own drug. But then he didn't. That's weird." Nick read further down the transcript. "The girl's disappearance was reported by her brother, a professor of mathematics at St Vincent's.

"He testified Candace Simmons had had an appointment with the head of the department, Roland Kane, to discuss a few academic matters and hadn't returned that night. The brother of the victim —"

Nick sat up straight. "Whoa."

"What?" Loiacono asked, bending forward. His thick black eyebrows formed almost a straight line across his forehead. "What?"

"The brother —" Nick continued reading and translating slowly, " — Tim Gresham, was worried when his sister didn't come back to her dorm. He reported her missing on the morning of the 28th. She was found at ten that morning naked in Lone Ridge Park with signs of violent rape.

"She remained in a coma for five days. Miss Simmons has been confined to a psychiatric hospital since November 10th."

Nick met Loiacono's eyes.

"Jesus Christ," Nick breathed, and Loiacono made a quick sign of the cross.

Tim's quiet words seemed to echo in the clear still air.

"Madeleine didn't kill Roland. I did."

Tim smiled again. "But you knew that, didn't you, Faith? You've known since last night. I could see it in your eyes. You recognized me. And to think I told you to get out, to go home. I was afraid this would happen."

"You—you left the note? Why?"

"Like I said. I knew that at some point you'd remember. That you'd recognize me."

Faith's mind was stumbling, tumbling. "I don't know what you're— *Recognize* you? Where? How? What are you talking about?"

"Last night." Tim's shoulder rubbed against hers. "Come on now...don't be coy. You and I both know what happened. You saw me coming and you recognized me."

She shook her head. "I still don't know what you're talking about. Coming where?"

Tim gave an exaggerated sigh. "All right. Think back. Last night, coming down *Via di Città* toward the square. I was with Paul Allen. You were further down the street. You saw us, and you froze. What were you thinking of?"

How perfect Nick was compared to you. How could she possibly say that? She couldn't. "I, ah—" She fumbled for words and his voice rode right over hers.

"Of course you recognized me. I realized that right away. I had no idea anyone had seen me that night until you told me. The perfect crime and here there was a witness." He shook his head. "I've been planning this for ten months, Faith. I'm sorry you had to get in the way."

Faith bristled. It was so like a man. She was being made to feel guilty for something she had no memory of doing. "Listen, Tim, I don't have the slightest idea what you're talking about," she began heatedly. Then stopped, because she did. Jesus Christ, she did. No wonder she'd been feeling so ill at ease around him.

"Oh, my God." It came out without thought. She flashed again on her first night in Siena. The maid carrying the tray with the bottle, strong calf muscles bunching as she walked. Broad back, no waist, stubby legs. *Tim.* "You—*you* were the maid I saw that night. *You* were the one who brought Roland that bottle of whiskey. You were the one—"

"—who killed Roland. I already told you that, Faith. Weren't you listening?"

Faith searched his eyes for signs of violence or madness, but all she saw was the same old Tim. A little agitated, a little excited maybe, but essentially the mild-mannered nerd she'd known for over a year. The first man she'd slept with, though that was hard to remember just now.

There was an immense silence, as if the whole world had suddenly gone away. For the moment, there were no tourists to be seen in the square, none of the police officers from the *Questura* around the corner lounging on the cathedral steps, sneaking a smoke, even the damned pigeons had disappeared.

Faith was suddenly conscious of being high up on a deserted walkway with a confessed murderer.

"But—but *why?* And how?" she blurted, then bit her lip. This was no time for explanations.

This was a moment for edging back into the museum, walking downstairs as quickly and quietly as possible, emerging into the central square and then making a run for the police station. The hand Tim clamped on her arm was as firm as shackles.

"Why?" Tim mused. He turned his gaze outward as if just now noticing how deserted the square was. He addressed the side of the cathedral and his profile was hard, tense. "The son of a bitch raped my sister, that's why. And got off scot-free, the fucker," he added viciously.

Faith had never heard Tim swear. And she had never seen that expression on his face.

"Your sister?"

Tim turned then. "You remember the girl who was raped last October? And then the whole thing was hushed up?"

"Yes." Faith kept her voice low. "Candace Simmons."

"That's right. Well, Candace Simmons was my sister. Stepsister. My mother married her father when she was seven and I was seventeen. She was a sweet girl, a little young for her age. Trusting, overly sensitive. We didn't spend much time together growing up because my mom divorced her dad soon after the marriage. But Candy and I kept in touch. Neither of us had siblings and, no matter what, she considered me her big brother."

A nerve twitched heavily along his cheek. "She wanted to go to college at St. Vincent's, to be near me. But she refused to let anyone know we were brother and sister, so she wouldn't get privileged treatment."

He gave a short bark of harsh laughter. "Well, she got privileged treatment all right. Roland Kane's special brand. That guy had radar and zoomed right in on the weak and vulnerable. You. Madeleine. Candace."

Faith frowned, trying to remember the story. "Your sister. Stepsister. She's still…alive isn't she?"

"Alive!" Tim slapped the balustrade with his free hand, startling the two pigeons who had come back to roost on the little tablets. They rose fluttering in the air, then slowly settled back down. "She was in a coma for days. When she came out of it, it was as if Candace, my sweet, little Candace had just…disappeared. She's completely psychotic. She'll be in a psychiatric hospital for the rest of her life."

"But—but if Kane did this, why isn't he—wasn't he—tried and put in jail? Why didn't you press charges? How could you let him get away with it?"

"Candace couldn't testify. And there was only my word she had been going to see Kane. Do you know what a decent defense lawyer can do with that? It's hearsay. And Kane could afford the best lawyer around.

"There might have been a trial and he might even have lost his job, but he'd have gotten off. And I didn't want him on trial anyway." He turned his head to look at her. "I wanted him dead. I've been waiting all year to do it."

Faith shivered. All last year, Tim had worked side by side with Kane. They had sat in academic councils together. They had discussed students together and had planned the Quantitative Methods Seminar together. And every second of every day, Tim had been planning Kane's death.

The day was hot, but she felt cold. "How?" she whispered through lips that had gone numb.

"What do you mean, *how?*" Tim frowned, annoyed. "You know how. You found him. I stuck a knife—oh." His brow cleared. "I see what you mean. Well, that part was easy. I came over the day before you guys arrived. I've been planning this for a long time now and I had it planned down to the last detail. Except for you. You almost ruined everything. I had no idea anyone had seen me."

He gave her a steely look and Faith almost apologized. *Sorry, Tim, I had no idea you were planning on killing Kane. If I'd known, of course I would've stayed home.*

She looked yearningly at the door. Tim's grip on her arm tightened.

"I've been to Siena seven times and I know the routine down pat. Roland goes up drunk to his room around ten, Grif takes a sleeping pill and sleeps like the dead, and Madeleine goes off to have her yearly affair with the night porter."

Faith jolted. Her gossip lobe took instant precedence over the survival instinct. "Madeleine's been having an affair? With the night porter?" she breathed. "How long has *that* been going on?"

"For seven years," he snapped. "Now pay attention."

She shut up.

"I entered early in the afternoon and hid in one of the rooms with the stiletto, the bottle and the maid's uniform." He frowned. "That threw me a little when I found out later that the caterers had changed. All the years before, there'd been an elderly maid." A look of anger crossed his face, then he shrugged. The CEO recalling a minor glitch in the company plan.

"They make such a big thing over here about never changing anything. Roland's room is always seventeen and there's no one else sleeping along his corridor until the delegates start arriving the next day. No one was supposed to see me. It went even more smoothly than I thought." Faith was creeped out by Tim's smile. "Roland was in a stupor, and he was barely conscious. He didn't recognize me. He wouldn't have recognized his mother. I was going to give him the bottle and wait for the drug in it to take effect, but it wasn't necessary. A little pressure on his neck and he went down.

"I sat in his room and watched him until after midnight, just enjoying the moment." Tim's fists clenched, the slug-pale skin over the knuckles turning white.

It was so creepy, listening to Tim's matter of fact voice. She could imagine the scene all too vividly. The dark cell, Kane lying on the floor and Tim, like some gigantic vulture, watching over him, waiting for the moment in which he'd kill his prey.

"Around one o'clock, I did it," he continued briskly, and the hairs on the nape of her neck stood up. "The door of the

Certosa isn't locked on the inside. The night porter was — busy. Humping Madeleine. I just walked out. I'd arrived that morning in Rome, rented a car and driven up to Siena. I left the car about half a mile away from the *Certosa*. That night I drove myself back to Rome airport in time for the morning flight out.

"I traveled under a different name. I have an English passport in the name of Timothy Dunham. I've kept it up. I always knew it would be useful one day to be somebody else. Timothy Dunham arrived back in Boston and two hours later, Tim Gresham took a flight to Rome.

"I have a perfect alibi. When Kane was killed, I was six thousand miles away, sick in bed with the flu. And no one will ever know the truth." He looked at her steadily and his chest rose and fell on a sigh. "Except for you."

"Oh, hey." Faith smiled reassuringly. She held up her hands. "Don't worry about a thing, Tim. I won't tell a soul. I swear."

"Of course not," he said gently. "Because you'll be dead."

And he pushed her over the balustrade.

Dante opened the door to the common room where Nick and Loiacono were working, slammed it closed and leaned against it wearily. "Damn," he said. "Madeleine Kobbel didn't do it."

Nick and Loiacono looked up. "What?" Nick said. "What do you mean? We had a whole *Certosa* full of geeks who saw her do it. Listen, she can't wriggle out of this one. She almost killed Faith."

"No." Dante stepped forward and leaned a hand on the desk. He stared down at his knuckles. "I don't mean that. I mean she didn't kill Roland Kane."

"She tried to kill Faith," Nick said hotly.

"Probably." Dante drummed his fingers once, violently. "But we can't prove it. Even if she tried to kill Faith, though, she didn't kill Roland Kane."

Nick cared far less about Roland Kane than he did about Faith. The only thing he knew, though, was that anyone capable of tilting a heavy vase over a wonderful woman's head was certainly capable of killing a nasty man. "Why do you say that? How do you know she didn't off the prof?"

"Because." Dante sighed. "The night Kane was murdered, Madeleine Kobbel was in bed with Egidio Pecci. All night. I just got off the phone with Egidio and he says they've been having an affair while she's in Siena for the past seven years." He shook his head. "Egidio says she's a tiger in bed."

Nick was stunned. "Egidio was having an affair with Madeleine Kobbel? What's the matter with the guy?" Nick couldn't fathom it. He turned the thought around in his head, but it still didn't make any sense. "I'd rather stick it into a rattlesnake's jaws."

Loiacono cleared his throat and turned his head swiftly, but not before Nick caught a smile on his face. Loiacono never smiled. The idea of Madeleine in bed wasn't a smiling matter.

"Amen." Dante shrugged. "Bottom line, though, is that Egidio swore she didn't leave his bed from 10:00 p.m. until seven in the morning. He says they didn't sleep at all." Dante looked pained. "So I guess that's that. We're going to have to look elsewhere for Roland Kane's murderer.

"Damn! Just when I thought I could wrap everything up in time for the *Pa*—" Dante glanced at Loiacono and coughed.

Nick slid the printouts of the Deerfield PD's emailed attachments over. "We might have another candidate for you, Dante."

Dante picked up the sheaf and leafed through it. "Is there a short version of this?"

"The short version is that Roland Kane raped Tim Gresham's sister. But first, Kane pumped the girl full of gamma hoomma hubba."

Dante straightened. "Gamma hydroxybutyrate."

"That's what I said."

"Gamma hydroxybutyrate is what was found in—"

"The bottle of whiskey in Roland Kane's room," Loiacono finished. "But not in Roland Kane's blood."

"Tim Gresham didn't arrive in Italy until after the murder. So we're back to square one," Dante said glumly.

Nick didn't feel like letting Gresham off the hook that easily. "How do we know that?"

Dante looked up from the printouts. "How do we know what?"

"How do we know he arrived after the murder?"

"He was seen arriving by about fifty people, that's how we know."

"Well…" Nick shifted from foot to foot, thinking furiously. He wasn't used to thinking without moving on ice, and felt dizzy. "Once Gary LeSabre forgot his anniversary. We were in Seattle and we had a big game the next day. He flew to Boston, bought some flowers, grabbed a cab to his house, gave his wife the flowers, kissed her, went back to the airport and grabbed the first flight back. We didn't even realize he'd been gone."

Dante stilled. "Do you think that's what Tim Gresham did? If he's the murderer, he'd be too smart not to have taken the flight he said he did. So the question is—did he catch an earlier flight to come over just long enough to kill Kane and fly back in time to catch the flight he says he was on?

"Loiacono, get Alitalia on the phone. Get their reservations office at Fiumicino and get the person in charge. Ask if their reservations show a Tim Gresham taking a short round trip from Boston to either Rome or Milan. Nick, who else flies from Boston?"

"Delta and World Airways," Nick answered.

Dante already had the phone in his hand. He nodded to another phone across the table. "I'll take Delta. You take World Airways."

"Okay." Nick picked up the receiver, his mind on overdrive.

Dante looked at him oddly. "This is a real long shot."

"Humor me," Nick said.

Dante started to dial twelve for information when he noticed that Loiacono wasn't on the phone to Alitalia. Loiacono usually sprang to obey orders. He was pounding furiously on the keyboard of his computer. "What are you doing, Loiacono? I thought I told you to query Alitalia."

Loiacono grunted, pressed "enter" with enough force to punch through the plastic and sat back, his eyes glued to the monitor. "It's quicker to hack into Alitalia's reservations computer, sir."

"Hacking into… Loiacono, isn't that illegal?"

"Yes, sir. Technically. Ahhh…" A smile creased his features and Nick wanted to shiver. It looked unholy. Loiacono looked up at Dante. "I'm in, sir. Do you want me to stop?"

"No." Shaking his head in wonder, Dante rounded the table to stand behind Loiacono. Nick joined him. "See if you can find a reservation for Tim Gresham, arriving June 30th."

Three seconds later, they had it.

"Okay." Dante leaned forward. "Now see if there's another reservation in that name the previous day."

Loiacono tapped and brought up another page. "Nothing, sir."

"Well, as I said, it was a long shot. But let's be thorough and try Delta and World Airways. Loiacono, do you think you could—"

"Certainly, sir." Loiacono bent over his keyboard.

"Wait!" Nick almost shouted, and both men frowned at him.

"What?" Dante asked plaintively.

Nick knew what a major effort Dante was making. He was straining with every cell in his body to be in the *piazza* now. But they needed to be thorough.

It was worth a try. "If it's quick, can Loiacono try to check for another name? Tim Dunham. D-U-N-H-A-M."

Dante shrugged. "Loiacono?"

"Yes, sir."

Ten seconds later, all three men stared at the data. Timothy Dunham had made a twenty-four hour trip from Boston to Rome and back on the 29th of June.

"*Tombola*," Loiacono said.

"Bingo," Nick echoed.

There was a clatter on the landing and the door burst open. A white-faced Nicoletti burst into the room.

"What's the matter, Nicoletti?" Dante moved toward the young officer. "You look like you've seen a ghost."

Nicoletti was panting, sweat dripping down his pasty face. "*Commissario!*" he gasped. "Miss Murphy, outside—oh, my God."

Nick was closest to the wall and had a knee brace, but he beat Dante out the door.

"Oh, my God. Oh, my God. Oh, my God."

Faith chanted the words to drown out the terror as she clung to the little stone tablet the pigeons had been perched on. She'd made a wild leap as Tim had pushed her off and had barely caught on to it. She scrabbled for a better handhold.

"Damn you!" Tim reached down and to the right. He tried to pry her fingers off the tablet.

With a whimper of terror, Faith edged her hands around until she was on the other side of the tablet, out of his reach. With a grunt of anger, he climbed out on the balustrade as far as he could, stretching dangerously out, hand scrabbling for hers. He could almost touch her.

He smiled.

Good, old Tim. My pal. The good guy who was doing his damnedest to kill her.

Tim stretched further and she could feel the brush of his fingertips against her hand. She whimpered and edged closer to the wall. Tim's arm was trembling. He lunged and slipped and almost fell.

There was a high-pitched scream, then another. A man shouted. Faith chanced a glance down at the square far, far below. People were congregating and a man had his arm lifted, pointing at them. Faith looked away. The view was terrifying and made her dizzy.

Another woman screamed and there was the sound of a loud police whistle.

Tim was edging his way back to the walkway. His feet hit the bricks with a slight thud. He straightened and looked at her. She looked back, numbly.

"It's made of stone, what you're holding on to," he said conversationally. "It's stone and porous and provides a bit of a grip. But you're sweating and soon you won't be able to hang on any longer. You'll never survive the fall.

"Everyone saw I tried to rescue you, but couldn't. So I went for help. It will take me a long time to find help. I expect that by the time I make my way downstairs, you'll be smeared all over the square. And, of course, I'll be a heartbroken colleague and former lover. Good-bye, Faith." His head disappeared.

She heard the click of the door closing.

Faith's fingers were throbbing. She slipped and her heart shot up into her throat. She wouldn't be able to hang on much longer. She'd never been an athlete. She had no strength in her arms and hands. Her hands slipped again and she caught herself just in time.

Her face was wet with tears and sweat, and drops of salty liquid burned her eyes. She was panting so hard the hot air burned her throat.

She looked down. There was a crowd gathering and she could hear the murmurs above the pounding of her heart. Two men were rounding the corner at a run, pushing their way through the people, two tall, broad-shouldered men...

"Nick!" she screamed. Her heart hammered and she had to shake the tears and sweat from her eyes to focus. It was crazy, but she felt that as long as she could see him, nothing bad could happen to her.

The sounds of boots clattering rose up. Some men were dragging over what looked like a large piece of canvas.

She sobbed. Her hands were going numb. She couldn't hold out much longer. "Nick!" she screamed again. "Help me!"

"Faith, hang on." Nick had a megaphone and his amplified voice carried in the still air. "We're setting up something to catch you. We're here. I'm here. You're going to be okay, honey. Just hang in there."

"Nick," she whimpered. Her arms were shaking with fatigue.

She saw four men holding the corners of a red and white striped piece of material. It looked like an awning, ripped off a storefront.

Her right hand slipped and she screamed. "Nick!"

"It's okay, honey." His voice drifted up, reassuring and strong. "We're almost—" She heard muffled sounds.

She was too terrified to look down. Suppose they weren't set up yet? She couldn't hold on for more than a few seconds. It would be impossible to survive a fall from this height. She was going to die. Her arms were trembling uncontrollably. She couldn't feel her fingers. Her wrists ached.

She was slipping…

"Faith!" Nick's voice boomed. She could barely concentrate and could hardly hear him over the pounding of her heart. "Listen to me carefully, sweetheart. On the count of three, I want you to let go. I want you to fall straight, then curl up like a somersault with your back down.

"You have to land on your back, honey, with your legs and head tucked in. Is that clear? You can't land on your stomach or you'll break your back. Faith? Can you hear me?"

"Yes," she whispered.

"Faith!"

"Yes!" she yelled.

"Okay, on the count of three. One, two, three…jump!"

Oh, God. Faith let go.

It lasted a century. It lasted a second.

For a moment, she seemed to hang suspended in air. Then a giant fist slammed into her, pushing her down, faster, faster…

She curled in on herself in the fetal position, hugging her knees, pulling backwards, and hit the canvas with her back, bouncing high at an angle, her limbs splaying out.

Her foot connected with something solid and the canvas slipped as one of the men fell from the force of her kick. She fell and bounced again, less violently this time, then again. Finally, she stilled.

There was a moment of silence, then several pairs of hands reached for her as the canvas was lowered to the ground. She was placed on her feet. She swayed and was grasped in two strong arms. Not Nick's. She would recognize Nick's embrace anywhere.

"Thank God!" Dante said, and held her at arm's length. His face was white and covered in sweat. "Jesus, you had us scared, girl."

Other police officers were crowding around and she was hugged half to death. Faith swiveled her head. Nick was usually larger than anyone else around and impossible to miss. Where was he?

"Where's Nick?" she asked, just as they heard a loud groan. They all turned to look.

"Shit!" He was on his back, clutching his leg. "I just busted my other leg!"

"Ow! That hurts!" Nick had always thought of himself as stoic. In the course of his hockey career, he'd bled, broken bones and sprained muscles with depressing regularity, and had just sucked it up. Usually, however, the doctors at least tried to make it better.

Nick was aware, however, that he'd violated Rule Number One of life in Siena — never, *ever* get sick on the day of the *Palio*. If you do — you're on your own.

"Quit bellyaching, Rossi," the doctor said curtly.

He was an orthopedic surgeon, and — most of the year, but not today — a friend of Dante's. Dante should have been here, but he was too busy booking Tim Gresham for murder.

The doctor had obviously drawn the short straw for duty this afternoon. His name was Giacomo Barzi, he was from the Giraffe *contrada*, and he had no sympathy for Nick's strained quadriceps whatsoever.

"Here, hold this." Dr. Barzi took Nick's hand, pressed it over the cold compress on his thigh and disappeared.

Two seconds later, Nick could hear the talking heads of the state broadcasting network, RAI, beginning their coverage of the *Palio* from Siena, starting up on a TV in the next room. The actual race wouldn't begin for another two hours, but the parade — men and boys dressed in meticulously correct silk and satin medieval costumes, gravely marching around the track to the stately beat of drums — had just begun.

Nick knew every step of it by heart, beginning with the tolling of the ancient bell atop the tower of city hall, the *sunto*. Each *contrada* would be represented, with a prize for the most elegant. There was no sense that this was an historical reenactment.

The men — and it was strictly a politically incorrect display of male power and plumage — wore their stunning costumes with no sheepishness. They walked, carrying rippling banners, or rode gloriously caparisoned horses, with the swagger of knights of a powerful city, the city Siena had once been, bigger, more powerful and richer than Paris.

No one wanted to miss the parade. Least of all Dr. Barzi.

Nick had been rushed to the *Le Scotte* hospital by four police cars, sirens screaming. Ever since then, he'd been receiving less than stellar care on this day of days. And here he was, sitting on a cot in the emergency ward, pants down around his ankles and no doctor in sight. The entire hospital seemed eerily empty.

"Poor Nick," Faith said softly. "Does it hurt a lot?"

Nick put on his bravely suffering face, Bogie in *Casablanca*, Ben Affleck in *Pearl Harbor*. There were worse things than being wounded and tended by a grateful woman who was pretty and smart.

Faith had refused any medical attention and had refused to leave his side. She'd ridden up with him and had sat with him through Barzi's ministrations.

Nick looked at her, measured angles, and said, "If you could just bend down and massage my thigh…"

"Sure." Faith bent obligingly and laid her soft, slim hands on his thigh and rubbed gently.

Ah. Nick breathed out. *Bliss.* It almost made the pain go away, which was a bonus since Barzi had been in too much of a hurry for painkillers. There was an added advantage in that Faith's sundress gaped open.

"A little lower," he murmured, and Faith bent down. He could see the tops of her pretty, conical and braless breasts, pink little nipples and all. Gave him a nice little buzz. *Hmmm.*

Faith stopped kneading, tracked his intent gaze and straightened, plastering a hand over the front of her sundress. "You're a sick man, Nick Rossi." She shook her head in mock sorrow. "If it weren't for the fact you saved my life, I'd leave you here to the tender mercies of the doctor."

"But I did, and you won't."

"Right." She smiled at him, her face glowing.

It was so great having her back, looking at him with softness in her eyes. Having Faith around was going to make the coming bleak winter bearable.

"We're going to have fun when we get back." Nick put his hand over hers. "We can—"

"Time to strap you up." Dr. Barzi came back into the room, a big roll of gauze in hand.

A touching show of concern, but Nick could hear that the RAI programming had gone to a commercial break. He knew that whatever medical care he was going to get was going to have to fit into two coffee commercials, a preview of that evening's shows and a cold remedy spot.

But it had been worth it. Worth getting hurt on the day of the *Palio*. Worth even a permanent limp. He'd never, ever forget the sight of Faith dangling by her fingertips, impossibly high up. So high up a fall would have spelled her certain death.

Nick had lightning reflexes. Speed was his trademark and more than one sports writer had written that some of his moves were too fast for the naked eye to track. But at that moment, seeing Faith a second or two from death, he had simply stood, frozen on the spot, totally incapable of moving or even breathing. He'd have sworn his heart had stopped together with his brain.

Thank God for Dante, who'd mobilized his men to rip the awning off the corner bar to form a safe landing for Faith. They'd acted just in time. Nick had been injured because his hands, sweat-slicked with terror, hadn't been able to maintain their hold on the awning.

The terror had lasted until he'd seen Faith bending over him, until he'd felt the tickle of a lock of her brandy-colored hair sweeping across his face, until her worried eyes had locked with his. And his own had closed in naked, heart-pounding relief.

"Ow!" Pain interrupted his thoughts. The doctor was pulling the broad band of gauze so tightly he was cutting off circulation. Nick needed a bandage, not a tourniquet. "Do you have to pull that so tight?" He glared at Dr. Barzi, who looked back at him indifferently.

Barzi rolled his eyes. "Dante told me you were an athlete. Athletes are supposed to be tough. Listen to me. You've got a sprained quadriceps. I have to bind you up tightly to avoid blood leaking out from the damaged muscle. I won't be doing you any favors if I don't do it right and you develop a massive hematoma."

"Let him do his job, Nick," Faith said softly. She slipped her hand in his.

Nick shut up. He gritted his teeth when Barzi adjusted the gauze, tightening it even more. He needed to think of something else.

"When does your flight leave?" he asked Faith. It was an idle question, simply to make conversation, but to his surprise, Faith removed her hand from his and stepped back.

Her voice was cool. "I, uh, haven't had a chance tell you, Nick. I'm, uh, not coming back to the States."

He felt like he'd received a hockey puck to the gut. *What the hell had happened?* One moment she was smiling at him as if he were her personal God, and the next she was dismissing him, her voice one degree above freezing on a hot and humid day. What the hell did that mean—she wasn't coming back?

Not coming back. Oh, God, she'd accepted some job somewhere. Maybe somewhere cold and awful like England. Or worse, she'd met someone—one of those geeks who talked math and stank of unwashed prof and number two pencil—and decided he'd be better company in the long run than Nick. Smarter.

Some vestige of when he'd been cool allowed him to ask, casually, "So where are you going?" when what he wanted to do was beat his head against the wall until it hurt as much as his leg. Legs.

"Siena," Faith answered, with a sly smile. "I've been offered a year's contract to work at a new foundation in Siena. If I can stay on after the contract expires, I will." She looked him straight in the eye. "There's not much for me back in Deerfield."

And just like that—bam!—he knew.

Nick realized he wasn't a deep thinker, a forward-looking thinker or a strategic thinker. He'd been led by instinct all his life and every instinct he'd ever had, honed by years of action on the ice, guided him now.

"Yeah?" he said casually. "What do you know? Me, too. There's a farm up for sale next to the land my grandparents own. The guy's ancient and his kids aren't interested in wine or olive oil. But it's some of the best land in Italy and I'm going to buy it. Farm it. Make the best wine and olive oil on the face of the earth."

Eventually. When he learned how to farm. Nick mentally crossed his fingers.

Faith glowed. "Yeah?" she breathed.

"Oh, yeah," Nick said.

Epilogue
‍ℬ

"They're gorgeous." Faith watched the charge of the *carabinieri* around the racetrack. Dressed in nineteenth-century uniforms, they were impossibly dashing, capes billowing, plumed helmets fluttering, outstretched swords glittering in the late afternoon sunlight.

Nick squeezed her waist. "Hush. Don't let Dante hear you. He's jealous because the *polizia* doesn't get to do the cavalry charge, only the *carabinieri*. And the *carabinieri* have snazzier dress uniforms than the police. He hates this part of the *Palio*."

Faith smiled at Nick. They were on the third floor of an ancient *palazzo* whose balcony overlooked the *campo*. Dante and two of his men had carried Nick up the stairs, Nick cursing all the way as they bumped him from wall to wall. He'd been sweating and white-faced by the time he'd been deposited on the balcony.

Their hosts were a charming, middle-aged couple who spoke excellent English and had instantly made Faith feel at ease. Various friendly Rossis drifted in and out until the cavalry charge, when they all jostled for space on the balcony.

Below them was a sea of excited Sienese, spilling out of balconies, shoulder to shoulder on the bandstands ringing the *piazza*, jam-packed in the center, where attendance was free, swaying and chanting and shouting.

"Who are they?" Faith asked suddenly, pointing to mysterious men with closed fantastical helmets.

"The *contrade morte*," Nick answered. "The dead *contrade*. They no longer exist except in the souls of the Sienese."

The crowd nearly drowned out the drum rolls as flag wavers, bearing the flags of the various *contrada*, came out. Faith watched, entranced, as the flags were thrown in the air and caught. The flag wavers executed complicated maneuvers with flawless grace. A roar rose up from various points of the crowd as each *contrada's* flag was borne by.

It was almost too much to take in — the bright colors, the handsome, solemn men marching gravely in their glorious velvets and silks, the flags rippling in the soft evening air, the drums beating in the cadence of a heartbeat and over it all, the bell tolling.

One last toss of the brilliant flags in the air, the bell stopped and the crowd held its breath. The track was cleared and Faith could feel the anticipation of the crowd vibrating in the air. Certainly she could see Nick and Dante trembling.

A roar from the crowd, and the jockeys riding bareback in brilliant silks started emerging onto the track. The horses glowed with health, prancing nervously as the crowd went wild. When the red-and-yellow silk of the Snail *contrada* appeared, Nick and Dante leaned against the balcony and started shouting.

Nine horses and jockeys lined up between two ropes, the tenth back several feet, allowed a galloping takeoff. The horses were nervous and it was difficult to keep them in the lineup. Finally, the jockeys were told to exit from the starting ropes and try again. They had to start over three times. Finally, by some alchemy, everyone was in position for a second, a boom sounded, and they were off!

Nick and Dante were shouting themselves hoarse and she found herself shouting, too, as Lina took second place and stayed there. The track had two sharp curves and two horses fell at the first curve. One regained its feet, riderless, and plunged back into the race. The noise was incredible, thousands of flashbulbs went off, and the entire square trembled with excitement.

The horses thundered by again, Lina still second, moving gracefully, her hooves barely touching the ground. Her jockey was crouched on her neck, a red-and-yellow blur, silks fluttering.

The third and last round. The horses had all moved up in a pack, gaining ground on the leader and Lina. The jockey tapped Lina twice on the hindquarters with his whip and she shot forward, galvanized, long slender legs flying. She drew even with the leader, another tap, her stride lengthened, she moved ahead...another shot from the gun and the crowd went wild.

Nick and Dante were pounding each other on the back, screaming, then pounding her on the back, as excited Snails jumped the fence and surrounded the horse and jockey. The jockey was lifted and carried away on the shoulders of wildly exulting men.

The Snail had won.

The End

About the Author

&

Elizabeth Jennings welcomes email from her fans at e.jennings@tin.it. Please visit her at her website: www.elizabeth-jennings.com

Elizabeth also welcomes mail from readers. You can write to her c/o Ellora's Cave Publishing at 1056 Home Avenue, Akron, OH 44310-3502.

Why an electronic book?

We live in the Information Age—an exciting time in the history of human civilization in which technology rules supreme and continues to progress in leaps and bounds every minute of every hour of every day. For a multitude of reasons, more and more avid literary fans are opting to purchase e-books instead of paperbacks. The question to those not yet initiated to the world of electronic reading is simply: *why?*

1. *Price.* An electronic title at Ellora's Cave Publishing and Cerridwen Press runs anywhere from 40-75% less than the cover price of the <u>exact same title</u> in paperback format. Why? Cold mathematics. It is less expensive to publish an e-book than it is to publish a paperback, so the savings are passed along to the consumer.

2. *Space.* Running out of room to house your paperback books? That is one worry you will never have with electronic novels. For a low one-time cost, you can purchase a handheld computer designed specifically for e-reading purposes. Many e-readers are larger than the average handheld, giving you plenty of screen room. Better yet, hundreds of titles can be stored within your new library—a single microchip. (Please note that Ellora's Cave and Cerridwen Press does not endorse any specific brands. You can check our website at www.ellorascave.com or

www.cerridwenpress.com for customer recommendations we make available to new consumers.)

3. *Mobility.* Because your new library now consists of only a microchip, your entire cache of books can be taken with you wherever you go.

4. *Personal preferences are accounted for.* Are the words you are currently reading too small? Too large? Too...**ANNOYING**? Paperback books cannot be modified according to personal preferences, but e-books can.

5. *Instant gratification.* Is it the middle of the night and all the bookstores are closed? Are you tired of waiting days—sometimes weeks—for online and offline bookstores to ship the novels you bought? Ellora's Cave Publishing sells instantaneous downloads 24 hours a day, 7 days a week, 365 days a year. Our e-book delivery system is 100% automated, meaning your order is filled as soon as you pay for it.

Those are a few of the top reasons why electronic novels are displacing paperbacks for many an avid reader. As always, Ellora's Cave and Cerridwen Press welcomes your questions and comments. We invite you to email us at service@ellorascave.com, service@cerridwenpress.com or write to us directly at: 1056 Home Ave. Akron OH 44310-3502.

THE
☥ ELLORA'S CAVE ☥
LIBRARY

Stay up to date with Ellora's Cave Titles in
Print with our Quarterly Catalog.

TO RECIEVE A CATALOG,
SEND AN EMAIL WITH YOUR NAME
AND MAILING ADDRESS TO:

CATALOG@ELLORASCAVE.COM

OR SEND A LETTER OR POSTCARD
WITH YOUR MAILING ADDRESS TO:

CATALOG REQUEST
C/O ELLORA'S CAVE PUBLISHING, INC.
1056 HOME AVENUE
AKRON, OHIO 44310-3502

Please be advised: Ellora's Cave is a publisher of erotic romance.
Our books as well as our website contain explicit sexual content.

CERRIDWEN PRESS

Cerridwen, the Celtic goddess of wisdom, was the muse who brought inspiration to storytellers and those in the creative arts.
Cerridwen Press encompasses the best and most innovative stories in all genres of today's fiction.
Visit our website and discover the newest titles by talented authors who still get inspired — much like the ancient storytellers did...
once upon a time.

www.cerridwenpress.com